"Axios."

He didn't respond to ~~the sound of~~ his name. He couldn't ~~take his~~ eyes off Andreos. His strong throat moved in a swallow and his pallor whitened as several expressions charged through his eyes.

Shock. Incredulity. Utter fury.

"What...what are you doing here?"

Finally, eyes the color of a dark arctic night clashed with mine. "What am I doing here?" he asked with icy incredulity. "This is what you have to say to me after the stunt you pulled?"

My insides shook, but I forced myself to hold his gaze. "You'll want to discuss this, I'm sure, but can it wait till—"

"I'll *want to discuss this*? Are you for real?"

A drowsy Andreos stirred in my arms, his senses picking up on the frenetic emotions charging through the air.

"Miss, would you like us to—"

"Leave us." Ax's tone was deep. Implacable.

I wasn't in the least bit surprised when the staff hurried away, carrying the remnants of my idyllic picnic. Already that seemed like a distant memory in the presence of the blisteringly furious man before me.

The Notorious Greek Billionaires

Seduced by a Greek billionaire!

A billionaire's reputation is *everything*. Part of Greece's most formidable family, Axios and Neo Xenakis headline every newspaper. But the arrival of two unexpected brides is about to turn their billion-dollar world upside down... Though it's the discovery of their one-night babies that will change their lives—forever!

Escape to Greece with...

Axios and Calypso

Claiming My Hidden Son

Available now!

Neo and Sadie

Coming soon!

Maya Blake

CLAIMING MY
HIDDEN SON

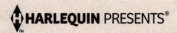 HARLEQUIN PRESENTS®

If you purchased this book without a cover you should be aware that this book is stolen property. It was reported as "unsold and destroyed" to the publisher, and neither the author nor the publisher has received any payment for this "stripped book."

Recycling programs
for this product may
not exist in your area.

ISBN-13: 978-1-335-47878-8

Claiming My Hidden Son

First North American publication 2019

Copyright © 2019 by Maya Blake

All rights reserved. Except for use in any review, the reproduction or utilization of this work in whole or in part in any form by any electronic, mechanical or other means, now known or hereafter invented, including xerography, photocopying and recording, or in any information storage or retrieval system, is forbidden without the written permission of the publisher, Harlequin Enterprises Limited, 22 Adelaide St. West, 40th Floor, Toronto, Ontario M5H 4E3, Canada.

This is a work of fiction. Names, characters, places and incidents are either the product of the author's imagination or are used fictitiously, and any resemblance to actual persons, living or dead, business establishments, events or locales is entirely coincidental.

This edition published by arrangement with Harlequin Books S.A.

For questions and comments about the quality of this book, please contact us at CustomerService@Harlequin.com.

® and TM are trademarks of Harlequin Enterprises Limited or its corporate affiliates. Trademarks indicated with ® are registered in the United States Patent and Trademark Office, the Canadian Intellectual Property Office and in other countries.

Printed in U.S.A.

www.Harlequin.com

Maya Blake's hopes of becoming a writer were born when she picked up her first romance at thirteen. Little did she know her dream would come true! Does she still pinch herself every now and then to make sure it's not a dream? Yes, she does! Feel free to pinch her, too, via Twitter, Facebook or Goodreads! Happy reading!

Books by Maya Blake

Harlequin Presents

Signed Over to Santino
Pregnant at Acosta's Demand
The Sultan Demands His Heir
His Mistress by Blackmail
An Heir for the World's Richest Man

Conveniently Wed!

Crown Prince's Bought Bride

One Night With Consequences

The Boss's Nine-Month Negotiation

Bound to the Desert King

Sheikh's Pregnant Cinderella

Rival Brothers

A Deal with Alejandro
One Night with Gael

Visit the Author Profile page
at Harlequin.com for more titles.

PROLOGUE

THE DRUMMING IN my ears was loud. So loud I had the fleeting thought that I was on the verge of suffering a stroke. Of doing myself irreparable harm and comprehensively ending this debacle once and for all.

But that would be too easy.

And the headline…

I could see it now.

Axios Xenakis Suffers Stroke Due to
Family Pressures!

They would have no clue as to the unreasonable part, of course. Despite the media outlets lauding the story of the Xenakis near-ruin to phenomenal rise on a regular basis these days, they would be swift to jump on past flaws. Old skeletons would be dragged out of closets. I would be deemed weak. Broken. Not quite up to the task of managing a global conglomerate.

Just like my father.

Just as my grandfather had been falsely labelled after that one risky move that had seen all his hard work whittled away to almost nothing.

He'd had to bear that one misfortune all the way to his grave.

Once a titan of his industry, a simple decision to align himself with the wrong partner had decimated him, leaving the Xenakis name with a stench of failure that had lingered long after his death, causing insidious damage.

Damage that had taken back-breaking hard work to reverse, with my refusal to allow my family name to sink without a trace spurring me to seek daring solutions.

The Xenakis name was no longer one to be ashamed of. Now it was synonymous with success and innovation— a global conglomerate that *Fortune 500* companies vied to be associated with.

However, the solution being proposed to me now was one set to resurrect the unsavoury ghosts of the past, with their talons of barefaced greed—

'Ax, are you listening? Did you hear what Father said?' asked Neo, my brother.

'Of course I heard it. I'm not deaf,' I replied, with more than a snap to my voice.

'Thank God for that—although you do a great stone statue impression.'

I ignored Neo and fixed my gaze on the man seated behind the large antique desk. My father was studying me with a mixture of regret and apprehension. He knew my precise thoughts on the subject being discussed.

No, not *discussed*.

It was being *thrust* upon me.

'No,' I replied firmly. 'There has to be another way.'

The tension in the room elevated, but this was too serious for me to mince my words. Too serious to let the elephant that always loomed in the room on occasions like this cloud my judgement.

I simply couldn't allow the fact that my grandfather had chosen me as his successor instead of my father to get in the way of this discussion. Nor could I allow the resentment and guilt that had always tainted my relationship with my father to alter my view on what was being proposed.

What was done was done. I'd turned the tides and restored the fortunes of my family. For that even my father couldn't object.

Which was why I was a little surprised when he emphatically shook his head.

'There isn't. Your grandfather was of sound mind when he made the arrangement.'

'Even though he was judged otherwise in other areas?'

Barely fettered bitterness filtered through my voice. The injustices dealt to my grandfather and mentor, the man who taught me everything I know, still burned like acid all these years after his untimely death.

'Now is not the time to reopen old wounds, Axios,' my father said, jaw clenched.

My quiet fury burned even as I accepted his words. 'I agree. Now is the time to discuss ways to get me *out* of this nonsense.'

And it *was* nonsense to expect an arrangement like this to hold water.

'A sweeping agreement where the other party gets to call the shots whenever they like? How come the lawyers haven't ripped this to shreds?' I demanded, striving to keep a tighter rein on my ire.

My father's lips firmed. 'I've spent the last month discussing it with our counsel. We can fight it in court, and probably win, but it'll be a protracted affair. And is now really the time to draw adverse publicity to the company? Or drag your grandfather's name through the mud again for that matter?'

My own lips flattened as again I grimly accepted he was right. With Xenakis Aeronautics poised for its biggest global expansion yet, the timing was far from ideal.

Which was exactly what Yiannis Petras had banked on.

'You mentioned you'd offered him ten million euros and he refused? Let's double the offer,' I suggested.

Neo shook his head. 'I already tried. Petras is hellbent on Option A or Option B.'

The breath left my lungs in a rush. 'Over my dead body will I go for Option A and hand over twenty-five percent of Xenakis Aeronautics,' I replied coldly. 'Not for the paltry quarter of a million his father bailed Grandpapa out with, while almost crippling him with steep interest repayments!'

The company I'd spent gruelling years saving was now worth several billion euros.

My brother shrugged. 'Then it's Option B. A full and final one hundred million euros, plus marriage to his daughter for minimum term of one year.'

A cold shudder tiptoed down my spine.

Marriage.

To a bride I didn't want and with a connection to a family that had brought mine nothing but misery, pain and near destitution.

During the formative years of my life I witnessed how a fall from grace could turn family members against each other. Clawing my own family out of that quagmire while other factions sneered and expected me to fail had opened my eyes to the true nature of relationships.

Outwardly, the Xenakis were deemed a strong unit now, but the backbiting had never gone away. The barely veiled expectation that everything I'd achieved would be brought down like a pile of loose bricks and that history would repeat itself was a silent challenge I rose to each morning.

While my extended family now enjoyed the fruits of my labour, and even tripped over themselves to remain in my good graces, deep down I knew a simple misstep was all it would take for their frivolous loyalties to falter.

I didn't even blame them.

How could I when my own personal interactions had repeatedly taken the same route? Each liaison I entered into eventually devolved into a disillusioning level of avarice and status-grabbing.

It was why my relationships now had a strict time limit of weeks. A few months, tops. Which made the thought of tying myself to one woman for twelve long months simply...*unthinkable*.

My chest tightened, and the urge to rail at my grandfather for putting me in this position seared me with shame before I suppressed it.

He'd been in an equally impossible position. I knew first-hand what the toll of keeping his family together had cost him—had watched deep grooves etch his grey face once vibrant with laughter and seen his shoulders slump under the heavy burden of loss.

Yes, he should have told me about this Sword of Damocles hanging over my head. But he was gone. Thanks to the ruthless greed of the Petras family. A family hell-bent on extracting another pound of flesh they didn't deserve.

'The hundred million I understand. But why insist

on marriage to the daughter?' I asked my brother as his words pierced the fog of my thoughts.

Neo shrugged again. 'Who knows how men like Petras think? Maybe he just wants to offload her. The clout that comes from marrying into the Xenakis family isn't without its benefits,' he mused.

I shuddered, the reminder that, to most people, my family and I were nothing but meal tickets sending a shock of bitterness through me.

'And did you meet this woman I'm to tie myself to?'

He nodded. 'She's…' He stopped and smiled slyly. 'I'll let you judge for yourself.' His gaze left mine to travel over my grey pinstriped suit. 'But I'm thinking you two will hit it off.'

Before I could demand an explanation my father leaned forward. 'Enough, Neo.' My father's gaze swung to me, steel reflected in his eyes. 'We can't delay any longer. Yiannis Petras wants an answer by morning.'

The pressure gripping my nape escalated—the effect of the noose closing round it ramping up my discord. Marriage was the last thing I wanted. To anyone. But especially to a Petras. Both my grandparents and my parents had been strained to breaking point because of the Petras family's actions, with ill-health borne of worry taking my grandmother before her time too.

There had to be another way…

'What's her name?' I asked my father—not because I cared but because I needed another moment to think. To wrap my head around this insanity.

'Calypso Athena Petras. But I believe she responds to Callie.'

Beside me, Neo smirked again. 'A dramatic name for a dramatic situation!'

I balled my fist and attempted to breathe through the churning in my gut. First they'd forced my grandfather's business into the ground, until he'd broken his family right down the middle by working himself into an early grave. Now this…

'Show me the agreement.' I needed to see it for myself, find a way to assimilate what I'd been committed to.

My father slid the document across the desk. I read it, my fingers clenching as with each paragraph the noose tightened.

Twelve months of my life, starting from the exchange of vows, after which either party would be free to divorce.

Twelve months during which the Petras family who, by a quirk of karma—if you believe in that sort of thing—had fallen on even harder times than they'd condemned my family to would be free to capitalise fully on their new status of wealth and privilege by association.

My lips twisted. I intended to have my lawyers draft divorce papers before I went anywhere near a church.

I exhaled, knowing my subconscious had already accepted the situation.

'Don't overthink it, brother. You're thirty-three next month. This will be over by your thirty-fourth birthday. If you bite the bullet,' Neo offered helpfully.

Slowly, I dragged myself back under control. 'I've worked too hard and too long to restore our family back to where it belongs to lose it to a greedy opportunist. If there's no other way…tell Petras we have a deal.'

My father nodded, relieved, before he sent me another nervous glance. The kind that announced there was something more equally unsavoury to deliver.

'What now?' My patience was hanging by a thread.

'Besides paying for the wedding, we also need to present the family with a...a dowry of sorts. Petras has asked for Kosima.'

I surged to my feet, uncaring that my chair tipped over. '*Excuse* me?'

My father's face tightened. 'No one has stepped foot on the island since your grandfather passed—'

'That doesn't mean I want to hand it over to the son of the man who caused his death!'

A flash of pain dimmed his eyes. 'We don't know that to be strictly true.'

'Don't we? Did you not see for yourself the pressure he was under? He only started drinking after the problems with Petras started. Is it any wonder his heart failed?'

'Easy, brother,' Neo urged. 'Father is right. The house is rotting away and the land around it is nothing but a pile of weeds and stones.'

But I was beyond reason. Beyond furious at this last damning request.

'Grandpapa loved that island. It belongs to us. I'm not going to hand it over to Petras. Isn't it enough that he's imposing this bilious arrangement on us?'

'Is it enough for you to drag your heels on this last hurdle?' My father parried.

Unable to remain still, I strode to the window of the building that housed the headquarters of Xenakis Aeronautics, the global airline empire I'd headed for almost a decade. For a full minute I watched traffic move back and forth on the busy Athens streets while I grappled with this last condition.

I sensed my brother and father approach. I didn't acknowledge them as they positioned themselves on either side of me and waited.

Waited for the only response that I could conceivably give. The words burned in my throat. Left a trail of ash on my tongue. But it had to be done. I had to honour my grandfather's request, no matter my personal view on it. Or I'd risk everything he'd built. Risk mocking the sacrifice that had taken the ultimate toll.

'Tell Petras he has a deal.'

My father's hand arrived on my shoulder in silent gratitude, after which he exited quietly.

Neo chose more exuberant congratulations, but even then I barely felt him slap my shoulder.

'Think of it this way. For twelve months you'll be free of all the scheming socialites and supermodels who've been falling over themselves to extract a commitment from you. I'll happily carry that burden for you instead.'

'Unless you wish to date one of those supermodels whilst sporting a black eye, I suggest you leave my office immediately,' I growled.

My brother's laughter echoed in my ears long after he'd slammed the door behind him.

But long before the echo died I made another silent vow to myself. Petras and his kin would pay for what they'd done to my family. Before the stipulated year of marriage was out they'd regret tangling with the Xenakis family.

CHAPTER ONE

'*Smile, Calypso. It's the happiest day of your life!*'

'*Here, let me put some more blusher on your cheeks... you're so pale. Perhaps a bit more shadow for your beautiful eyes...*'

Beneath the endless layers of white tulle that some faceless stranger had deemed the perfect wedding gown material and gone to town with my fingers bunched into fists. When the tight clenches didn't help, I bit the tip of my tongue and fought the urge to scream.

But I was past hysteria. *That* unfortunate state had occurred two weeks prior, when my father had informed me just how he'd mapped out the rest of my life. How it was my turn to help restore our family's honour.

Or else.

The cold shivers racing up and down my spine had become familiar in the last month, after a few days spent in denial that my father would truly carry out his intentions.

I'd quickly accepted that he would.

Years of bitterness and humiliation and failure to emulate his ruthless father's dubious acclaim had pushed him over the edge once and for all.

The soft bristles of the blusher brush passed feverishly over my cheeks. The make-up artist determined to transform me into an eager, blushing, starry-eyed bride.

But I was far from eager and a million miles away from starry-eyed.

The only thing they'd got right in this miserable spectacle was the virginal white.

If I'd had a choice that too would have been a lie. At twenty-four I knew, even in my sheltered existence, that being a virgin was a rare phenomenon. At least now I realised why my father had been hell-bent on thwarting my every encounter with the opposite sex. Why he'd ruthlessly vetted my friendships, curtailed my freedom.

I'd believed my choices had been so abruptly limited since the moment my mother fell from grace. Since she returned home the broken prodigal wife and handed my father all the weapons he needed to transform himself from moderately intolerable to fearsome tyrant. I thought I'd been swept along by the merciless broom of wronged party justice, but he'd had a completely different purpose for me.

A purpose which had brought me to this moment.

My wedding day.

The next shudder coagulated in my chin, making it wobble like jelly before I could wrestle my composure back under control.

Luckily the trio of women who'd descended on our house twenty-four hours ago were clucking about pre-wedding nerves, then clucking some more about how understandable my fraught emotions were, considering who my prospective husband was.

Axios Xenakis.

A man I'd never met.

Sure, like everyone in Greece I knew who he was.

A wildly successful airline magnate worth billions and head of the influential Xenakis family. A family whose ill fortune, unlike mine, had been reversed due the daring innovation of its young CEO.

It was rumoured that Axios Xenakis was the kind of individual whose projections could cause stock markets to rise or fall. The various articles I'd read about him had boggled my mind—the idea that any one person could wield such power and authority was bewildering. To top it off, Axios Xenakis was drop-dead gorgeous, if a little fierce-looking.

Everything about the man was way too visceral and invasive. Just a simple glance at his image online had evoked the notion that he could see into my soul, glean my deepest desires and use them against me. It was probably why he was often seen in the company of sophisticated heiresses and equally influential A-listers.

Which begged the question—why the Petras family? More specifically, why *me*?

What did a man who dated socialites and heiresses on a regular basis, as was thoroughly documented in the media, have to gain by shackling himself to me?

I knew it had something to do with the supreme smugness my father had been exhibiting in the last several weeks but he had refused to disclose. Somehow, behind the sneers and bitterness whenever the Xenakis name came up over the years, my father had been scheming. And that scheming had included me.

In all my daydreams about attaining my freedom, marriage hadn't featured anywhere. I wanted the freedom to dictate who I socialised with, what I ate, the pleasure to paint my watercolours without fear of recrimination, without judgement… The freedom to live life on *my* terms.

The hope of one day achieving those things had stopped me from succumbing to abject misery.

But not like *this*!

I forced my gaze to the mirror and promptly looked away again. My eyes were desolate pools, my cheeks artificially pink with excess rouge. My lips were turned down, reflecting my despair since learning that I was promised to a stranger. One who'd demanded a wedding within twenty-eight days.

My flat refusal had merely garnered a cold shrug from my father, before he had gone for the jugular—my one weakness.

My mother.

As if summoned by my inner turmoil, the electric whine of a wheelchair disturbed the excited chatter of the stylists. The moment they realised the mother of the bride had entered the bedroom, their attention shifted to her.

Taking advantage of the reprieve, I surreptitiously rubbed at my cheeks with a tissue, removing a layer of blusher. The icy peach lipstick disappeared with the second swipe across my lips, leaving me even paler than before but thankfully looking less of a lost, wide-eyed freak. Quickly hanging the thick lace veil over my face to hide the alteration, I stood and turned, watching as the women fawned over my mother.

Iona Petras had been stunningly beautiful once upon a time. Growing up, I was in awe of her statuesque beauty, her vivacity and sheer joy for life. Her laughter had lit up my day, her intelligence and love of the arts fuelling my own appreciation for music and painting.

Now, greying and confined, she was still a beautiful woman. But along with her broken body had come a broken spirit no amount of pretending or smiling, or even gaining the elevated position as mother of the bride, soon to marry a man most deemed a demigod, could disguise.

She withstood the stylists' ministrations without complaint, her half-hearted smile only slipping when her eyes met mine. Within them I saw ravaging misery and the sort of unending despair that came with the life sentence she'd imposed on herself by returning when she should have fled.

But, just as I'd had to remain here because of her, I knew my mother had returned home because of me. And somewhere along the line Iona Petras had accepted her fate.

'Leave us, please,' she said to the stylists, her voice surprisingly steely.

The women withdrew. She wheeled herself closer, her face pinched with worry. For the longest minute she stared at me.

'Are you all right?'

I tensed, momentarily panicked that she'd learned what I'd hidden from her for the last few weeks. As much as I'd tried to ignore the ever-growing pain in my abdomen, I couldn't any more. Not only had it become a constant dull ache, it had become a reminder that even health-wise my life wasn't my own. That I might well be succumbing to the very real ailment that had taken my grandmother—

'Callie? Are you ready?'

Realising she was talking about the wedding ceremony, I felt the urge to succumb to hysteria pummel me once again. As did the fierce need to be selfish just this once…to simply flee and let the chips fall where they may.

'Is anyone ever ready to marry a man they've never met?' I asked. 'Please tell me you've found out why he's demanding I do this?' I pleaded.

Eyes a shade darker than my own lapis-lazuli-coloured ones turned mournful as she shook her head. 'No. Your father still refuses to tell me. My guess is that it has something to do with your grandfather and old man Xenakis.' Before I could ask what she meant, she continued, 'Anyway, Yiannis will be looking for me, so I need to be quick.'

She reached inside the stylish designer jacket that matched her lavender gown and produced a thick cream envelope, her fingers shaking as she stared at it.

'What's that?' I asked when she made no move to speak.

Within her gaze came a spark of determination I hadn't seen in years. My heart leapt into my throat as she caught my hand in hers and squeezed it tight.

'My sweet Callie, I know I've brought misery to your life with my actions—'

'No, Mama, you haven't. I promise,' I countered firmly.

She stared at me. 'I'm not sure whether to be proud or to admonish you for being such a good liar. But I know what I've done. My selfishness has locked you in this prison with me when you should be free to pursue what young girls your age ought to be doing.' Her fingers tightened on mine. 'I want you to make me a promise,' she pleaded, her voice husky with unshed tears.

I nodded because…what else could I do? 'Anything you want, Mama.'

She held out the envelope. 'Take this. Hide it in the safest place you can.'

I took it, frowning at the old-fashioned cursive lettering spelling out my name. 'What's this?'

'It's from your grandmother.'

'Yiayia Helena?' A tide of sorrow momentarily washed over me, my heart still missing the grandmother I'd lost a year ago.

My mother nodded. 'She said I'd know when you needed it. And even if I'm wrong...'

She paused, a faraway look in her eyes hinting that she was indulging in all those might-have-beens that sparked my own desperate imagination. When she refocused, her gaze moved dully over my wedding dress.

'Even if this...alliance turns out to be tolerable, it'll help to know you were loved by your grandmother. That should you need her she'll be there for you the way I wasn't.'

I held on tighter to her hand. 'I know you love me, Mama.'

She shook her head, tears brimming her eyes. 'Not the way a mother should love her child, without selfish intentions that end up harming her. I took the wrong turn with you. I left you alone with your father when I should have taken you with me. Maybe if I had—' She stopped, took a deep breath and dabbed at her tears before braving my worried stare again. 'All I ask is that you find a way to forgive me one day.'

'Mama—' I stopped when she gave a wrenching sob.

Her gaze dropped to the envelope in my hand. 'Hang on to that, Callie. And don't hesitate to use it when you need it. Promise me,' she insisted fervently.'

'I... I promise.'

She sniffed, nodded, then abruptly turned the wheelchair and manoeuvred herself out of my bedroom.

Before I could process our conversation I was again surrounded by mindless chatter, unable to breathe or think. The only solid thing in my world became the envelope I clutched tightly in my hand. And when I found that within the endless folds of tulle the designer had fashioned a pocket, I nearly cried with relief as I slipped the envelope into it.

Even without knowing its contents, just knowing it came from my grandmother—the woman who'd helped me stand up to my father's wrath more times than I could count, who'd loved and reassured me on a daily basis during my mother's year-long absence when I was fifteen years old—kept me from crumbling as my father arrived and with a brisk nod offered his stiff arm, ordered me to straighten my spine…and escorted me to my fate.

The chapel was filled to the brim, according to the excited chatter of the household staff, and as my father led me out to a flower-bedecked horse-drawn carriage I got the first indication of what was to come.

Over the last three weeks I'd watched with a sense of surrealism as construction crews and landscapers descended on our little corner of the world to transform the church and surrounding area from a place of rundown dilapidation into its former whitewashed charming glory.

The usually quiet streets of Nicrete, a sleepy village in the south of the island of Skyros, the place generations of the Petras family had called home, buzzed with fashionably dressed strangers—all guests of Axios Xenakis. With the main means of getting on and off the island being by boat, the harbour had become a place of interest in the last few days.

Every hotel and guest house on the island was booked solid. Expensive speedboats and a handful of super-yachts had appeared on the horizon overnight, and now bobbed in the Aegean beneath resplendent sunshine.

Of course the man I was to marry chose to do things differently.

My carriage was halfway between home and the church when the loud, mechanical whine of powerful rotors churned the air. Children shouted in excitement and raced towards the hilltop as three sleek-looking helicopters flew overhead to settle on the newly manicured lawns of the park usually used as recreational grounds for families. Today the whole park had been cordoned off—evidently to receive these helicopters.

Beneath the veil I allowed myself a distasteful moue. But the barrier wasn't enough to hide my father's smug smile as he watched the helicopters. Or his nod of satisfaction as several distinguished-looking men and designer-clad women alighted from the craft.

I averted my face, hoping the ache in my heart and the pain in my belly wouldn't manifest itself in the hysteria I'd been trying to suppress for what seemed like for ever. But I couldn't prevent the words from tumbling from my lips.

'It's not too late, Papa. Whatever this is… Perhaps if you told me why, we can find a way—'

'I have already found a way, child.'

'Don't call me a child—I'm twenty-four years old!'

That pulse of rebellion, which I'd never quite been able to curb, eagerly fanned by Yiayia when she was alive, slipped its leash. She'd never got on well with my father, and in a way standing up to him now, despite the potential fallout for my mother, felt like honouring her memory.

His eyes narrowed. 'If you wanted to help then you should've taken that business degree at university, instead of the useless arts degree you're saddled with.'

'I told you—I'm not interested in a corporate career.'

Nor was I interested in being constantly reminded that I wasn't the son he'd yearned for. The one he'd hoped would help him save Petras Industries, the family company which now teetered on the brink of bankruptcy.

'*Ne*—and just like your mother you let me down. Once again it has fallen to *me* to find a way. And I have. So now you will smile and do your duty by this family. You will say your vows and marry Xenakis.'

I bit my lip at this reminder of yet another bone of contention between us. I'd fought hard for the right to leave the island to pursue my arts degree, only returning because of my mother. The small art gallery I worked at part-time on Nicrete was a way of keeping my sanity, even as I mourned my wasted degree.

'After that, what then?'

He shrugged. 'After that you will belong to him. But remember that regardless of the new name you're taking on you're still a Petras. If you do anything to bring the family into disrepute you will bear the consequences.'

My heart lurched, my fists balling in pain and frustration—because I knew exactly what my father meant.

The *consequences* being my father's ability to manipulate my mother's guilt and ensure maximum suffering. His constant threats to toss her out with only the clothes on her back, to abandon her to her fate the way she'd briefly abandoned her family. But while my mother had deserted her child and marriage in the name of a doomed love, my father was operating from a place of pure revenge. To him, his wife had humiliated and betrayed him, and he was determined to repay her by keeping her prisoner. Ensuring that at every waking moment she was reminded of her fall from grace and his power over her.

The reason that I'd been roped in as a means to that end was my love for my mother.

Eight years ago, when he'd returned home with my absentee mother after the doctors in Athens had called and informed him that she'd been in a crash, and that the man she'd run away with was dead, he'd laid out new family rules. My mother would stay married to him. She would become a dutiful wife and mother, doing everything in her power to not bring another speck of disgrace to the family. In return he would ensure her medical needs were met, and that she would be given the finest treatment to adjust to her new wheelchair-bound life.

For my part, I would act the devoted daughter…or my mother would suffer.

The horses whinnying as they came to a stop at the steps leading to the church doors dragged me to the present, pushing my heartache aside and replacing it with apprehension.

The last of the guests were entering while organ music piped portentously in the air. In less than an hour I would be married to a man I'd never exchanged a single word with. A man who had somehow fallen in league with my father for reasons I still didn't know.

I glanced at my father, desperate to ask why. His stony profile warned me not to push my luck. Like my heartache, I smothered my rebellion.

My father stepped out of the carriage and held out his

hand. Mine shook, and again I was glad for the veil's cover to hide my tear-prickled eyes.

A small part of me was grateful that my father didn't seem in a hurry to march me down the aisle because he was basking in the limelight that momentarily banished the shadow of scandal and humiliation he'd lived under for the past eight years. For once people weren't talking about his wife's infidelity. Or the fact that the woman who'd deserted him had returned in a wheelchair. Or that he'd taken her back just so he could keep her firmly under his thumb in retribution.

Today he was simply the man who'd seemingly bagged one of the most eligible bachelors in the world for his daughter—not the once illustrious but now down-trodden businessman who'd lost the Petras fortune his father had left him.

The doors to the church yawned open, ready to receive their unwilling sacrifice. My footsteps faltered and my father sent me a sharp look. Unable to meet his eyes without setting off the spark of mutiny attempting to rekindle itself inside me, I kept my gaze straight.

I needed to do this for my mother.

I spotted her in the front row, her head held high despite her fate, and it lent me the strength to put one foot in front of the other. The slight weight of my grandmother's envelope in my pocket helped me ignore the rabid curiosity and speculative whispers of three hundred strangers.

Unfortunately there was only one place left to look. At the towering figure of the man waiting in perfect stillness facing the altar.

He didn't twitch nor fidget. Didn't display any outward signs of being a nervous groom.

His broad back and wide shoulders seemed to go on for ever, and his proud head and unyielding stance announced his power and authority. He didn't speak to the equally tall, commanding figure next to him, as most grooms did with their best man. In fact both men stood as if to military attention, their stance unwavering.

My gaze flicked away from Axios Xenakis, my breath stalling in my throat the closer I approached. Even without seeing his face I sensed a formidable aura—one that forced me again to wonder why he was doing this. What did he have to gain with this alliance?

He could have any woman he wanted. So why me?

And why had several butterflies suddenly taken flight within my belly?

Wild instinct urged me to fan my rebellion to life. *Fight or flight.* Pick one and deal with the consequences later.

But even as the thoughts formed they were discarded.

I had no choice. None whatsoever.

But maybe this man I was marrying would be a little more malleable than my father. Maybe—

He turned. And the feeble little hope died a horrible death.

Eyes the colour of polished gunmetal bored into me as if they were with fierce, merciless hooks. They probed beneath the veil with such force that for a moment I imagined I was naked—that he could see my every weakness and flaw, see to the heart of my deepest desire for freedom.

His lips were pressed into a formidable line, his whole demeanour austere. Axios Xenakis could have been in a boardroom, preparing to strike a deal to make himself another billion euros, not poised before an altar, about to commit himself to a wife he'd never met.

I catalogued his breathtaking features. Wondered if that rugged boxer's jaw ever relaxed—whether the cut-glass sharpness of his cheekbones ever softened in a smile. Did he maintain constant control of those sleek eyebrows so they were permanently brooding? Did his nose ever wrinkle in laughter?

Why was I interested?

I was nothing but part of a transaction to him—one he didn't seem entirely thrilled about, judging by his icy regard. So it didn't matter that the olive vibrancy of his skin drew from me more than a fleeting look, or that he was without a doubt the most strikingly handsome man I'd ever seen.

He was a world removed from the boys I'd sneakily dated at university, before my father had found out and ruthlessly thwarted my chances with them before anything resembling a relationship could form.

Axios Xenakis belonged in a stratosphere of his own. One I was apprehensive about inhabiting.

My footsteps stalled and I heard my father's sharp intake of breath. It was swiftly followed by the tight grip of his hand in warning.

Don't disgrace the family.

Defiance sparked again.

But then I saw my mother's head turn. The ubiquitous misery filmed her eyes, but alongside it was a look so fierce it might have been a reflection from my grandmother's eyes.

It was a look that infused me with courage.

It's up to you, it said. *Do this...or don't.*

My heart thundered. The need to turn around and simply walk away was a wild cyclone churning through me.

At the altar, Axios's eyes never shifted from me, his stance unchanging in the face of my clear reluctance. It was as if he knew what I'd decide and was simply waiting me out.

And, since I was playing in a game whose rules no one had bothered to apprise me of, there was only one move I could make.

I would play this round, then fight my corner later.

With that firm promise echoing inside me, I stepped up to the altar.

I saw a fleeting disappointment in his eyes before he masked his features. He was *disappointed*? Did that mean he didn't want this?

Wild hope flared within me even as bewilderment mounted. If he didn't want this then there might be room to negotiate. Room to get what I wanted out of this.

Realising I was staring, and that my father had been dispatched and I was now the sole focus of Axios Xenakis' eyes, I hurriedly averted my gaze. But not before acknowledging that up close he was even more electrifying. Perhaps it was the severity of his grey suit. Or the fact that the hand he held out to me screamed a silent command.

The last strains of the hymn trailed away, leaving behind a charged silence. With each second it weighed heavier, pressing down on me.

His hand extended another inch, and heavy expectation thickened the air.

With a deep breath, inevitably I slipped my hand into his—and joined the stranger who was to be my husband.

Almost immediately he released me. But the sensation of his touch lingered, and a sizzling chain reaction I was unprepared for travelled up my arm, flaring wide.

It was enough momentarily to drown out the intonation of the priest's voice as he began the ceremony.

I rallied long enough to murmur the words I'd reluctantly memorised and, when the time came, to pick up the larger of the two platinum wedding bands.

With fingers that still trembled I faced Axios. The impact of his eyes, his towering frame, the much too handsome face momentarily erased the words from my brain.

In silence he held out his left hand, his laser eyes boring into me as he simply…*waited.*

'I take thee…'

'For better or worse…'

'With my body…'

'Love, honour, cherish…'

'Till death…'

With each spoken vow my heart squeezed tighter, the mechanical delivery I'd expected to give morphing into a whispered outpouring wrapped in consternation.

The second I was done he reached for the other ring without taking his eyes off me, again holding out his hand for mine.

And then Axios Xenakis spoke for the first time.

'I, Axios Xenakis, take thee, Calypso Athena Petras…'

The rest of his words were lost to me as the deep, hypnotic cadence of his voice struck like Zeus's thunderbolt into a place I didn't even know existed until that moment.

His voice was…*sexy.* Alluring. Magnetic.

It seemed impossible that a voice could be all those things, and yet I felt every one.

The cold brush of platinum on my skin brought me back to myself just in time to hear the priest announce us as man and wife. To say that my new husband could now kiss me.

I started to turn away. Because this was a far cry from a normal wedding ceremony. And we were far removed from two people in love.

Large, firm hands cupped my shoulders, shocking me into stillness. Unable to stop a cascade of light shivers, I held my breath as he lifted the heavy veil and draped it behind me with unhurried movements. I watched his gaze take in my bound hair, the small headband made of tiny diamonds and pearls that had belonged to Yiayia Helena and the similar necklace adorning my throat.

Had he been anyone else I might have entertained the notion that Axios Xenakis was reluctant to look into the face of the woman he'd just committed himself to. Because when his piercing grey eyes finally settled on me, I caught a momentary confusion, then his eyes widened and his jaw slackened for a split second before he reasserted supreme control.

Any fleeting pleasure I'd felt at gaining some unknown upper hand fled as heat suffused my face at his intense, almost shocked scrutiny.

Admitting that I should have left the make-up artist's work alone didn't help my urge to squirm under his candid regard. But I forced myself to hold his gaze, ignore the consternation in his eyes and the humiliating thud of my heartbeat.

Just when I thought he intended to drag the torture out for ever he slid one finger beneath my chin to nudge my head upward. Caught in the mysterious hypnosis of his gaze, I watched his head descend, so close that heat from his skin singed mine.

I braced myself, my stomach churning with emotions I couldn't name.

I'd been kissed before. Those university colleagues I'd toyed with before my father's bitter reach had scared them away. None of them had elicited this level of shivery anticipation.

His kiss arrived, subtle as a butterfly's wing and powerful as a sledgehammer. Sensation rocked through me like an earthquake, dizzying and terrifying, leaving me with nothing to do but to brace my hands on his chest, anchor myself to reality somehow.

But all that did was compound my situation. Because the solid wall of his chest was like sculpted warm steel, inviting the kind of exploration that had no place in this time and space.

Pull away.

Before I could, he gave a sharp intake of breath. In the next moment I was free of him and he was turning away.

Back to earth with a shaky thud, I fought angry bewilderment even as I strove for composure before our three-hundred-strong audience.

The feeling lingered all through our walk down the aisle, through our stiff poses for pictures and then the ride back up the hill to the crumbling mansion overlooking the harbour—the only home I'd ever known.

The horse and carriage had been swapped for a sleek limousine with darkened windows and a partition that ensured privacy. Beside me Axios maintained a stony silence, one I wasn't inclined to break despite the dark, enigmatic looks he slanted me every now and then.

When it all became too much, I snatched in a breath and faced him. 'Is there something on your mind?'

One eyebrow quirked. 'As conversations go, that's not

quite what I expected as our first. But then I'm making many surprising discoveries.'

He wasn't the only one! 'What's that supposed to mean?'

He didn't reply immediately. Then, 'You're not what I was led to expect.'

I couldn't help my lips twisting. 'You are aware of how absurd that sounds, aren't you?'

He stiffened, and I got the notion that once again something about me had surprised him. 'No. Enlighten me,' he replied dryly.

'Not what you were *led to expect*?' The slight screech in my voice warned me that hysteria might be winning but I couldn't stop. 'Let me guess—you thought you were getting some biddable wallflower who would tremble and trip over herself to please you?'

You were trembling minutes ago, when he kissed you.

I ignored the voice and met his gaze.

He'd turned into a pillar of stone. 'Considering the ink isn't dry on our marriage certificate, perhaps we should strive not to have our first disagreement. Unless you wish to break some sort of record?' he rasped, gunmetal eyes boring into me.

Apart from our marriage, I still didn't know the precise details of the deal between my father and my new husband and it momentarily stalled my response. But the fire burning inside me wouldn't be doused.

'I get the feeling you're just as...*invested* in this thing as my father is, so it bears repeating that you're *not* getting a simpering lackey who will jump through hoops to amuse you.'

His eyes narrowed. 'Your *father*? Not you?'

Short of revealing my ignorance on the matter, I had to prevaricate. 'I'm a Petras—same as he.'

Something that looked very much like contempt flickered through his eyes. 'Consider me forewarned,' he replied cryptically.

Before I could query what he meant the limo was pulling up to the double doors of my family home. Liveried footmen hurried to throw our doors open.

Inside the rarely used but hastily refurbished ballroom guests drank champagne and feasted on canapés and my father gave a painfully false speech. I only managed to sit through it by reaching into my pocket and clutching the envelope within.

The moment the speeches were done Axios was swarmed upon by fawning acquaintances, eager to engage the great man in conversation. I told myself that my primary emotion was relief as the stylists, also roped into acting as my attendants, rushed to straighten my veil and train, twitching and tweaking until they were satisfied that I'd been restored to their vision of bridal beauty.

But just when I thought I'd have a moment's reprieve Axios's gaze zeroed in on me, his eyes falling to the barely touched food on the plate that lay next to my untouched glass of champagne.

One brow rose. 'Not in the mood for celebrating? Or are you trying to make some sort of point by not eating?'

I couldn't eat—not when the inkling was deepening that Axios Xenakis was far from a willing participant in this devilish deal. And if that was the case, what had I let myself in for?

I pushed the anxious thought away and let my gaze fall on his equally full plate. 'You should talk.'

He lifted his champagne and took a healthy gulp.

'Unlike you, this occasion isn't one I feel inclined to celebrate.'

My breath caught, but before I could ask him to elaborate, he continued.

'And in the interest of clarity let me warn you that neither you nor your father have any cards left to play. Should you feel inclined to make *more* demands.'

Christos, what exactly had my father done?

But even as the question burned fire boiled in my blood. 'Are you threatening my family? Because if you are, please know that I will fight you with everything I've got.'

His lips twisted at my fierce tone. 'What a fiery temper you have. I wonder what other surprises you're hiding beneath those unfortunate layers of… What *is* that material?'

As much as I hated my wedding dress, his remark sparked irritation. 'It's called tulle. And you should know. You paid for it, after all.'

The barest hint of a sardonic smile lifted his sensual lips. 'Writing a cheque for it doesn't mean I pay attention to every single detail of a woman's wardrobe. I have better things to do than concern myself with the name of the fabric that comprises a wedding gown.'

'But this is *your* wedding too,' I taunted, knowing my mockery would aggravate.

Something about this towering hunk of a man, who'd made it clear that this was the last place he wanted to be, riled me on a visceral level, firing up a need to dig beneath his formidable exterior.

'Isn't it supposed to be one of the momentous occasions of your life?'

Every trace of humour disappeared. Piercing grey

eyes pinned me in place, and the tension vibrating from him was so thick I could almost touch it.

'Momentous occasions are highly anticipated and satisfactorily celebrated. You'd have to be delusional or deliberately blind to imagine I'm in such a state, Calypso Petras.'

The way he said my name, with drawling, mocking intonation, fired my blood. Along with other sensations I couldn't quite name.

'It's Calypso Xenakis now—or have you already forgotten?' I fired back, taking secret pleasure in seeing the irritated flare of his nostrils.

'I have not forgotten,' he answered with taut iciness.

'If this is such an ordeal for you, then why all this?' I waved my hand at the obscenely lavish banquet displayed along one long wall, the champagne tower brimming with expensive golden bubbles, the caviar-laden trays being circulated, and the designer-clad guests, shamelessly indulging their appetites.

'Because your father insisted,' he replied, his voice colder than an arctic vortex. 'As *you* well know.'

I opened my mouth to tell him for once and for all that none of this made sense to me because no one had bothered to consult me about my own wedding.

The sight of my mother's face, staring at me from one table away, pain and misery etched beneath her smile, dried the words in my throat.

For whatever reason fate had tangled the Xenakises and the Petrases in an acrimonious weave and my mother and I were caught in the middle. I could no more extricate myself than I could turn my back on her.

A tiny, tortured sound whistled through the air and I realised it came from my own throat—a manifestation of that hysteria that just wouldn't die down. I stood abruptly, knowing I had to get away before I did something regrettable.

Like climb on top of the lavishly decorated lonely high table, set apart from everyone else to showcase the newly married couple in all their glory, and scream at the top of my lungs.

That just wouldn't do. Because while I might have acquired a new surname, it was dawning on me that until I learned the true nature of what I was embroiled in I would be wise to keep a firm hold of my feelings.

And an even firmer hold of my wits.

CHAPTER TWO

Money makes the world spin.

I swallowed my champagne, careful not to choke on it as I dispassionately observed the guests indulging in the revelry of my sham of a wedding.

Money had made this happen, and in the exact time frame I'd requested it.

Money had put that smug smile on Yiannis Petras's face.

Money had made the family, decimated by my grandfather's fall from grace, rally together for the sake of enjoying the rejuvenated fruits of my labour.

I'd seen first-hand how the lack of it could cause backbiting and untold strain. Ostensibly solid marriages crumbled under the threat of diminished wealth and influence. I'd seen it in my parents' marriage. It was why I'd never have freely chosen this route for myself.

My gaze shifted to my brand-new wife.

Had money influenced her agreement to this fiasco?

Was she getting a cut of the hundred million euros?

Of course she was. Had she not proclaimed herself a true Petras?

For those seconds as she'd hesitated at the altar I'd

entertained the notion that she shared my reluctance, had imagined the merest hint of resistance in her eyes.

Her words had put me straight.

A cursory investigation had revealed that while she'd graduated from Skypos University with a major in Arts, she'd done nothing with her degree for the last two years. Her father's daughter through and through, sitting back and taking the easy route to riches.

So what if outwardly she wasn't what I expected?

I snorted under my breath at this colossal understatement. Calypso Petras...*ochi*, make that Calypso Xenakis...was beyond a surprise. She was a punch to my solar plexus, one it was taking an irritatingly long time to wrestle under control.

Even now my senses still reeled from what I'd uncovered beneath her veil. She was far from the drab little mouse I'd assumed.

'I believe there's a rule somewhere that states you shouldn't scowl on your wedding day.'

I resisted the urge to grind my teeth and faced my brother. 'You think this is funny?'

'This whole circus? No. I believe that ring on your finger and the look on your face makes it all too real.' Neo affected a mocking shudder intended to rile me further.

It worked.

'I'm talking about your implication that my... Calypso.' *Thee mou*, why did her name sound so...erotic?

Neo's eyes widened before glinting with keen speculation. 'If I recall, I didn't give you any specifics.'

There was a reason Neo was president of marketing at Xenakis Aeronautics. He could sell hay to a farmer.

My fingers tightened around my glass. 'You deliberately let me to think she was…unremarkable.'

She was quite the opposite. Hers was the confounding kind of beauty one couldn't place a finger on. The kind that made you stare for much longer than was polite.

Neo shrugged. 'No, I didn't. And don't blame me for the dire state of your mind, brother,' he answered.

The low heat burning through my blood intensified. And while I wanted to attribute it to this conversation, I knew I couldn't. Ever since I'd pulled that hideous veil off her face and uncovered the woman I'd agreed to marry a different irritation had lodged itself deep inside me. One I wasn't quite ready to examine.

But that wasn't to say I was ready to let Neo off the hook for…

For what?

Making obfuscating observations about Calypso Petras that had made me dismiss her from my mind, only to be knocked off-kilter by her appearance?

Granted, she still wasn't my type. Her eyes were too large…much too *distracting*. They were the type of turquoise-blue that made you question their authenticity. Framed with long eyelashes that begged the same question. And then there were her lips. Full and sensual, with a natural bruised rose hue, and deeply alluring despite the absence of gloss.

The dichotomy of fully made-up eyes and bare lips had absorbed my attention for much too long at that altar. And it had irritated me even further that since our arrival at the reception those lips had been buried beneath a hideous layer of frosty peach.

But it hadn't stopped me puzzling over why the two aspects of her initial appearance had been so at odds with each other. Or why she'd seemed…startled by our very brief kiss on the altar.

False innocence wrapped around her true character? A character that contained more than a little fire.

My mind flicked to other hints I'd glimpsed over the last few hours. While I was yet to discover what lay beneath the layers of the wedding gown, there were more than enough hints to authenticate her voluptuousness.

Yet to discover…

The peculiar buzz that had been ignited during that fleeting kiss notched up a fraction, the fact that the brief contact still lingered on my lips drawing another frown.

'Your new wife is looking a little…unhappy. Perhaps you should see about fixing that?'

About to state that I had nothing to fix, that her happiness was none of my concern, I found my gaze flicked to the table. Despite the picture of poise she was trying to project she looked pale, her eyes flitting nervously. A quick scrutiny of our guests showed she was the object of several stares and blatant whispers.

A helpless prey in a jungle of predators.

My feet moved almost of their own accord, the niggling urge to reverse that look on her face irritating me even as I moved towards her, effectively silencing the whispers with quelling stares.

Regardless of how this union had come about, rumours couldn't be allowed to run rife. This was how undermining started.

As I neared, silence fell. Her gaze shifted, met mine. Her chin lifted, a wisp of bewilderment and skittishness evaporating and her eyes flashing with defiance.

For some absurd reason it sparked something to life inside me. Something I fully intended to ignore.

Defiance or bewilderment, the deed was done. She
and her family had capitalised on an agreement made
under duress and bagged themselves a windfall. She
should be celebrating.

Instead I caught another trace of apprehension as I
stopped beside her chair. Eyes growing wide, she looked
up at me. The graceful line of her neck—another alluring feature that seemed to demand attention—rippled
as she swallowed.

Thee mou, if this was an act then she was a good ac-
tress!

Aware of our audience, and a burning need to find
out, I held out my hand to her. 'The traditional first
dance is coming up, I believe.' The earlier we could
get this spectacle out of the way, the quicker I could resume my life.

Her gaze darted to the dance floor, her reluctance
clear. 'Is that…really necessary?'

Something about her reluctance and her whole demeanour grated. She was behaving as if I was contami-
nated!

'Enough with this pretence. That wide-eyed innocent
thing will only work for so long. Give it up, Calypso.'

She offered me her hand, but the eyes that met mine
as she stood sparkled with renewed fire. 'No one calls
me Calypso. My name is Callie,' she stated firmly.

I attempted to ignore the slim fingers in mine, the
smooth softness of her palm and the way it kicked to
life something inside me as I led her to the middle of
the dance floor.

'I'm your new husband—surely I don't fall under the
category of *no one*?' I curled my arm around her waist,

a singular need to press her close escalating inside me as the band struck up a waltz.

She stiffened. 'Are you insinuating that you're *special*?'

For some reason my lips quirked. 'By your tone, I'm guessing I'm not. Not even special enough for you to grant me the simple gift of addressing you as I please?'

Her lips firmed again, drawing my attention to their plumpness. Reminding me of that all too fleeting taste of them.

'And what am I to call *you*? Other than *stranger* or *husband*?'

For some reason the fiery huskiness of her voice drew another smile. A puzzle in itself, since humour was the last emotion I should have been experiencing. I was in this situation because of money and shameless greed.

'Call me Axios. Or Ax, as most people do. I doubt we will reach the stage of coining terms of endearment.'

'On that I think we're agreed,' she replied, her gaze fixed somewhere over my shoulder.

Another scrabble of irritation threatened to rise, but I suppressed it when I noticed that once again, beneath the show of sharp claws, she was trembling, her wide eyes a little too bright. As if she was holding on to her composure by a thread.

'Is something wrong?' I asked. Again I questioned my need to know. Or care.

'What could possibly be wrong?'

She didn't bother to meet my gaze. If anything, she attempted to detach herself, which ought to have been impossible, considering how close we were dancing. But I was learning that my new wife had several…interesting facets.

'It is polite to look at me when you address me.'

She maintained her stance for another few seconds, then her blue eyes rose to mine. The urge to stare into them, to commit every fleck and expression to memory, charged through me, this time bringing a wave of heat to my groin.

I inhaled slowly, forcing myself to ignore that unsettling sensation and address her as I would any acquaintance.

Even though she wasn't.

Even though she'd taken my name and we were effectively bound together for twelve long months.

'This thing will go smoother if we attempt to be civil with one another. Don't you agree?'

'I'm not a puppet. I cannot act a certain way on command.'

'But you *can* dispense with that little-girl-lost look. And I find it curious that you would choose to refer to puppets. Perhaps you're familiar with knowing exactly which strings to tug to get what you want?'

Unlike me, she didn't attempt to disguise her frown. 'What are you talking about?'

'This whole scheme, orchestrated by you and your family, has gone off without a hitch. Feel free to stop acting now.'

She inhaled sharply, her eyes darting to the guests dancing around us. 'Please keep your voice down.'

'Afraid you'll be found out? Are you really so blind to the fact that every single guest is speculating wildly about how two people who've never met are now married?'

Her plump lips pressed together for a moment. 'I can't

control what other people think. But I do care about per-petuating unfounded rumours.'

'Do you, *yineka mou*?'

Her blue eyes shadowed and her gaze quickly flicked away. 'Can you not call me that, please?'

'Why not? Are you not my wife?'

The more the term fell from my lips the deeper it bored into me, as if rooting for a place to settle. Of course the search would be futile, because this was far from what I wanted.

The strain and stress of trying to save his failing company while keeping his family and his marriage together had driven my grandfather into an early grave, his spirit broken long before the heart attack that had suddenly taken him. It was the same stress that had nearly broken my own father, forcing him to step down after a mere two years as CEO.

I didn't intend to weigh myself down with similar baggage.

I refocused on Calypso, attempting to ignore the effect of her soft curves against my body as she asked, 'So, what happens after this?'

'"This"?'

'After we're done here,' she elaborated.

Unbidden, my thoughts flew ahead. To when the evening would turn exclusive and intimate. When wedding euphoria traditionally took on another, more carnal dimension.

A traditions I *wouldn't* be indulging in.

'Do you plan on getting back into your helicopter and leaving me here?'

The carefully disguised hope in her voice threw me back to that day in my father's office a month ago, when an agreement that bore all the hallmarks of blackmail had crash-landed into my life and threatened the Xenakis name and business. Did she really think she and her family could take financial advantage and then sail off into the sunset?

The silent vow I'd taken that day to ensure neither Calypso nor her father escaped unscathed resurged as I looked down into her face. A face struggling for composure and a body twitching nervously beneath my hand.

I pulled her closer, steadied her at her slight stumble, and lowered my lips to her ear.

'It's our wedding night, *matia mou*. How would it look if we didn't stay under the same roof? Sleep in the same bed?'

My lips brushed the delicate shell of her ear and she shivered. A moment later wide, alluring eyes sought mine.

'Sleep in the same bed? But you don't even know me. What…what's the rush?'

I opened my mouth to tell her there was no rush. That giving her my name was the final payment she and her family would extract from me. Instead I shrugged, noting absently that a part of me was enjoying this a little too much.

'Other than ensuring there will be nothing to be held over my head when the whim takes your father? Are you suggesting a period of getting to know one another before we decide if we must consummate this marriage?'

She gave a little start. '*If*? Don't you mean *when*?' she whispered fiercely, her eyes wider, searching.

Again the words to answer, to state that this dance was as close as we would get for the duration of our agreement, remained unsaid on the tip of my tongue.

If she believed I would further compound this debacle by gracing her bed, so be it. She would discover differently later.

Absurdly, the pleasure in that thought of delivering disappointment never arrived. Instead I was unarmed by a disturbing throbbing in my groin, by the temptation to take a different approach. To gather her closer, breathe in the alluring perfume that clung to her silken skin.

I did just that, nudging her close with a firm clasp on her lower back. And heard her sharp intake of breath.

Pulling back, I glanced at her pale face. 'Are you all right?'

Her swift nod assured me that she was lying, and the wild darting of her gaze confirmed that belief.

'Calypso?'

'I… I'm fine. Just a little headache. That's all.'

I frowned. 'Then why are you touching your stomach?'

Her hand quickly relocated from her midriff to my shoulder, her smile little more than a grimace. 'It's nothing, I assure you.'

About to refute that assurance, I was forestalled by the end of the music and the applause that followed. And then by the arrival of Iona Petras.

My introduction to Calypso's mother, along with everyone else in the Petras clan, had been stiff and perfunctory, with no disguising exactly what this bloodless transaction was.

Everyone except Calypso.

'May I have a private moment with my daughter?' the older woman asked, although I got the feeling it was more an order than a request, giving me a momentary glimpse of where Calypso had inherited her quiet fire.

My fingers started to tighten on Calypso's waist, as a peculiar reluctance to let her go assailed me. I strenuously denied it and released her. 'By all means.'

A silent conversation passed between mother and daughter before Calypso held out her hand. Without so much as a glance my way, they exited the ballroom.

A fine irritant, like a tiny pebble in my shoe, stayed with me throughout all my inane conversations with people I didn't know and another five-minute ribbing from Neo. By the time my father approached I had the notion that my jaw would crack from being ground so tight.

'Am I mistaken or do you two seem to be getting along?' my father asked.

'You are mistaken,' I quipped, unwilling to admit how that dance and the feel of Calypso in my arms had fired up my blood.

He grimaced. 'I was hoping this would be less of an ordeal for you if you got along.'

'I said I'd do what needs to be done. And I will.'

Despite that small, startling flame of anticipation burning inside me.

Despite the fact that I'd completely dismissed any occurrence of a wedding night until exactly five minutes ago.

That sensation of her slender back beneath my hand…that pulse beating at her throat… The shivers she couldn't control.

The fire of anticipation flared higher, resisting every attempt to dampen it down.

But did I need to?

This abhorrent agreement hadn't, thankfully, included a stipulation for consummation. But would it be a true marriage without it?

Enough!

Wrestling with myself over this was beneath me. Everything Yiannis Petras had asked for had been delivered. They would get nothing more from me.

That declaration lasted until my new wife walked back into the room and attempted to dismiss me with a vacant smile, even while her eyes challenged me.

Something locked into place inside me.

A challenge that needed answering.

Without stopping to question the wisdom of doing it, I crossed the wide room to where she stood. Took the hand loosely fisted by her side and brushed my lips over her knuckles.

Satisfaction sizzled through me when her breath caught. 'Say your goodbyes, Calypso. It's time to leave.'

'So what now?' I cringed inwardly at the nerves in my voice.

The helicopter ride—my first—from Nicrete to Agistros, the large island apparently owned entirely by Axios, had been breathtaking and exhilarating, and thankfully had not required much conversation. Largely because Axios had piloted the aircraft and I'd felt too nervous to disturb him, even if there'd been anything to talk about.

My mind was still a jumble after our charged snippets of conversation and that little slip on the dance floor, when he pulled me close and the ache in my belly manifested itself, and my last unsettling conversation with my mother.

But most of all it was the look in Axios's eyes before he'd whisked me away from the reception and down to the waiting helicopter that kept my heart banging against my ribs.

That look was far too unsettling and electrifying for me to rest easy.

Especially not after landing on a dedicated cliff-side helipad on this island that boasted its own dormant volcano and a jaw-dropping villa that seemed almost too beautiful to be real.

I thought it was the setting sun that leant it that fairy tale look and made the unevenly staggered storeys seem to go on for ever. But every single facet of it turned out to be real, from the blush-hued stone, the towering arched windows, the rooftop infinity pool that seemed to blend into the sky and the endless reception rooms and bedroom suites, each holding priceless ancient works of art interspersed with the work of new cutting-edge artists whose work I loved.

Every jaw-dropping fact I'd read about Axios Xenakis had seemed amplified the moment he'd stepped out of the helicopter, and his aura was intensifying with each second as he walked me around Villa Almyra, exuding flawless power and authority.

Now, standing in the luxury sitting room adjoining what I assumed to be the master bedroom, I couldn't hold my words back.

He didn't answer for the longest time. He shrugged off the bespoke jacket he'd worn for the wedding ceremony. Then strolled over to the extensive drinks cabinet.

'Would you like a drink?' he asked.

About to refuse, I stopped. It would buy me time to ease my nerves. 'Mineral water, thanks.'

He poured my drink, then a single malt whisky into

a crystal glass, handing mine to me before taking his time to savour his first sip.

The feeling that he was waiting, biding his time for… *something* threatened to overwhelm me, even while my senses skittered with alien excitement. Slowly it grew hotter, more dangerous.

His gaze raked over my wedding dress for a charged few seconds. 'Now we do whatever you want. It's *your* wedding night after all,' he drawled.

I got the feeling he was testing me. For what, I didn't know. And I wasn't sure I was ready to find out.

'The modern art pieces all over the house. Did you pick them yourself?'

His eyes widened fractionally, as if I'd surprised him. 'Yes,' he bit out. Then, on a softer note, 'Good art rarely loses its value.'

A layer of my nerves eased as I nodded. 'And pieces from emerging talent only appreciate with time.'

He strolled to the massive fireplace in the living room and leaned one muscular shoulder against the mantel. 'Masterpieces from the greats are all well and good, but modern art has its place too. They should be appreciated side by side.'

Just as he had placed them all over the house. I took a sip of water, settling deeper into my seat. 'I agree. Does that theme echo in all your properties?'

'Yes, it does.'

Before I could express pleasure in the thought, the gleam in his eyes arrested me.

'Is this how you wish to spend your wedding night, Calypso? Discussing art?'

The nerves rushed back and my hand trembled. 'What if it is?'

'Then I suggest you might want to be in more comfortable attire than that gown?'

Again, his eyes raked me, sending heat spiralling through me.

'Is this a ploy that usually works for you?'

One corner of his mouth lifted before his eyes darkened. 'Like you, I've never been married, so we both find ourselves in strange waters. Either way, the dress is going to have to come off one way or the other.'

'And if you don't like what is underneath…?' I dared. 'Will you send me back?'

His eyes narrowed. 'Is that what you're hoping for?'

Was it? I could have sworn my answer would be yes until actually faced with the question. But the word stuck in my throat, refusing to emerge as he sauntered towards me, taking a moment to discard the crystal tumbler so both his hands were free to capture my shoulders when he stopped in front of me.

'What I'm hoping for is that you will stop dishing out those enigmatic smiles and tell me what you meant earlier,' I said.

He frowned. 'You've lost me,' he drawled.

'When you said *if* we were to consummate this marriage? Are you incapable of doing so? If so perhaps you should get one of your staff to show me where I'm to sleep.'

His eyebrows rose. 'If I didn't know better I'd think you just issued me a challenge,' he drawled, in a voice that ruffled the tight nerves beneath my skin.

His scent filled my nostrils, his calm breathing propelling my attention to his sculpted chest, to the pulse beating steadily at his throat. To the magnificent vitality of his skin and the sheer animalistic aura breaching my tightly controlled space. Screaming at me to notice his masculinity. And not just to notice. He drew me with a power I'd never known before. I didn't just want to breathe him in. I wanted to touch. Explore. Taste.

That sensation was so strong I stepped back, eager to diffuse it.

The hands that held me stemmed my movement, and hard on the heels of my immobility came the realisation that I wanted to stay right where I was. But I didn't want him to know that.

'Well? *Are* you?' I taunted.

A mysterious smile tilted one corner of his lips before his hands slid down to my elbows. 'It should be easy enough to prove, *matia mou.*'

Just like that I was hit with the reality that this was my wedding night. That I was all but taunting him into… *possessing* me.

The thought sent a shiver through me. Coupled with something else. Something way too close to the forbidden desire that had coursed through me when I'd allowed myself to dream of this day some time in the dim and distant future, when I was out from under my father's thumb and free to have a boyfriend. A lover. A *husband*.

But how could that be? The man I'd imagined bore no resemblance to this formidable man, who wore arrogance and power as if it were a second skin. *Theos*, even his frown was attention-absorbing.

'Are you cold?' he asked.

I shook my head. Like everything else in this stunning villa, the temperature was perfect, blending with the early summer breeze.

'Then what's wrong?' he rasped, his eyes turning

speculative again, as they had when I almost gave my-self away on the dance floor.

The pain had thankfully receded, but other questions loomed just as large. The subject of my virginity and how that would factor into things, for one.

I pushed it away, seizing on another pressing need. 'I want you to tell me exactly what your agreement with my father is.'

One eyebrow rose. 'Isn't that a case of shutting the barn door after the horse has bolted? What's the point of rehashing the subject?'

It was time to come clean. 'I… I may have let you operate under the assumption that I know what's going on.'

Surprise flickered through his eyes before they narrowed. 'Are you saying you don't?'

'Not the exact details, no.'

Scepticism flared. 'You expect me to believe that? When you walked willingly by his side up the aisle?'

'Tell me you've never done something against your will and I'll call you a liar,' I replied.

The flare of his nostrils confirmed what I suspected—that this marriage was as much without his approval as it was without mine.

'Assuming it was solely your father who pushed for this, what steps did you take to stop him?'

None. Because my protests, like everything else, had fallen on deaf ears. I didn't say the words out loud, his timely reminder that, despite the promise I'd made, my mother's fate was in my father's hands, stilling my tongue. My hesitation gave Axios the answer he needed.

'I didn't, and the details don't matter. We are where we are. But I know there's an agreement between you.

I simply want you to spell it out for me so I know what I'm dealing with.'

He stared at me, his measuring gaze weighted. I shouldn't have been relieved, even a little pleased to see the cynicism fade a little, but I was.

'Maybe he didn't tell you. How very like Petras to want to keep the spoils all for himself,' he muttered almost absently, before dropping his hands from my arms to say abruptly, 'Under an agreement signed between your grandfather and mine, Yiannis Petras, or any appointed representative after his death, can collect on a debt owed by my family. Your father wanted twenty-five percent of my company or the cash equivalent. We settled on one hundred million euros. And you.'

I couldn't hide my gasp at the confirmation that I'd been sold like a chattel.

Again, his cynicism receded. 'He really didn't tell you? Are you saying you're a victim in this?' he breathed.

The label smarted. 'I'm not a victim. But, no, he didn't tell me.'

Jaw gritted, he shoved a hand through his hair. 'So you don't know that under the terms of the agreement he'll also receive the deeds to Kosima?'

'What is Kosima?'

A bleak expression darkened his face. Whatever Kosima was, it held an emotional attachment for him.

'It's the private island where my grandfather was born. It was his favourite place on earth. Your grandfather knew that when he and my grandfather struck their unholy agreement. I assume he passed the information on to your father.'

My heart lurched with guilt, and for a wild moment

I wanted to ease his pain. 'And my father demanded it as part of the agreement?'

Again his lips twisted, before his gaze slanted over me from head to toe. 'Of course. Just as he demanded that I marry *you*.'

This time my heart lurched for a different reason. He truly hadn't wanted this marriage—was entangled in it against his will just as I was.

About to stress that I had known absolutely nothing about this, that my father's avaricious demands were nothing to do with me, I heard that stern warning from my father slam into my brain. I didn't doubt that he would make my mother's life even more of a living hell than it was now.

The realisation that nothing had changed, that nothing *would* change, settled on me like a heavy, claustrophobic cloak.

'Why did you go through with it?' I asked. When he frowned, I hurried to add, 'You obviously hate what my family has done to you, so why…?'

My disjointed thoughts rumbled to a halt, my insides twisting with dread. A caged lion was an unpredictable creature, and from the first moment I'd set eyes on him I'd felt his banked fury.

Now I knew why.

His eyes blazed grey fire at me. 'You think I didn't try to find a way that didn't involve tying myself down for twelve months or handing over a multi-million-euro pay-out your father has done *nothing* to earn?' he sliced at me.

My breath caught. 'Why twelve months? Why not three…or even six?'

His mouth tightened. 'Ask your father. He had the

power to nullify some or all aspects of this agreement. He chose not to. And he counted on me not fighting this in court because adverse publicity is the last thing my company needs right now. Your grandfather was an unreasonable man who my own grandfather had the misfortune of partnering with.'

'I know they started the airline business together, but—'

'Your grandfather wasn't interested in an airline business. He wanted to invest in boats, despite knowing next to nothing about them,' he spat out the words. 'But because they were tied together my grandfather was forced to work twice as hard to maintain both arms of the business. The only way Petras would agree to dissolve the partnership was to leave without taking his quarter-of-a-million-dollar share of the business immediately. If he had done so he would've bankrupted the company. But that didn't stop him from demanding crippling interest on the loan, and an agreement promising a percentage of Xenakis Aeronautics should he or any other Petras need a future bail-out. But even then, it was too late. My grandfather had spread himself too thin, trying to maintain two suffering businesses, but he was too proud to declare bankruptcy. The strain broke his marriage and his family, and after my grandmother died his heart just…gave up.'

My heart twisted at the anguish in his voice. 'I…'

What could I say? *I'm sorry*? Would Axios even believe me? What did it matter? My father had cunningly used the past against him. Against both of us.

'I didn't know any of this.'

His jaw rippled. 'My grandfather was my mentor. He taught me everything I know. But he withheld the extent of how bad things were until it was too late. Until I had to watch him wither away.'

After an age of losing himself in the bleak past, his eyes zeroed in on me.

'Why? If you didn't know all this, why present your-self to me at that altar like a sacrificial lamb?'

The cynicism was back full force. 'I'm not a lamb!'

One corner of his mouth lifted. 'No, I'm learning that my initial impression was mistaken. But I still want to know why,' he pressed with quiet force.

How could I tell him without speaking of the very thing I'd done all this to avoid? If my father had man-aged to pressure a powerful man like Axios Xenakis to do his will, what would he do to my mother if he found out I'd been divulging family secrets?

'Perhaps I had something to gain too,' I responded truthfully, knowing how it would be viewed.

True to form, his eyes slowly hardened, and that dis-appointment I'd briefly spotted at the altar flashed across his face.

As one of his hands slowly rose to cup my face, it seemed he wanted to delve deeper, perhaps even at-tempt to understand how we had become caught in this tangled web. But then he slowly withdrew, his demean-our resigned, even a little weary.

An urge to soothe him spiked through me. I man-aged to curb it, barely managing not to fidget under his piercing scrutiny.

'Did the agreement stipulate that we needed to…to consummate the marriage?' I asked.

He froze, and a sizzling, electrifying look entered his eyes. I got the feeling that he'd been waiting for this…

that somehow coming to this point was what that sense of heightened expectancy had been all about.

'Not specifically, no.'

'But you don't know that it won't be held against you…against us…further down the line?'

He gave an indolent shrug even while his eyes continued to pin me in place. 'He's *your* father, Calypso. You tell me.'

I couldn't rule it out. And I suspected Axios knew that.

'Maybe he will. Maybe he won't. But I can't take the risk.'

With my mother's words echoing in my heart, my hunger for freedom grew with every second.

He took a slow, steady step towards me. His hands at his sides, he simply stared down at me, his only movement the deep rise and fall of his chest.

'What does that mean, Calypso?' he queried softly.

'It means I want there to be no room for misunderstanding later.'

Slowly, his hand rose again, his knuckles grazing my cheek. My shiver made his eyes darken.

'I need to hear the words, so there's no misunderstanding now.'

Heat suffused my face, as if chasing his touch. But his gaze wouldn't release me. Not until the words trembling on my lips fell free.

'I want to consummate this agreement. I want you to…take me.'

The full force of the words powered through me, shaking me from head to foot. Dear God, this wasn't how I'd imagined losing my virginity. None of this was how I'd dreamed it. So why did my insides twist themselves with…*excitement*?

For the longest time he simply stared at me, a myriad of emotions crossing his face. Eventually that dark gleam returned in full force, his presence filling the room as he turned his hand and brushed a thumb over my lips.

'Are you sure you don't wish to discuss…art?'

The thickness of his voice displaced any levity his words attempted. And it drove home that this was happening. My wedding night. No, it wasn't the one I'd dreamed about, but really, if life was fair, would my father have tossed me in as part of a hundred-million-euro deal?

That thought was buried beneath the turbulent need climbing through me as he dragged his digit back and forth over my lip.

'I'm sure,' I answered, in a voice that sounded nothing like mine.

He tilted my gaze to his, making a gruff sound at whatever it was he saw on my face. His head started to lower—just as the other delicate subject raced to the forefront of my mind.

Tell him. He's going to find out soon enough.

'There's something you should know.'

One eyebrow rose in silent question.

'I'm a virgin.'

His fingers froze beneath my chin, his whole body turning to marble. 'What did you say?'

I swallowed the knot in my throat, praying the shivers would stop coursing through my body. 'I've never done…never been with a—'

A curse fell from his lips, raw and stunned. 'Why?'

Finally—*finally*—that burst of hysteria filtered through. 'You're asking why your wife is a virgin? Isn't that an odd question?'

'*Ne*—and it is precisely why I want to know why a twenty-four-year-old who looks the way you do is still untouched.'

Heat flowed through me. 'Looks the way I do...?'

The faintest colour washed his cheekbones. 'You must be aware of your beauty, Calypso,' he rasped, and his deep, husky voice set fire to my belly.

I blushed at the raw intensity in his words that reached into a secret part of me and took control of it. Hot tingles raced over my skin, warming me from the inside, tightening low in my belly and hardening my nipples. A gasp tore from my throat. His gaze dropped to my parted lips, his eyes darkening with each charged second that ticked by.

Then his eyes narrowed. 'Surely Petras didn't keep you under lock and key simply for this possibility?' Incredulity racked his voice.

Pain lashed through me, because the same thought had occurred to me. My father might not have visited the ultimate indignity upon me by spelling it out in black and white, but by thwarting all my previous attempts at a relationship he'd ensured his deal would be sweetened with my virginity. Another indication as to how little he cared for me.

Despite the anguish racking me, I raised my chin, pride insisting I did not confirm his suspicion. 'Does it not occur to you that I've simply not met anyone interesting enough?'

Shrewd grey eyes conducted a slow scrutiny. 'Your pulse is racing. Your face is flushed. I don't need a crystal ball to tell me you're excited. It is safe to say that, regardless of why you've remained untouched before, you're definitely interested now, Calypso.'

I silently cursed my body for betraying me but I wasn't ready to be cowed yet. 'You want me to bolster your ego by admitting I find you attractive?'

His head went back, as if he was surprised by the question. Of course he did. Good looks. Power. Influence. All attributes that made him irresistible to women. The stunning parade of women he'd purportedly dated was evidence that his effect on the opposite sex was woven into his DNA.

A sexy, arrogant smile curved his lips. 'I don't need you to *tell* me, *matia mou*. I *know* you do.'

My gasp was swallowed by the simple act of his head swooping down and his mouth sealing mine in a hot, savage possession that snatched the breath from my lungs. If that kiss in the church had been spine-tingling, this complete mastery was nothing short of earth-shattering.

The bold sweep of his tongue over my sensitive lower lip fired electricity in every cell. When he followed that with the lightest graze of his teeth, in another clever tasting, a tiny hunger-filled sound left my throat.

Axios muttered something beneath his breath before the fingers capturing my chin moved to my lower back, tugging me closer, until the hard column of his body was plastered against mine and the wide stance of his powerful legs cradled me. Until the hot brand of his manhood was unmistakably imprinted against my belly, in a searing promise of what was in store.

His lips devoured mine with unapologetic hunger. And when one hand grasped mine and redirected it to his chest I gave in to the heady desire and explored him.

Tensile muscle overlaid by his expensive cotton shirt was warm and inviting, and after a tentative caress, I sighed and gave in to *more*. The ultra-masculine line of his shoulder and neck drew my fingers, and that mysterious hunger built up into something that both terrified and thrilled me.

He made a gruff sound when my fingers brushed his warm, supple throat. It was enough to startle me. Enough to remind me that I didn't really know what I was doing. That, while I understood the mechanics of sex, I wasn't well-versed in its nuances.

Nerves dulled by the fire of arousal resurged, breaking free by way of a helpless whimper.

He raised his head and stared at me for the longest time before catching my hand in his. 'Come,' he commanded huskily.

I snatched in a much-needed breath. We both knew where we stood—that we were products of my father's machinations—surely we were going into this with our eyes open, in the knowledge that this was a one-time thing…weren't we?

Molten grey eyes watched me. When I slid my hand into his, he led me to some wide, imposing double doors. With casual strength he pushed them open to reveal the most magnificent bedroom I'd ever seen. While it bore unashamed signs of masculinity, the Mediterranean blue hues of the furniture blended with solid wood and gold-trimmed furnishings in the kind of design afforded only to the rich and influential.

But of course the centrepiece of the huge space was the bed. Emperor-sized, with four solid posts, its only softening effect was the muslin curtains currently tied back with neat ribbons.

Axios released me long enough to toss away extraneous pillows and pull back the luxury spread before he recaptured me. This time both hands went to my waist, his gaze dropping down to where he held me. He muttered something under his breath that I couldn't quite catch and when our gazes reconnected flames danced in the dark grey depths.

My knees weakened and I lifted my hands to rest them on his shoulders. He drew me closer while his hands searched along my spine, located the zip to my dress and firmly drew it down.

The dress gaped and he drew in a harsh breath, his gaze trailing over my exposed skin to linger on my barely covered breasts. Through the silk his hands branded my skin, making me squirm with a need to feel them without any barrier. As if he heard my silent wish, he took hold of the straps and eased them down my arms. The material pooled at my feet, leaving me in the scrap of lace panties and matching strapless bra.

One expert flick and the bra was loosened. Instinctively, I moved to catch it. Moved to delay this exquisite madness unfurling inside me.

Axios caught my hand, drew it firmly back to his shoulder. 'I want to see you, Calypso. I want to see everything.'

Unable to stand the raw fire in his eyes, I fixed my eyes on his chest. On the buttons hiding that steel and muscle from me. Again he read my wants with ease.

'Take my shirt off, *yineka mou.*'

Yineka mou. My wife.

Why did my insides dance giddily each time he called me that? Especially when we both knew this was an enforced, transient thing?

'Don't keep me waiting.'

The husky nudge brought me back to him. With fingers that had given up being anywhere near steady, I reached for his sleekly knotted tie, tugged it free and released his top shirt button. It was simpler to avoid his eyes as I concentrated on my task, but halfway down, when my fingers brushed his abs, he hissed under his breath.

Impatience etched on his face, he took hold of the expensive cotton and pulled the shirt apart. That raw display of strength tossed another log onto the flames building inside me. By the time he lifted me free of my wedding gown and took the few steps to the bed I'd lost the ability to breathe.

Riveted, I watched him shrug off the shirt, followed by his other clothing, before prowling to the bed. With the ease of a maestro he caught me to him, his fingers sliding up my nape and into my hair to release the three pins that secured the thick strands. His eyes raked my body as he slowly trailed his fingers through my hair. The effect was hot and hypnotising, the need to melt into him surging high.

So when he settled his expert lips over mine all I could do was moan and hold on, shudder in shocking delight when his chest grazed my hardened nipples.

But soon even that grew insufficient. Tentatively I parted my lips, in anticipation of the next decadent sweep of his tongue. When it grazed mine the zap of electricity convulsed my whole body.

Axios tore his lips from mine, incredulous eyes burning into me. 'You truly *are* innocent…' he muttered.

Mercifully, he didn't require an answer, or he was too impatient. After another searing kiss, in which his tongue breached my lips and brazenly slicked over mine, he trailed his lips over my throat.

Each pathway he claimed over my skin sent a pulse straight between my legs, plumping and heating my core until I thought I would explode. Large hands moulded my breasts, his fingers torturing the peaks. I cried out, my senses threatening to splinter.

The feeling of delving into another dimension, one where only pure pleasure existed, swelled through me, drawing me into a place of wonder. A place where I could give expression to what I was experiencing.

'That's...so amazing. How is this feeling possible?'

Had I said that out loud? Axios momentarily froze, but I was too caught up in bliss to find out why. Then his caresses continued, his mouth pressing kisses on my midriff, my belly, along the line of my panties.

When he tugged them down, my breath stalled.

He parted my thighs, trailed kisses up one inner thigh, then another.

'Your stubble feels...incredible.'

Again I felt him still.

'Am I doing something wrong? Please...'

Long fingers grazed the swollen nub, sending feverish pleasure racing through my body. Without him close to anchor me I grabbed hold of the sheets. Anything to keep me from disintegrating beneath the force of pleasure ramping through me.

Except that force tripled when his mouth settled with fierce intent on my feminine core. Brazenly, he tasted me with a connoisseur's expertise, teasing and torturing and dragging me to the brink of madness.

Until a new tightness took hold of me.

'Ah...it's too much... I... I can't take it...'

'Yes, you can,' he declared huskily.

His lips went back to wreaking their magic, to piling on that enchantment, until I simply…blew apart.

Bliss such as I'd never known suffused my body, convulsions rippling over me before sucking me under. I was aware of the cries falling from my lips, was aware that Axios had returned to my side, and I gripped him blindly, needing something solid to hang on to.

When he moved away I started to protest before I could stop myself. His kiss settled me for the few moments while he left the bed. The sound of foil ripping barely impinged upon my enchanted calm, my senses only sparking to life when he resumed his overwhelming presence between my thighs.

The intensity of the eyes locked on mine was almost too much to bear. I sought relief elsewhere. But there was none to be found in the wide expanse of his shoulders, the ripped contours of the chest I suddenly yearned to explore with my mouth, or… *Theos mou*…the fearsomely impressive evidence of his maleness.

The tiniest whimper slipped free. And while it brought an arrogant little twitch to his lips, there was also a slight softening of his fierce regard.

'Look at me, Calypso.'

The low command brought my gaze back to his. To the lock of hair grazing his eyebrow that I yearned to brush back. The slightly swollen sensual lips I wanted to kiss.

'Do you want this?' he asked.

The thought of stopping now was unthinkable. 'Yes,' I answered.

He gripped one thigh, parting me with unwavering intent.

The first shallow thrust stilled my breath. The second threw me back to that dimension where only sensation reigned.

Apprehensively, I exhaled. Axios moved his powerful body, withdrawing before penetrating me. Once. Twice.

On the third glide the sting was replaced by a different, jaw-dropping sensation, one that dragged me deeper into that dimension.

'You're…so deep. It feels…incredible.'

Above me, Axios hissed, his fingers digging into my thigh as he held himself, still and throbbing, inside me. The sensation was indescribable. But…

'Why aren't you moving? Do *I* need to? Maybe if I roll my hips…'

Tentatively I experimented, then cried out as pleasure rained over me.

'That was…sensational. I want to… Would you mind if I did it again?'

'No. I wouldn't,' he said thickly, then met my next thrust with an even more powerful one.

What the hell was happening?

I stared down at Calypso. Her eyes were shut in unbound pleasure.

My fraying control took another hit, the feeling that this little witch with her wide streak of innocence that had turned out not to be a clever trick was responsible for my curious state driving confusion through me.

The giving and taking of carnal pleasure was far from new to me but this…

I wanted to tell her to open her eyes. To centre her to me. To—

'Why are you stopping? Please don't stop. I want more.'

Her husky, innocent plea ramped up my arousal, the enormity of what was happening lending a savage edge to my hunger I'd never experienced before.

But just to be sure she was right there with me I leaned closer, flicked my tongue over her nipple. 'Do you like this, Calypso?'

Short blunt nails dug into my back. 'Yes!'

'And this?' I pulled the tight bud into my mouth, suckling her sweet flesh with fervour.

'*Ne*. That… You do that so well. I never want it to end.'

Theos. Did she not know what she was doing? That this kind of uncensored commentary could drive a man over the edge?

But she wasn't doing it with another man. She was doing it with *me*. The man she was bound to for the next twelve months.

Her husband.

Knowing I was her first shouldn't be sending such primitive satisfaction through my blood. And yet it was, settling deep inside me with such definitive force it threw up a shock of bewilderment.

I was thankful to avoid examining it in that moment. Because the utter nirvana of taking her, hearing her unfettered pleasure, was creating an unstoppable chain reaction inside me. One that kept me thrusting into her snug heat, my pulse racing to dangerous levels as her delicious lips parted and another torrent of words ran freely.

'*Glykó ouranó*… I'm on fire… What you're doing to me… Please… I need… I *need*…'

My teeth gritted as I hung on to control with my fingertips. As her sweet body arched beneath mine and her head thrashed on the pillow.

'You need to let go, Calypso.' I sounded barely coherent to my own ears.

With a sharp cry she gave herself over to her bliss, her sweet convulsions triggering mine. The depth of my climax left me gasping, the stars exploding across my vision unending.

Leached of all power and control, I collapsed onto the pillows, stunned by the sorcery I'd just experienced. A unique experience I wanted to relive again. Immediately.

Soft arms curved around my waist and I reached for her before I could stop myself—before I could question the wisdom of lingering when I normally exited. Pulling her into me when I normally distanced myself.

I will. In a moment.

Once I'd gathered myself. Once this experience had been dissected and slotted into its proper place.

I would have fought any future attempt by Yiannis Petras to further line his pocket, but Calypso's way of sealing all avenues had been…better. Pleasurable, even.

Or foolish?

I tensed, unwilling to accept that perhaps I could have found another way. Not succumbed to this bewitchment so readily.

So draw a line under it. Leave!

Her soft breathing feathered over my jaw. Sleep was stealing over her slightly flushed face. The urge to join her whispered over me—another wave of temptation that lingered for far too long, making me close my eyes for several minutes before common sense prevailed.

So what if the sex was sublime? It was just sex. Come

tomorrow my life would resume its normal course. This whole day would be behind me.

I'd done my duty. Had ensured Petras would no longer be a threat to my family. For now the night was still young. There was no rush to go anywhere...

Except temptation was ten times stronger when I woke in the early hours of the morning. In the murky light of dawn I caught the faintest glimpse of the slippery slope my grandfather had been led down by another Petras.

A road I couldn't risk.

I put words to definitive action by rising and leaving the bed, gathering my clothes and walking out of the master bedroom.

Because my business with my wife was over.

CHAPTER THREE

My TRANSITION FROM sleep to wakefulness was abrupt, bracing in the way that fundamental change manifested itself. Confirmation that I hadn't dreamt any of it registered in unknown muscles throbbing with new vigour. The sheets also bore evidence of what had happened, and confirmed that Axios had left some time in the night.

Had he chosen to sleep somewhere else? Or had his helicopter taken off during one of the brief stretches of time when I'd fallen asleep?

Although my agitated thoughts wanted to latch on to the fact that it was the sex that had driven him away, intuition suggested otherwise. Axios might not have wanted to experience the depth of chemistry that blazed between us but he'd been caught up too. Maybe a little bit too much?

Because I was reeling from the wildness of our coming together, the sheer abandonment that still rocked me to my core. The sheets might have cooled in his absence but his possession still remained. As did my growing consternation.

Last night my decision had seemed so clear-cut. Close all avenues by which my father could further interfere in my life. But the experience had been nothing like clear-cut. The experience of sleeping with Axios had been…unparalleled.

And now he was gone.

I refused to allow the dull thudding of my heart to dictate my disappointment. Whatever my future held, it was time for action.

About to get out of bed, I paused as my last conversation with my mother replayed one more time.

'You will know very quickly if this is the right choice for you. If it isn't, don't be like me. Don't accept it as inevitable. Do what is right for you.'

'What are you talking about, Mama?'

'Find your own happiness, Callie. Don't let your father's actions dictate the rest of your life. Your grandmother said the same thing to me on my wedding day and I didn't listen.'

'I don't think I have a choice. You… Papa—'

'Forget about me! There's nothing your father can do that will hurt me any more. Knowing you're unhappy because of me will break my heart. Promise me you'll put yourself first.'

'Mama—'

'Promise me, Callie!'

My promise weighed heavy on my heart as I rose from the bed. For a moment I swayed in place, my limbs weak with recollection and my body heating after every little wanton act of last night.

But, lips firmed, I approached what I hoped was the bathroom. There, further signs that this was Axios's domain were everywhere—from the luxury male products to the thick dark robe hanging next to the shower.

Trying not to let the intimacy of his belongings get to me, I quickly showered. Thankful for the voluminous towel that covered me from chest to ankle, I was contemplating the less than palatable thought of wearing my wedding dress again when a soft knock broke into my thoughts.

I cleared my throat. 'Come in.'

One of the younger staff members who helped manage the villa entered with a shy smile. She'd been introduced to me last night, when my senses had been grappling with unfolding events.

With a strained smile, I pulled the robe closer around me and returned her greeting.

Her gaze passed quickly over my towel. 'May I assist you with anything, *kyria*?'

'If you could direct me to where my belongings are, I'd appreciate it.'

'Of course. This way, please.'

Expecting her to leave the room, I was surprised when she crossed to the opposite side and opened another door.

I followed her through a short hallway into another impressive suite, complete with living room, bathroom and dressing room.

An adjoining suite.

'I came to ask if you would like some breakfast, Kyria Xenakis?'

The title added another layer of shock to my system and it took me a few seconds to answer with a question of my own. 'Um…is Kyrios Xenakis still here?'

She nodded. 'Yes. But he will be leaving soon. So if you wish to—'

'Yes, I would very much like to. Can you wait for me to get dressed?'

Her eyes widened a touch, probably at the request.

But I didn't care. I needed answers. Needed to know how he intended the next twelve months to proceed. And, if necessary, insist on taking back control of my life.

My father had shown me that he cared nothing about me except as a pawn to further his needs. Regardless of my commitment to Axios, I didn't intend to be pushed around any more.

That affirmation anchored deep as I concentrated on getting dressed.

The small suitcase that had accompanied me when I left Nicrete was empty, its contents sitting on a lonely shelf in the vast dressing room. But those weren't the only contents of the large, opulent space. Rack upon rack of clothes were displayed in fashion seasons, with matching shoes arranged by colour, height and style.

Awestruck, I stared. It was by far the most extensive collection I'd seen outside a clothes store. Simply because I didn't know who the clothes in the closets belonged to, I fished out a simple shirt dress from my own belongings, added comfortable flats and caught my hair in a ponytail.

The maid led me down the stairs and through several halls before stopping at a set of double doors.

'He's in there,' she said softly. Then melted away.

The faint sound of clinking cutlery reached my ears as I paused to take a fortifying breath. But, aware that no amount of deep breathing could prepare me for the morning after last night, I pushed the door open.

He was seated at the head of a long, exquisitely laid table. Impeccably dressed in formal business attire, minus the jacket, with the sun streaming down on him.

I almost lost my footing at the sheer visceral impact of his masculinity. It really was unfair how attractive

Axios Xenakis was. How the simple act of caressing his bottom lip with his forefinger, his brow furrowed in concentration, could spark fire low in my belly.

You're not here to ogle him.

Fists tightening at the reminder, I approached where he sat. 'We need to talk.'

He took his time to look up from the tablet propped up neatly next to his plate, to power it down with a flick of his finger before cool grey eyes tracked over me from head to toe and back again.

'*Kalimera*, Calypso. Sit down—have something to eat.'

His even tones threw me. He wasn't behaving like a man who'd left his marriage bed after bedding his virgin wife. In fact, he seemed far too confident. Far too... *together* for my liking.

When I didn't immediately obey he rose, his gaze resting on me as he pulled out a chair and...waited.

I sat, because hysteria would achieve nothing. What I intended to say to him could be said standing or sitting. Besides, this close, the potent mix of his warm body and his aftershave was making my head swim. Reminding me of what it had been like to stroke that warm body, to cling to it as fevered bliss overtook me.

'What's on your mind?' he enquired as he poured exquisite-smelling coffee into my cup, then nudged platters containing sliced meats, toast and cheeses towards me.

Cool. He was far too cool.

Something was going on here. I probed his face and saw the slight tension in his jaw. The banked emotion in his eyes. I might have known Axios for less than twenty-four hours, but I'd quickly deciphered that his eyes gave him away. Right now, they were far too shrewd.

My heart jumped into my throat.

'My father may have put us both in this position, but there's no reason why we should remain like this.' Relief welled as my voice emerged strong and steady.

His nod of agreement stunned me. 'You're right,' he said.

'I am?'

He shrugged. 'The agreement states that we should be married for a year minimum—not that we need to be in each other's pocket. Of course that's not to say it's cart blanche for you to do as you please.'

'What does *that* mean?'

'It means that for the time being Agistros is yours to enjoy. We will revisit our circumstances again when I return in a few weeks.'

His announcement was still resonating inside me when he rose from the table and strode, his head proud, shoulders stiff, towards the door.

'When you return? Where will you be?'

He paused, his tall, imposing body swivelling towards where I sat, frozen. 'In Athens, where my business is, and where I intend to stay for the foreseeable future.'

Despite sensing this had been coming, I found the announcement took me by surprise. 'You're leaving me here on my own?'

Theos—could I sound any more alarmed?

He gave a curt, unfeeling nod. 'It is the best decision.'

I pushed my chair back and stood, feeling a yearning spiralling inside that wouldn't be silenced. A yearning to know that his condemnation of my father meant that he was different. That, despite tarring me with the same brush as my parent, he wouldn't punish me too.

'Why can't I live in Athens too?' *With you.*

It would be the perfect place finally to put my art degree to good use. To start a career.

His hardening features broadcasted his displeasure at that question even before he spoke. 'Why force us to endure one another when we don't have to?'

'I'm perfectly happy living on my own. I can rent a flat, get a job in an art gallery—'

The twist of his lips reminded me again of how hot his kisses could be. 'What's the point of staging an elaborate wedding to fool the world if my wife immediately moves into an apartment?'

'Then why did you do it?' I challenged.

'Your father timed his strike to perfection—because my company needs stability now more than ever.'

Invisible walls closed in on me. 'So this is a *business* decision?'

His jaw clenched. '*Everything* that has transpired between us has been based on a business decision.'

Even last night?

My heart lurched and I was glad I was sitting down. 'There has to be another way.'

'There is. You stay here, in our purportedly happy home. You'll want for nothing. Your every wish will be catered for. Buy as much art as you wish to—or even make it if you want.'

Yesterday the promise of freedom from this nightmare would have brought boundless relief. Today, all I felt was…trapped.

'I can't. I can't live like that.'

The words were uttered more for myself than for him.

Born from my deep desire never to fall under another's command the way my father had forced me to live under his.

'How long am I to stay in this gilded *prison*?'

His eyes darkened. 'If this is a prison, *yineka mou*, it is not of my making. I tried for months to make your father listen to reason. *He* caused this situation, not me. If you want a way out of this, then find one.'

With that, he walked out, leaving my insides cold as ice.

Axios's words echoed through the long days and nights that followed his departure from Agistros. Long after the days in the luxurious paradise had begun to stretch in brain-numbing monotony.

My new husband, having made his feelings clear about our forced marriage, didn't bother to come home. The stunning villa had indeed become my prison, and its elegant walls and priceless furnishings closed in on me more with every day that dragged by.

And the more my world became narrow, the louder my mother's words and the contents of my grandmother's letter clamoured.

By the end of the second week dejection had me in a constricting hold. But alongside it was the discomfort in my abdomen, which wouldn't let up. Telling myself it was a psychosomatic reaction to my current situation began to feel hollow when I knew my grandmother had felt similar symptoms in the year before her death.

Then the housekeeper informed me one sun-drenched morning that Axios had left a message to say that he would be away on business in New York for another ten days. It seemed like the ominous catalyst I needed.

In the privacy of my suite, I quickly considered and discarded the things I wouldn't need. My large hobo bag was big enough to hold the most crucial essentials, and the small stash of cash I'd saved from my allowance was more than enough to see me through the first few days of my unknown adventure.

After that…

My heart lurched as I attempted to hold down my breakfast the next morning. I took my time, ensuring I was well-sustained before I left the table. Aware of the housekeeper's keen eye, I calmly drank another cup of tea, then helped myself to fruit before drawing back my chair.

'Agatha, I'm thinking of visiting friends. I'm not sure how long I'll be. A few days—maybe longer.'

Surprise lit the housekeeper's eyes. 'But Kyrios Xenakis said you were to stay here—'

'Kyrios Xenakis isn't here. And he's not coming back for ten days. I seriously doubt he'll miss my absence in the meantime.' I slapped on a smile to take the sting out of my words.

She gave a wary nod. 'When do you wish to leave? I'll tell Spiros to ready the boat.'

'Don't bother. I'll grab a water taxi from the harbour. The walk down will do me good.'

Disapproval filmed her eyes. '*Kyria*, I don't think that's a good idea.'

One of the few facts I'd learned about my absent husband was that he was far wealthier than I'd imagined. The members of the Xenakis dynasty basked in the sort of wealth that required bodyguards and well-orchestrated security for them to travel. Exactly the sort of attention I didn't need.

'I appreciate your concern, but it's not necessary, Agatha. Thank you.'

I walked away before she could respond. And, since I wasn't entirely sure she wouldn't alert Axios at the very first opportunity, I rushed up to my suite, grabbed my bag and hurried back down.

Two hours later I stepped up to the sales counter at the airport on the mainland. 'One-way ticket to Switzerland, please.'

The attendant eyed me for what seemed like for ever before issuing my ticket. But if I thought that was nerve-racking, discovering what my grandmother had left for me once I arrived at the Swiss bank left me shamelessly sobbing in a cold and grey bank vault.

And then everything that had gone before paled in comparison to the fear that gripped my heart when I sat before a Swiss doctor three days later.

Dr Trudeau, a short, grey-haired physician with kind eyes, peered at me over his rimless glasses, gentle fingers tapping the file in front of him before he sighed.

'Miss Petras, I have good news and bad news. Although I'm not entirely sure how welcome the good news will be once I explain what I believe is happening with you. I'm so sorry.'

CHAPTER FOUR

One year later

THE TURQUOISE WATERS of the Pacific were so blindingly beautiful they brought tears to my eyes. Or perhaps it was the stinging salt from the spray.

It definitely wasn't because today was my first wedding anniversary.

No. Most certainly not that.

On the list of the most forgettable things to happen to me in the last year, my hastily arranged wedding and the shockingly cold ceremony was right at the top. Not to mention the trapped groom who couldn't wait to walk away from me. The man I now had the dubious pleasure of calling my husband.

My heart leapt into my throat even as I pushed Axios's image away. He would need to be dealt with soon.

But not just yet.

I lifted my face to the blazing sun, willed it to pierce through my desolation and touch my wounded soul. I needed brightness and mirth, sunshine and positivity. If only for a little while longer… It might all be gone soon, slipping through my fingers like mercury.

Gripping the railing of the sleek sailboat transporting

me from an exclusive Bora Bora resort to the adjoining uninhabited island where I'd ordered my picnic, I mentally went through my list from bottom to top.

Number five: Take control of my life. *Check.*

Contrary to my fears, walking away hadn't doomed me or my mother. My monthly phone calls reassured me that she was fine. My father, now a hundred million euros richer, was engrossed in yet another business venture. Better still, he hadn't challenged any of the terms of the contract he'd made with Axios.

Number four: Do something worthwhile with my painting. *Check.*

The past year had been frightening in some ways but immensely fulfilling in the exploration of my talent. I was still basking in the knowledge that I could have had a career if fate hadn't pushed me down a different path.

Number three: Accept that my condition might not have a happy ending and that my prognosis might follow my grandmother's. *Check.*

It had been a difficult acceptance, often pitted with tears and heartache and grief for all the things I might never have. For what this would do to those I love.

Number two: Cherish my precious gift for as long as I can. *Check. Check. Check.*

The last item on my list filled me with equal parts desolation and trepidation. But it needed to be done.

Number one: Hand over my precious gift to Axios Xenakis.

As if that gift knew he was in my thoughts, a soft cry rippled through the sun-drenched breeze, followed by a sharper one, demanding attention.

Smiling, I turned from the railing and crossed the deck to the shaded lounge. There, lying amongst the cushions, was the reason for my heartbeat. The reason I needed to keep fighting for my unknown future.

'Are you awake, my precious boy?'

At the sound of my voice Andreos Xenakis kicked his plump legs, his arms joining in his giddy response as his searching eyes found mine. For an instant my breath caught. The similarity between the piercing grey eyes of father and son was so visceral, I froze.

Another insistent cry had me reaching for him. His warm, solid weight in my arms quieted the worst of my trepidation, and soon even that evaporated beneath the sheer joy of cradling him, feeding him, doing such mundane things as changing his nappy and handing him his favourite toy, basking in his sweet babbling while I enjoyed the stunning view and just...*being*.

Pushing away the terrifying news the doctor had given me that day in Switzerland and the choice I'd had to make, I breathed in relief when the boat slowed and a staff member approached with a courteous smile.

'We're here, miss. Your picnic is set up for you on the shore.'

Whatever the future held, I would deal with it.

After all, I'd dealt with so much this past year.

Except the future had found me before I was ready. And it came in the form of a solitary figure with furious gunmetal eyes and a gladiator stance, waiting with crossed arms on the jetty as the sailboat returned to the exclusive resort.

My heart leapt into my throat, my breath strangled to nothing as I watched the figure grow larger, more broody, more formidable.

More everything.

He'd grown harder. Edgier. Or perhaps that was all

imagined. A product of those feverishly erotic dreams that frequently plagued me.

Whatever… The man who watched me in silent condemnation as the boat gently butted the wooden planks on the jetty had zero mercy in him. And when his gaze shifted to Andreos and widened with chilled shock I had the distinct notion that I'd played this wrong.

I'd been too selfish.

Taken too much time for myself.

Too much time with my son.

'Axios.'

He didn't respond to my whispered utterance of his name. He couldn't take his eyes off Andreos. His strong throat moved in a swallow and his pallor increased as several expressions charged through his eyes.

Shock. Amazement. Utter fury.

'What are you doing here?' I asked.

Finally eyes the colour of a dark arctic night clashed with mine. 'What am I *doing* here?' he asked with icy incredulity. 'This is what you have to say to me after the stunt you have pulled?'

My insides shook but I forced myself to hold his gaze. 'You'll want to discuss this, I'm sure, but can it wait till—?'

'I'll *want to discuss this*? Are you for real?'

A drowsy Andreos stirred in my arms, his senses picking up on the frenetic emotions charging through the air.

'Miss, would you like us to—?'

'Leave us.' Axios's tone was deep. Implacable.

I wasn't in the least bit surprised when the staff hurried away.

'How did you find me?'

It seemed a monumental feat for him to drag his gaze from Andreos.

'Through an act of sheer coincidence. The owner of this resort happens to be a business acquaintance of mine. He was on a rare tour of his property when he spotted you. Had he not chosen to take his yearly tour this last week...' He stopped, shaking his head as if grappling with the sheer serendipity of the occurrence that had led him to me.

My chalet was on the beach, and I made the short walk to the gorgeous timber-clad structure aware of his every step behind me.

'I intended to come back—I promise.'

'You *promise*? Why should I take your word on anything? You told the staff you were visiting friends when all along you intended to abscond from our marriage. And now you're hiding in a resort on the other side of the world under a false name. Not to mention you seem to have had a child during that time. I am assuming the child is yours?'

'Of course he his. Who else's would he be?'

He went as rigid as an ice statue, and what little colour had flowed back into his face on the walk from jetty to chalet receded momentarily before fury reddened his haughty cheekbones once more.

'So I can add infidelity to your sins?'

'Infid—? What are you talking about?' Shock made my voice screech.

Andreos whimpered as I laid him down in his cot, and then went back to sound sleep.

'We used contraception on our wedding night, as I recall,' he rasped with icy condemnation.

'Well, I wasn't on birth control. I never have been.

And, while I'm not an expert, I'm sure there's a caution that states that condoms aren't one hundred percent foolproof.'

'And I'm suddenly to accept that the protection that has never failed me before suddenly malfunctioned with *you*?'

I wasn't sure why the reference to other lovers drilled such angst through me. His lovers, past or present, were of no consequence to me. I had no hold over him, nor did he over me, when it came right down to it. All that had brought us together was my father's greed and manipulation.

'I don't know what to say to make you believe me but I know the truth, Axios. Andreos is yours.'

Piercing eyes locked on mine for the better part of a minute. 'If he's mine, why have you hidden him from me for the better part of a year?'

His voice had changed, turned grittier, and he even looked a little shaken as his gaze swung again to Andreos. He started to walk towards the cot as if compelled, then stopped, shook his head.

'Why is he here on the other side of the world when he should be in Greece, with his family?'

It would have been so easy to blurt out everything that had happened to me since that dreaded visit to the doctor in Switzerland. and the urgent summons to hear my diagnosis three gut-churning days later, when it had been confirmed that there was indeed a growth in my cervix.

But I was also told I was pregnant, and that any further exploration, even an initial biopsy to ascertain its malignancy or benignity, would jeopardise my baby.

I could have told him about the latest scans I had in

my suitcase, taken by Dr Trudeau in Switzerland, and his recommendation to take action.

But if Axios's presence here wasn't warning enough that the time I'd bought for myself was over, the look in his eyes said I wouldn't escape scot-free.

Nevertheless, I wasn't the same woman he'd married. Harrowing decisions made in the cold grip of fear had a way of changing a person.

'Why does it matter to you, anyway? I thought you would be glad to see the back of me for ever.'

A ferocious light glinted in his eyes for a heart-stopping second before he took a step towards me. 'You married a Xenakis, Calypso. You think simply packing your bag and walking out through the door is the end of it? That you simply had to hightail it to the other end of the world for your marriage vows to cease to have meaning?'

I stemmed my panic as his words rankled. 'Our vows had *meaning*? I could've sworn you challenged me to find a way to make them *stop* having meaning.'

His eyes narrowed. 'You think *this* was the answer?'

'It was *my* way!'

'Perhaps I should've added an addendum that finding a way needed to involve discretion and consideration. Nothing that would throw a spotlight on me or my family. My mistake. Tell me, Calypso, do you think disappearing off the face of the earth for over a year screams discretion or consideration?'

I shrugged with a carelessness I didn't feel. 'You didn't stick around long enough to hash out another course of action. I did what was best.'

'What was best for *you*, you mean?'

My senses wanted to scream *yes!* Caution warned

me to remain calm. To talk this through as rationally as the tower of formidable fury in front of me would allow.

'You still haven't told me why you're here.'

He made another sound of incredulity. 'Because you're my wife! Because the whispers need to cease. Because you will not jeopardise everything I've worked for. And that's just for starters.'

'Ah, *now* we're getting to the bottom of it. You're here because of what my absence is doing to your business? Is that it, Axios?'

With lightning speed warm fingers curled over my nape. His hold wasn't threatening, simply holding me in place so that whatever point he needed to make would be accurately delivered.

'While no one would dare say it to my face, rumours of my wife fleeing our marital home has caused ripples in my life. The kind I can do without. So make no mistake: I intend to remedy that. Whatever point you intended to make, it ends now.'

Each word contained a deadly promise—an intention to have his way that stoked the rebellion that had gone dormant in the last year back to life.

'Believe it or not, my walking out had absolutely nothing to do with you.'

'Enlighten me, then, *matia mou*. What was it all about?'

The soft cadence of his voice didn't fool me.

'What could possibly have driven you from the life of luxury and abundance your father battled for so cunningly?'

The mention of my father brought my goals back into focus. Reminded me why I hadn't been able to stomach staying under Axios's roof for one more day. That feeling of a loss of control. Of suffocation. Of not being able to live my life on my own terms. My choices being taken away from me without so much as a by your leave…

'I'm not my father,' I stressed, with every cell in my body.

'No, you're not. But while I was prepared to give you the benefit of the doubt before, your actions have led me to form a different opinion about you. So whatever your reasons were, tell me now.'

'Or what?'

He didn't speak for the longest moment. Then his attention shifted to the cot where Andreos slept, lost in baby dreams. My heart tripped over itself as I watched Axios's face. Watched him speculate with that clever mind financial analysts rhapsodised over.

'Is he the reason?'

'What do you mean?'

His jaw rippled. 'If there was an indiscretion, I urge you to confess it now rather than later.'

His words shouldn't have scraped my emotions. Considering what my mother had done, and the fall-out and gossip that had followed, I knew all too well how assumptions were made, judgements passed without verification. But the reality that he suspected Andreos wasn't his lanced a soft spot in my heart.

A fierce need to protect my child's honour ploughed through me. 'We may not have known each other before we met at the altar, but you should know that I would rather cut off my own arm before attempting to lie about my child's parentage. Whether you're willing to accept it or not, he's yours.'

If I'd expected my fervour to melt his coldness, I was sorely disappointed.

'Your vigorous defence of your child is admirable. But, as you said, we were virtual strangers before we came together. If you want me to believe you, tell me where you've been. Every single thing you've done in the past year. Then perhaps I'll consider believing you.'

The list reeled through my head.

Finding the bank account in Switzerland my grandmother had left in my name.

Seeing the private doctor who'd treated me.

Getting the results and feeling the soul-wrecking fear that my fate would echo my grandmother's.

Making the choice I had to make.

Andreos's arrival.

Saying the fervent prayers for *more*. One more day. One week. One month.

One year.

I couldn't tell Axios any of that. Even the simple joy of rediscovering my love of painting and finding the shops and galleries I'd sold my watercolours to seemed too sacred, too private to share with the man who looked at me with rancour and suspicion. Whose every breath seemed like a silent pledge to uncover my secrets.

My life. Lived on my terms.

That was what I'd sworn to myself that rainy afternoon in my hotel room after leaving Dr Trudeau's office. For the most part, it had been.

Axios's arrival had simply shortened the time I'd given myself before checking off the last item on my list.

'You'll consider believing me after you've triple-checked everything I say?'

The unapologetic gleam in his eyes told me he intended to do exactly that. Tear through every new, unconditional friendship I'd formed along the way, every haven I'd sought refuge in.

My stomach churned at the thought of Axios finding out the true state of my health and exploiting it the way my father had done with my mother. It was that terrible thought more than anything else that cemented my decision to keep my secret.

If he found out my condition, he would wonder if the state of my health affected my suitability as a mother. Unlike my mother, my flaws weren't outward. For the precious time being, I could hang on to that.

As for when I couldn't…

'All you need to know is that Andreos is yours and I'm prepared to return to Greece. If that's what you want?'

His nostrils flared and his gaze raked my face for long sizzling seconds before his lips twisted. 'Oh, yes, wife. The time has most definitely come for that. And whatever it is that you're keeping from me, rest assured, I'll find out.'

With that he stepped back.

Thinking he was going to leave me to grapple with the turmoil his unexpected arrival had caused, I watched, my heart speeding like a freight train, as he headed to the cot where Andreos slept.

Silence disturbed only by the slow stirring of the ceiling fan throbbed in the room as Axios stared down at the son he hadn't accepted was his. His jaw clenched tight and his throat moved convulsively as he watched the rise and fall of the baby's chest.

He remained frozen for so long I feared he'd take root there. When he turned abruptly and tugged a sleek phone from his pocket my senses tripped.

'What are you doing?'

Eyes the colour of a stormy sky met mine as he hit a number and lifted the handset to his ear. 'Getting the answers I need.'

The sharp orders he gave in Greek when the phone was answered didn't surprise me. The irony that the one truth I'd told him was the one he was having a hard time accepting wasn't lost on me. But, conversely, I understood. I too had wondered why fate would choose to lay both joy and sorrow on me in one fell swoop, leaving me with a choice that had seemed both simple and terrifying.

After all, my actions pointed to behaviour that would've left *me* suspicious too. And, considering what my own mother had done for the sake of freedom and love—an act that was an open secret in Nicrete—I didn't blame Axios for wanting to verify that the baby he'd helped create was truly his.

When he was done making an appointment for his private doctor to visit his home in Athens the moment he returned, to take DNA samples for a paternity test, he hung up, his piercing regard staying on me as he tucked his phone away.

I ignored the blatant challenge and asked the question more important to me. 'Is it going to hurt him?'

For the most fleeting second the charged look in his eyes dissipated. 'No. I'm told all it requires is a swab from his cheek.'

I nodded. 'Very well, then.'

He frowned, my easy acquiescence seemingly throwing him. But his face returned to its formidable hauteur in moments, and his strides were purposeful as he strode to the house phone and picked it up.

Before he dialled he turned to me. 'Is the child okay to travel on a plane?'

'The *child's* name is Andreos. And I'd thank you not to make any plans without discussing them with me first.'

A muscle ticked in his jaw. 'Why? Did you not tell me that you intended to return to Greece?'

'Yes, I did.'

'When exactly were you proposing to do that? When he was a year old? When he was five or perhaps ten?' he grated out.

The cold embrace of knowing that time wasn't on my side stalled my answer for several seconds. 'I was thinking days—not months or years. My booking at this resort is only for a week. I was going to fly back to Athens from here.'

His lips flattened. 'I don't plan on leaving you behind, Calypso. My good faith where you're concerned is gone. When I fly out of here in three hours you and the child will be by my side. And that state will continue until such time as you choose to come completely clean about your actions for the past year or I furnish myself with the information.'

After that, there really wasn't much more to say.

Moments after Axios left my suite the head concierge arrived with instructions to get as many staff as I needed to help me pack. I almost laughed, considering my meagre belongings and everything Andreos needed could fit in one small suitcase.

I dismissed the staff and was done with my packing in twenty minutes. The rest of the time I spent sitting beside Andreos's cot, hoping against hope that my time with him going forward would be just as peaceful as the past precious months had been. Because I didn't intend to be separated from him for a second. Time was too precious. Too special. And I would fight for every moment.

As if aware he was at the centre of my thoughts, he stirred and woke, his face remaining solemn for a few seconds before a toothless smile creased his chubby face. Blinking back the tears of joy that just looking at him prompted, I scooped him up and cradled him close.

By the time Axios knocked on the door we were both ready.

After another taut spell of staring at Andreos with turbulent eyes, he eyed the single suitcase with grating consternation. 'This is all you have?'

'I believe in travelling light.'

His expression darkened. 'What about safety equipment for the baby? A car seat?'

'I find it easier to hire what I require as and when I need it. And, before you disparage my methods, I research and make sure everything I use is of the highest safety standard.'

His gaze remained on me for another second before he nodded at the porter.

My suitcase was quickly stowed on a sleek private boat. Within minutes my last sanctuary had become a dot on the horizon.

I'd forgotten just how ruthlessly efficient Axios Xenakis could be. I received another rude reminder when, upon our arrival at the jetty, a smiling courier presented me with a gleaming state-of-the-art buggy and car seat combo, already assembled.

I braced my hand on Andreos's back, tugged him closer to where he nestled snugly in his papoose. 'That won't be necessary. The airline I'm flying with will have all the equipment I need.'

Axios stepped forward and took hold of the push-chair. 'You think I'm going to let you out of my sight now I've found you?'

'But I have a ticket—'

'And I have a private jet.'

Of course he did.

I'd blocked so many things out of my mind for the sake of pure survival. But the world had kept on turning. Axios had remained a powerful mogul with looks that weakened women's knees. And, as a billionaire who commanded an airline empire, didn't it stand to reason he'd possess his own plane?

A short SUV ride later we arrived at the private area of the airport, where an obscenely large aircraft bearing the unique Xenakis family logo stood gleaming resplendently beneath the French Polynesian sun.

'So what's it to be? Athens or Agistros?' he asked silkily.

I stared at him in surprise. 'You're giving me a *choice*?' It was more than he had the last time. More than my father ever had. Not that I planned on reading anything into it.

He shrugged. 'The location doesn't matter. Whichever you choose will be home. *For all of us*,' he added succinctly.

I chose Athens.

A mere twenty-four hours later we drove through the imposing gates of Axios's jaw-dropping villa. A different set of staff greeted us, and an even more opulent set of adjoining master suites had been readied for the prodigal wife's return.

I was standing in the middle of cream and gold opulence when I felt his presence behind me. Not wanting to look into those hypnotising eyes, I kept still, my precious bundle safely tucked in my arms.

My skin beginning to tingle wildly, I snatched in a breath and held it when his mouth brushed over the shell of my ear and he said, in a low, deep whisper, 'Welcome home, *yineka mou*. And rest assured that this time you will not get away from me that easily.'

CHAPTER FIVE

MY SON.

I have a son.

My chest squeezed tight. The emotions tumbling through me were…indescribable.

Back on Bora Bora everything inside me had prompted me to accept Calypso at her word—accept that the child was mine. Only I'd made the mistake before of thinking I could manage her, that she was a victim when she was anything but. She was cunning. Intelligent and resourceful enough to disappear without a trace for a whole year.

And apparently to take what is mine with her.

The result of the paternity test spelled out in stark indelible ink confirmed that, in this at least, Calypso had spoken the truth. But swiftly on the heels of that knowledge came a mystifying mix of searing fury and heady delight—the former for what I'd been deprived of and the latter for the astounding gift I hadn't even realised I wanted.

My son.

She kept him from me. Deliberately. Chose to leave my home and have my baby on her own, with no care as to what my feelings were in the matter. Why? Because

I'd left her on Agistros? In the lap of the kind of luxury most people only dreamed about?

But did you give her any choice?

I swallowed the bite of guilt as my eyes locked on the paper.

Andreos.

Even as a part of my brain tested the name out and accepted that it fitted him my fingers were shaking with the enormity of everything I'd missed. Things I'd never have thought would matter suddenly assumed colossal importance.

His first cry.

His first smile.

His first laugh...

Did babies his age laugh? I'd been robbed of the opportunity to find out for myself.

I tossed the document away and stood. Sudden weakness in my legs stopped me from moving. One hand braced on the polished wood surface, I sucked in a deep breath, attempted to bring myself under control.

Control was essential. Over my erratic emotions. Over my wayward wife and over the belief that she should take such actions without consequence. To deprive me of my own flesh and blood...

Why?

The deeply visceral need to know straightened my spine.

I found her in the smallest living room—the room farthest from my study and the one she seemed to have commandeered for herself and Andreos since her return. He lay on a mat on the floor, his fists and legs pumping with abandon as Calypso crouched over him. A few toys were strewn nearby, momentarily forgotten as mother and son indulged in a staring game of some sort. One that amused Andreos...*my son*.

So babies his age did smile. They also returned their mother's stare with rapt attention until they were tickled, then dissolved into heaps of laughter.

Something stirred raw and powerful within me as I stared into the eyes that had seemed familiar to me from the start, even as I cautioned myself against full acceptance. The feeling intensified as I watched Calypso's utter devotion, saw the bond between mother and son, the unit I'd been excluded from.

The unit I wanted to belong to—

Sensing my presence, Calypso's gaze flew to mine, then immediately shadowed.

Theos mou, was I really that frightful?

'You can be.'

I dismissed the uncanny sound of Neo's voice in my head.

Too bad. I'd given her four days to settle in. Four days of swimming in the uncharted waters of her re-entry into my life with a son...*my son*...in tow.

It took me but a moment to summon Sophia, one of several household staff who'd been infatuated with Andreos since his arrival.

To Calypso, I said, 'We need to talk. Come with me. Sophia will look after Andreos.'

Her clear reluctance lasted for the moment it took for her to spot the piece of paper clutched in my fist. Then she slowly rose.

About to head back to my study, I changed my mind and headed up the stairs.

'Where are we going?'

The hint of nervousness in her voice rankled further.

'Where we won't be disturbed,' I replied as evenly as I could manage.

'But…'

I stopped and turned. 'Do you have a problem with being alone with me?'

The faintest flush crept into her cheeks, but her head remained high, her gaze bold. 'Of course not.'

Truth be told, perhaps my suite wasn't the best choice. Amongst everything I'd imagined might happen when I finally located my wayward wife, discovering that the chemistry that had set us aflame on our wedding night still blazed with unrelenting power was the last thing I'd expected.

The fact that I couldn't look at the curve of her delicate jaw without imagining trailing my lips over her smooth skin, tasting the vitality of the pulse that beat at her throat or palming her now even more ample breasts was an unwelcome annoyance that nevertheless didn't stop my mind from wandering where it shouldn't.

Did unfettered pleasure still overtake her in that sizzling, unique way it had during our one coming together? Did she go out of her head with unbridled passion at the merest touch? If so, just who had been stoking that particular flame in her year-long absence?

It took every ounce of control I had to contain my searing jealousy at the thought. Answers to those questions would come later. *This* was too important.

Without stopping to further examine the wisdom of the venue, I made my way into the room.

She followed, making a point to avoid looking at the bed as she passed through into the private living room. From my position before the fireplace I watched her take a seat and neatly fold her hands in her lap. Had her pulse not been racing in her throat I would have been fooled by her complete serenity.

'He's mine.'

Just saying the words dragged earth-shaking emotion through me, robbing me of my next breath. That a small bundle could do that—

'I told you he was.'

There was a new defiance in her demeanour, a quiet, fiery strength that had been there a year ago but had matured now.

'I've never lied to you.'

'Then what do you call *this*?' I tossed the report on the coffee table.

She paled a little, her throat moving in another swallow. And why did I find that simple evidence that she felt *something* so riveting?

'You were always going to know your son, Axios. I simply took a little time before informing you.'

Rejection seared deep. 'No. I should've been informed the moment you found out you were carrying my child.'

'Why? So we could discuss it like a *loving married couple*? Or so you could treat it as another *business* transaction, like our arranged marriage? I'm sure you'll forgive me for choosing neither option, since the former was a farce and the latter was unpalatable.'

The accusation scored a direct hit, making my neck heat with another trace of guilt. Over the last year I'd gone over everything that had happened in those twenty-four hours. Accepted that perhaps I could've handled things differently. But was this the price I had to pay for it?

'I had a right to know, Calypso.' My voice emerged

much gruffer than I'd intended. And deep inside me something like sorrow turned over.

Her lashes swept down, but not before I spotted the sea of turmoil swelling in the blue depths. My nape tightened and my instincts blared with the notion that she was hiding something.

'What if I told you that I didn't know what I wanted?' she asked.

A white-hot knife sliced through me at the thought that it would have decimated me had she taken a different route than bearing my son.

'Calypso…'

Her name sounded thick on my tongue. I waited until she raised her gaze to mine.

'Yes?'

'Regardless of this…disagreement between us, you will have my gratitude for choosing to carry our son for ever.'

Her eyes widened in stunned surprise. 'Um…you're welcome,' she murmured.

Once again her gaze swept away from mine—a small gesture that disturbed and confounded me. And then that defiant bolt of blue clashed with mine and absurd anticipation simmered in my gut.

'He's here now. Can we not put what has gone on in the past behind us and move on?'

'Certainly we can. As soon as you tell me what I want to know I'll take great strides to put it all behind me.'

Again that mutinous look took her over, sparking my own need to tangle with it. To stoke her fire until we both burned.

'Are you prepared to do that, Calypso?'

For several moments she held my gaze. Breath stalled,

I awaited an answer...*one* answer...to quell the questions teeming inside me. But then that unnerving serenity settled on her face again.

'It's not important—'

'*Not important?* You leave my home under cover of a blatant falsehood, then you disappear for a year, during which time you bear my son, and you think your absence isn't *important*?'

'Careful, Axios, or I'll be inclined to wonder whether you actually missed the wife you bothered with for less than a day before walking away.'

I sucked in a stunned breath. A year ago she'd warned me that she wouldn't be biddable. Discovering she was innocent had clouded that warning. But this kitten had well and truly developed claws. Sharp ones. I was tempted to test them. Intellectually and...yes...*physically.*

Unbidden, heat throbbed deep in my groin, stirring desires I'd believed were long dead until one glimpse of my wayward wife from a jetty in Bora Bora had fiercely reawakened them.

That unholy union of sexual tension and unanswered questions propelled me to where she sat, cloaked in secrets that mocked me.

Her slight tensing when I crouched in front of her unsettled me further, despite the fact that I should've been satisfied to see that she wasn't wholly indifferent to me.

'You want to know about the inconvenience your absence caused, Calypso?'

She remained silent.

'Some newspaper hack got wind that my wife wasn't in Agistros, enjoying her first weeks of marital bliss. Nor was she with friends, as she'd led everyone to believe.

To all intents and purposes she seemed to have fallen off the face of the earth.'

A delicate frown creased her brows. 'Why would that be of interest to anyone? Especially when you intended to banish me to Agistros for the duration of our arrangement anyway?'

'You're my wife. Everything you do is news. And appearing to have deserted your marriage was definitely newsworthy.'

She blinked. '*Appearing* to have?'

'I have an outstanding PR team who've had to work tirelessly to put a lid on this.'

There was no hint of remorse on her sun-kissed face. Instead she looked irritated. 'If you've managed to somehow spin my absence to suit our narrative then there's no problem, is there?'

I allowed myself a small smile, one her gaze clung to with wary eyes. 'You would like that, wouldn't you? To escape every unpleasant fall-out from your actions?'

'You don't have the first idea of what I want, Axios.'

My name on her lips sent a punch of heat through me. Thinking back, I couldn't recollect her ever saying it before Bora Bora. Not when she'd spat fire at me, not when she'd confessed her untouched state, and not when she'd been in the complete grip of passion. Certainly not when she'd asked me to take her with me to Athens.

There had been far too many times over the last year when I'd regretted not doing so—not because of that infernal hunger that had long outstayed its welcome, but simply because it would have curtailed her actions.

But the past was the past. There was still the future to deal with. And my new reality.

My son.

'For the sake of probability, and if I were in the mood to grant wishes, what exactly would you want, *matia mou*?'

Wariness made her hesitate, but slowly defiance laced with something else pushed through. 'I'd want a divorce. As soon as possible.'

Stunned disbelief rose in me like a monumental wave I'd once ridden on the North Shore, and then just as swiftly crashed on the beach of her sheer audacity and shock. It was all so very dramatic.

I couldn't help it. I laughed.

Her pert little nose quivered as she inhaled sharply. 'What's so funny?'

Affront and defiance flushed her skin a sweet pink, drawing my attention to her alluring features. My wife was now all woman. An arrestingly feminine woman who'd just demanded…*a divorce*.

'Why you, my dear, and your continued ability to surprise me.'

'I'm glad you're amused. But I'm deadly serious. I want a divorce.'

Humour evaporated as abruptly as it had arrived. Leaning forward, I grasped her upper arms and fought not to be distracted by her smooth supple skin or the need to caress her and reacquaint myself with her.

My once sound argument about staying away from her had backfired spectacularly. I'd left her on Agistros thinking that she'd be safe and I'd be saved from temptation. Look how that had turned out.

Even with sex off the table I should have kept her close. I could have prevented her fleeing. Instead I'd borne the subtle snipes of those who had been quick to point out my failure. Quick to compare me to my grandfather and test me to see whether I'd crack under the same pressure.

With Calypso gone I'd experienced a taste of what he'd gone through—sometimes even with members of my own family.

Now she was back…and asking for a divorce.

'We seem to have veered a little off-track to be indulging in hypotheticals. You'll recall that, according to the agreement, this marriage needs to last at least twelve months.'

'Yes, I remember.'

'Twelve *ongoing* months. Not twelve absentee months.'

She swallowed and my fingers moved, some compulsion driving me to glide my fingers up her neck, trace the colour flowing back into her cheeks. She made a sound under her breath, bearing a hint of those she'd made on our wedding night.

Before I could revel in it she pulled back abruptly. My hands dropped back to her arms.

'My father hasn't contested the agreement,' she said.

'So you took the time to check on his activities?' Disgruntlement rumbled through me at the thought.

Her flush gave me my answer. 'What are you saying, Axios?'

'I'm saying the clock stopped the moment you walked out. But, fortunately for you, your father is no longer in the picture. For one thing he can't prove that you've been an absentee wife—unless you apprised him of your intentions?'

'No, I didn't,' she muttered, her eyes not quite meeting mine.

I'd long suspected that while she might have avoided contact with her father, her mother was a different story.

But Iona Petras had remained resolutely closed-lipped about the whereabouts of her daughter.

'Good—then the ball, as they say, is in my court.'

She met my gaze boldly, read my clear intent and gasped. 'You mean you have the power to give me a divorce but…?' Her voice dried up, a telling little shiver racing through her body.

'But I won't, sweet Calypso. Not until a few things are set straight.'

'What things?'

'For starters, my PR company didn't make *all* the problems go away. While I frustrated the news media enough to make them chase other headlines, my competitors and my business partners were another story. Your absence fuelled enough rumours about instability to stall my latest deal.'

A peculiar expression that resembled hurt crossed her face. 'So this is about stocks and shares again?'

The disparaging note in her voice grated. 'Why? Did you want it to be something more?'

She stiffened. 'No.'

Her firm, swift denial rankled, but again I dismissed it. 'There will be no divorce. Not until I'm completely satisfied that there will be no permanent fall-out from your actions. And not until we've thoroughly discussed the impact this will have on Andreos.'

She stiffened. 'Does it occur to you that I might be doing this for him? That this arrangement might not be the best environment for him?'

'Then we will strive to make it so. You'll get your divorce, if you wish it. It could be as early as a month from now or it could be the year you were supposed to give me. In that time, wherever I go, you and my son will go also. He will be your priority. But when called upon you will be at my side at public functions and you will play the role of a devoted wife. And you will do all of that without the smallest hint that there's dissent between us.'

Her sweet, stubborn chin lifted in a clear defiance. 'And if I don't? What's to stop me giving the newspapers what they want? Telling them the true state of this so-called marriage?'

Why did her rebellion fire me up so readily? In truth, very few people got to display such attitude towards me. Neo tried me at the best of times, but even he knew when to back down. The rest of my family fell in line, because ultimately I held the purse strings.

But it seemed my errant wife's fiery spirit turned me on. Made me want to burn in the fire of it.

I caught her chin in my hand, my thumb moving almost of its own volition to slide over the dark rose swell of her lower lip. She shivered, this time unable to disguise her arousal. I intensified the caress, a little too eager to see how far she was truly affected. Blue eyes held mine for another handful of seconds before they dropped. But her breathing grew more erratic, her pulse hammering against the silken skin of her throat.

I held still, my groin rudely awakening as the little eddy of lust whipped faster, threatened to turn into a cyclone.

'You really wish to defy me? You think that now you and your family have received what they want they can simply sit back and enjoy the spoils of their ill-gotten gains? Do you think that I will let you get away with it?'

She glared blue fire at me. 'I won't be ordered about, Axios. I won't be dictated to like one of your minions!'

'I would never mistake you for a minion. But a little hellcat, intent on sinking her claws into me? Definitely.'

For a charged moment she returned my stare. Then her gaze dropped to my lips.

A sort of madness took over. A breathless second later our lips met in a fiery clash, the hot little gasp she gave granting me access to the sharp tongue that seemed intent on creating havoc with my mood and my libido.

Caught in the grip of hunger, I slicked my tongue against hers, took hold of one hip to hold her in place. She attempted to smother her moan, attempted not to squirm with the arousal I could already sense. I needed more. Needed confirmation of…*something*. Something that bore a hint of the torrid dreams that had plagued me almost nightly for a solid year. Something to take away the disarming hollowness that had resided in me since I'd got the call in New York that my wife had fled Agistros.

My teeth grazed the tip of her tongue when it attempted to issue a challenge. This time she couldn't hold back her moan. Couldn't stop herself from straining against me, from gasping her need.

And when she did I took. Savoured. Then devoured.

Her moans fuelled my desire, and the scramble of her hands over my chest, then around to my back facilitated the urgent need to lay her on the sofa so I could slide over her, to once again experience the heady sensation of having Calypso beneath me.

Her nails dug in deeper as I lowered myself over her, felt the heavy swell of her breasts press again my chest. The recollection that she'd borne my child, that she still nurtured him, was a powerful aphrodisiac that charged through me and hardened me in the most profoundly carnal way.

Could I get any more primitive?

Yes, my senses screamed.

The deepening urge to claim and keep what was mine thundered harder through me, drawing me away from the naked temptation of her lips to the seductive smoothness of her throat, her vibrant pulse, the exquisite valley between her breasts.

It took but a moment to slide the thin sleeve of her sundress off her shoulder, to release the front clasp and nudge aside the cup of her bra to bare her delicious flesh to my ravenous gaze. To mould the plump mound in anticipation of drawing that stiff, rosy peak into my mouth.

Beneath me, Calypso's breath caught. Her eyes turned a dark blue with the same fiery lust that was causing carnage wit in me, then snapped to mine and stayed there.

Slowly, with an ultra-feminine arching of her back that held me deeply enthralled, she offered herself to me, somehow turning the tables on me. Because for all that this was supposed to be a punitive lesson, a way to remind her who held the power now, after her actions had swung the tide to my advantage, I was caught in a vortex of desire so voracious I couldn't have stopped even if I'd wanted to.

So I lowered my head and with a powerless groan sucked the bud into my mouth.

Savage hunger exploded inside me, all my senses lost as her fingers locked in my hair and held me to my delightful task.

'Oh… *Theos mou*,' she gasped.

The memory of our one night together, of her unreserved responsiveness and the unique way she'd expressed her pleasure, sharpened my hunger, sparking a desire to relive that experience. I slid one hand beneath her body, urged her even closer. She answered by arching higher, offering more of herself to me.

'Tell me what you're feeling,' I urged thickly, aware that my voice was hoarse, barely intelligible.

She froze, the eyes that had rolled shut mere seconds ago flying open.

Watching her, I lazily caught that peak between my teeth, felt a carnal shudder unravel through her. 'You taste exquisite.'

Arousal and denial warred in her face, and then her fingers flew from my hair as small but effective hands pushed at my shoulders. 'No! Stop!'

For a moment I considered a different tactic. Negotiation. Talking her round to my way of thinking. Satisfying this need that dogged us both. But hadn't my family and I given the Petrases enough in this lifetime? This was supposed to be the time to extract *my* pound of flesh after what they'd done to my grandfather. Besides, sex was what had led us here in the first place. Was I really going to fall into the well of temptation I'd counselled myself against a year ago when I should be dealing with the reality of my son?

The reminder was enough to propel me off her and across the room. Even then it took several control-gathering breaths to master my raging libido. It didn't help that her reflection in the window showed her naked breasts for another handful of seconds before she righted her clothes.

When she was done, she rose. She didn't approach—which was a good thing, because I wasn't sure I wouldn't have given in to the urge to finish what we'd started.

'Axios…'

I gritted my teeth, the discovery that my name on her

lips was its own special brand of hell driving my fingers through my hair.

This had gone on long enough. 'This is no longer purely business, Calypso. I want to know my son.'

I caught another expression on her face—one that sent a different type of emotion charging through me.

I turned around, wanting to verify it more accurately, but whatever it was had gone, her face a composed mask.

'Of course. I won't stand in the way of that.'

Why didn't that agreement satisfy me?

Why did that hollowness still remain?

'Good. Then we shelve discussion of divorce until further notice.'

That gruff, shaken tone was gone. It was almost as if that little display of emotion over his son had never happened. As if the wild little tumble on the sofa less than five minutes ago was already a distant memory.

But, no...there were tell-tale signs. Signs I didn't want to notice. Like how deliciously tousled his dark, luxuriously wavy hair was now, courtesy of my restless fingers. How colour still rose in his chiselled cheekbones.

And that definitive bulge behind his fly—

With a willpower that threatened to sap the last of my composure I averted my gaze from the pillar of temptation he represented, and reminded myself why we were here in the first place. Dear heaven. I needed to be done with this before the desire I'd believed eroded by distance and absence made a complete fool of me.

'I need your word, Calypso.'

The implacable demand centred my thoughts. Reminded me that this wasn't over. Contrary to what I'd believed, twelve months of living apart from him had done nothing to lessen my sentence. I was back to square one, with a child to think about.

A child Axios fully intended to claim.

'Where exactly does Andreos feature in your grand plan?' I asked, belatedly focusing on the most precious thing in my life. On safeguarding his welfare before I embarked on fighting for my survival.

Axios's head went back, as if the question offended him. 'He is my son. He will be brought up under our care with the full benefit of the Xenakis name at his disposal for as long as he needs it.'

Through all of this I'd held on to the secret fear that Andreos might suffer. Over the past year I'd meticulously researched the Xenakis dynasty, with Andreos's needs at the forefront of my mind.

Outwardly, they appeared a close unit—but, as with most super-wealthy and influential families, rumours of acrimony abounded. Once or twice it had been rumoured that Axios's status as CEO had been challenged by a daring cousin or uncle. None had succeeded, of course.

'You give me your word that you'll protect Andreos, no matter what?'

'Of course. I vow it.' His voice was deep and solemn and immediate.

Relief weakened my knees, and for some absurd reason I wanted to throw my arms around him. 'Thank you.'

His frown deepened, speculation narrowing his eyes. I turned away before he could read my anxiety. Now wasn't the time to think about my precarious health… about the tough road ahead. About the battle my grandmother had fought against cervical cancer and eventually lost.

And it certainly wasn't the time to dwell on the fact

that the pain in my abdomen remained, its presence edging into my consciousness with each passing day.

'Possible cancer... Prognosis uncertain if you choose to keep your baby...'

Dr Trudeau's words broke free from the vault I'd kept them in. Along with the frighteningly easy decision I'd made to keep my baby for as long as I could instead of chasing risky surgery. The tearful gratitude for every day Andreos had nestled in my womb, growing despite the unknown threat to his life and mine.

And his sweet cry the moment he was born.

I'd learned quickly that for my son's sake I needed to compartmentalise. His keen intelligence and sensitivity, even at such a tender age, had focused me on giving him my very best—always. But giving him my best included fighting to remain in his life. Even if I had to temporarily entrust him to Axios in order to do so.

'Do you agree?' Axios pressed, his gaze probing mercilessly.

'I'll give you what you want on one condition. Take it or leave it.'

After a moment he jerked his head in command for me to continue.

'I'll stay until your precious deal is done. On condition that you don't attempt to interfere in my relationship with my son.'

'What gives you the impression that I'd wish to do anything of the sort?'

My shrug fell short of full efficiency under his heavy frown. 'It's been known to happen.'

'Who? Your father?'

I could have denied it, kept up the years-long pretence. But time was too precious to waste on falsehoods. So I nodded. 'Yes.'

Axios moved towards me, his frown a dark cloud. 'What did he do to you?'

I hesitated now, because on the flipside I didn't want to bare my all to him. The desire to continue living on my own terms hadn't diminished an iota since my return to Greece. And even if I intended to agree to Axios's demands I would always keep one small corner of my life free from his interference.

'He manipulated every relationship I ever had in some way. I don't want that to happen with Andreos.'

The grey gaze boring into mine stated blatantly that he wanted more. Mine declared I'd given him all I intended to.

'I've seen you with Andreos. He thrives under your care. I'd be a fool to jeopardise that.'

Before I could breathe my relief he stepped closer, bringing that bristling magnificence into touching distance. I balled fingers that tingled with the need to feel his vibrant skin under my touch again.

'You have my word I will not interfere. Will you give me yours?'

Again I was mildly stunned that it was a question rather than a declaration. But the searing reminder that giving in to one emotion around Axios was simply the gateway to a flood of other sensations I needed to keep a tight leash on, had me swallowing the desire.

'I will stay for as long as it takes to give you what you need,' I offered.

He accepted it with a simple nod, as if it was nothing to celebrate. And perhaps in the grand scheme of things it wasn't. We were picking up where we'd left off with the added inconvenience of needing to put out more fires than he'd initially anticipated.

After several skin-tingling moments during which he simply stared at me, as if probing beneath my defences to read my secrets, I twisted away, eager to escape those all-seeing eyes.

'I need to get back to Andreos.'

'We're not quite done, Calypso.'

About to ask what else we needed to talk about, I felt my tight throat close even further when he stepped closer. His scent curled around me, reminding me of what had happened on the sofa a short while ago. Had things really got out of hand so quickly? My body still hummed with unspent energy, and my heart hadn't quite settled into its steady cadence.

'I'll come with you to visit my son.'

The throb of possessiveness in his voice sent my senses flaring wide with warning. What exactly that warning was refused to surface as we left his suite.

As it turned out it wasn't necessary to return to the ground floor. Sophia was carefully navigating the stairs, with a sleepy Andreos in her arms. We followed her as she entered the opposite wing of the villa, where a nursery had been set up by a team of designers on the first day of my return.

Seeing us, she smiled. 'We played for a while, but I think he's ready for his nap, *kyria*,' she said softly.

The sight of Andreos fighting a losing battle to stay awake drew a smile from my heart. Handing him over to Sophia even for such a short while had made my heart ache. I knew it would be a million times worse when I had to leave, but somehow I trusted Axios with his care. Sophia's clear devotion to him was an added bonus.

I reached out for him but Axios stepped forward.

'Do you mind?' The demand was gruff but gentle.

In stunned surprise I nodded. Still smiling, Sophia handed son over to father and discreetly melted away.

The sight of Axios holding his son for the first time shouldn't have brought a thick lump to my throat. The sight of his strong, powerful arms carefully cradling my baby, his throat moving in a convulsive swallow, shouldn't have fired a soul-deep yearning through my body. A yearning for things to be different. For fate not to be so cruel.

Why? Did I wish for things to be different between Axios and I?

Absolutely not.

As for other yearnings—hadn't I already been granted more than enough? I'd prayed for a healthy son and been given the child of my heart. I'd prayed for a little more time and had enjoyed almost four beautiful months.

But the thought of leaving him, even to fight for my health—

'What's wrong?'

I jumped, my gaze rising to see Axios watching me.

'Am I holding him wrong?'

The touch of uncertainty in his voice caught a warm spot inside me and loosened another smile from me as I approached, unable to stop myself from reaching out, kissing Andreos's forehead and cheek, breathing in his sweet and innocent scent.

'No, you're not doing anything wrong.'

Grey eyes so very similar to his son's dropped to the now sleeping Andreos, and his chest slowly expanded in a long breath before he headed over to the brand-new, state-of-the-art cot set out for our baby.

With the utmost care he transferred Andreos from his arms to the cot, barely eliciting any protest from him. Arms thrown up beside his head in angelic abandon, Andreos slept on as his father draped a soft cotton blanket over him, drew a gentle finger down his cheek and straightened.

Still smiling, I glanced over at Axios—and my heart leapt into my throat. Gone was the gentle look he'd bestowed on his son. In its place was a bleak visage full of loss and yearning that made me gasp. Made that pulse of guilt rise again.

The sound drew his attention to me. When he took hold of my arm and steered me out of earshot I tried to think past the naked tingles his touch brought. To think how I could contain the relentless waves of turbulent emotion bent on consuming us.

'I'd like answers to a few questions, Calypso. If you feel so inclined?' he rasped.

Seeing no way to avoid it without collapsing the agreement I'd struck, I nodded.

His hand dropped to my wrist. 'We'll discuss this further over lunch.'

Lunch was an extensive selection of *meze* fit for a small banquet—not the intimate setting for two laid out on one of the three sun-splashed terraces.

Axios must have spotted my surprise as he pulled out my chair because he shrugged. 'I didn't know your preferences so I instructed the chef to prepare a large selection.'

'Oh…thank you.'

His gaze rested on me as he lowered himself into his own chair. 'Again, you sound surprised. Believe it or not I want things to go as smoothly as possible for both of us.'

The knowledge that this included simple things such as what I ate widened the warm pool swelling inside me. Even cautioning myself that it was foolish to entertain such a sensation didn't do anything to stem it as I helped myself to pitta bread and tzatziki, feta cheese and chickpea salad and succulent vine leaves stuffed with lamb and cucumber.

'Where was Andreos born?'

His deep voice throbbed with one simple emotion—a hunger to know. And for the very first time since my decision to live life on my terms, twelve long months ago, I experienced a deep stirring of guilt.

But along with that came a timely warning not to divulge everything. Knowledge was power to men like Axios. Men like my father. And every precious uninterrupted moment with my son was as vital to me as the breath in my lungs.

Although in the past four days since my return, Axios had seemed a little more...malleable. While the man who'd laid down the law and walked away from me in Agistros still lurked in there somewhere, this Axios tended to ask more and command less.

But still I carefully selected the bits of information that wouldn't connect too many dots for him and replied, 'He was born in a small clinic in Kenya, where I was volunteering. He came a week early, but there were no complications and the birth was relatively easy.'

He didn't answer. Not immediately. The glass of red wine he was drinking with his meal remained cradled in his hand and his expression reflective and almost... yearning as he stared into the middle distance.

'I would've liked to be there,' he rasped. 'Very much.'

The warm pool inside me grew hotter, turning into a

jet of feeling spiralling high with emotions I needed to wrestle under control before they got out of hand.

But even as the warning hit hard I was opening my mouth, uttering words I shouldn't. 'One of the nurses filmed the birth…if you'd like to see it?'

What are you doing sharing your most precious moments with him?

He's Andreos's father.

Axios inhaled sharply, the glass discarded as he stared fiercely at me. 'You have a video?'

I jerked out a nod. 'Yes. Would you—?'

'Yes.' The word was bullet-sharp, and the cadence of his breathing altered as his gaze bored into me. 'Yes. Very much,' he repeated.

For the longest time we remained frozen, our gazes locked in a silent exchange I didn't want to examine or define. Soon it morphed into something else. Something equally intimate. Twice as dangerous.

Perhaps it was in the molten depths of his eyes, or in the not so secret wish to relive what had happened upstairs ramping up that ever-present chemistry. Whatever it was, we'd brought it alive on that sofa and now it sat between us, a writhing wire ready to sizzle and electrify and burn at the smallest hint of weakening.

Forcing my brain back on track didn't help. Hadn't we been discussing childbirth? The product of what had happened in a bedroom the last time we were both present in one.

'I'll let you have the recording after lunch,' I blurted, then picked up my water glass and drank simply to distract myself.

From the corner of my eye I watched him lounge back

in his seat, although his body still held that coil of tension that never dissipated.

After a moment he picked up his glass and drained it. '*Efkharisto*,' he murmured. 'Now, on to other things. Arrangements are being made to equip you with a new wardrobe. My mother tells me the things you left behind are hopelessly out of date.'

I frowned, the change of subject from the soul-stirring miracle of Andreos's birth to the mundanity of high fashion throwing me for a few seconds. 'I don't need a new wardrobe.'

'Perhaps not—but might I suggest you let the stylists come anyway? Who knows? You might find something you like for our first engagement on Saturday,' he replied.

The last tendrils of yearning had left his voice, to be replaced by the cadence I knew best. One of powerful mogul. Master of all he surveyed. Despite the pleasant heat of the sun a cool breeze whispered over my skin, bringing me harshly back to earth.

'What's happening on Saturday?'

'It's been four days since you returned. It's time we presented you properly to the world. My mother has organised a party in your honour. She was unwell when we married last year, and couldn't make it to the ceremony. She's anxious to meet you. And, of course, she's yet to meet her grandson. Call this a belated welcome, if you will, but several business acquaintances will be there, so it's imperative that everything goes smoothly.'

'Is it really necessary to parade me before your friends and family?'

'I think it's best to put the rumours to rest once and for all. Then we can concentrate on our son.'

While his attention to Andreos warmed my heart, the prospect of being paraded before his family and business didn't. 'And how do you propose we do that? Is there a storyline I need to follow, chapter and verse?'

He smiled as if the thought of playing out a role so publicly was water off his back. 'Leave that to me,' he stated cryptically. 'All I require from you is to present a picture-perfect image of loving wife and mother. I trust I can count on you to do that?'

For the sake of uninterrupted bonding with my son I would go to hell and back. 'Yes.'

Perhaps my agreement was too quick. Perhaps the depth of feeling behind it was too revealing. Whatever, his gaze grew contemplative, stayed fixed on me.

And when he walked away, moments after the meal was done, I got the distinct feeling there were more bumps and curves on this peculiar road I'd taken than I'd initially realised.

CHAPTER SIX

A PRE-PARTY FAMILY MIXER.

A harmless-sounding statement until you were confronted by the full might of the formidable Xenakis clan.

The gathering had been deceptive. Over the course of two hours they'd trickled in—some by car, others by boat. And Axios's formidable-looking brother Neo, looking a little distracted and a lot harassed, had come by sleek helicopter, with the iconic Xenakis Aeronautics logo emblazoned on its side.

Inexorably the trickle became a stream, and then a torrent. By four p.m. the largest salon in the villa, the surrounding terrace and the perfectly manicured lawn were overflowing with aunts, uncles, cousins and distant offshoots—some from as far afield as Australia and New Zealand.

Fascinatingly, despite the low buzz of tension surrounding their interactions, there were no overt signs of dissent.

Perhaps because I was their main focus.

I didn't want to admit it, but the six-hour makeover session I'd endured earlier in the day boosted my confidence now, as impeccably dressed men and couture-

clad women approached the place where I stood next to
Axios, with a wide-eyed Andreos nestled in my arms.

My hair had been brought back to shoulder-length,
layered and trimmed into loose stylish waves that
gleamed with new vitality. And the rails upon rails of
new clothes hanging in the closets of my vast dressing
room, complete with matching accessories and priceless
jewellery, were the *pièce de résistance*.

After months of wearing flats and tie-dye sundresses,
and ponytailing my hair, the transformation took a little getting used to. While the teardrop diamond necklace glittering just as bright as the pristine white linen
shift dress and tan platform shoes were making me feel
intensely aware of the kind of circles I'd married into.

The most striking of the women within those intimidating circles was Electra Xenakis—Axios's mother.

Her hair was a distinctive grey, which had been used
to enhance her beauty rather than been dyed away, and
it framed an angular face, highlighting superb cheekbones and the striking grey eyes she'd passed on to her
sons. Tall and slender, with a ramrod-straight posture,
she was formidable—until she gave a rare smile. Then
warmth radiated from her every pore, and the icy grey
palazzo pants and matching top she wore were suddenly
not so severe.

On meeting Andreos she dissolved into hearty tears.
And that unfettered display of love for her grandchild
thawed the cold knot of apprehension inside me, easing
my anguish at the thought of a permanent separation
from my child.

The distance I'd needed to get my composure back
after handing Andreos over to his grandmother lasted
mere minutes before I sensed a presence beside me. It

wasn't as visceral and all-encompassing as Axios's, but it demanded attention nevertheless.

I glanced up to find Neo Xenakis standing before me.

'I never quite got the chance to welcome you into the family last year.' His tone was measured, his eyes just as probing as his brother's.

'I guess the circumstances weren't exactly…conducive,' I replied.

'*Ochi*, they weren't. But your disappearing act didn't help matters, I expect?'

I stiffened. 'I had my reasons,' I replied.

Without answering, he dropped his gaze to the contents of the crystal tumbler he clutched. 'Whatever they were, I hope it was worth keeping a father from his child?'

Again his tone was more appraising than censorious, as if he was attempting to understand my motives. Again my guilt resurfaced. And this time brushing it away wasn't easy.

Before I could formulate a response, a deeper and more visceral voice asked, 'Is everything all right?'

For me not to have sensed his arrival spoke volumes of the kind of magnetism the Xenakis men possessed. And now Axios had arrived next to me the force of their presence had doubled. Their sole focus was on me, but one set of grey eyes was vastly more potent than the other, sending my composure into free fall.

I took a long, steadying breath to reply, 'We're fine.'

Axios's gaze slid from mine to his brother, a clear question in his eyes.

Neo's expression clouded for a moment, then he shrugged. 'Like your wife said, we're fine. No need to go Neanderthal on me.'

Before either of us could enquire what he meant, he

excused himself and struck out for the large gazebo on the south side of the garden, currently decked out with fairy lights and free of guests.

'Is he okay?' I felt compelled to ask.

Axios's gaze stayed on him long enough to see his brother lift a phone to his ear before he turned to me. 'His issues aren't mine to disclose, but Neo is touchy on the subject of babies. Like the rest of the family, news about his nephew's existence surprised him. But, since Andreos is single-handedly winning everyone over, I suspect the circumstances of his arrival will be forgiven soon.'

Had he deliberately excluded himself from that statement? Unwilling for him to see the bite of anguish that distinction brought, I turned my gaze to where the majority of the Xenakis clan had now gathered, choosing to see the bright side.

Andreos was indeed holding centre stage, tucked into his favourite blanket and nestled lovingly within his grandmother's arms. The absolute devotion on the older woman's face eased my heartache, but in the next moment the sudden thought that my own mother hadn't met my son hit me with tornado-strength force.

'What is it?' Axios asked, the eyes that hadn't left my face since his brother's disappearance narrowing.

The fleeting thought to shrug off his question came and went, and I couldn't help the small shaft of pain that came with it. 'My parents haven't met him yet.'

His face tightened, the mention of Yiannis Petras drawing a reaction I would have preferred to leave out of the already fraught atmosphere. I held my breath, ready to fight my corner.

'We can arrange a visit for your mother later…if you wish?'

Surprised by that response, I blinked. 'I do. Thank you.'

After another minute of assessing scrutiny he nodded. 'Whatever your reasons for fleeing Agistros, I accept that I could've handled our last meeting a little better,' he said, his voice a deep rasp.

My lips were parted in shock when another wave of Xenakises wandered over. Axios's droll look and almost-smile told me he'd seen my shock at his apology.

I managed to get my emotions under control beneath his family's probing glances, watching their silent musing as to what had transpired with Axios's stray wife. I was grateful for their circumspection because, as baptisms of fire went, it could have been worse.

It was with far more trepidation that I contemplated my extensive closet three hours after everyone had disappeared into their various guest rooms and private homes to get ready for the main event. The knock on the door barely snagged my attention. Absent-mindedly I responded, my fingers toying with the tie of my bathrobe as I contemplated the stunning array of clothes.

'As much as you seem to enjoy simply staring at them, you do actually have to pick an outfit to wear for the party, you know?' Ax drawled, his deep tone more amused than I'd ever heard him.

I jumped and turned around, barely able to hold back a gasp at the sight of him, standing a few feet away, wearing half of a bespoke tuxedo. His pristine snow-white shirt was half buttoned, but neatly tucked into his tailored trousers, and his bowtie was strung around his neck.

The intimate knowledge of what resided beneath his clothes dried my mouth as I stared, slack-jawed, several superlatives crowding my brain.

Debonair. Breathtaking. Insanely gorgeous.

Slowly the silence thickened and he raised one sleek eyebrow. 'Can I help with anything?'

The hand I waved over my shoulder at the closet was irritatingly fluttery. 'I can't decide what to wear. Meeting your family was one thing… This is a different ball-game.'

His gaze travelled from the top of my hair, which still held its earlier style, thanks to the expertise of the stylist, then lingered at the belt holding my robe closed, before moving to my bare feet. Each spot his eyes touched triggered fiery awareness.

'You handled my family admirably and won them over with Andreos. Even Neo—and he's a handful at the best of times,' he added dryly. 'You'll excel just as well tonight.'

The deeply spoken reassurance made my heart lurch. To hide its effect I scrambled for something else to concentrate on, and spotted his dangling sleeves and the cufflinks in his hand.

'Do you need help with those?' I asked, even though assisting him would involve stepping closer, breathing in the intoxicating scent that clung to him and never failed to send my senses haywire.

He held out his arms. 'If you wouldn't mind?'

Breath held, in the hope that it would mitigate the erotic chaos stirring to life inside me, I reached for the two halves of his shirtsleeve in one hand and held out the other for the cufflinks. The tips of his fingers brushed my palm as he handed them over, and every inch of my skin responded as if set alight.

Intensely aware that my nipples were hardening, and that a pulse had started throbbing between my thighs, I hurried to finish my task, my own fingers brushing the inside of his wrist in the process.

Axios inhaled sharply, an incoherent sound rumbling from his chest.

Could we not even exchange a common courtesy without feeling as if the world was about to burst into flames?

Evidently not.

Which was probably all the warning I needed to keep my distance. Never to repeat what had happened on his sofa.

'*Efkharisto,*' he murmured, his voice deep and thick.

His eyes were molten, as heated as that needy place between my legs. Unable to withstand his gaze, for fear I'd give myself away, I turned to face the rack of clothes. Of course my senses leaped high when he stepped next to me, then took another step closer to the open closet.

To my shaky memory this was perhaps the first time I'd been this close without having his laser eyes on me. The opportunity to give in to the urge to stare was too hard to resist.

The breadth and packed strength of his shoulders.

The vibrancy of his lustrous hair.

The sharp, mouthwatering angle of his freshly shaved jaw.

Too busy fighting the way every inch of Axios triggered this unwanted but unstoppable reaction, I didn't notice he'd made a selection until he pivoted, the momentary gaping of his shirt delivering one final punch of his sheer magnetism before he drawled, 'You'll look beautiful in any one of these gowns. But this one will do, I think.'

Heat engulfed my face as I reached out and snatched the gown from his hand, hastily stepping back. 'I... thanks.'

'You need help with the zip?' he asked, in a voice thicker than before.

Aware of the dangerous waters I was treading, I shook my head. 'I think I'll manage. Thanks.'

He hesitated for a stomach-churning moment, then nodded. 'I'll return in fifteen minutes. We will go downstairs together, if you wish.'

I nodded my thanks.

Contrary to his stealthy arrival, I was conscious of Ax's departure for the simple reason that he seemed to take the very air out of the room with him, leaving me breathless as I shrugged off the robe and slipped the gown over my head.

Barely paying attention to the design, I zipped it up and stepped into the heels that had been helpfully paired with the dress, spritzed perfume on my neck and wrists, and was adding the finishing touches to my make-up when his knock came.

Very much aware of the silk clinging to my hips and breasts, I prayed my body wouldn't give me away as I opened the door.

For the longest time he simply stared at me. 'Beautiful,' he finally stated, and the sizzling gleam in his eyes only lent him a more dangerous air, rendering all my efforts for composure useless as I accepted there was no level this man couldn't reach in the drop-dead gorgeous stakes.

'Thank you,' I replied, my voice a husky mess.

He held out his arm. I took it, and was still in a semi-daze when we exited the limo at the entrance to the six-star luxury hotel in the middle of Athens where the party was being held.

The moment Ax and I stepped into the ballroom silence fell over the guests, every eye fixed on me.

'I don't know whether to smile or scowl. What's *de rigueur* these days?' I murmured.

'Just ignore them. That's what I do when I feel out of place.'

I laughed, mostly to hide his unabated effect on me. Besides, I couldn't help it, because picturing Axios as a fish out of water was like attempting to imagine what the landscape inside a black hole looked like.

'Something funny?'

'You wouldn't look out of place amongst a clutch of nuns in a prayer circle.'

He smiled, and just like that my body went into free fall, breaking one tension while ratcheting up another. And as I was crashing down, towards some unknown destination, it struck me that this was the first time I'd seen any semblance of a smile from the man I called my husband.

'An unusual compliment, I think, but thank you all the same,' he said.

'You should've told me the whole of Athens would be here tonight,' I said, a little desperate to maintain a disgruntled distance from him.

He lowered his head even closer to murmur in my ear, 'Put your claws away, *pethi mou*. You look much too beautiful to pick a fight.'

'I'm sure we can find something to fight about if we look hard enough.'

Was I really that desperate to start a fight? Simply to stop this unruly attraction in its tracks?

His amusement disappeared, to be replaced with the unwavering regard that never failed to trigger mini-earthquakes inside me. My breath snagged in my throat as he stepped closer, until there was nothing but a whisper of space between us. To anyone observing us we'd look as if we were sharing an intimate moment. But I knew what was coming even before he spoke.

'Keep tossing those little challenges at me, Calypso, and I'll delight in picking you up on one.'

The electric promise in those words sent a bolt through me. It lingered through all the introductions to influential individuals, A-list celebrities and even more of the Xenakis clan and it slowly began to re-energise, that spark of rebellion re-ignited.

For some reason I *wanted* to challenge him.

So when I found a moment's reprieve I looked up from my untouched glass of champagne into his face. 'Do you know what I think, Axios?'

A simple but effective hitch of his brow commanded me to continue.

'I don't think you will pick me up on any challenge. I don't think you'll do anything to risk this reputation you're bent on protecting.'

'Are you brave enough to test your theory, I wonder?' he asked, and something untamed pulsed beneath his civil exterior. Something that made the glass in my hand tremble wildly.

His gaze dropped to it before returning to my face. With a wicked smile he raised one imperious hand and traced his knuckles down my heated cheek.

'Pick your battles with care, Calypso. You look stun-

ning in this dress—every eye in the room keeps returning to you time and again, and I'm the envy of every
man here. You should be celebrating that, not picking a
fight with your husband.'

With that, he leaned even closer, replaced his hand
with his mouth for the briefest of moments...

And then he walked off.

Leaving me shaking with a cascade of emotions.

The only reason I felt out of sorts was because that
little incident in my dressing room had thrown me—
shown me a different side to Axios that had intensified
the illicit yearning inside me. And while standing next
to Axios wreaked havoc with my equilibrium, watching
him, the most prominent man in the room, walking away
left me with a yawing hollow in the pit of my stomach.

Did I really want him? Or was I just terrified by the
knowledge that the only eyes I wanted on me were his,
not the guests' who kept coming up to me, some blatantly questioning why the great Axios Xenakis had tied
himself down to *me*.

I shook my head, hoping to clear it of these confus-
ing thoughts.

'I hope you're not shaking your head because you
wish to deny me your company?'

I attempted to control my bewildering thoughts before
turning towards another one of Ax's cousins.

At my blank look he said, 'I'm Stavros. We met earlier.'

I nodded, attempted to smile. 'Hello.'

His smile was reserved, but genuine. I found myself
wishing for another smile. One that was edged in sizzling grey. I was really losing it.

'Having fun?'

I shrugged. 'I'm in a room full of some of the most

powerful people on earth, sipping champagne and enjoying the status of hostess with the mostest. What's not to love?'

As with most of the Xenakis clan, his expression grew speculative. 'You sound…distressed. Is everything all right?'

About to answer, I looked across the room to where Ax had been talking to the trade minister moments ago. He was staring directly at me, as if he could see to the heart of my jumbled emotions.

That he could do that from across the room panicked me and irked me. Nevertheless, I had to hold on to what was important. And that was Andreos. Regardless of my personal situation, I couldn't afford for anything to jeopardise my time with my child.

With a deep breath, I forced a smile and turned to Stavros. 'I'm absolutely fine, Stavros. Sorry if I sounded a little off. Chalk it up to missing my baby.'

'Ah, a little separation anxiety, *ne*? As the father of young children, I remember that state well, too.'

'Yes… Speaking of which, would you mind excusing me? I'd like to call and check on him.'

This time Stavros's smile was a little tight. 'Of course. But I hope you'll honour me with a dance when you return?'

For some reason his request made me glance at Ax. He was once again engrossed in conversation with a clutch of men who were no doubt hanging on his every word.

That spark of rebellion returned and I answered Stavros's smile. 'Maybe. We'll see…'

Excusing myself, I wove through the crowd, my pinned-on smile beginning to fray a little more at the edges every time I was stopped by a well-meaning guest wishing to very *belatedly* congratulate me on my marriage and Andreos's birth, while subtly probing for cracks in my demeanour.

True to his word, Axios had taken care of all the speculation and chosen the most direct explanation for my absence.

'My wife wished to have a peaceful pregnancy and took the time she needed to safely deliver our son.'

Only the most daring would choose to probe my absence after that.

All evening I'd watched him hold court, effortlessly exuding power and charm over hardcore businessmen and moguls I'd only read about in the newspapers.

And while the wedding last year and the family gathering earlier had already shown me his authority and charisma, watching him speak to and mingle with some of the most influential people in the world truly rammed home to me the almost frightening power he wielded.

He was a powerful man whom my father had managed to bend to his will. A man whose reputation I'd put in jeopardy with my disappearing act.

Had I been fooling myself by striking a deal with him?

Enough! Running rings around my decisions was futile.

I stepped out onto the thankfully empty terrace of the grand hotel ballroom and called Sophia. Reassured that all was well, my thoughts flew as they often did when I thought of Andreos to the battle that awaited me. To the fear that my time with him would be cut short.

My hand dropped to linger over my stomach, to the dull ache residing deep inside…

'Are you all right?' Axios demanded with a gravel-rough voice.

I jumped and whirled around, hastily dropping my hand when his gaze moved to it. 'You're spying on me now?'

He sauntered towards me. 'I came to check on you because I didn't want you to feel neglected. And I haven't forgotten that you fled your marriage after one day and didn't return for a year,' he returned with sizzling fire.

'Because you were happy to leave me alone on your island without a care for what *I* wanted. Have you forgotten that? Did it even occur to you that I might want a different life for myself other than what *you* chose for me?'

For the longest time he didn't reply. Then, 'That was an error in judgement. One I regret,' he intoned solemnly.

The unequivocal apology had the same effect as the one earlier. My jaw dropped. 'You...do?'

'*Ne*,' he drawled.

For another charged moment he stared at me. Then his gaze dropped to my phone.

Almost dazedly I stared at it. 'You can stand down your spies. I was simply calling Sophia to check on my son.'

A deeply possessive look glinted in his eyes. 'He's *our* son, *pethi mou*. Yours and mine and no one else's.'

The very idea of Andreos being anyone else's child but Axios's was so profoundly impossible I almost laughed out loud. And then that notion faded under the weight of the electrified atmosphere crackling between us. The feeling of being caught on the edge of a lightning storm that never quite went away.

It didn't take a genius to see that Axios was in an equally edgy mood.

Attempting to dissipate it, I waved the phone at him. 'He's fine, by the way. According to Sophia, he went down without a fuss.'

Axios shrugged. 'He's almost four months old. I believe that as long as he's warm and well fed he has very little to worry about.'

'It's a little more complicated than that. He needs love and laughter. He's also at the stage where he'll really start recognising his mother's absence.'

Bleakness flashed across his face, momentarily slashing my insides. 'What about his father's? And whose fault is it that I'm not fully equipped with that information, Calypso?' His voice throbbed with raw emotion.

'Axios—'

His hand slashed through the air a split-second before he closed the gap between us and settled his hands on my shoulders. 'I want to move on from this. But there are questions you still haven't answered.'

My heart dipped. 'Like what?'

'What's the big secret about your whereabouts? I hunted for you high and low. My investigators visited Nicrete—discreetly, of course, since I had to protect my family from untoward gossip. The general consensus there was that Calypso Petras was far too level-headed, far too considerate to have made such a selfish move. At least without assistance or coercion of some sort. Perhaps from a source no one considered.'

'What source?'

His tension heightened, his whole body seemingly caught in a live electric feed. 'You tell me.'

'Maybe a secret admirer? Perhaps even another man?' I taunted.

A fierce little muscle ticked in his jaw. 'Was it? Considering you were a virgin, I wasn't inclined to think you would jump into another man's bed that easily. Tell me I wasn't wrong,' he bit out.

He hadn't thought the worst of me.

The idea of it left me nonplussed for several seconds, considering he still had no idea of my whereabouts for the past year. Considering he had to have overheard some of the blatant whispers at the party.

'Why the interrogation? I thought you were all about keeping up appearances? Convincing the world that my absence was a well-orchestrated plan?'

'That's been taken care of. The results will be evident soon enough. Let's discuss us,' he said, then immediately frowned as if he hadn't expected to say that.

Perhaps he hadn't. After all, wasn't he the man who'd never engaged in a relationship that lasted more than a few weeks?

'*Us?* Are you sure? You seem as surprised by that word falling from your lips as I am to hear it.'

For the longest time he stared at me. Then he shrugged. 'Only a fool stays on a course that's doomed. Perhaps I'm embracing new changes. Attempting to be… different.'

My heart lurched, even as I tamped down fruitless hope. All this meant nothing. Not if my prognosis was as dire as my senses screamed that they were. Not if this marriage was ticking down to dissolution.

'Can we not do this here? I'd like to go back in.'

'Why? So Stavros can succeed at working his angle?'

I blinked in surprise. 'What are you talking about?'

He edged me back a step, following me so we were wedged against the stone balustrade. 'Just a heads-up. His marriage is on the rocks. He's attempting to raise his stature by undermining my authority every chance he gets—chances which, unfortunately for him, haven't been readily available. I'd rather not see you be his pawn,' he breathed, his voice absolutely lethal while being so soft.

Too late, I accepted that the fire inside me was building out of control. His body surged closer, reminding me in vivid detail of the hard-packed, streamlined definition of muscle beneath his bespoke suit. And the fact that his body could render me speechless with very little effort.

'You can stand down. I can take care of myself.'

'*Ne*, I'm beginning to see that,' he murmured, and again there was the barest hint of grudging acceptance in his eyes.

But I didn't get the chance to explore the discovery because his head slowly lowered.

Hot, sensual and commanding, his lips slanted over mine. With a gasp that was way too husky and way too revealing I threw up my hands. Somewhere in the back of my head I was aware that I'd dropped my phone. But it didn't seem to matter, because his tongue was delving between my lips, seeking entrance I was helpless to deny.

He tasted me with a brazenness that struck a match to the desire that had been straining to be freed after that episode on his sofa. With effortless ease he set it ablaze between one snatched breath and the next.

His tongue stroked mine with a possessiveness that took control of my whole body, so that when one hand slid from my shoulder and down my back to draw me into sizzling contact it felt as if I was made of warm, pliant dough, ready to mould myself to any shape of his bidding.

When his other hand angled my head to deepen the kiss it was all I could do to slide my own hands around his neck. To hold on tightly as the dizzying journey zipped like a rollercoaster ride I never wanted to end.

With a helpless moan, I parted my lips wider, strained onto my toes the better to absorb more of the experience.

Ax made a gruff sound that disintegrated beneath our frenzied kiss. His hold intensified until we were plastered together from chest to thigh. Until the unmistakable imprint of his thick, aroused manhood blazed hot and potent against my belly.

My fingers convulsed in his hair as the memory of him inside me, possessing me, surged into life. Feverish need pooled between my thighs, hunger prising another moan from my throat.

Before it could be anywhere near sated Ax was pulling away, his gaze searingly possessive as it moved from my damp and tingling mouth to my eyes.

'Now that we've shown the world how hot we still are for each other, will you come inside with me and dance with your husband?' he asked, his tone husky but firm.

Did he really want to dance with me or had he kissed me just for show?

The eyes burning into mine seemed to be attempting to read me just as hard as I was trying to reading him.

What was he looking for?

What was *I* looking for?

My scrambling senses flailed, and I was aghast at how easily and completely he'd overtaken my senses. How even now, with a few snatched breaths, I still couldn't think beyond the need to experience that kiss all over again. Yearning for more than just a kiss.

Realising he was awaiting a response, I scrambled the appropriate words together. 'Yes. If I must.'

He swooped down to pick up my discarded phone, then linked his fingers with mine before tugging me after him.

The crowd parted at our re-entrance, and some of the gazes I met were alight with the knowledge of what we'd been doing out on the balcony.

Being mired in my confused emotions saved me feeling embarrassment at those looks. It also made me pliant enough to survive half of the slow waltz with Axios before my senses began to return.

The reality of finding myself plastered to my husband once more, with the effects of that kiss still lingering in the form of my peaked nipples and erratic breathing, made me glance wildly around, avoiding his gaze as I tried to gather my shredded composure.

'Look at me, Calypso,' he instructed gruffly.

Almost helplessly I met his gaze.

His expression was studiously neutral but his eyes glinted with residual emotion. 'What just happened is nothing to be ashamed of,' he said gruffly. 'In fact, some might think it…fortunate that we're compatible in some ways.'

I wanted to laugh, because he was oh, so savvy about such things. While I continued to flounder.

'Don't you think it's a touch…*needy* to feel you have to be the centre of everyone's attention?' I asked.

The arrogant smile he slanted down at me said he didn't care one way or the other what people thought.

'I don't wish to be the centre of everyone's attention. Just yours,' he drawled.

For the sake of our audience, I sternly reminded myself, even as my insides lurched and jumped with misguided giddiness.

To mitigate that sensation I pressed my lips together and swayed in his arms, hoping the music would soothe my ragged nerves and spirit the rest of this infernal night away.

But, as fate had shown me time and again, hopes and dreams belonged in fairy tales. Axios danced me through three more tunes before conceding the fourth to the mayor.

Thereafter, quickly reclaimed by my so-called doting husband, we moved from group to group, his hand firm on my waist and his piercing grey eyes smiling down at me through each introduction.

His acting skills were exceptional. Our guests lapped up every soft caress, indulgently smiling at my every recounting of why I'd been away as if it was a true Greek love story.

We stopped within every circle long enough to project an image of cordiality before moving on. And I regurgitated the practised story of my absence until I feared I was blue in the face. Until I was ready to scream the truth to the whole world.

Perhaps his shark-like instincts sensed my frazzling composure. Because Ax turned to me as I impatiently waved away another offer of champagne and started to open my clutch.

'What is it?' he asked.

Remembering he had possession of my phone, I looked at him. 'Can I have my phone back? I want to check on Andreos.'

His gaze rested on my face for several beats. Thinking he wasn't going to answer, I was surprised when he turned to the business acquaintances he'd been talking to.

'It's time for us to take our leave. My beloved cannot bear to be away from our son for long, and I find that I'm not far behind her in that sentiment.'

Indulgent laughter followed, quick goodbyes were said, and before I knew it we were heading out to the waiting limo.

Settled into the back seat, I found my senses once again crowded with the sight and sound of Axios. My inability to dismiss him.

'I could've gone home on my own. You didn't need to leave with me.'

One sleek eyebrow spiked. 'You wanted me to stay there and reverse the effect of everything we've achieved this evening?' he replied.

'You seem to be a master at convincing everyone that the moon is made of caviar. I'm sure they'll believe whatever you tell them.'

He gave a low, deep laugh. Which drained away as his eyes latched to my face. 'Perhaps I do have this unique gift you speak of, but I also meant what I said. I've missed months of my son's life. I don't intend to miss any more.'

'For how long?'

His whole body froze. 'Excuse me?'

'How long do you think this phase of yours will last?'

'You have lost me…'

A thought that had been niggling me despite his assertion rose to the fore. 'You didn't want this marriage and we never got around to discussing children. We're only here because a condom failed at the crucial juncture.'

'And you think those circumstances beyond my control preclude me from assuming my mantle of responsibility towards my son? Did it you?'

'I… It's different.'

'How?' he challenged.

'I love him! I would do anything for him. While you…'

'What? Speak your mind, *glikia mou*.'

'You just want to show off your virility.'

After several tense seconds he settled back in his seat. 'You're right. I do want to show him off. He is my son, after all. As for showing off my virility—again, the evidence is there for all to see. But, while you're wrong if you think you're the only one invested in Andreos's existence, I'm aware that only time will prove what I say to you. So I guess the ball's in your court on that one.'

'How so?'

'You're the one who's in a hurry to leave. You say you were always going to come back? I'm choosing to believe you. If you want to ensure my devotion to my son is as strong as yours, then you need to rethink the urgency of your divorce demands, do you not, *pethi mou*?'

Despite his silky tone his eyes bored into mine in the dark interior of the car, and the notion that he was attempting to see right into my soul assailed me.

The thick lump wedged in my throat stalled my answer. Because *time* was the one commodity I might not have.

CHAPTER SEVEN

THE LIMO SWEEPING through the gates of his Athens mansion drew from me a breath of relief. But I soon realised I wasn't going to be set free from Ax's presence when he trailed me up the stairs to the door of Andreos's room.

I hesitated before the doors—partly because I didn't want to bring charged tension into Andreos's presence and partly because a tiny part of me wanted space to dissect everything that had happened this evening. But the greater part of me wanted to keep my son all to myself. Just for a little while.

A sharp cry from within dissipated every thought.

As Ax held the door open for me I entered the room in time to see Sophia lifting Andreos from his changing mat.

She stopped and smiled when she saw us. 'Good evening, Kyria Xenakis. You're just in time for Andreos's midnight feed. Would you like me to warm the bottle for you?'

I waved her away and Ax strode forward to take Andreos from her arms. 'Go to bed, Sophia. I'll take care of it.'

With a smiling nod, the young girl retreated to the adjoining bedroom, shutting the door behind her.

Ax adjusted his hold on Andreos, his strong hands lifting him aloft so they were face to face. My breath caught and, recalling his words in the car, I watched father and son stare at each other, one expression showing unabashed curiosity while the other probed with raw intensity as Axios absorbed his son's every expression as if hoarding it for his memory.

A little ashamed at questioning his motives in the car, I bit my lip as something settled inside me. No matter our personal angst, Axios cared for his son. Perhaps in time he'd love him almost as much as I did.

In that moment I wanted to tell him he would have years of special moments like this if I didn't manage to defuse the time bomb ticking inside me, but the words remained locked tight in my throat, the need not to have this time diluted with unwelcome outside influence stilling my tongue as I joined them.

Sensing another presence, Andreos turned towards me, his chubby arms windmilling as he babbled in delight. Then delight turned into familiar irritation as hunger kicked in and he whimpered his displeasure.

'Someone is impatient for his feed,' Ax mused, before his gaze dropped pointedly to my chest.

A fierce blush suffused my face. My breasts had been growing heavier in the last couple of hours. Even without the need to feed him myself I would have needed to express some milk before going to bed.

Expecting Ax to hand him over, I watched in surprise when he headed to the antique rocking chair I used for feeding Andreos. 'You're staying?'

'Unless you have an objection?' he asked, and I realised it was a genuine query.

About to say yes, I stunned myself by shaking my head.

A look flitted across his face faster than I could decipher it before he nodded. Once I was seated in the chair, which I'd discovered had been in his family for generations, Ax handed Andreos over. Then he started to move towards the adjacent sofa.

'Um…' I said.

He turned immediately. 'What is it?'

'Can you help me with my dress?'

Piercing grey eyes darkened a fraction as they moved to the halter neck of my dress. He gave a brisk nod, and in one deft move freed the fastening.

I caught the front before I was completely exposed, but there was no hiding from Ax's focused attention as I positioned Andreos on my lap.

He latched on with greedy enthusiasm, one fist planted firmly on my breast while both chubby legs jerked up to wrap around the forearm of the hand I'd laid on his plump belly to steady him.

The familiar action tugged at my heartstrings and drew a smile.

'Does he always do that?' Ax rasped, his voice gruff with emotion.

For a precious few seconds I'd forgotten he was there, watching my every move, absorbing his son's routine. Now my gaze met his and I nodded shakily, strangely overcome to be sharing this little snippet of time with the man who'd helped create my precious son.

'Since he was two and a half months old. I think it's his way of telling me to stay put. He'll let me go when he's satisfied.'

Ax lounged back in his seat and crossed his legs, a curious, heart-stopping little smile playing at his sensuous lips. 'He's a Xenakis. He knows what he wants.'

That display of unabashed male pride would have been unbecoming from any other man. From Ax it was a solid statement acknowledging his progeny. Progeny that would be completely his if I lost my fight.

The lance of pain to my heart made my breath catch.

'What is it?' Ax asked sharply. 'Does it cause you pain?'

My gaze flew to his and I had to swallow before I could answer. 'The breastfeeding? No, it doesn't.'

His narrowed gaze moved from Andreos and back to me. 'Then what is it?'

I flailed internally as I tried to find a plausible response. 'I was just remembering our conversation in the car. Perhaps I was…a little harsh.'

One brow quirked, but it was minus the mockery I'd become used to. *'Perhaps?'*

'Okay, I was. I… I don't want us to butt heads over Andreos.'

His hands spread in a manner that suggested a truce. 'Neither do I, Calypso.'

As milestones went, this was another sizeable one in an evening filled with small earthquakes of surprise. My breath caught. Andreos whimpered. I looked down to find eyes so much his father's wide and curious upon me. Reading my every expression just as intently as his father probed beneath my skin.

'Maybe we should discuss this further later?'

'I agree,' Ax responded, then proceeded to watch me with hawk-like intensity all through the feed.

When I transferred Andreos to my other breast Ax's gaze tracked my blush after dropping once to my nipple. But this time my self-consciousness was reduced. The natural act of providing sustenance for my baby was one I realised I didn't mind sharing with his father.

Just as abruptly as he'd wrapped his sweet limbs around my arm Andreos dropped his legs and he detached with a loud plop.

Ax rose and sauntered over, wordlessly securing my dress as I sat Andreos on my lap and rubbed his back. I was rewarded with a loud burp three minutes later.

With a gentle caress of his son's head, Ax stepped away. 'I have a few phone calls to make. I'll meet you in my suite when you're done here.'

The reminder that our suites were interconnecting and the memory of what had happened in his sent a pulse of electricity through me as I watched him walk away.

His icy indifference had receded. Something had happened on that balcony tonight. The realisation that Ax didn't tar me with the same brush as my father had eased something in me.

I was pondering the new path this might lead to as I laid a sleepy Andreos back in his cot and then entered the suite forty-five minutes later.

Both the living room and bedroom in Ax's suite were empty. Entering my own suite, I crossed to the dressing room, quickly undressed, then slid on my night slip before throwing a matching silk gown over it.

I was brushing my hair at my dressing table when Ax walked in, both hands in his pockets.

He paused in the doorway, his eyes holding a skin-tingling expression and resting on me for a long moment before he prowled forward. He stopped behind me and I waited, my breath locked in my throat as one hand reached out, tugged the brush from me and slowly dragged it through my hair.

For a full minute he said nothing, and the hypnotic sensation of his movements flooded my system with torrid lust.

'You'll be pleased to know our strategy worked,' he drawled eventually. 'My family and friends believe we are happily reunited. I expect my business partners to fall in line by morning.'

Something shook inside me. The easy way he laid his hand on me was a stronger warning that things were shifting. That the conversation on the balcony had indeed sparked much more than a rebellion and the need to answer it in both of us.

Before I could heed the warning he nudged me to my feet, slid his hand down my arm to link with my fingers. 'Come with me.'

Even the imperious tone had altered, become less... autocratic.

I followed him into his living room.

There, on a wide screen, he'd set up the video I'd given him. 'Ax...?'

'I haven't had a chance to watch this yet. Or perhaps I was putting it off,' he said, with a hint of vulnerability in his voice that stunned me enough to take the seat next to him when he settled on the plush sofa.

'You want to watch it now?' I asked.

His eyes met mine, held me in place. 'Yes,' he stated simply.

With a flick of his finger on the remote the video came to life. The simple but clean walls of the hospital room in Kenya came into view before the camera swung over the machines to rest on my heavily pregnant form.

My breath strangled into nothing as the uniquely intimate and life-changing event unfolded on the screen, tugging at the very heart of me.

Beside me Ax caught his breath audibly as he watched a contraction hit me, and the hand that still held mine tightened. This footage had been taken about ten minutes before Andreos's birth. Ax watched every frame without taking his gaze off the screen, his whole body rapt as Andreos was laid in my arms for the first time. He watched me kiss his wrinkled forehead, heard me murmur, 'My little miracle,' as tears of joy spilled down my face.

His throat moved in a swallow when the video ended, and he immediately hit 'rewind' and watched it all over again.

Then his gaze shifted to me.

'Ax...'

He shook his head, raised my hand to his mouth, gently kissed the back of it. 'It was a magnificent birth.'

Deep inside me something *essential* melted, pulling me into a dangerous spell I wasn't entirely certain I wanted to fight. Emotion clogging my throat, I smiled.

'He's a beautiful boy,' he rasped, a throb of deep pride in his voice.

I blinked unbidden tears away. 'Yes. He is.'

'As beautiful as his mother.'

As my breath caught all over again, his thumb rubbed across my knuckles.

'Again you have my thanks—especially since you had to go through that alone.'

'I'd do anything for him,' I replied, and I knew the fervent well of my emotion had registered with him.

For the longest time he simply stared, then his gaze returned to the screen, his vision going a little hazy.

'The reality of him—' He stopped. 'He may be an unexpected arrival in my life, but I want the chance to do right by him. To do things differently—'

Again he stopped, prompting questions I couldn't halt.

'Differently from what? Your father? I noticed your stiff interaction at the wedding, then again at the family mixer, and assumed *I* was to blame.'

He shook his head. 'Our issues go back a little further. I was still a teenager when my grandfather announced that I was to be his successor. In his eyes my father didn't have what it took to make the tougher decisions.' A muscle ticked in his jaw as his lips firmed. 'My father disagreed. He attempted to prove my grandfather wrong.'

I frowned. 'How?'

'My grandfather temporarily handed him the reins of the company. Six months later my father suffered a breakdown brought on by extreme stress. He didn't take the prognosis well.'

'What did he do?'

'He believed my grandfather had humiliated him. And when my grandfather made it known that he'd seen me as his successor all along, my father…didn't take it well. His resentment festered irreparably.' His lips twisted. 'Which, in a nutshell, is the story of my whole family.'

'But you all seem so…*united*—give or take the odd vibe or two.'

He shrugged cynically. 'Self-interest, especially where wealth is concerned, has a way of binding even the most dissenting individuals. My father may not like the status quo but he's had to accept it.'

'Is there no way to repair your relationship?'

A hint of bleakness came and went in his eyes within a heartbeat. 'We've accepted our strengths and our weaknesses. My father may resent me for seemingly usurping him, but he doesn't want the role.'

'You offered it to him?'

His lips thinned. 'A few years ago I suggested a partnership. He refused.'

'He wanted all or nothing?'

His lips twisted. 'Don't we all?'

Pain lashed me. 'Not all of us. Our fathers, maybe.'

Grey eyes met mine and a moment of affinity lingered between us, threatening to burrow into vulnerable places.

I cleared my throat. 'Is that why you're determined to try with Andreos?'

He'd said on the balcony that he was attempting to be different. The part of me that wasn't terrified of what the future held desperately craved to see that difference.

The question took him aback, and a naked yearning blanketed his features before he mastered it. 'Is it wrong to wish for a better outcome with my son than that between my father and I?' he rasped.

Again, a deep, sacred sensation pulled at me. Harder. Stronger. Making it impossible to breathe.

Despite the danger of falling under the silken spell he was weaving, I laid my hand on his arm. 'No, it's not.'

His gaze dropped to my hand. Silence charged with electricity filled the room as something flashed in his eyes. Primal and fierce. The video and our conversation had done something to him. Shifted the dynamic.

I was tempted to run. To hide from it. But I was just as determined not to regress.

'So…where do we go from here? After tonight, I mean?'

His eyes dropped to my lips, then moved back up to seize mine.

'Now we consolidate on what we've started,' he murmured huskily.

I wanted to ask for clarity. Wanted to ask whether he meant us or the larger world. But his fingers wound tighter around mine, his free hand rising to slide into my hair, dragging over my scalp in a wickedly evocative move that snatched the air from my lungs and hardened my nipples into aroused peaks.

Those penetrating eyes tracked my every reaction, his nostrils flaring when he caught the visible signs of my agitated state.

'And how do you propose to do that?' I asked.

'By making things real both inside and outside of the marriage bed,' he stated, his voice deep and sure.

Lightning-hot excitement charged through me, the need to experience this altered Axios overwhelming me. Would the change he wanted with his son manifest itself with me too, even in the short time I might have?

Only one way to find out.

I tugged myself free and stood to my feet.

Mutiny flashed in his eyes.

When he started to reach for me, I held up a hand. 'If you want me to change my mind convince me that you're worth it,' I said.

Then I fled.

I went after her like a beast possessed.

She was mine.

My wife.

All evening I'd caught tantalising glimpses of her. The way she moved, the thoughtful way she responded to strangers' rabid curiosity, even accommodating Stavros…

I'd run the gamut from telling myself I didn't care about all the facets of herself she was revealing to feeling a determination to pin her down and extract every last secret from her.

But that video…

Her father was in possession of a hundred million euros. My name could have commanded an entire wing in a plush private hospital. And yet Calypso had chosen to deliver our son in a state-run hospital in Kenya with third-rate equipment. And, not only that, she'd done all that with an inner strength that shone through the footage, surrounded by people who had clearly held her in high regard.

She'd spent some of the past year volunteering. I couldn't name a single member of my family who would devote their time to charity unless it came with a tax write-off or a star-studded gala where they could show off their diamonds.

And besides the awe-inspiring act of giving birth, the most striking thing about Calypso Xenakis was the determination I'd seen on her face in that video.

It had sparked something inside me. A need for… *more*.

That intoxicating little incident on the sofa this afternoon, compounded by the kiss on the balcony this evening and watching her nurse our son, was what had finally fully awakened the primitive beast inside me. The video was evidence of her strength and resilience, despite my less than stellar behaviour last year.

Even confessing the true relationship between myself and my father—a subject I'd never discussed with another living soul—had felt…liberating. That we were both products of our circumstances had triggered an affinity in us that had in turn laid out a different way to approach what had been thrust on us.

Perhaps it didn't need to be finite.

That admission to do things differently this time had surprisingly settled deep inside me.

The Calypso I'd married had possessed a banked fire.

The woman who'd returned from her mysterious absence was flame and grit.

Heat I was unashamedly drawn to. Grit I wanted to explore.

Both characteristics drove me after her.

I arrived in the suite just as she was entering her own bedroom. I stopped her with the simple act of capturing her delicate wrist. The electricity of contact simply reaffirmed my decision.

She waited, one eyebrow elevated.

Theos mou, did she know how alluring she was, with her blue eyes daring me even as her agitated breathing announced that she wasn't unaffected by this insane chemistry?

'I want you, Calypso. And unless I'm wildly off-base you want me too.'

'That's it? Surely you have better negotiating skills than that, Axios?' she taunted.

The breathless sound of my name on her lips escalated the heat pounding through my bloodstream. I wanted to kiss her. To prove with deeds instead of words how combustible this thing between us was.

'You're not the same woman I left on Agistros last year. I see that now.'

More than that, she had the power to walk away again if she chose.

The strange sensation of being on slippery ground forced me into further speech, even as I questioned the wisdom of the route I was taking.

'Come to my bed—not because of our agreement or because of your ultimatum. Do it because you want to. Because we can make each other feel things we've never experienced before.'

Her lips parted in a soft gasp. 'You… I do that to you?'

I couldn't help the hoarse laughter that was ejected from my throat. I dropped her wrist and removed myself several mind-clearing paces away.

'Barely two hours ago, I was close to saying to hell with propriety and taking you on that balcony. What do *you* think?'

Despite the heat flaming up her face her shoulders went back, accepting her power over me. It was all I could do to remain standing where I was and not stride across the room to demonstrate just how much the hunger inside me lashed through her too.

But this was too important.

I wasn't an animal, and she needed to grant me clear acknowledgement of her desire before it would work. But it *was* going to work. There were no viable alternatives to allay this…this insane *craving* inside me save for the highly unsatisfactory avenue of self-pleasure, which I wasn't willing to consider any more.

'I'm a man with healthy appetites, Calypso. And I

haven't had sex since our wedding night. Do you know that?'

She gave another gasp, this time a heated one that went straight to my groin. She backed against the door, as if putting distance between herself and the live wire of desire lashing us would work.

Eyes wide, she lifted her chin in further challenge. 'How do I know that's true?'

Frustration threatened to erupt. I tamped it down. 'I don't make a habit of lying, *yineka mou*. Regardless of how we came together, I took a vow I intend to honour until I'm no longer bound by it. But if you don't believe me I can give you the number of a top investigator and you can discover the truth for yourself.'

'Even if I believe you, maybe you didn't seek another woman's bed because you didn't want to jeopardise your precious deal.'

She was really good at pushing my buttons. And the curious thing was that I preferred this version of Calypso to the one who'd glided down the aisle a little over a year ago.

I shrugged off my tuxedo, watched her gaze cling to my torso before another blush pinkened her smooth skin. 'Whatever my reason for staying celibate, I wish it to end now.'

'Because you decree it?'

'Because you're woman enough to admit you want me too. Because *when* you come to my bed it'll be because your needs are as strong as mine and you're not ashamed to give in to them.'

Tossing the jacket aside, I gave in to the urge and returned to her, my senses jumping at the promise of decadent friction when she swallowed but stayed her ground.

And then, because I wasn't above playing dirty to get my way, I unbuttoned one shirt stud. Then another.

Brazenly, I revelled in the tremor that went through her lush frame as her eyes followed my undressing with abashed appreciation. A layer of femininity which might have been there all along or I might have missed called to the beast in me.

'I want to lay you on my bed…make you cry out my name in climax.'

Her eyelashes fluttered before sweeping down. That tell-tale sign that she was hiding something nearly derailed me. It certainly froze me in place, congealing my insides with the knowledge that, far from being a forward-thinking man, some things were sacred to me.

'Tell me what you're thinking.'

She remained silent for far too long. In real time it was probably a handful of seconds. But it was enough to unnerve me. Enough that when she deigned to lift those hypnotising eyes to mine all that remained in me was a frenzied roar.

I watched her lips move but didn't hear the words she uttered. Her eyes grew wider, possibly at my expression. She started to step back.

I closed the gap between us and tugged her to me. With her heavy magnificent breasts pressed against my chest all I wanted was to lose myself in her. To slay this terrible *need*.

Her nostrils quivered as she inhaled rapidly. Against my chest her hands fluttered, and a trembling I wanted to believe had nothing to do with sex seized her.

'Axios…'

'I said I want to be different, Calypso. Take this leap with me?'

But even as her eyes widened at my words she hesitated, her lower lip caught between her teeth, taunting me with the prospect of unaccustomed denial.

And all the while my insides churned with emotions I didn't want to examine.

All the while delicate tremors filtered through her body and her breathing grew more erratic with her undeniable arousal.

I was on the very edge of my sanity when Calypso's fingers whispered over the button above my navel, toyed with the stud for a second before fluttering away again. Eyes that refused to meet mine remained fixed on my chest.

She released her lip and I fought the urge to lean down and bite the plump, wet curve.

Before her wicked hands could further wreck me, I caught them in one hand. 'Calypso, look at me.'

After an eternity her lashes lifted. Dark blue hypnotic pools pulled me in, threatening to drown me.

'Say the words. I want to hear them,' I pressed, aware that my voice was a gravel-rough mess.

She inhaled. 'I'll take the leap with you. For now.'

I had to hand it to her—she knew how to time her negotiations to maximum effect. But I'd given my word and I wouldn't go back on it. Besides, the earlier we excised this fever from our systems the earlier we could start the extrication process.

The earlier I could return to my life as I knew and preferred it.

The punch of satisfaction I expected never arrived.

More...

'For now?' I repeated, dismissing the hollow echo of the words.

I steeped myself deeper in the moment. Revelled in the fingers gripping my shirt as if the small scrap of cotton would ground her. She swallowed again, then gave a nod.

I crooked a finger under her chin and nudged her head upward. 'Tell me, *pethi mou*,' I insisted.

'I want you,' she whispered.

The breathy little sound washed over my chin and throat, making something frenzied and untamed leap inside me, filling me with the prospect of what 'more' could mean.

'More...' I pressed, wanting irrevocable confirmation that she wanted this.

Her chin lifted, her eyes gleaming boldly. 'I want to be in your bed. I want you to take me.'

I slid my hand up her delicate spine to tangle in her hair. To grip it and keep her attention on me. 'I want to make you mine again. Tell me you want that.'

Her fists bunched, a breathy little sound escaping her throat as she swayed closer. 'I want to be yours.'

Like over a breached dam, a torrent swelled inside me. Removing her silk dress was as simple as catching the fragile material and ripping it off her body.

She gasped, staring down at the tattered fabric at her feet before attempting to glare at me. 'I don't believe you did that.'

A smile caught me unawares. 'I didn't think you were that attached to it. If so, I'll buy you a dozen more,' I vowed thickly. Because the sight of her body, displaying changes after bearing my son in the form of slightly thicker hips, a rounded softness in her belly and, best of all, the heaviness of her breasts, had intensified the throbbing in my groin.

I was barely aware of sinking to my knees, framing her lush hips and pulling her to me. I welcomed the fingers clenching tight into my hair as my lips found the sensitive flesh below her navel and brazenly tasted her creamy skin. When she sagged against the door I went lower, removing her panties before catching one leg and throwing it over my shoulder so I could find the heart of her, the true feminine core that called to me with the strength of a dozen sirens.

'Ax!'

Her sweet cry urged me on, her taste a drug surging with unstoppable force through my bloodstream. I didn't relent until she was splintering in my arms, her moans music to my ears. Only then did I scoop her up and carry her to my bed to begin all over again.

Her head rolled on the pillow, her hair fanning out in a dark silken halo as her lips parted on hot little gasps as I rediscovered every delightful inch of her body.

'*Omorfi…*'

The word tumbled unbidden from my lips as I caught one pearled nipple in my mouth. And she *was* beautiful, with a certain indefinable layer of femininity and strength adding to her allure.

'When you glided up that aisle like an obedient wraith I had no idea you were hiding this…this steel and sensuality beneath that frothy gown.'

Her eyes widened in dazed surprise. 'Was that why you left the next morning? Because I wasn't what you expected?'

It was my turn to be stunned. To ponder how events had unfolded through her eyes. But now wasn't the time to admit I'd been unnerved then too. Just as I was now.

'No. My delivery wasn't great, but I believed leaving was best. However, *this*…' I slid a hand down her ribcage, revelled in her unfettered response '…was certainly a surprise.'

And the fact that she was even more responsive now threatened to annihilate my self-control completely.

Before I was entirely consumed I reached for a condom, donned it and accepted the enthralling welcome of her parted thighs. I slanted my lips over hers, unwilling to leave any feast unsatisfied as I entered her in one deep, glorifying thrust.

Pleasure detonated in a shower of fireworks as I seated myself deep within her. Felt her tighten around me, drawing me deeper. When she sought to shatter me further with needy whimpers and greedy hands I tore my lips from hers, gritted my teeth in an effort to make this last.

But of course the next layer of sweet torture waited in the wings. With her mouth free, and the nirvana of a higher plane of pleasure waiting, I watched her slide into that unique dimension, that place where her unfiltered pleasure rippled from her alluring lips.

'My God, you're so big. *So* deep. I feel every inch of you…'

A muted roar rumbled up my throat as her words threatened to completely unravel me.

Her nails sank into my back, ripping away another layer of control. And just like on that night I'd never been able to put out of my mind I realised she was unaware of herself, that pleasure had transported her into another dimension.

'Shall I roll my hips like that first time? That was incredible.'

'Calypso…' I wasn't sure whether saying her name

was warning or encouragement. Either way, she didn't respond. She continued her mind-altering commentary. Commentary that fired a white-hot blaze inside me alongside the fiery one already raging from possessing her.

I stared down into her stunning, unguarded face as I pushed in and out of her, racing both of us towards that special peak.

Another man would have taken advantage of the situation, prised secrets from her subconscious while she was in this state. But that was an invasion my conscience wouldn't let me stomach for longer than a nanosecond.

So I refocused on the words tumbling from her lips, revelled in them for another reason altogether. Because they turned me on. Because no other woman had brought this unique, exquisite surprise to my bed. Because hearing her vocalise her pleasure charged mine in a way I'd never thought possible.

Increasing the tempo of my thrusts, I lowered my body to hers, drew her tighter against me. 'Wrap your legs around my waist, *omorfia mou*.'

With gratifying speed, she complied.

'Now, tell me more,' I growled in her ear. 'Tell me everything you're feeling.'

Whether she heard me or not, I didn't know, but the words spilled out.

Unmanned by her unfiltered longing, I kissed the corner of her luscious mouth and groaned when she chased mine when I withdrew.

'Kiss me. Please kiss me.'

'Say my name, *matia mou*. Say my name and I'll kiss you.'

'Axios,' she moaned. 'Kiss me, *please*, Axios.'

Unable to resist the sultry demand, I kissed her again. Felt her tighten around me in response and gritted my teeth to keep myself on that dizzying plateau for one more second. She was eroding every ounce of my willpower, pushing me towards the zenith long before I was ready.

And there was little I could do to stop it.

Especially not when my mind was already flying to the next time, to the next position.

She would be on top. Yes, she would ride me, her heavy breasts high and proud, while those unfettered words fell from her lips. The image was so potent, so vivid, I lost the ability to think straight.

My unguarded growl in response to that scenario pushed her higher. Her nails dug into my shoulders, her head thrashing on the pillow.

'Let go, Calypso. Now!'

The command set her free. With a sharp, sweet cry, she dissolved into uncontrollable convulsions, her body writhing beneath mine in innocently uncoordinated movements that finally shattered my control.

With a roar torn from deep within I succumbed to exquisite, untrammelled bliss. Time ceased to matter. I was aware I'd collapsed on top of her, one propped arm the only thing stopping me from crushing her. But her own arms were wrapped tight around me, as if holding me together.

The singular, searing thought that I wanted to remain here *indefinitely* charged through my daze, forcing me to move. Forcing sanity back into this madness.

But even as I gathered her to me after my return from the bathroom she was unravelling me again, the hand on my chest reaching deeper as she turned her face to me.

'Ax?'

'Hmm?' Unfamiliar dread clenched my gut, escalating the notion that somewhere along the line I'd fallen under her mercy and her whim.

Her breath fluttered out in an almost reverent exhalation as her eyes lifted to mine. 'You're the only man I've ever been with. I just thought you should know.'

That gift, freely given when it could have been withheld in light of our circumstances, punched and winded me. The notion that opening up to her had possibly earned me this unsettled me even more.

Questions and wants and needs surged higher than before, racing to the tip of my tongue before circumspection halted them. I wanted more from her. But did I have more to give to her and to Andreos?

I pushed back the dismaying sensation.

She was staying…for now.

That unsettling little addendum would be tackled later. After much-needed regrouping.

'*Efkharisto.*'

The word emerged deeper, graver than I'd expected. I did nothing to offset it. Nothing but accept that things *had* to be different.

Nothing I'd seen of the marriages around me had fuelled a need to embroil myself in one—not when they strained so easily and threatened to break at the smallest hint of adversity.

But, in the hypothetical scenarios where marriage *had* crossed my mind, I'd known that unshaken faithfulness and stalwart support would be the cornerstone of its success. Not the kind of marriage held together by financial worth—the kind my grandfather had struggled to hold on to and ended up paying dearly for.

That reminder cooled my jets long enough to let in rational thought. Long enough to know that Calypso and I needed a base of trust from which to operate.

Which meant getting her to open up about her secrets…

I decided to come at it from a different angle. 'Are you ready to tell me why you chose to leave Greece?'

Her eyes shadowed and her lashes swept down. But before I could catch her chin and redirect her attention on me she lifted her gaze, her eyes boldly meeting mine with a resolution I wasn't sure whether to welcome or battle.

'Okay.'

Relief stunned me. 'Okay?'

She nodded. 'I want whatever time we have remaining to be peaceful.'

I forced my teeth not to grit at the reminder of a timescale. 'Good.'

A touch of nerves edged her features. When she went to move out of my arms, I caught her back. 'It would please me if you stayed right here for this.'

CHAPTER EIGHT

HE WAS UNRAVELLING ME with his low-voiced requests. With this side of him that hinted at the kind of man I'd dreamed of calling husband and father to my child. The kind of man who asked me to take a leap even when I knew that ultimately my path might lie elsewhere.

Tell him.

Maybe this could all turn out differently.

You could have more nights like this, far into the future.

But what if the worst happened? I couldn't put Andreos through that.

Besides, while Ax had readily agreed to my stipulation...for now...he'd given me no insight as to what would happen beyond that.

But I'd bought myself a little more time—and, *Theos mou*, I wanted to experience this again. And again. Without angst or acrimony.

Even now, with my limbs weak from their physical and emotional expenditure, hunger was slowly gathering force, anticipation adding fuel to a fire which didn't seem in a hurry to burn itself out. And if all it took was a simple recounting of my year, where was the harm?

I pushed away the voice urging caution and when I

opened my mouth the words that tumbled out surprised even me.

'My grandmother was a feminists' feminist. She hated every aspect of a patriarchy that dictated what she could and couldn't do. She especially hated it when my grandfather died and everyone expected her to re-marry because she had a young daughter to care for.'

I caught the edge of Ax's puzzled frown and couldn't help the smile that tugged at my lips.

'She never did remarry, but after she lost her house she was forced to live with my parents. I grew up in the shadows of her rebellion. She urged me to stand my ground. To question everything.'

His frown cleared, a droll look entering his grey eyes. 'Ah. I see.'

'Needless to say she butted heads with my father al-most on a daily basis.'

Ax tensed. Not wanting the mood tarnished, I passed my hand over his chest—a soothing gesture that worked with Andreos but might not work with his father. My breath caught when he exhaled after a handful of sec-onds.

'Anyway, I found out on my wedding day that she'd left me an envelope. My mother was to give it to me when she thought I needed it.'

A trace of regret flashed across his face. 'She thought you'd need it the day you married me.'

It wasn't a question, more of an acceptance of how things had turned out.

I shrugged. 'Besides my father, none of us knew much about you. What little I knew before we met at the altar I found out online,' I said, recognising but unable to stop the hint of censure in my tone.

The regret in his eyes deepened as he nodded. 'I accept that. So your father really kept you in the dark about everything?'

'Yes. And it wasn't anything new. He did that most of my life.'

'Why?'

The whisper of family shame slithered over my skin. 'Surely you've heard the rumours?'

'I prefer facts to rumours,' he stated.

I didn't bother to ask what he'd heard. I wanted this discussion over as quickly as possible.

'My mother left home when I was fifteen. She'd met another man and was planning on leaving my father. But they were involved in an accident. The man died. My mother survived—obviously—but she suffered a spine injury and... Well, you've seen her. My father brought her back home and promised to take care of her—under certain conditions.'

The hand that had been lazily trailing through my hair froze. 'It seems your father makes a habit of using people's misfortunes against them.'

I couldn't deny that truth. And when Ax used his hold to gently propel my gaze up to his I couldn't hide it from him.

Whatever he saw in my face made him exhale again. 'I used to think that was an encompassing Petras family trait,' he murmured.

'*Used* to?' Did that mean he'd changed his mind? That he *wasn't* tarring me with the same brush as my father any more?

He continued to stare at me for a long stretch. 'You're nothing like him. You have a formidable inner strength that he doesn't—clearly inherited from your grandmother,' he said.

The low, gruff words opened up a fountain of emotion inside me that stopped my breath, especially when he brushed his lips over mine, as if wanting to seal the words in.

Getting carried away would have been so easy, but I forced myself to pull back. 'Anyway, I moved from under my father's thumb to under yours without any intermission—'

He stiffened, his face growing a shade paler. 'Under my thumb? I made you feel like that?'

I shrugged. 'You dictated where I would live. How I would live. Without giving me a say. So when you told me to find a way... I did.'

His jaw tightened and after a moment he nodded. 'I don't blame you for staging a rebellion. I would have in your shoes too. Perhaps not with anonymity but... that's understandable considering my reaction to our marriage.'

Tears prickled my eyes, threatening to spill at the thought that he was seeing things from my side. 'Anyway, my grandmother's letter left details of a Swiss bank account in my name. I went to Switzerland to see what it was all about. She'd left me the means to live under a new identity if I chose. There was also a box with some of her things in it.'

'That's how you were able to live without detection for a year?' he said.

I nodded. 'I think she meant me to use it more as a way to rebel against my father than a way—'

'For you to escape your new husband?' he finished with terse amusement.

'Either way, it seemed like a sign.'

A touch of hardness entered his eyes. 'Leaving your husband tearing his hair out for a year.'

'You weren't my husband. You especially weren't interested in being one the morning after the wedding. You married me to save your precious company, so don't pretend my absence caused you any personal slight or even—heaven forbid—any *anxiety*!'

'You carried my name. You were supposed to be under my care. Believe me, your disappearance was punishment enough—especially when I was left imagining the worst,' he rasped in a raw tone.

Plastered to him as I was, I felt the shudder that shook his frame, and his set jaw and the flash of bleakness in his eyes spoke to a vulnerability I'd never have imagined him capable of until tonight.

I stopped breathing, because... No, I hadn't quite thought about it. 'It wasn't just our forced marriage, Axios. My father was threatening my mother too.'

Fury flashed in his eyes. 'What?'

'He wanted to keep me in line through her. But she made me promise I wouldn't stay if I was unhappy. It all got a bit too much.'

'Did he carry out his threat?'

I shook my head. 'I'm guessing he was too busy playing with his windfall.'

The monthly phone calls with my mother had assured me she was okay, and had been all the wind beneath my wings I'd needed to stay away.

He bit out a tight curse and threw an arm over his forehead. 'Your father has a lot to answer for, but he's saved himself a trouncing by leaving your mother alone,' he growled. After a moment, his gaze pierced mine again. 'My investigators eventually traced your flight from Greece to Switzerland and assured me that my wife had simply chosen to run away of her own accord. At least now I know how you managed to avoid detection after you left Geneva, but perhaps you'd be so kind as to finish telling me where you went?'

The pulse of anguish still underlined his anger, but knowing it wasn't directed at me made it easier to finish my retelling.

'I took a train to Strasbourg and then wandered through Europe for a time before heading to South-East Asia. After that I made my way through Africa.'

All the while keeping in touch with Dr Trudeau and praying for my baby's continued health.

'When did you know you were pregnant with Andreos?' he rasped.

My stomach hollowed out in remembrance, and it took every ounce of self-control not to show how that fateful day still affected me. How the possibility that I would never meet my child had left me broken and sobbing for one day straight, until the fervent prayers had begun.

'I found out early. In Switzerland.'

He waited, his gaze imploring me for more. But I had nothing more to give. Nothing that wouldn't see the precious time I had left with Andreos compromised.

And it would be. It was clear Axios was deeply possessive and protective of his son. Over the past few days I'd learned just how meticulous and all-powerful he could be. I couldn't afford for the time I had with my baby to be compromised.

Or, on the flipside, he simply wouldn't care.

Pain snaked through me, dulling my heartbeat. No, he was better off not knowing.

'Why Kenya?' he asked, tugging me back to the present.

'Because I was seven months pregnant when I got there. Because I loved it there and knew I wouldn't be able to travel. I chose to stay and have Andreos there.'

Again, he lapsed into contemplative silence, those piercing grey eyes pinning me to the bed. Then, 'Thank you for telling me,' he said simply. Gruffly.

Tears prickled. To hide them, I lowered my head until our lips were a whisper apart. He didn't protest. His eyes simply went molten and his hard body stirred beneath mine as I closed the gap and helped myself to the magic of his kiss.

He allowed my exploration for a minute. Allowed the tentative probe and the slide of my tongue against his in a deeper kiss while the hand around my waist moved in a slow caress up and down my back, until he boldly cupped my bottom and brought me into brazen contact with his impressive arousal.

Then he flipped me over and took complete control, effectively emptying my brain of everything but the naked desire snaking through my body, setting me alight with a need so acute all I could do was let it wholly consume me.

Nevertheless, his warning ricocheted in my head long after our bodies had cooled. Long after his deep, steady breathing indicated sleep.

Because telling myself I didn't care what my actions had caused Axios after I took up the fight for my health, that I wasn't important enough to cause a ripple in his existence, didn't quite ring true in my head. I cared. Even if marrying him and taking his name had been a transaction dictated by my father for financial gain, our coming together had produced a son. And that mattered. Whether I liked it or not, Axios mattered to me. More than perhaps was wise.

The intensifying ache inside that reminded me I might have less time than I imagined added to the turmoil churning inside me, keeping me awake as dawn approached. Eventually mental exhaustion won out, and I fell into a sleep fuelled with pleasure and pain, blissful happiness and acute sadness.

Thankfully I was in a state of happiness when I resurfaced from sleep to the sound of a cooing baby.

'*Kalimera*, my angel,' I murmured, my drowsy awakening made all the better by my sweet baby's enthusiastic babble and the innocent smell of his freshly bathed body.

Eyes still closed, I felt my heart bursting with a joy that widened my smile.

'He's been very patient as he waited for his mama to wake, but I fear that state is about to be over,' drawled the deep, masculine voice of my baby's father.

My eyes flew open, the reminder of where I was and what had transpired last night fracturing my smile as I encountered the arresting image of a rudely vibrant Axios, one hand propping up his head and the other resting lightly on his son's stomach.

Andreos, his curious gaze switching between his father's face, mine, and just about every bright object it could touch upon, wriggled with impatience and babbled some more before letting out a cry that signalled he was well and truly done with waiting to be fed.

My lungs flattened with surprise and an unexpectedly sharp yearning as Ax shifted onto his back, lifted his son and held him aloft, a drop-dead gorgeous smile breaking out on his face as father and son stared at each other.

'You've made it this far, *o moro mou*. Give it another half-minute and you will be rewarded, hmm?' he teased.

I sat up, unable to help my blush and self-consciousness at the reminder that I was naked under the sheets.

After anointing his son's forehead with a gentle kiss, Axios turned to watch me sit up and arrange the pillows around me in preparation to feed an increasingly impatient Andreos.

When I was settled, Axios handed him over. And, just like last night, he didn't seem in a hurry to leave. In fact, he settled back on his pillow, his gaze unashamedly fixed on me as I settled our son at my breast.

Sunlight streamed through the partially opened curtain, bathing the parts of Axios I could see in mouth-watering relief—mainly his very naked, very chiselled torso. The effort it took to drag my gaze away and avoid the incisive eyes was depressingly monumental.

'I… What time is it?'

'It's a little after nine,' he answered, reaching out to caress his son's bare, plump foot. 'You were out of it when the monitor signalled that Andreos was awake. Sophia was about to give him a bottle, but I thought I'd bring him to you instead.'

I nodded, my throat clogging at the picture of togetherness and domestic bliss his words painted. Before I could stop myself, might-have-beens crowded my heart and I stared down at Andreos, painfully aware of Ax's presence in the pictures that filled my mind.

A little desperately, I reminded myself that this was all temporary. A short stretch of time to enjoy with my son before—

'Calypso?'

I blinked, unable to stop myself from being compelled to meet his gaze.

His eyes narrowed and he waited a beat before asking, 'What's wrong?'

I shook my head. 'It's nothing. I'm just a little tired, that's all.'

His shuttered gaze said he knew I was being evasive. But he let it go. 'Not too tired to spend a few hours out of the city, I hope?'

Surprised, I stared at him. 'Out of the city?'

He nodded. 'I thought we could fly to Agistros for the afternoon. Agatha will organise a picnic for us and we'll spend a little time by the water.'

'Why?' I blurted.

He tensed slightly. 'On the rare occasion that I find myself with free time, I wish to spend it with our son. With you. I thought you might enjoy it. Am I wrong?'

I flushed. 'I… No.'

I'd planned nothing except spending a lazy day with Andreos. But the thought that Axios had plans, that he wanted to include us, kicked a wild little thrill into my bloodstream. A *dangerous* thrill. One I needed to nip in the bud sooner rather than later.

'I was planning on heading down to the beach here, but one beach is as good as any other, I suppose.'

A sly smile tilted one corner of his lip. 'I beg to differ. The beaches on Agistros rival the best in the world.'

My cheeky need to tease grew irresistible. 'According to *you*.'

His smile widened. 'Since I own it, my opinion is the only one that counts.'

The statement was so unapologetically arrogant I laughed. The sound seemed to arrest him, his eyes turning that molten shade that sent heat pulsing through my blood as we stared at each other.

'I believe this is the first time I've heard you laugh,' he rasped, his gaze raking over my face to settle brazenly on my mouth, almost effortlessly calling up another blush that suffused my face. 'I like it.'

Without warning his hand rose, his fingers trailing down one hot cheek and along my jaw before dropping down to recapture his son's foot.

Something heavy and urgent and profound shifted inside me. The thought that I didn't know this facet of the man I'd married and that I wanted to hit me square in the midriff, before flaring a deep yearning towards all the dark corners of my heart.

My smile felt frayed around the edges as I fought to maintain my composure, fought not to blurt out another prayer for things I didn't deserve.

I'd been given so much already.

Gloom wormed through my heart, the fear of what lay ahead and of fighting an uphill battle I might not win casting shadows over the gift of another day.

I was still struggling to banish it when a knock came on the door.

'Ah, right on time,' he murmured.

With another heart-stopping smile Axios launched himself out of bed. Naked and gladiator-like in all his glory, he walked across the suite, stopping long enough to pull on a dark dressing robe before heading for the door.

He returned a minute later, wheeling a solid silver trolley loaded with breakfast dishes. Bypassing his side of the bed, he stopped the trolley close to me before hitching up a thigh and settling himself next to me.

I tried and failed not to watch him pour coffee for himself, tea for me, and lift a large, succulent bowl of ripe strawberries.

He waited until I'd put Andreos over my shoulder and begun rubbing his back to elicit a burp before he shifted closer. Dipping one end of a strawberry into a bowl of rich cream, he leaned forward and then held the plump fruit against my lip.

'Taste.' His voice was deep, low. Hypnotising.

I leaned forward, parted my lips and took the offering. He watched me chew with the kind of rapt attention that could wreak havoc with a woman's sensibilities. Only after I'd swallowed did he help himself to a piece— minus the cream.

He alternated between feeding me and himself until the bowl was empty, and then he set about piling more food on a plate.

'I can't eat all that,' I protested as I laid a very satisfied Andreos down beside me.

Axios shrugged, setting the tray in my lap. 'Our son is very demanding. And I get the feeling that state is only going to get more challenging. You'll need all the advantages you can get.'

About to tell him there was nothing I was anticipating more, the words stuck in my throat, and a bolt of heartache clenched my heart in a merciless vice.

Thankfully Axios was in the process of lifting a newspaper from a side pocket of the trolley, granting me a scant few seconds to get my emotions under control before he straightened and flicked the paper open.

Then a different sort of tension assailed me.

Seeing the pictures gracing the front page, I felt my gut twist. While I'd known we'd be under scrutiny last night, it hadn't occurred to me that we'd actually make front-page news.

The first picture had been taken when we'd first entered the ballroom. With our heads close together, Ax's masculine cheek almost touching mine, it hinted at an edgy intimacy between us that was almost too private.

From the look on Axios's face, he didn't feel the same.

He turned the page and my insides churned faster. There were more pictures, including some of us on the balcony, his hand splayed on my back, right before he pulled me in for that toe-curling kiss.

Axios stared at the pictures with something close to smug satisfaction.

'Did you know we were being photographed?' I asked, biting into a piece of ham-layered toast and concentrating on stirring my tea so I wouldn't have to look at the picture. At how the sight of Axios in a tuxedo continued to wreak havoc with my equilibrium. Nor face the fact that a very large part of me was wondering what true intimacy with this man whose name I'd taken would feel like.

He shrugged. 'I suspected we might be.'

That he was very much okay with it—had perhaps even wanted us to be photographed—was evident.

'And has it achieved what you meant it to?' I needed the reminder that this was all for a reason. For a definitive purpose which *didn't* include getting carried away with fairy tales.

With a flick of his fingers he folded the paper and picked up his coffee. 'If you mean are my business partners back on board, then, yes. But let's not rest on our laurels just yet,' he said.

Did that mean more socialising? More moments like

those on the balcony? And why didn't that fill me with horror? Why was my belly tingling with thrilling anticipation?

Questions and sensations stayed with me through a quick shower and lingered while I chose a bikini set, pulled a floaty spaghetti-strap sundress over it and slipped my feet into stylish wedge shoes.

Stepping out to join Axios and Andreos two hours later, on the landscaped lawn that led to the helipad, I noticed we were flying in a different, larger chopper.

Axios caught my questioning look. 'This one is more insulated. To better protect Andreos's delicate eardrums,' he said, casting an indulgent glance at the baby nestled high in the crook of his arm.

Of course he *would* have a special helicopter that catered for babies!

With the sensation of having woken up in an alternative universe from which I couldn't escape, I walked beside him to the aircraft.

The trip, unlike last time, flew by, and before I knew it we were skimming the beaches of Agistros, the azure waters of the island sparkling in the sunlight.

The villa was just as breathtaking as it had been a year ago, and this time, without deep trepidation blinding me, I was better able to appreciate it. Granted, there were other equally precarious emotions simmering beneath my skin, but just for today I let the dazed dream wash over me, revelling in simply *being* as Axios stepped out of the helicopter, reached to help me out and took control of Andreos's travel seat.

Expecting tension, in light of the way I'd departed the villa the last time, I breathed a sigh of relief when the staff, headed by Agatha, spilled out with welcoming smiles. It was obvious that news of Andreos had travelled as they cooed over him.

When Agatha carried him off to the kitchen to supervise the picnic preparation, I drifted into the living room with Axios.

Dressed in the most casual attire I'd seen him in so far—high-spec cargo trousers and a navy rugby shirt—he nevertheless still looked as if he'd stepped straight off the cover of a magazine.

To keep myself from shamelessly ogling him, I drifted over to the set of framed photos on one of the many antique cabinets gracing the room. There was a slightly faded one of an old man, his distinguished and distinctive features announcing him as Theodore Xenakis. Ax's grandfather. The man who'd been forced under duress to make an agreement that had changed lives—including mine.

Perhaps it wasn't the best choice of subject matter to bring up on what was meant to be a lazy day by the beach. But after hearing Axios open up about his father, I wanted to know more. Yearned to learn what had formed the man whose name I bore.

Once we'd made our way down to a private beach, tucked into the most stunning bay I'd ever seen in my life, I found myself asking, 'Did your grandfather ever live here on Agistros?'

He stiffened, but his tension eased almost immediately. 'In the latter part of his life, yes.'

There was more to that statement. 'Why? I mean, I've seen your family. I know you're dispersed all over Athens, and on several family-owned islands. I also know that Agistros belongs to you. So why did he live here? Did he need care?'

For the longest time I thought he wouldn't answer. When he did reply, his tone was low. Deep. As if remembering was painful.

'Before his company fell on hard times my grandfather invested in real estate and gifted islands to every family member. Neo has an island twenty miles from here.'

At the mention of his brother it was my turn to stiffen. 'I don't think Neo likes me.'

Ax's eyes glinted, a hard kind of amusement shifting in their depths. 'He's going through a…a situation.'

'A "situation"?'

'Something's been taken from him that he wasn't quite ready to part with,' he said cryptically.

I frowned. 'Someone's stolen from him?'

'In a manner of speaking.'

Recalling our conversation, I frowned. 'A woman?'

Again, dark amusement twisted Ax's lips. 'Yes. And a formidable one, I hear.'

Realising he wasn't going to elaborate, I pressed gently, 'So…about your grandfather…?'

A trace of bleakness whispered across his face. 'He left Kosima, his favourite island, for many reasons. But mainly because the strain of trying to save his company took a toll on his family, especially my grandmother. After she died we didn't deem it wise for him to remain on Kosima by himself. So he came to stay here.'

I wanted to probe deeper, find out why the once booming Xenakis empire had swan-dived to the brink of bankruptcy three years before his grandfather had died. But I held my tongue because I suspected my own family had had a hand in the Xenakis family's misfortune. Also, that flash of bleakness resonated inside me, his pain echoing mine.

Not wanting the day ruined by revisiting the animosity between our families, I stared at the stunning horizon, a different urge overtaking me. 'I wish I could paint this,' I murmured, almost to myself.

Ax turned to me. 'When was the last time you painted?'

Unsurprised that he knew of my passion, I answered, 'All through my pregnancy, and a short while after Andreos was born.'

'Why didn't you pursue your painting before?'

I shrugged. 'There wasn't much call for it on Nicrete.'

His silence was contemplative. 'You wanted to do something with it in Athens. Do you still want to?' he asked, a trace of guilt in his voice.

Not if I don't have much time left.

'Perhaps not full-time but…yes.'

'I would like to see you paint.'

Something melted inside me and I couldn't help my gasp. 'You would?'

He gave an abrupt nod. 'If you would allow it…very much.'

Again something tugged inside me, harder this time—a feeling of my world tilting, making me sway towards him.

To counteract it before I did something supremely unwise, I tugged my dress over my head. 'I'm going for a swim.'

With every step from sand to sea I felt his gaze burn into my skin, heating me up from the inside out. Thigh-deep, I dived into the cool, exquisite water, hoping it would wash away the discordant emotions zinging through me.

This really shouldn't be difficult. All we had to do was exist in the same space until I was absolutely certain Andreos would be safe and cared for, before I returned to Dr Trudeau in Switzerland to face my fate.

All I had to do was prevent myself from falling under Ax's spell. Surely it wasn't that hard?

Yes, it is. I feel more for him with every passing minute!

The weight of that verdict was so disturbing I didn't sense his presence until the second before he wrapped a strong arm around my waist.

His hair was slicked back, throwing the sharp, majestic angles of his face into stunning relief. Droplets of water sparkled on his face, a particularly tempting one clinging to his upper lip, evoking in me a wild need to lick it off.

'Andreos!' I protested.

'He's fine,' he said with hard gruffness as he pulled me closer, tangled my legs with his.

I looked over and sure enough our son was well-insulated by plump pillows, shaded by a large umbrella, happily playing with his rattle.

'Calypso…'

My name was a thick demand I couldn't resist. And when he pulled me into his arms and slanted his sensual lips across mine I gave in, my conflicting thoughts melting away under the heat of mounting passion.

Afterwards we returned and spread out on the blankets. A trace of trepidation returned, tingeing the closeness wrapping itself around us, a closeness I wanted to hang on to despite the uncertainty lurking in the future.

Because this version of Axios, who wanted to see me paint, who had opened up about his grandfather, was a version who could so easily worm his way into my heart.

On the Monday morning after our first trip to Agistros I arrived downstairs to find six high-spec easels and an assortment of expensive paints and brushes. Stunned, I blinked away tears as Axios presented them to me.

'You…you shouldn't have.'

He shook his head. 'You've denied your passion long enough,' he said. 'A year longer than necessary because of me,' he added heavily.

Next he organised special transportation for my mother to visit. Having not seen each other for a year, our reunion was tearful, her joy over her grandson boundless.

Seeing her, reassuring myself that she was all right despite the pain still clouding her eyes, lifted a weight off my shoulders. And that melting sensation returned full force when Axios set out to charm her—a ploy that worked to dissipate the lingering tension between them once and for all.

From my father I heard nothing. And, frankly, it didn't overly bother me.

After that our lives fell into a pattern.

Weekdays were spent at the villa in Athens, with at least three evenings of the week spent at one social engagement or another, which inevitably made front-page news, while Saturday and Sunday were spent on Agistros.

It was almost idyllic—the only fly in the ointment Dr Trudeau's increasingly urgent emails and the knowledge that now I was assured of Ax's complete devotion to our son I had no cause to put my health issues on hold.

It was on one weekend a few weeks later, in the place we'd now designated our picnic spot, when he glanced over at me as he reclined on a shaded lounger with a sleepy Andreos dozing on his bare chest. Father and son were besotted with each other, the growing bond between them a source of untold joy to me.

'I'm flying to Bangkok on Tuesday for business.'

Since he never discussed his business arrangements with me I met his gaze in surprise, unwilling to expose the sharp sting that had arrived and lodged in my midriff. 'Okay…'

'You and Andreos can come with me.'

The swiftness with which the sting eased was dismaying—and a little terrifying. Enough to trigger a waspish response. 'Is that a question or a command?'

The flash of flint in his eyes stunned me. Hard on its heels came the realisation that I much preferred his blinding smiles. The sexy growls when he was aroused. Even his sometimes mocking tones.

Theos, I'd fallen into a highly dangerous state of lust, complacency, and a host of other things I didn't want to name. One in particular had been gaining momentum, clamouring for attention I was too afraid to give it. It was there when I woke. It blanketed me before I fell asleep and teased my dreams. It was there now, pulsing beneath my skin as Ax's gaze locked on mine and another blinding smile made an appearance.

'It's whichever you find easiest to comply with.'

For some absurd reason my heart flipped over even as I wondered whether he was asking me along because the thought of being separated from us for any length of time was disagreeable to him or because of appearances.

His expression was mostly unreadable, but there was

something there. A touch of apprehension I'd never seen before. And, though it was highly unwise to latch on to it, I found myself leaning towards it, indulging myself in the idea that he *cared* whether I agreed or not.

'How long is this trip going to last?'

'It's to finalise a new airline deal I've been working on for a year. It's been challenging at times, so I expect both sides will want to celebrate after the deed is done. Prepare to stay for the better part of a week. Did you travel to Thailand on your trip?' he asked, but his almost flippant query didn't fool me for one second.

Axios was a master at subtle inquisition. Over the past weeks he'd dropped several questions unexpectedly.

'No. My coin-flip landed in favour of Indonesia instead of Thailand, so I went to Bali.'

'Then this will be your chance to explore another country,' he replied smoothly, despite the trace of tension in the air.

Andreos chose that moment to make his displeasure at the charged atmosphere known. Axios absently soothed a hand down his small back, but his eyes remained fixed on me.

When I reached for him Ax handed him over. Then he stayed sitting, his elbows resting on his knees.

'Will you come with me?' he asked, his eyes boring into mine.

And because that undeniable yearning for *more* wouldn't stop—because I craved this...*togetherness* more than I craved my next breath—I answered, 'Yes.'

CHAPTER NINE

TIME IS RUNNING OUT...

The unnerving sensation that time was slipping through my fingers had arrived like a thief in the night and stayed like an unwanted guest, permeating my every interaction with Calypso. I couldn't put my finger on *why* and nor did I have a clear-cut solution.

The sensation left me off-kilter and scowling as I climbed the steps into my plane two days later.

A lot of things I'd believed to be cut and dried had become nebulous in the past few weeks. The idea of marriage...of *staying* married, for instance...didn't evoke the same amount of resistance it had done a year or even a month ago. As for being a father...

Thoughts of Andreos immediately soothed a fraction of the chaos inside me. My son's existence had brought a deeper purpose to my life I wouldn't have believed possible had I not experienced it for myself. The chance to pass on my heritage to him, to teach him about the sacrifices his grandfather had made filled a bleak corner of my soul.

As for his mother...

The warmth I'd enjoyed with her over the past few weeks, watching her joy in painting and simply basking in the unit she and Andreos presented had subtly altered, leaving me with more questions than answers. Even more acute was the feeling of exposure after revealing so much of myself and the anguish her family's actions had caused mine.

Yes, but only one member of her family...not all of them...

My chest twinged with another sting of guilt. I'd learned from my grandfather's mistakes, applied his good mentoring to my life and avoided the bad. Shouldn't the same apply to Calypso? Especially when she'd been caught in the same web of greed as I had?

The urge to hash this out with her grew stronger. And yet the fear of repeating the mistakes of last year, driving her away, stopped me.

It didn't help that over the last day or so she'd seemed under the weather, thereby curtailing any serious conversation I'd felt inclined to have or my reaching for that final resort of last resorts—tugging her into my arms in the dark of night and letting the mindless bliss of having her melt every fractious thought away.

Harmony and unstinting passion—it was a combination I would never have associated with her a few weeks ago, but I now craved to have it back.

My gaze fell on her as I entered the living area of the plane. She was chatting to one of the attendants, her alluring smile sparking heat in my bloodstream as she nodded to whatever was being said.

Unable to help myself, I let my gaze trail over her. The cream form-fitting jumpsuit caressed her luscious body from shoulder to ankle, its emphasis of her supple behind and lush breasts drying my mouth and reminding me that it had been three long days since I'd had the pleasure of her body.

The attendant departed, and as Calypso turned to sit I noticed the top buttons securing the front were left undone to reveal her impressive cleavage. My groin stirred harder and it was all I could do not to give a bad-tempered, frustrated groan.

I approached, dropping into the seat opposite her. She held Andreos like a buffer, her gaze stubbornly avoiding mine even though she was aware of my presence.

'The silent treatment isn't going to work where we're headed. You do know that, don't you?'

The blue eyes that finally deigned to meet mine were shadowed, her face still showing a hint of the paleness that raised an entirely new set of ruffled emotions inside me.

'Don't worry, Axios. I'll put on the appropriate performance when needed.'

Even her voice had lost a trace of that passionate lustre that fired up my blood.

'Are you all right?' The words were pulled from a deep, *needy* part of me.

Her eyes widened, then she nodded abruptly and her gaze dropped to Andreos. 'I'm fine. Just a slight… stomach ache.'

The unsettling sensation deepened, the niggling feeling that I was missing something escalating. 'Did you take anything for it? I'll get the attendant to bring you—'

She shook her head hastily when I reached for the intercom button, but I didn't miss the shadow that crossed her face, the knuckles that whitened in her lap.

'It's… I'm fine, Ax. I think I'll go and lie down with Andreos for a while after we take off.'

True to her word, the moment we reached cruising altitude she unbuckled herself, rose, and headed to the back of the plane with Andreos.

The urge to follow, to demand answers to the teeming questions ricocheting in my brain, was so strong I clenched my gut against the power of it.

I stayed put, forcing rationality over impulse. I had business to take care of, conference calls to make. And yet somewhere on that endless to-do list the looming issue of our agreement ticked louder.

An agreement I'd lately found myself re-examining with growing dissatisfaction.

Restlessness drove me to my feet. At the bar, I poured myself a cognac and tossed it back, hoping the bracing heat would knock some sense into me. All it did was emphasise the expanding hollow inside me and quicken this alien need demanding satisfaction.

Setting the glass down, I started to walk back to my seat—and then, unsurprised, I found myself moving towards the back of the plane.

After my soft knock elicited no response I turned the door handle. Lamps were dimmed, the window shades drawn, but still I saw them. Both asleep.

One with small, chubby arms thrown above his head in innocent abandon.

My son. My world.

The other curled on her side with one arm braced protectively over Andreos and the other draped over her belly.

My wife.

But not for much longer. Unless I took steps to do something about it.

Resolution slid home like a key in a lock I didn't even

realise needed opening. Now I did—now the possibility of *more* beckoned with a promise I didn't want to deny.

Shaking out a light throw, I tucked it over both of them, then stepped back.

Calypso made a distressed sound in her sleep, an anxious twitch marring her brow for a second before it smoothed out and her breathing grew steady.

Was her stomach still bothering her? I frowned as that niggling returned.

My hand clenched over the door handle.

Were her secrets disturbing her sleep? Could that be the last stumbling block I needed to overcome to make this marriage real? If so, could I live with it?

The breath locked in my lungs was released, along with the bracing realisation that, regardless of what the secret was, it needn't get in our way. If she was prepared not to let it.

Very much aware that several things hung in the balance, I stepped out, shut the door behind me and returned to the living room. But through all my strategising and counter-strategising my resolution simply deepened.

My grandfather had sacrificed and nearly lost everything in his dealings with one Petras.

But perhaps it was time to draw a line underneath all that, let acrimony stay in the past where it belonged.

Perhaps it was time to strike yet another bargain.

A more permanent one.

Thailand was magical.

Or as magical as a place could be when I knew that dark shadows crept ever closer. Knew that my stolen time was rapidly dwindling away.

It marred my ability to enjoy fully the sheer magnificence of our tropical paradise except on canvas, with the paints Axios had supplied me with, which conversely helped in keeping my true state under wraps for a little longer.

The discomfort in my abdomen which he had erroneously assumed was my period kept him from the jaw-droppingly stunning master suite of our Bangkok villa at night. And when we were required to make an appearance together at one of the many events marking the successful merger of Xenakis Aeronautics and a major Thai-owned airline he was painfully solicitous, showering me with the kind of attention that made the tabloid headlines screech with joy.

The kind that made my heart swell with a foolish longing that I knew would make the inevitable break all the more agonising.

The kind he'd showered me with over the last few weeks but that now came with a speculative look in his eyes. As if he was trying to solve a puzzle. As if he was trying to make our situation *work*.

But my guilt at the subterfuge was nothing compared to the grief tearing my heart to shreds at the thought of leaving Andreos.

When, after four days in Bangkok, Axios announced that we were relocating to Kamala in Phuket for the remaining three days, for a delayed honeymoon, I knew I couldn't hide from my feelings any longer.

I was in love with Axios.

Even knowing he didn't feel the same couldn't diminish the knowledge that I'd been falling since that night on the balcony. Since I'd agreed to *for now*. But, contrarily, accepting my true feelings meant I couldn't in good conscience burden him or my precious baby with the battle ahead.

I was in love with my husband. And to spare him our marriage had to end.

Tucked inside the bamboo shelter of a rainforest shower, I gave in to the silent sobs tearing my heart to pieces, letting the warm spray wash my tears away. When I was wrung out, I carefully disguised the tell-tale signs of my distress with subtle make-up before leaving the suite.

In bare feet and a floaty white dress that whispered softly around my body, I approached the sound of in-fant giggles, a deep, sexy voice and the playful splash of water.

Axios was enjoying a lazy swim with Andreos. And, as much as I wanted to stop and frame the beautiful pic-ture father and son made, so I could carry it in my heart, I knew my emotions were far too close to the surface to risk detection.

Instead I made my way past the pool and through the glass hallway that led to another stunning wing of the multi-tiered luxury villa. To the special place I'd dis-covered on our arrival.

The suspended treehouse was accessed by a heavy plank and rope bridge from the second level of the villa and a broad ladder from the level below. I took the walkway, enjoying the swaying movement that made me feel as if I was dancing on air, and entered the wide space laid out with polished wooden floors, wide rect-angular windows and a roped-off platform that gave magnificent views of the Andaman Sea and the Bay of Bengal.

A riot of vivid colour brush-stroked the horizon, signalling the approach of night. Silently awed, and my breath held, I watched the colours settle into breathtaking layers of a purple and orange sunset.

I wasn't sure how long I stood there, lost in my turbulent thoughts, selfishly praying for things I couldn't have. And even when I sensed Axios's approach I didn't turn around, didn't give in to the raw need to fill my senses with the sight and sound of him.

Instead I gripped the rope barrier until my knuckles shrieked with just a fraction of the pain shredding my insides.

Whether he sensed my mood or not, Axios didn't speak either. But when he stopped behind me I felt the intensity of his presence. And when he slid an arm around my waist and engulfed me in the poignant scents of father and son I couldn't help the scalding tears that prickled my eyes.

With a soft moan I sagged into his hold, and the three of us stood on the platform, staring at the horizon as the bright orange ball of the sun dipped into the sea and a blanket of stars started to fill the sky.

'Come,' he said eventually, his voice low and deep. 'The chef is almost done preparing dinner. Let's go put our son to bed, hmm?'

Throat tight with locked emotion, I nodded, making sure to avoid his probing gaze as we made our back into the villa. After putting a dozing Andreos in his cot, we retraced our steps to the open terrace, where a candlelit dinner had been laid out.

There, Axios pulled out a chair and I sat, my stomach in knots and my heart bleeding, as I looked at the face of the man I was hopelessly in love with.

The man I could never have.

* * *

Theos mou, she was gorgeous.

The breath that had stalled in my lungs fought to emerge as I watched candlelight dance over her face and throat. Even the veil of melancholy shrouding her didn't detract from the captivating mix of fire and calm I wanted to experience for a very long time.

For ever.

Our three-course dinner had passed in stilted conversation, and our appetites had been non-existent. She'd refused dessert and I'd downed my aromatic espresso in one go.

But it was time.

Business pressures had forced this conversation to the back burner for the last four days. It was time to lay my cards on the table.

'About the divorce you requested: I would like to renegotiate...'

A vice tightened my sternum when wild panic flared in her eyes. The hand resting on the table began to tremble and she snatched it away, tucking it into her lap as she exhaled sharply. 'What do you mean, "renegotiate"? You gave me your word!'

For the first time I felt a visceral need to take it all back, to smash it to pieces and rebuild something new, something lasting from the rubble created from greed and blind lust. Because there was something more here. This...*distance* between us had cemented my belief that this wasn't just sex. That I'd fallen deeper, farther than even my imagination could fathom. Perhaps even into that dimension where Calypso could exist.

The thought of that ending...of never experiencing it

or her at some point in the future…twisted in something close to agony inside me.

The state was further evidenced by the quiet panic this very argument was fuelling inside me—the fine trembles coursing through my body, taunting me with the possibility that this might be the one deal that eluded me. That my actions last year and since finding her on Bora Bora might have doomed me in her eyes. The very thought that I might fail where I'd succeeded at everything else. Everything that mattered…

No.

'I know what I promised, but I no longer think it's—'

'No!'

She surged to her feet, and the trembling in her hand seemed transmitted to her body as eyes steeped in turmoil centred on mine. But when she spoke her voice was firm, the most resolute I'd ever heard her. And that only twisted the knife in deeper. Because I sensed a dynamic shift in her the like of which I'd never experienced before.

She seemed to falter for a moment, her hand sliding to her stomach, before she shook her head. 'You made a promise, Axios, and I'm going to have to insist you deliver on that promise.'

That gesture…

'Tell me why, Calypso. Give me a reason why you won't even hear me out,' I challenged, feeling the ground slip away beneath my feet even as I rose and faced her across the dinner table.

'Why?' he grated again when words failed to emerge from my strangled throat in time to answer his question.

His features were changing from a determined sort of cajoling to frighteningly resolute.

'Are you pregnant?' he added hoarsely, and there was a blaze of what looked like hope in his eyes as they dropped to my stomach.

'What? No, I'm not pregnant,' I blurted, dropping my hand.

Was that disappointment on his face?

'Can we take a breath and discuss this rationally?' he asked.

The desire to do just that—to let him talk me into dreaming about an impossible future—was so heart-wrenchingly tempting it took the sharp bite of my nails into my palm to stop agreement spilling from my lips.

'No. I'm all talked out, Axios. All I want now is action. For you to stick to your word and…and let me go.'

His grey eyes went molten for a handful of seconds before his jaw clenched tight. 'Why? We've proved in the last few weeks that we're completely compatible. As parents to Andreos. And in the bedroom.'

Desperately, I shook my head. 'We…we can love Andreos as much together as apart. As for the bedroom… it's just sex. Basing a marriage on it is delusional.'

'I beg to differ. The kind of compatibility we have is unique. Don't be so dismissive of it. Besides, how would you know? I'm the only lover you've ever had,' he tossed in arrogantly.

And he would be the only one for me. 'That still doesn't mean I want to give up everything for the sake of—'

A throat clearing on the edge of the terrace interrupted me. Sophia, now Andreos's official nanny, had travelled with us to Thailand, and she looked supremely nervous.

'What is it?' Axios demanded.

'There's a call from Switzerland for Kyria Xenakis. They say they've been trying to reach you.'

I felt the blood draining from my face as Axios frowned. *Dr Trudeau, tired of waiting for me to contact him.*

'Tell them I'll call back tomorrow,' I said hastily.

The second Sophia hurried away, Axios's gaze sharpened on me. 'Why are you getting a call from Switzerland?'

'I still have business there,' I replied, hoping he'd let it go.

For a terse moment I thought he'd push, but then he sighed. 'What were you going to say before? For the sake of what, Calypso?'

For the sake of unrequited love.

Mercifully, the words remained locked deep inside me, the only hint spilling out in my strained voice as I fought to remain upright, to fight for this vital chance to do this on my own terms.

'I can't—I don't *want* anything long-term. I want to be free.'

To fight for the chance to return whole. Even to dream of starting again with a clean slate.

Hope dried up as Ax's face turned ashen, his eyes darkening with something raw and potent. Something I wasn't sure I wanted to decipher, because it resembled the helpless yearning inside me.

But that couldn't be. Axios not only hated what my father had done to him, he despised what my family had done to his grandfather. I was the last person he could be contemplating hitching himself to for the long term. Which meant that whatever his proposal was it still had an end date. That even if Dr Trudeau had a sliver of hope for me I might not have a chance with Ax.

Nonetheless, temptation buffeted me until I had to hold on to the edge of the table to keep from falling into it.

'Free to live your life? What about our *son*, Calypso?' he demanded scathingly, his voice ragged. 'Do you intend to drag him along on another freedom jaunt? Are you so blinkered to his needs that you would rip him from me to satisfy your own needs?'

'Of course not!'

The searing denial was the final thread holding my emotions together. I felt the hot slide of tears and could do nothing to stop it. So I stood there, my world going into one final free fall, and set the words I despised but *needed* to say spilling free.

'He…he's happy in Athens. He's a Xenakis. You love him. He belongs with you. You can…' *Keep him. Love him. The way I might not be able to.*

The final words dried in my throat, the final selfless act of handing over my precious son unwilling to be given voice. But still he *knew*.

Knew and condemned me absolutely for it.

Brows clamped in horror, he stared at me. 'Are you—?' He stopped, shook his head in abject disbelief. 'You're leaving him behind? Your quest for freedom is so great that you intend to completely abandon your son?'

His voice was bleak, his eyes pools of bewilderment.

'Or it is something else, Calypso? Is it me? Have I not proved I can be a good husband, provide for you and our son?'

There was my chance. Say no and this would be over.

Tell him he'd failed me and it would be done. But I couldn't. Because even if he didn't love me, he hadn't failed me.

'Please, Axios—'

'Please what?' he asked urgently, stalking around the table towards me. 'Make it easier for you to walk away from your child? From me?'

His chest rose and fell in uncharacteristic agitation, his eyes dark, dismal.

'I watched my grandfather's world crumble around him. You want me to let you do the same to mine?' he rasped jaggedly.

I squeezed my eyes shut. 'Please don't say that.'

'Why not?' he demanded, his expression hardening. 'You want easy? Let me make it simple for you. Take one step out through the front door and you will never set eyes on Andreos again. I will make it my mission to erase your name from his life. It will be as if you never even existed.'

Choked tears clogged my throat and my world turned inside out with sorrow.

'You would do that? Really?'

He hesitated, one hand rising to glide roughly over his mouth and jaw before he shook his head. 'Make me understand, Calypso. What could possibly be out there that you won't get with me? What could be more important to you than to care for our child? To watch him grow and thrive under our care?'

I pressed my lips together, the agony of keeping the naked truth locked inside me so it wouldn't stain Andreos killing me. 'My…my freedom. I want what I've wanted for as long as I can remember, Axios. I want to be free.'

For the longest time he simply stared in stark disbelief. Then his breath shuddered out. And with it the last of the bewilderment in his eyes. Now he saw how set I was on bringing this to an end, his jaw clenched in tight resolution.

'Is that your final decision?' he grated.

My balled fist rose from the table, rested on my abdomen and the possible time bomb ticking inside me. 'Yes. It is.'

'Very well. You'll hear from my lawyers before the week is out.'

My breath strangled to nothing. *It was over. Just like that?*

'Axios—'

'No!' His hand slashed through the air. 'There's no room for bargaining.'

And in that moment, presented with his bleak verdict, I felt the words simply tumble out. 'I'm sick, Axios. I have a lump…in my cervix.'

He froze, his eyes widening with shock as he stumbled back a step. 'What?' he whispered, his face ashen.

'I suspected it last year—a few weeks before we married. The doctor in Switzerland who confirmed I was pregnant also confirmed the presence of the lump. My… my grandmother died of cervical cancer—'

'Why have you waited this long for treatment?' he railed.

'Andreos. I wanted to make sure he was safe. And loved.'

He went even paler, his eyes growing pools of horror and disbelief. 'You've known this…you've carried this for a year…and you didn't tell me?' he rasped, almost to himself as he gripped his nape with a shaky hand.

'Why? Because you were testing me? Because I let you down? Because you don't trust me?'

No! Because I love you. Because I can't let you both watch me die.

'Because I didn't want to put Andreos through what might happen. He was a miracle, Ax. I couldn't…didn't know if I could carry him to term, but once I knew I was pregnant I knew I had to *try*.'

'You found out about the lump the same day you found out you were carrying Andreos?' he asked, his voice still stark.

I nodded. 'I just… I couldn't lose him, Ax. I couldn't risk a biopsy to find out whether my prognosis was the same as my grandmother's. But I agreed to frequent scans that wouldn't harm the baby. When the first one showed that the pregnancy was stopping the lump from growing—'

'You chose to stay pregnant,' he finished, awed disbelief in his voice.

I sniffed back tears and nodded again. 'You see, Andreos was a miracle in so many ways. Conceiving him bought me time, and once he was born… I just couldn't let him go.'

'But the lump is still there. It's causing you pain, isn't it?' he asked, even though the knowledge blazed in his eyes. 'That's why you touch your stomach. That's why you were unwell on the plane. And the timing of your return… That was your plan all along—to hand over Andreos and go off and fight this on your own?'

'Yes,' I answered simply. 'I've had one scan since Andreos was born. It showed a small growth rate. But it's… it's time for further tests. Axios, I watched my grandmother suffer in the last months of her life. I can't…

won't put Andreos through that if that's what I'm facing.
I *have* to leave. I would prefer it if you didn't fight me.
But…what you said…about erasing me from his life—'

Axios cursed and shoved both hands through his hair.
'That was an idle threat. You'll always be his mother and
he'll know you as such. He'll know your courage and
what you did for him,' he intoned in a low, solemn voice.

At my sob of relief his lips firmed and he stared at
me for an age. 'Andreos,' he said heavily, with a final-
ity that struck real fear into me. 'He's the only reason
you're doing this.'

It was a statement—as if he already knew the answer.
He took a step back. Then another. Until an unpassable
chasm yawned between us.

'Very well. If you've made your choice then so be it.'

I'd expected this to come, but still I stood in utter
shock as Axios blazed one last searing look at me, then
turned and stalked away.

Shock turned into numbing self-protection when,
upon waking up alone in the master suite the next day,
I learned from Sophia that Ax had left. That he'd left instructions for Andreos and I to return to Athens alone.

As if the staff knew things had changed drastically,
from the moment we walked through the front door of
the Athens villa the atmosphere seemed altered. The
only one who thankfully remained oblivious was Andreos. Having mastered the art of rolling over, he was
now determined to conquer sitting up in record time, and
thus provided the only source of delight in the house.

In a bid to make the most of whatever time I had with
him, before Ax returned, I all but banished poor Sophia
as I greedily devoured every precious second.

Two days turned to three.

Then four.

And then came the news from the housekeeper that Ax was expected mid-afternoon.

The urge to delay my exit, to see his face one last time, pummelled me. But, knowing I couldn't delay the inevitable, I booked my flight to Switzerland. The bag I'd hastily packed while Andreos napped stood like a silent omen at the foot of my bed.

'The car's waiting, *kyria*,' Sophia informed me, her face wreathed in worry.

Unchecked tears streamed down my face as I leaned down and brushed my lips over Andreos' plump cheek. 'Promise me you'll look after him?' I managed through a clogged throat.

Sophia's anxious gaze searched mine. 'I… I promise. But, *kyria*—'

I shook my head, knowing I'd break down if this was prolonged. 'That's good enough for me. Thank you, Sophia.'

Bag in hand, I hurried out, flew down the stairs to the waiting car. Blind with tears, I didn't register his presence until the car was pulling away.

'I will allow those tears for now, *pethi mou*. But for what comes next I'll need that formidable resilience I've come to know and adore.'

CHAPTER TEN

'Axios! What...what are you doing here?'

His face was as gaunt and ashen as the last time I'd seen it. But in his eyes purpose and determination blazed in place of horrified anguish.

Even so, the sight of him shook me, his presence unearthing a cascade of emotions through me.

When he didn't answer, when all he seemed to want was to absorb every inch of my face, I tried again. 'I thought you'd gone...that I'd never see you again.'

His chest heaved in a mighty exhalation. 'I had to go,' he replied gruffly.

Despair and disappointment slashed me wide open. 'Oh. I understand.'

He gave a grating self-deprecating laugh that was chopped off halfway through. '*Do* you? Do you understand how utterly useless and powerless I felt? How I had to walk away because I knew I'd failed you again?'

'What? Why would you—?'

'We will dissect that later. But for now...' my breath caught as his thumb brushed away my tears, '...it's tearing me apart to see these tears,' he grated roughly.

Which only made them fall harder.

'Andreos... Leaving him...that's tearing *me* apart.'

'Just Andreos?'

The question was deep and low. But heavy with unspoken emotions.

I lifted my gaze to find him watching me with hawklike intensity, his eyes burning with a new light. One that made my insides leap.

'Ax...'

Before I could answer his hand seized mine, his eyes steadfast on me.

'Will you give me the chance to make things right, Calypso? Trust me just for a little while?' he demanded with a hoarse plea.

About to answer, I paused as we pulled up at the private airstrip and stopped next to his plane. 'Axios, where are we going?'

He alighted and held out his hand. I slid out of the car, still in a daze, and didn't resist when he pulled me close.

'You've lived in fear for over a year, while bearing and caring for our son. You've loved him unconditionally when you could've taken a different option without judgement. But you don't need to be alone in this. You never need to be alone again,' he vowed.

The depth of his words made my heart pound with tentative hope. That hope turned to shock when I spotted the middle-aged man standing at the door of the plane.

'Dr Trudeau...what are you...? What's he doing here?' I asked Ax.

'He's here to help. As are the others.'

Taking my hand, he led me onto the plane. And my shock tripled.

'Mama?' Seated amongst three other distinguished-looking men was my mother. When she smiled tremulously and held out her arms a broken sob ripped through me as I rushed forward and threw myself into her embrace.

'Your husband rightly felt that you should be surrounded by those you love in your time of need.'

Did that include him?

Fearing I'd give myself away if I looked his way, I kept my gaze on my mother.

'You should've told us, Callie.'

I shook my head. 'I couldn't risk not having Andreos.'

And that seemed to settle the matter with her. She nodded, then looked over my head. I didn't need the signal to know that Ax was approaching.

'Let me introduce you, Calypso.'

Swiping my hand across my cheek, I composed myself and stood. Besides Dr Trudeau, the three men were all doctors too, specialising in everything to do with the cervix.

'Your mother has been instrumental in providing details about your grandmother's condition. With your permission, we'll head to Dr Trudeau's clinic and start the tests.'

I gasped, my gaze finding Ax's. 'That's what you've been doing the last three days? Rounding up specialists?'

He nodded, that blaze burning brighter in his eyes. 'You are far too important, *yineka mou*. I'm leaving nothing to chance.'

I swayed. He caught me, held me tight.

After pinning me with his gaze for several seconds, he glanced around. 'We're about to take off,' he said. 'I would like to talk to my wife in private, so I trust you can all amuse yourselves?' At their agreement, he turned to me. 'Calypso?'

I nodded, a million hopes and dreams cascading through my brain as I followed him into the master suite.

He waited long enough for me to be seated and buckled in before stalking over to the drinks cabinet. Dazedly, I watched him pour a glass of cognac, grimace, and pour a thimbleful into a second glass. Walking over, he handed the smaller drink to me.

'A small sip won't hurt,' he stated gruffly, almost pleadingly.

With another befuddled nod I accepted it, took the tiniest sip and shuddered my way through swallowing it down. As the spirit warmed my insides, another sensation filtered through. But the joy bubbling beneath my skin fizzled out when Axios sank onto his knees before me.

'Was it just about Andreos?' he asked starkly. 'Were you leaving only because of him or did I feature anywhere in your thoughts?'

'Ax—'

'I know I didn't give you the wedding of your dreams, or make the time after that palatable. But did I drive you away completely, Calypso?'

There was a layer of self-loathing in his voice that propelled me to grip his hand. 'I just didn't want to burden you—'

'Burden me? You're my *wife*!'

'One who was a stranger when we exchanged vows! I didn't know how…what you would do…'

'What I would *do*? What other option was there besides seeking medical—' His curse ranged through the room. 'Did you think I'd exploit you the way your father did your mother?'

'I didn't know then.'

For an eternity he simply stared at me. '*Then?* Does that mean you know different now?' he asked, his voice awash with hope and his eyes alight with a peculiar kind of desperation that tore through me.

I didn't realise my nails were digging into the sofa until he set his hand on mine, stilling my agitation. I wanted to cling to him. *Theos* did I want to. But the fear of fanning false hope, triggering another torrent of might-have-beens that would further shatter my heart, stopped me.

Discarding his drink, he took both my hands in his. 'Tell me, please, if I have a chance with you. No matter what happens I intend to stay and fight this thing along with you. But after that—'

I pressed a hand to his lips. 'We might not have a future,' I whispered. 'It wasn't just about Andreos. I didn't want to put *you* through that.'

His fingers tightened around mine, and when his eyes fused with mine, I felt the live wire of his desperation.

'That's why you tried to leave me again this time?'

Suspecting I wouldn't be able to speak around the lump in my throat, I nodded.

A hoarse breath shuddered out of him. 'I never thought I'd be so relieved at such a reason for being dumped.'

He stopped abruptly, caught my face between his hands and blazed me a look so intense my insides melted.

'I love you, Calypso. I fell in love with your defiance in Bora Bora. Fell in love with you when I saw your love for our son. I adored your strength when I watched that video. Watching you paint, seeing your talent…awed me. Despite the odds, you have fought and continue to fight for what you want. One day our son will grow up to learn what an inspiration you are. He'll watch you and know he has the best mother in the world.'

The tears came free and unchecked. 'Oh, Ax...'

'Getting the call that you'd gone the morning after our wedding altered something inside me. I wasn't ready to admit it, but I knew I'd failed you. That I'd failed myself. Your agreeing to take a leap with me felt like a second chance. And with every breath I vow to make it worth your while.'

'Was...was this what you were going to tell me in Thailand?'

'Yes. I knew I was in love with you. I planned on begging you to give our marriage a chance. But—'

'But I chopped you off at the knees before you could lay out everything my own heart and soul wanted to tell you. That I loved you and would've given anything to remain your wife.'

He froze. 'Say that again, please?' he begged.

'I love you, too, Ax. Even before the possibility of Andreos and the possibility of love I was drawn to you. Something inside me made me put *you* at the top of my bucket list. I was always going to come back, even if only for a short time, because my heart knew I belonged to you. And these last few weeks have felt like a heaven I didn't want to leave. I may have been devastated when you left me the morning after our wedding, but watching you leave me in Thailand...'

He closed his eyes for a single moment. 'I knew I was making a mistake even before I got on the helicopter after our wedding night. But when I left this time I knew

I was coming straight back. That nothing would stop me. Because you're my heart, *pethi mou*. My very soul.'

To cement that vow he slanted his lips over mine, kissed me until we were both breathless.

'Tell me again,' I commanded.

His eyes burned with feeling. 'I love you. With all that I am and everything in between.'

He kissed me again as the plane sped down the runway and soared into the sky.

When I broke away to look out of the window, he gently caught my chin in his hand. 'What is it?'

'Andreos.'

A warm smile split Ax's face. 'He has Sophia and a dozen other staff curled around his plump little fingers. They will take care of him until we send for him in the morning. He's our little miracle and we will fight this thing together. All three of us. For now, you will let me take care of you. You will allow me the privilege of helping to make you better. Please, my love?'

I nodded, but still hesitated. 'What if it's too late? What if they can't…?'

He slid his thumb across my lips, silencing my doubts. 'Whatever happens we face it together. For better or worse, you have me for life. I will never leave your side and I will never fail you again.'

His words unfurled my joy. This time I wasn't alone. I had my precious baby and the husband of my heart. I intended to fight with everything I had for the chance to ensure my days were blessed with nothing but love, health and happiness.

At cruising altitude, Axios swung me into his arms and strolled to the bed. I curled my arms around his neck and looked into molten eyes blazing with love.

'I love you, Calypso,' he said again, as if saying the words filled him with as much happiness as it filled my heart.

'*Se agapo*, Axios.

EPILOGUE

A year later

'WHAT ARE YOU DOING?'

'Starting on your payback,' Axios drawled, striding across the master bedroom in Agistros to lay me down on the king-sized bed before trailing his lips over my shoulder to the sensitive area beneath my earlobe.

'What?' I gasped, delightful shivers running through me at the wickedness he evoked.

'You owe me a full pregnancy experience. I can't think of a better time to start than now. I want to experience it all—from morning sickness to the moment our baby enters the world.'

I made a face. 'Morning sickness isn't very sexy.'

He dropped a kiss on the corner of my mouth. 'Perhaps not. But I made you a promise to be here for the good as well as the bad, *eros mou*. So I will be on hand to hold your hair when you throw up. To massage your feet when the weight of our child tires you. And everything you need in between. If that's what you want too?' he asked, hope brimming in his voice.

I curled my arms around his neck. 'More than anything in the world.'

The operation to remove what had turned out to be a benign lump in my cervix six months ago had been a resounding success, with every trace of it gone and quarterly scans showing it hadn't returned.

Today Dr Trudeau had given us the all-clear to try for another baby—a statement Axios seemed determined to capitalise on immediately. And with a doting grandmother to help care for Andreos, in the form of my mother, life couldn't have been better. Her decision to leave my father hadn't been easy, but I'd supported her. Yiannis Petras hadn't resisted for long, busy as he was with frittering away his millions on one bad investment after another.

Ax groaned. 'Don't cry. It rips me up when you do.'

I laughed tremulously. 'Oh, God, then prepare yourself. Because I'm very hormonal during pregnancy.'

'Hmm, I will have to think of ways to counteract that.'

'What did you have in mind?'

'Why, endless seduction, of course. I can think of nothing better than making love to my beautiful wife while she nurtures our baby in her womb.'

More tears flowed. With another groan, he sealed his lips to mine—most likely to distract me. It worked. Within minutes I was naked and gasping, lost in the arms of my true love.

And when, at the height of feeling, he looked deep into my eyes and whispered, 'I love you, Calypso,' he went one better and kissed my tears away.

The power of him moving inside me, possibly planting his seed inside me, triggered fresh tears.

I was still emotional when our breaths cooled. When he pulled me close and whispered in my ear.

'Our adventure is only just beginning, *eros mou*. And I couldn't have wished for a better partner at my side to experience it all but you, Calypso Xenakis.'

'Nor I, you, my love,' I returned, with every ounce of the love I held in my heart.

* * * * *

If you enjoyed
Claiming My Hidden Son
you're sure to enjoy these other stories
by Maya Blake!

His Mistress by Blackmail
Sheikh's Pregnant Cinderella
Crown Prince's Bought Bride
An Heir for the World's Richest Man

Available now!

COMING NEXT MONTH FROM

HARLEQUIN Presents.

Available November 19, 2019

#3769 THE GREEK'S SURPRISE CHRISTMAS BRIDE
Conveniently Wed!
by Lynne Graham

Letty can't let her family fall into financial ruin. A convenient Christmas wedding with Leo is the ideal solution! Until their paper-only arrangement is scorched...by the heat of their unanticipated attraction!

#3770 THE QUEEN'S BABY SCANDAL
One Night With Consequences
by Maisey Yates

Mauro is stunned to discover the beautiful innocent who left his bed at midnight three months ago is a queen...and she's pregnant! He's never wanted a family, but nothing will stop this billionaire from demanding his heir.

#3771 PROOF OF THEIR ONE-NIGHT PASSION
Secret Heirs of Billionaires
by Louise Fuller

Ragnar's chaotic childhood inspired his billion-dollar dating app. He must keep romantic attachments simple. But when Lottie reveals their heart-stopping encounter had consequences, there's no question that Ragnar *will* claim his baby...

#3772 SECRET PRINCE'S CHRISTMAS SEDUCTION
by Carol Marinelli

Prince Rafe is floored by his unexpected connection to chambermaid Antonietta. All he can offer is a temporary seduction. But unwrapping the precious gift of her virginity changes *everything*. Now Rafe must choose—his crown, or Antonietta...

HPCNMRA1119

#3773 A DEAL TO CARRY THE ITALIAN'S HEIR
The Scandalous Brunetti Brothers
by Tara Pammi

With her chances of finally having a family in jeopardy, Neha's taking drastic action! Approaching Leonardo with her outrageous request to father her child by IVF is step one. Step two? Ignoring her deep desire for him!

#3774 CHRISTMAS CONTRACT FOR HIS CINDERELLA
by Jane Porter

Duty has always dictated Marcu's actions, making free-spirited Monet, with her infamous family history, strictly forbidden. But when their long-simmering passion burns intensely enough to melt the snow, will Marcu claim his Christmas Cinderella...?

#3775 SNOWBOUND WITH HIS FORBIDDEN INNOCENT
by Susan Stephens

Snowed-in with Stacey, his best friend's untouched—and very off-limits!—sister, Lucas discovers temptation like no other. And as their mutual attraction grows hotter, Lucas has never been so close to breaking the rules...

#3776 MAID FOR THE UNTAMED BILLIONAIRE
Housekeeper Brides for Billionaires
by Miranda Lee

Being suddenly swept into Jake's world—and his arms!—is an eye-opening experience for shy maid Abby. But when Jake's number one rule is *no long-term relationships*, how can Abby possibly tame the wild billionaire?

YOU CAN FIND MORE INFORMATION ON UPCOMING HARLEQUIN® TITLES, FREE EXCERPTS AND MORE AT WWW.HARLEQUIN.COM.

HPCNMRB1119

Get 4 FREE REWARDS!

We'll send you 2 FREE Books plus 2 FREE Mystery Gifts.

PRESENTS.

USA TODAY BESTSELLING AUTHOR
Annie West
Sheikh's Royal Baby Revelation

Presents.

NEW YORK TIMES BESTSELLING AUTHOR
Maisey Yates
His Forbidden Pregnant Princess

Harlequin Presents® books feature a sensational and sophisticated world of international romance where sinfully tempting heroes ignite passion.

FREE
Value Over
$20

YES! Please send me 2 FREE Harlequin Presents® novels and my 2 FREE gifts (gifts are worth about $10 retail). After receiving them, if I don't wish to receive any more books, I can return the shipping statement marked "cancel." If I don't cancel, I will receive 6 brand-new novels every month and be billed just $4.55 each for the regular-print edition or $5.80 each for the larger-print edition in the U.S., or $5.49 each for the regular-print edition or $5.99 each for the larger-print edition in Canada. That's a savings of at least 11% off the cover price! It's quite a bargain! Shipping and handling is just 50¢ per book in the U.S. and $1.25 per book in Canada.* I understand that accepting the 2 free books and gifts places me under no obligation to buy anything. I can always return a shipment and cancel at any time. The free books and gifts are mine to keep no matter what I decide.

Choose one: ☐ **Harlequin Presents®**
Regular-Print
(106/306 HDN GNWY)

☐ **Harlequin Presents®**
Larger-Print
(176/376 HDN GNWY)

Name (please print)

Address   Apt. #

City   State/Province   Zip/Postal Code

Mail to the **Reader Service:**
IN U.S.A.: P.O. Box 1341, Buffalo, NY 14240-8531
IN CANADA: P.O. Box 603, Fort Erie, Ontario L2A 5X3

Want to try 2 free books from another series? Call 1-800-873-8635 or visit www.ReaderService.com.

---

*Terms and prices subject to change without notice. Prices do not include sales taxes, which will be charged (if applicable) based on your state or country of residence. Canadian residents will be charged applicable taxes. Offer not valid in Quebec. This offer is limited to one order per household. Books received may not be as shown. Not valid for current subscribers to Harlequin Presents books. All orders subject to approval. Credit or debit balances in a customer's account(s) may be offset by any other outstanding balance owed by or to the customer. Please allow 4 to 6 weeks for delivery. Offer available while quantities last.

Your Privacy—The Reader Service is committed to protecting your privacy. Our Privacy Policy is available online at www.ReaderService.com or upon request from the Reader Service. We make a portion of our mailing list available to reputable third parties that offer products we believe may interest you. If you prefer that we not exchange your name with third parties, or if you wish to clarify or modify your communication preferences, please visit us at www.ReaderService.com/consumerchoice or write to us at Reader Service Preference Service, P.O. Box 9062, Buffalo, NY 14240-9062. Include your complete name and address.

HP20

If you purchased this book without a cover you should be aware
that this book is stolen property. It was reported as "unsold and
destroyed" to the publisher, and neither the author nor the
publisher has received any payment for this "stripped book."

Recycling programs
for this product may
not exist in your area.

ISBN-13: 978-0-373-62348-8

The Last Single Garrett

Copyright © 2017 by Brenda Harlen

All rights reserved. Except for use in any review, the reproduction or
utilization of this work in whole or in part in any form by any electronic,
mechanical or other means, now known or hereinafter invented, including
xerography, photocopying and recording, or in any information storage
or retrieval system, is forbidden without the written permission of the
publisher, Harlequin Enterprises Limited, 225 Duncan Mill Road,
Don Mills, Ontario M3B 3K9, Canada.

This is a work of fiction. Names, characters, places and incidents are
either the product of the author's imagination or are used fictitiously,
and any resemblance to actual persons, living or dead, business
establishments, events or locales is entirely coincidental.

This edition published by arrangement with Harlequin Books S.A.

For questions and comments about the quality of this book,
please contact us at CustomerService@Harlequin.com.

® and TM are trademarks of Harlequin Enterprises Limited or its
corporate affiliates. Trademarks indicated with ® are registered in the
United States Patent and Trademark Office, the Canadian Intellectual
Property Office and in other countries.

Printed in U.S.A.

The inadvertent contact made him groan.

Tristyn backed up. "You're in my space." When Josh didn't step away, she said, "Could you please get out of my space?"

"I could..." Instead, he stepped forward, breaching the distance between them.

"Twelve years," he murmured as he caught her chin in his hand. "It's a long time to wonder, don't you think?"

"I guess that depends on what you're wondering." Her tone was neutral but he caught her breathlessness.

"The same thing you are."

She was trembling. Not with fear, she realized. With desire. But going down that path with Josh now would be dangerous. Still, she played along.

"And what is that?" she asked.

He didn't say the words. He simply brushed her lips with his.

And with that kiss, any thought of resistance fizzled away. In that moment there was only Josh. And the intoxicating sensation of his kiss.

Twelve years ago she would've given anything to experience this. Twelve years ago she'd been totally unprepared for this. Even now, she wasn't sure what to do with the desire that pulsed through her veins.

All she knew was that if she touched him now, she wouldn't be able to stop.

* * *

THOSE ENGAGING GARRETTS!—
The Carolina Cousins

Dear Reader,

As the mother of teenage sons, I sometimes find myself scratching my head over the things they say and do—which reinforces my belief that men and women are indeed from different planets. My brother is in a similar situation with three young daughters, and that gave me an idea...

Josh Slater has no interest in marriage or children—and no clue what to do with the three little girls who are left in his care for the summer. Then Tristyn Garrett shows up at his door.

While Tristyn would never turn away from a friend in need, she has concerns about spending too much time with the man who was the (not-so-secret) object of her schoolgirl fantasies. On the other hand, maybe a summer fling is just what Tristyn needs to get over her longtime crush on Josh...

But playing house makes Josh appreciate the benefits of home and family—and yearn for the forever after he's never admitted that he's always wanted with Tristyn...

I hope you enjoy reading their story as much as I enjoyed writing it!

All the best,

Brenda Harlen

PS: Although Tristyn is indeed *The Last Single Garrett*, I hope you look forward to meeting the new cast of characters in my next miniseries Match Made in Haven, coming soon from Harlequin Special Edition!

Brenda Harlen is a former attorney who once had the privilege of appearing before the Supreme Court of Canada. The practice of law taught her a lot about the world and reinforced her determination to become a writer—because in fiction, she could promise a happy ending! Now she is an award-winning, national bestselling author of more than thirty titles for Harlequin. You can keep up-to-date with Brenda on Facebook and Twitter or through her website, brendaharlen.com.

Books by Brenda Harlen

Harlequin Special Edition

Those Engaging Garretts!

Baby Talk & Wedding Bells
Building the Perfect Daddy
Two Doctors & a Baby
The Bachelor Takes a Bride
A Forever Kind of Family
The Daddy Wish
A Wife for One Year
The Single Dad's Second Chance
A Very Special Delivery
His Long-Lost Family
From Neighbors...to Newlyweds?

Montana Mavericks: The Baby Bonanza

The More Mavericks, The Merrier!

Montana Mavericks:
What Happened at the Wedding?

Merry Christmas, Baby Maverick!

Visit the Author Profile page
at Harlequin.com for more titles.

For my readers—thank you!
XO

Chapter One

Tristyn Garrett didn't get paid to keep tabs on Josh Slater. Though her responsibilities at Garrett/Slater Racing seemed ever growing and changing, that wasn't one of them. So when Dave Barkov came into the building for his nine-thirty meeting with her too-sexy-for-his-own-good boss, she buzzed Josh's office. As a co-owner of the race team, Josh didn't always keep regular hours, but he was always there when he needed to be.

So why wasn't he there now?

"Excuse me for a minute," she said to Mr. Barkov, and made her way down the hall to Josh's office. The door was open, but the lights were off and the chair behind his desk was empty. His computer, which was always on, was flashing a reminder of the meeting with Dave Barkov, which Josh wasn't there to see.

Across the hall, her cousin's office was also empty, but she knew that Daniel was at the wind tunnel with Ren D'Alesio and his crew chief. She had received no communication from Josh to explain his absence.

Ordinarily she wouldn't worry about where he was, what he was doing or even who he was with, but Mr. Barkov was a potential new sponsor and this tour of the facili-

ties in Charisma, North Carolina, had been set up weeks ago. She knew because she'd set it up, after ensuring that the date and time worked for Josh. Right now, she was silently cursing the fact that she worked for him.

Their relationship was a mostly, if not strictly, professional one. Josh had been friends with her cousin Daniel for as long as she could remember, and over the past several years, he'd become a regular fixture at family events. He was, in many ways, like another cousin to her, except that she got along really well with all her cousins and her relationship with Josh wasn't always so amicable.

At the shop, they worked well together because each was focused on the performance of their respective duties. But away from GSR, there was often an uncomfortable… friction…between them.

She blamed Josh for that friction. He seemed to enjoy saying and doing things for the sole purpose of riling her, and even aware of that fact, she couldn't always control her reactions. Her sisters liked to tease that it was sexual tension and suggested that Tristyn could alleviate the problem by getting naked with Josh, but that wasn't going to happen—no way, no how, not ever.

But his failure to show up for a scheduled meeting with a new sponsor was completely out of character. Because as much as she occasionally accused him of being immature and unreliable, when it came to the business aspects of GSR, he was the poster boy for responsibility. Of course, he'd sunk a large portion of his own money—courtesy of his interest in Slater Industries, the company owned and operated by his parents—into the business and had convinced her cousin to do the same.

While Mr. Barkov waited, Tristyn called Josh's cell phone. She also sent a text message and an email, but he didn't respond to any of her attempts at communication. So she put a smile on her face and apologized to the spon-

sor, explaining that both the team's owners were tied up in a meeting elsewhere and offering to either reschedule or give him the promised tour of the facilities herself.

Mr. Barkov opted for the tour.

Two hours later, when he had finally gone and Daniel had returned from his meeting, she gave a perfunctory knock on her cousin's open door before she stepped through it and into his office. "Where the hell is he?"

Daniel looked up from his computer screen, his dark brows drawing together. "Who?"

She rolled her eyes. "The Slater half of Garrett/Slater Racing."

"I haven't seen him yet this morning," Daniel admitted.

"Because he's AWOL," Tristyn said, not even trying to hide her irritation.

"A few hours late is hardly AWOL," he chided.

"It's not a few hours," she argued. "Nobody has heard a single word from him since he left the track Saturday afternoon."

"He said something about having to deal with a family crisis," her cousin told her.

Concern immediately edged aside her irritation. "What kind of family crisis?"

Daniel shrugged. "I didn't ask. I figured that came under the heading of 'personal' business, which means it's none of mine—and none of yours, either."

Tristyn considered that for a minute before nodding in acknowledgment of the point. "Okay—it's none of my business," she agreed. "But I think you should call him."

"Why?"

"Because I've tried calling, texting and emailing, with no response, so I'm wondering if there's a reason that he's ignoring me."

Her cousin's brows winged up. "Is there?"

"Not that I'm aware of," she said. "But he's never ig-

nored my communications or been out of touch for so long before."

Daniel hit the speakerphone button, then punched in his friend's number. The call went immediately to voice mail—as each of hers had done.

You've reached Josh Slater. Please leave a message and I'll get back to you.

The beep sounded, then Daniel began to speak. "Hey, Josh. Give me a call when you get this message. I've got Tris in my office with a worried look on her face because she can't get in touch with you."

"I'm only worried that I'll have to cover for him when Dave Barkov shows up to meet the crew and tour the facilities," she interjected. "Oh, wait—I already did."

Daniel disconnected the call and slid her a look. "And you wonder why he might be ignoring you," he noted drily.

"He blew off a meeting with a potential sponsor," she said again.

"He'll check in soon," her cousin assured her, but she suspected he was trying to convince himself as much as her.

"Let me know when he does," she suggested.

Tristyn went back to her desk. As the administrative assistant and head of PR for the team, she had more than enough work to keep herself busy for the rest of the day. By three o'clock, when Josh hadn't checked in with her or returned Daniel's call, she picked up her purse and stopped by her cousin's office again.

"I'm going to detour past his place on my way home," she said.

Daniel glanced at his watch, frowned. "You're really worried about him, aren't you?"

Maybe she was a little concerned, because it wasn't like Josh to be out of touch. The man practically lived with his phone in his hand, answering calls when they came in

and responding to emails and text messages right away. But she wasn't going to admit her concern to her cousin.

"I'm annoyed," she said, because that was true, too. "I had to work through my lunch today to make up for the time I spent with your sponsor because Josh was a no-show."

"I'm sure Dave Barkov was more grateful than annoyed," her cousin said. "After all, you're a lot prettier than Josh is."

She kissed his cheek. "I'll see you tomorrow."

As she drove toward Josh's condo, she thought about her cousin's parting remark. While it was true that no one would ever apply the "pretty" label to Josh Slater, there were several others that came to mind. At six feet two inches, with dark blond hair, smoky gray eyes and a mouth that promised all kinds of wicked pleasure, he was tempting. Tantalizing. Hot.

Oh, yes, he was very definitely hot.

And she'd already been burned.

Josh Slater stared at the disaster zone that used to be his kitchen and tried to decide if he should wade into the mess or call a hazmat team. In addition to the pile of dishes from breakfast and lunch, there was a long drip of dried pancake batter on the oven door, toast crumbs on the counter, Cheerios on the floor and a pot with the congealed remnants of mac and cheese stuck to the bottom. He waded into the mess and had just filled the sink with soapy water when a knock sounded at the door.

He wasn't expecting any more visitors—he'd already had more than he'd anticipated this weekend and wasn't eager to add to the number. He decided to ignore the summons and pretend he wasn't home.

The knock sounded again, louder and more insistent this time. He frowned, thinking that if a knock could ex-

hibit personality traits, this one was brisk and impatient, very much like…Tristyn Garrett.

Because she was on his mind, he wasn't the least bit surprised to hear her voice come through the door. "If you're in there, Josh, you better open this door before I call 911 and have the fire department break it down."

Since she didn't usually issue idle threats, he wiped his hands on a towel and opened the door. "What are you doing here, Tristyn?"

"Nice greeting." Her deep green eyes narrowed as they skimmed over him, silently assessing. "You look like hell."

He scrubbed a hand over his face, felt the rasp of stubble on his jaw. Apparently he'd forgotten to shave this morning. But at least he'd showered. He was pretty sure he'd showered.

Tristyn, by contrast, looked stunning. With her slender build, deep green eyes and perfectly shaped mouth, she could easily have made a fortune in front of a camera. Of course, as a Garrett, she was already heir to a fortune. Still, she worked as hard as anyone else at GSR, often exceeding even his expectations—as she'd done again by showing up at his door.

"I didn't get much sleep last night," he finally responded to her comment.

He saw the cool derision in her eyes fade. "Are you sick?" She took a step forward and lifted her hand as if to check his temperature.

He stepped back, forcing her to drop her hand. Since she'd been enticed by her cousin Daniel to work for Garrett/Slater Racing two years earlier, he'd been forced to acknowledge that his best friend's little cousin was all grown up. But she was still his best friend's cousin, which meant that even if she looked like every man's fantasy, she was off-limits to him.

That knowledge hadn't stopped him from dreaming of

her hands on him—frequent and explicit dreams. But he didn't want her touching him because she felt sorry for him. It was much better if they both respected the walls she'd built between them.

"No, I'm not sick," he told her. "I'm just exhausted from trying to keep up with three very demanding females."

As he'd expected, the casual—and yes, deliberately provocative—words erased any hint of sympathy from her pretty green eyes. Now they glittered like emeralds—hard and sharp. "Seriously? You blew off a scheduled meeting with a sponsor because you're recovering from a weekend orgy?"

Before he could respond, a tiny voice piped up to ask, "Whatsa orgy?"

Ah, hell.

Josh cringed at the sound of the adult word coming out of the little girl's mouth as he turned to face his five-year-old niece. "I thought you were watching a movie in the bedroom," he said.

Emily shook her head. "I don't like the movie—it's scary."

"It's a princess movie," he pointed out. "How scary can it be?" Although he'd never seen it himself, he'd found it in one of the half dozen suitcases his sister had dumped in his foyer along with her three daughters, so he'd assumed it was suitable for the kids.

"It's scary," she insisted.

"This is my niece Emily," Josh said. "Emily, this is Tristyn."

"Hi," the little girl said shyly.

Tristyn crouched down so that she was at eye level with the little girl—inadvertently providing him with a perfect view down the open vee of her blouse. And the view was perfect: sweetly rounded curves peeking over the edge of

delicate white lace. He didn't look away until the lower part of his anatomy began to stir with appreciation.

"What movie are you watching?" Tristyn asked.

"*The Princess and the Frog.*"

"Are you at the part where the prince goes to see the witch doctor?" she asked.

Emily nodded solemnly, her big blue eyes wide and worried.

"That is a scary part," Tristyn admitted. "But I watched the movie just a couple of weeks ago with my niece, so I can tell you that the scary part will be over soon, then there are some funny parts and the movie has a happy ending."

Emily chewed on her lower lip. "For real?"

"For real," Tristyn promised.

"You wanna watch the movie?" the little girl asked.

"I would love to watch the movie," she said. "But I need to talk to your uncle for a little bit first, okay?"

"Okay," Emily agreed, and reluctantly headed back to the bedroom where the "scary" movie was playing.

Tristyn stood up again, tugging down the hem of the short skirt that had ridden up her thighs. She had spectacular legs to go with her tempting feminine curves—an almost irresistible package.

"Is she one of the females who kept you up all night?" she asked him now.

"Yeah," he admitted, with obvious reluctance. "Emily is my sister's middle daughter. She has two sisters, Charlotte, who is a couple years older, and Hanna, who is younger."

Tristyn curled her hand into a fist and punched him in the arm. She put some force behind the motion, but her effort glanced off his biceps.

He lifted a brow. "What was that for?"

"Because you're an idiot." She opened her hand, flexed her fingers. "Jeez—your arm is as hard as your head."

"You've often accused me of being an idiot," he pointed

out, ignoring her latter comment. "But it's never driven you to violence before."

She just shook her head. "What is wrong with you that you would rather let me believe you spent the weekend participating in an orgy than admit you were taking care of your sister's kids?"

"Maybe I didn't want to disillusion you."

"Into thinking that you had a heart in addition to your hormones?"

He shrugged. "We both know that our relationship is… safer—" he decided "—when you don't have any illusions about me being a nice guy."

"Don't worry—discovering that you spent a weekend with your nieces isn't going to change my opinion of you."

"Good to know," he said.

"Although I am curious about why they're here—and where your sister is."

"Long story."

"And why haven't you been answering your phone?" she asked.

"Because I can't find it," he admitted.

"You're kidding."

He shook his head. "I remember answering a text message when I was scooping up ice cream for the girls last night, but I haven't seen it since then."

"I assume you've looked in the kitchen?"

He hesitated, just a fraction of a second. "Yeah."

"That didn't sound very convincing."

"The kitchen is a bit of a mess right now," he admitted. "But I'm hoping the phone will turn up as I clear things away."

"I'll give you a hand," she offered, already moving toward the kitchen.

Josh followed, enjoying the sexy sway of her hips—

and nearly ran right into the back of her when she halted abruptly in the doorway.

She slowly turned to face him. "This is a *bit* of a mess?"

"I didn't have a chance to clear away breakfast dishes before it was time for lunch," he admitted.

"But you have a dishwasher," she pointed out.

"Still filled with clean dishes from yesterday."

She shook her head despairingly. "I'll put those away while you get the rest of this chaos organized."

He should have refused her offer of help, but the truth was, he was grateful. He was also appreciative of the fact that every time she bent forward, he could see down her top. Because Tristyn Garrett might be a pain in his ass a lot of the time, but she had a body that seemed to have been designed to fuel male fantasies.

She removed the cutlery basket and set it on the counter, then paused. He gestured to the drawer on the other side of the dishwasher, assuming that she didn't know where to put the clean forks and knives. But she made no move to open it.

"Um…Josh."

He immediately shifted his gaze from the nicely rounded curve of her butt to her face, hoping like hell she hadn't seen him looking where he had no business looking. "What?"

She lifted something out of the basket and held it up. "I found your phone."

Chapter Two

While his response was a harshly muttered four-letter expletive, Tristyn had to press her lips together so that she didn't laugh. Because it wasn't funny.

Well, it was *kind of* funny.

Because Josh's phone was as essential to him as the air he breathed into his lungs and the blood that flowed through his veins. A fact that was evidenced by the apoplectic expression on his face.

He snatched the device out of her hand and marched purposefully down the hallway. Curious to see how he would handle this incident, Tristyn followed, her steps faltering when she realized she was in the doorway of the master bedroom.

Josh's bedroom.

Part of her wanted to turn away, to let his private sanctuary remain private. Another part urged her to take a peek. That part won.

Her gaze moved around the space, noting the enormous king-size platform bed centered on the far wall and flanked by a set of night tables that matched the wardrobe, long dresser and entertainment stand. She glanced up at

the ceiling—nope, no mirrors. So maybe he wasn't quite the degenerate she'd always believed him to be.

And while there was no denying this room was a man's domain, the decor was simple but inviting. Walls painted in a pale neutral tone that reminded her of the sand on a pristine Caribbean beach; pale floors that she guessed were bamboo and that contrasted nicely with the dark walnut finish of the classic mission-style furniture she recognized from the Garrett catalog.

Usually a man's domain, she clarified, as her attention shifted to the three girls snuggled together on the bed, propped up on a mountain of pillows against the head-board. Emily—the one who hadn't wanted to watch the scary movie—was on the side closest to the door. In the middle was Hanna—a preschooler, Tristyn guessed, with big blue eyes focused on the screen and uneven blond pig-tails sprouting out of the sides of her head. On the far side was Charlotte—obviously the oldest sibling, also blond and blue-eyed, wearing ripped jeans and a black T-shirt with some kind of picture on the front that Tristyn couldn't see because the girl's arms were folded across her chest in a posture that she recognized as pure unhappy female attitude.

None of them paid any attention to their uncle. It was as if they weren't even aware that he was facing them from the foot of the bed. But that might be because they were all mesmerized by the animated feature playing on a tele-vision screen that was probably ten inches bigger than the one Tristyn had in her living room.

Josh scooped up the remote and thumbed a button to pause the movie, which finally succeeded in drawing the girls' eyes to him.

Charlotte opened her mouth as if to say something, then saw the phone in Josh's hand, slid a quick glance toward

the sister snuggled up beside her and closed it again without saying a word.

"Anyone?" Josh prompted.

"I talk," Hanna offered, crawling to the end of the mattress and reaching her hand up for the phone.

"That would be great, wouldn't it?" he said, his gaze moving over each of them in turn. "But someone put it in the dishwasher."

His littlest niece nodded solemnly. "Make it c'ean."

Tristyn saw a muscle in his jaw flex. "It didn't need to go in the dishwasher to be cleaned," he said through gritted teeth. "It was already clean."

This time Hanna shook her head. "I dwop ice cweam on it."

Josh blew out a frustrated breath and scrubbed his free hand over his face.

"You did say that you didn't want to find sticky fingerprints on any of your things," Charlotte pointed out in defense of her sibling.

"Meaning that I didn't want any of you to touch any of my things," he clarified.

His eldest niece shrugged. "Hanna tends to take things literally."

"She killed my phone."

The little girl looked up at him. "I so-wee, Unca Josh." She reached up to take the phone, puckered her lips and kissed the screen before handing it back to him. "All better?"

He sighed again as he dropped the now useless device into the side pocket of his cargo shorts, but one side of his mouth curved in a half smile. "It's not that easy, kiddo." He tapped a finger to his cheek. "You have to give a kiss here to make it all better."

She smiled and held her arms in the air. He slid one of his around her torso, and the natural ease with which he

lifted the little girl onto his hip made something inside Tristyn's chest flutter. She wasn't usually the type to get quivery over a man, but apparently seeing this strong, sexy male cuddle with a sweet little girl was all it took for her to feel warm and fuzzy inside.

Hanna wrapped both her arms around his neck and gave him a smacking kiss on the cheek. Then she drew her head back, her nose wrinkling with obvious displeasure. "You're scwatchy," she told him.

"Yeah, I forgot to shave this morning," he admitted, setting her on the bed again.

She immediately returned to the pile of pillows, then smiled at him again. "Movie?" she asked hopefully.

"After your movie is done and the kitchen is clean, we're going to have to go out so that I can buy a new phone," Josh told them, as he picked up the remote again.

Tristyn turned to follow him back down the hall. "If I hadn't seen it with my own eyes, I never would have believed it."

He glanced over his shoulder. "Believed what?"

"That you're a marshmallow."

He stopped then and turned to face her, his brows drawing together over smoke-colored eyes. "I am not."

"Yes, you are," she insisted. "You're all soft and squishy—like the Stay Puft Marshmallow Man."

Those eyes narrowed dangerously, the only warning she had before he took two slow and deliberate steps forward. She automatically took two steps back. He laid his palms flat on the wall on either side of her, then leaned in, so that his body brushed against hers. His undeniably lean and very hard body.

"Do I feel soft and squishy to you?" he asked, his mouth close to her ear.

She lifted her palms to his chest, where his heart was beating in a rhythm much steadier than her own, to hold

him at a distance. She had to moisten her suddenly dry lips with her tongue before she could reply, but she managed to keep her tone light and casual when she said, "In here." And tapped her fingers against his rock hard chest. "Your heart is soft and squishy."

"Because I didn't yell at a three-year-old?" he challenged.

"You not only didn't yell," she pointed out. "You melted. That little girl looked at you with those big blue eyes and said, 'I so-wee, Unca Josh,' and it was as if you completely forgot she destroyed an eight hundred dollar phone."

"It's just a phone," he said, conveniently ignoring the monetary value.

"Well, at least now I know why you didn't answer any of my calls, text messages or emails today," she noted.

He was still crowding her, standing so close that she could feel the heat emanating from his body. So close she had only to lean forward to touch her mouth to his strong square jaw. Her lips tingled with anticipation; her body whispered "yes, please." She clamped her lips firmly together and pressed herself back against the wall.

"Were you worried about me, Tris?" he asked, the silky tone of his voice sliding over her like a caress.

"No," she denied. Lied. "I was annoyed that I had to give Dave Barkov the tour of GSR."

"I never doubted that you could handle it," he told her.

"That's not the point," she said, ducking under his arm and walking away.

He, naturally, followed. "Do you want an apology? Okay—I'm sorry I was out of touch for a few hours."

She shook her head as she returned to the kitchen to resume the task she'd abandoned earlier. "You don't get it, do you? It's not just that you didn't tell anyone you wouldn't be at work today—you didn't even tell your friends what was going on here."

He held her gaze for a long moment. "Is that what we are, Tris…friends?" he asked, in that same silky voice that could make any woman go weak in the knees.

Any woman but her, of course, because she was immune to the considerable charms of Josh Slater.

"Maybe not," she finally said, determined not to give any hint of the feelings churning inside her. "A friend probably would have known you have three nieces."

"It's not something that often comes up in conversation," he pointed out. "And since my sister moved to Seattle when Charlotte was a baby, I don't get to see them very often."

"That's why you go to Washington every Christmas," she realized.

"Not every Christmas." He picked up the soapy cloth to wipe down the stovetop. "But I go when I can."

She finished unloading the clean dishes and began to load the dirty ones. "So why are they here now?"

"Lucinda's manager decided, at the last minute, to send her to Spain. The company she works for is setting up a new distribution center there and her pregnant boss, who was supposed to supervise the setup and train the staff, was recently put on bed rest by her doctor, so the company tapped Lucy to go."

"Why did I always think your sister worked at Slater Industries?"

"My older sister, Miranda, does," he told her. "She lives in London with her husband and their kids and manages the office there."

Which meant that he probably didn't get to see them very often, either, and perhaps explained why he was always hanging out at Garrett family events. Something to think about.

"How did you end up with so many dishes from two meals?" she asked, as she continued to fill the dishwasher.

"Each of the girls wanted something different for breakfast," he admitted.

"And you indulged them," she guessed.

"Well, Emily was up first and she asked for dippy eggs with toast sticks, so I figured I would make eggs for everyone. Then Charlotte woke up and informed me she doesn't eat eggs—except if they're in pancake batter. So while Emily was eating her eggs, I found a recipe for pancakes and started making those for Charlotte. By this time, Hanna was awake, too. But she just wanted cereal and seemed perfectly happy with the Cheerios I put on the table in front of her—until I made the mistake of pouring milk into the bowl."

Tristyn's lips curved as she pictured the scene he'd described. "Did she scream like a banshee?"

"I thought the neighbors would be knocking on my door—or Family Services," he admitted.

"Kylie went through a dry cereal stage," she told him. "Except for Rice Krispies, because they 'talk' when you put milk on them."

"And this—" he said, scraping the remnants of a pot into the garbage can "—is what's left of the mac and cheese they all had for lunch."

"Well, that's a score," she noted. "Pleasing all three of them with the same food."

"Except that Charlotte likes hers with ketchup mixed into it, Emily doesn't like it with ketchup at all and Hanna's ketchup has to be squirted on top of the pasta in the shape of a smiley face."

Tristyn smiled at that image, too. "And how long are they staying?"

"Eight to ten weeks."

Her brows winged up. "What are you going to do with them for two months?"

He wiped his hands on a towel, then folded it over the

handle of the oven door. "I'm thinking I should talk to my grandparents, to see if they're willing to take them for the summer."

"Didn't your grandmother just celebrate her eightieth birthday a few weeks back?"

He nodded.

"And your grandfather's a couple of years older than she is," Tristyn pointed out.

"Yeah," he admitted. "But they both play golf several times a week."

"Which is impressive," she acknowledged, "but still not as physically demanding as chasing after three kids. And considering that your sister entrusted *you* with the care of her children, I don't think she'd be too happy to learn that you dumped them on someone else."

"So what am I supposed to do? Hire a sitter to take care of them when I'm not here? Which is most of the time during race season," he reminded her.

She shook her head. "That's not an ideal situation, either."

"Do you have a better idea?"

"Not off the top of my head," she admitted, closing the dishwasher.

"Well, let me know if you think of something," he said. "They've hardly been here twenty-four hours, and I'm desperate enough to consider almost anything."

As Tristyn watched the last half hour of the movie with Josh's nieces, she tried not to think about the fact that she was in Josh's bed. *On* Josh's bed, she hastily amended. As if that clarification made any difference.

She wondered how many women had passed through that same doorway, laid on this same bed. Then pushed the question aside, deciding she didn't want to know. Still, she felt as if she shouldn't be here. She knew now why he

hadn't shown up at work today, and why he would be jug-gling his schedule for the rest of the week—and possibly the rest of the summer. And now that her questions were answered, there was no reason for her to stay.

No reason except that she'd made an impulsive prom-ise to a little girl. A little girl who was even now pressed against her side, her face turned away from the screen as the Shadow Man's spirit was taken away by the demons. But truthfully, her promise to Emily was only part of it. She was also intrigued by the opportunity to glimpse a corner of Josh's personal life and curious to see him in-teract with the little girls.

She vaguely remembered Lucy Slater from Hillfield Academy. Josh's younger sister had been two years be-hind Tristyn—a popular girl who liked to party more than study. She got kicked out midway through her sophomore year and wound up pregnant a couple years after that. By that time, Tristyn was mostly keeping her distance from Josh, so any information she had was secondhand from her cousin Daniel. There had apparently been a hasty wed-ding, and an even hastier divorce.

Obviously Lucy had gone on to have two more children and was now the mother of three beautiful girls. Three beautiful girls who were in Josh's care for the summer. Tristyn smiled a little at the thought of how the respon-sibilities would put a crimp in his usually active social life. Maybe she could offer to help with the girls, because it might be fun to have a front-row seat to the fireworks while he figured out how to mesh his life with the needs and demands of his three nieces.

Except that spending too much time in close proxim-ity to Josh was a risk. Sure, they were friends—or at least friendly—most of the time, but there was also that un-comfortable friction that occasionally reared up between them—seemingly more frequently in recent years.

As Daniel's best friend and business partner, Josh was almost an honorary Garrett. Because his parents traveled a lot to oversee the various offices and interests of Slater Industries—a multinational investment company—he was often on his own for national holidays, and Daniel's mom, Jane, always included him in whatever plans the Garretts made. As a result, Tristyn had spent a lot more time with him over the past two decades than she'd sometimes wanted to.

In many ways, Josh had been like another cousin, and almost as bossy and annoying as most of her cousins were—at least from the perspective of a ten-year-old girl who hated to be excluded from their activities because of her age and her gender. She didn't look at him any differently than she looked at Daniel or Justin or Nathan or Ryan. Not until the summer after she'd turned thirteen, when suddenly being around him made her heart beat just a little bit faster. And she would blush and stutter in response whenever he spoke to her.

Her sisters teased her about her crush on Daniel's best friend, which she vehemently denied. He was just an idiot boy like the rest of their idiot cousins and all the other idiot boys she knew. Of course, Lauryn and Jordyn didn't believe her denials. And when Tristyn saw Josh making out with Missy Harlowe (aka Missy Harlot) beneath the bleachers of the football field, she felt as if she'd been stabbed in the heart. This unexpectedly fierce reaction forced her to acknowledge the truth of her feelings, if only to herself. She was in love with Josh Slater.

Later, she'd realized that what she'd thought was love was only an infatuation. Regardless of what she called it, there was no denying that he'd been her first real crush. And seeing him with other girls—and there were *a lot* of other girls—had broken her heart each and every time. She cried when he graduated from Hillfield Academy, because

she would no longer see him at school every day. And she cried again when he went away to college, certain that her broken heart would never heal.

By the time Josh came home with Daniel for Thanksgiving, she had a boyfriend. Mitch Harlowe—Missy's younger brother—was a varsity athlete and an honor roll student with curly brown hair and eyes the color of melted chocolate. And he looked at her in a way that Josh never had—as if she was the most beautiful girl in the world and he was the luckiest boy in the world just to be with her.

She dated Mitch for more than a year and a half, but they never went "all the way." She was tempted, but she didn't want to be one of "those girls." They did a lot of other things, and Mitch was mostly patient with her—and undeniably relieved when she suggested that, maybe, after prom, they could finally "do it." He was first in line the day prom tickets went on sale.

She smiled a little at the memory, but her smile faded when her thoughts skipped ahead to that night—and an ending that neither of them had planned.

"You were right," Emily said, drawing Tristyn's attention back to the screen where the human-again couple were sealing their wedding vows with a kiss. "It does have a happy ending."

"It's not over yet," Charlotte told her sister. "It's not over until they show all the names of the people in the movie."

But a few minutes later, it was over.

"Okay, girls," Josh said from the doorway. "Time to get your shoes on."

"That's my cue to head out," Tristyn said to them.

Josh looked slightly panicked as she made her way toward the door. "Do you have to go?"

"You're leaving, too," she pointed out.

"But I was thinking—hoping," he admitted, "that you might come with us."

She didn't delude herself into thinking that he wanted her company. The simple and obvious truth was that he had no clue what to do with the three little girls left in his care and he was desperate for help with them. And yet she couldn't resist turning his own words around on him.

"Why is that?" she asked, blatantly fluttering her eyelashes. "Does keeping up with three females require more stamina than you possess?"

Chapter Three

Josh slid an arm around her back and drew her closer. So close that her breasts rubbed against his chest. Even through the layers of clothing that separated them, she felt her nipples tighten and strain against the lace of her bra. She lifted her eyes to his, and the intensity in his gray gaze nearly made her shiver.

"Do you want a demonstration of my stamina?" he asked.

She wanted to push him away, but she wouldn't give him the satisfaction of knowing that his touch affected her. Instead, she rolled her eyes. "Not even in your dreams."

His lips curved into a slow, dangerous smile. "You have no control over my dreams."

"Then definitely not in any version of reality," she amended.

"Are you sure about that?" he asked, finally releasing her.

"Positive," she said, taking just a half step back so that she could breathe without his proximity short-circuiting her brain.

And clearly her brain had short-circuited or she wouldn't have baited him in such a way. Because even if she was no

longer a teenager experiencing her first infatuation, compared to Josh Slater she was still a novice when it came to the games that men and women played.

"In that case, there's no reason you would object to accompanying me and the girls," he suggested.

He was right. For the past dozen years, most of their public interactions had been civil—if occasionally adversarial. It was only when they were alone together—which she tried to avoid, if at all possible—that they tiptoed around one another. But if she went along, they would have the barrier of three little girls to prevent them from rubbing one another the wrong way and creating a familiar and dangerously tempting friction.

"Let's go get you a phone," she agreed.

As soon as they stepped through the doors of the electronics store, Charlotte and Emily made a beeline toward the video games on display. Josh opened his mouth to call them back just as a young salesman stepped up and Hanna announced, "I has to go potty."

With an apologetic glance toward the store employee, he shifted his attention to his youngest niece. "Why didn't you go before we left home?"

"I didn't has to go before," she said with unerring logic. "I has to go now."

He looked at the salesman, who shook his head. "Sorry, we don't have any public restrooms here."

"There's a coffee shop next door," Tristyn pointed out. "I'll take her there."

"Thank you," Josh said.

As they turned around and went back out the door, he caught up with Charlotte and Emily. "You can stay here to look at the games or whatever," he told them. "But stay together."

"Okay," they agreed, each already with a controller in hand and attention fixed on the demo game system.

The hopeful employee was still hovering beside him—no doubt working on commission. "Can I help you find something, sir?"

"I need a new phone," he admitted, and handed over his dead—albeit squeaky clean—iPhone 7.

Tristyn returned with Hanna just as the tech guy—who had been attempting to work magic on Josh's SIM card—gave him the bad news: none of the information could be salvaged. Which wasn't really a surprise but a disappointment nonetheless.

"All of those names and numbers…gone?" Tristyn asked, feigning horror. "The cute little messages with kissy-face emojis from all of your girlfriends…gone? Your electronic little black book…gone?"

He slid her a look. "No worries—I have a real little black book for all of the important names and numbers."

"I have no doubt," she said.

Josh passed his credit card to the salesman. A few minutes later, he walked out of the store with his new phone, which indicated the time to be 5:26 p.m.

"I'm hungry, Uncle Josh," Emily said.

"It's not even five thirty," he noted. "What time do you guys usually eat?"

"Five thirty," Charlotte told him.

"I guess that means it's dinnertime," he acknowledged, mentally inventorying the contents of his refrigerator to determine if he had anything left to feed them. "What do you like to eat?"

"Pizza," Emily announced.

"Chicken fingers," Charlotte countered.

"S'ghetti," Hanna chimed in.

"Well, at least we have a consensus," he said drily.

"What's a sen-sus?" Emily asked.

"It means agreement," he told her.

Her little brow furrowed.

"He was being sarcastic," her older sister explained.

"Oh," Emily said. Then, "What's scar-tas-tic?"

"Sarcastic." Tristyn enunciated the word for her. "And it's your uncle Josh's way of trying to be funny, but he's not."

"S'ghetti," Hanna said again.

"You had pasta for lunch," Josh reminded her.

"Not s'ghetti," she argued.

"What's your vote, Tristyn?"

A peek at her watch made her grimace. "Actually, I—" she glanced at the girls' hopeful expressions "—I think going out to eat would allow everyone to choose what they wanted."

"And it would give my kitchen a reprieve," he agreed.

"I just need to make a quick call first," Tristyn said.

He offered his new phone.

"I've got my own," she reminded him, tapping the screen as she stepped away.

"Can we go eat now?" Emily implored. "I'm hungry."

"Me, too," Charlotte said.

"As soon as Tristyn's finished with her phone call, we'll go." He didn't pretend he wasn't eavesdropping on her call, and though he heard only bits and pieces of one side of the conversation, it was enough pieces to put together and figure out she was canceling plans for dinner with someone else.

"You had a date," he said, when she'd disconnected the call.

She nodded.

"You didn't have to cancel," he told her, though he was secretly pleased that she'd done so. And grateful that she would be sticking around to help him out with the girls for a little while longer.

"Well, my car's still at your place, and by the time we drove back there and then I drove home to change, I would have been late, anyway."

"I'm sure your date wouldn't mind waiting…especially if you promised to make it up to him later."

"So what's the plan for dinner?" she asked, deliberately ignoring his comment.

The question was answered with renewed calls for "pizza," "chicken fingers" and "s'ghetti."

"All of those are on the menu at Valentino's," Tristyn pointed out.

"But what do you want to eat?" he asked her, as he led the girls back to his truck.

"Are you buying?"

"It seems the least I can do to thank you for your help today," he told her.

"Then I want steak," she decided. "A nice thick juicy steak."

He buckled Hanna into her booster seat, then stepped back so that Emily could climb into hers while Tristyn opened the door on the other side for Charlotte. "From Valentino's?"

"No, from The Grille. So I'll have the seven-layer lasagna tonight and take an IOU for the steak."

He lifted a brow. "You're trying to wrangle a date, aren't you?"

"Ha!"

"Is that where you were supposed to go for dinner tonight?" he asked, settling behind the wheel and securing his own seat belt.

"I'm not discussing my plans with you," she told him.

"Who was your date with?"

"Refer to previous answer."

He should let it go. It really was none of his business, but he was curious. "Was it a first date?"

"Refer to previous answer," she said again.

"Because I haven't heard you mention that you were dating anyone."

"Should I add my social engagements to the itinerary of GSR's monthly meetings?"

"That would be helpful," he agreed.

"Well, it's not happening," she told him.

Her response didn't surprise him. What surprised him was how much he sincerely wanted answers to his questions. But for now, he decided to be satisfied with the knowledge that she'd canceled her date to have dinner with him.

The waitress introduced herself as Sydney, recited the daily specials as she handed out menus and filled their water glasses, then left them alone to peruse the offerings.

Valentino's didn't specifically have a children's menu, but they did offer child-sized portions of any of their entrées.

Charlotte frowned as she scanned the options. "There's no chicken fingers on the menu."

"The cook will make them," Tristyn assured her.

"How do you know?"

"Because he's made them for my niece before."

"I want pizza," Emily reminded them all.

Tristyn pointed to the section of the menu that listed the various options and toppings, but Emily wanted only cheese.

"Pep-ro-ni," Hanna said.

"You said you wanted spaghetti," Josh reminded her.

His youngest niece shook her head. "P'za."

"Pizza with pepperoni?" he asked, seeking clarification. She nodded, and then said, "I has to go potty."

"You just went when we were at the store," he reminded her.

"I has to go agin," she insisted.

He looked at Tristyn, who sighed. "This is the real reason you offered to buy me dinner, isn't it? So that you could escape bathroom duty."

"Well, I can't take her into the men's room, and there's no way I'm walking into the women's," he pointed out.

"I hafta go, too," Emily said.

"Charlotte?" Tristyn prompted.

She shook her head.

"Why don't you come, anyway, to wash up before dinner?" Tristyn suggested.

So she herded the three girls off to the ladies' room, leaving Josh alone at a table for five. Thankfully, he knew what everyone wanted, so when Sydney passed by the table again, he was able to place their order.

Charlotte and Hanna returned first, and Josh was settling his youngest niece into the booster seat again when Tristyn's sister Jordyn came over. Jordyn was married to Marco Palermo, whose grandparents had started serving pasta in the original downtown location of Valentino's almost fifty years earlier. Recently, Marco had spearheaded the expansion of their business with Valentino's II. He and his wife had also recently expanded their family with the addition of twin boys, who were now about nine months old.

"Gemma told me that Josh Slater had come in with four gorgeous females, which I thought was a little excessive—even for you." Jordyn winked at him before turning her focus to the girls.

"These are my nieces Charlotte and Hanna," he told her. "Emily must still be in the bathroom."

"She stuck her hands up under the faucet and sprayed water all over her shirt," Charlotte explained. "Tristyn's drying it off under the hand dryer."

Jordyn's brows lifted as she turned back to Josh. "My sister Tristyn?"

"She's the only Tristyn I know," he acknowledged.

"She was supposed to have a date with Rafe tonight." Then she shook her head. "Apparently her plans changed."

"That might be my fault," he acknowledged. "She saw that I was overwhelmed by the prospect of cooking another meal for three fussy kids and obviously took pity on me."

"We're not fussy," Charlotte interjected. "We just like what we like and don't like what we don't."

"Which is exactly what their mother used to say when she refused to eat what was put on the table," he acknowledged.

"How long have you been staying with Uncle Josh?" Jordyn asked Charlotte.

"We got here yesterday, and we're supposed to stay for the whole summer," she said, her glum tone clearly indicating her displeasure.

Josh wasn't overjoyed, either, but he couldn't see a way out of the situation for any of them. "My sister's in Spain on business for the next eight to ten weeks."

"The whole summer with Uncle Josh," Jordyn mused. "That should be...interesting."

"For all of us, I'm sure," he remarked drily.

But Charlotte was shaking her head. "He doesn't have any cool stuff *and* I had to sleep with Emily."

"In *my* bed," he pointed out. "While I slept on the sofa."

Jordyn chuckled softly. "Oh, yes, it will be an interesting summer."

"How are Henry and Liam?" he asked.

"If I had my phone handy, I'd bore you with a thousand pictures," she said, her deep green eyes—so similar to her sister's—suddenly going soft and dreamy. "They are the lights of my life."

"Along with your darling and devoted husband," Marco said from behind her.

Jordyn grinned as she glanced over her shoulder. "Along

with my darling and devoted husband," she dutifully intoned.

The aforementioned spouse slid an arm across her shoulders. "You said you wanted to have a quick word with Gemma while I went to the kitchen to grab a tray of lasagna for the potluck tomorrow, and when I came out of the kitchen, you were gone."

"Gemma told me that Josh was here, so I came over to say hi. And now I've met his nieces Charlotte and Hanna—and this must be Emily," she said, as his third niece and Tristyn made their way back to the table.

"And now we really have to go," Marco urged. "We've already been away longer than we planned and your mom has a ton of things to do before the picnic tomorrow, none of which she is getting done with Henry and Liam underfoot."

"You're right, we have to go," she agreed. But she gave her sister a quick hug before she turned to Josh again. "Are you taking the girls to the parade tomorrow?"

"I hadn't really thought about it," he admitted. But if he had, he would have answered with a resounding no. He'd barely been able to keep track of them in an electronics store; he didn't want to imagine the nightmare of trying to keep them together in the midst of the crowds that gathered to celebrate the Fourth of July.

"What parade?" Charlotte asked.

"The Independence Parade is part of Charisma's 'Food, Fun & Fireworks' celebration," Jordyn explained.

"I wanna see the fireworks," Charlotte told Josh.

"I wanna see the fun," Emily chimed in.

"I wanna see some food," Tristyn interjected. "Tonight. I'm starving."

"I starvin', too," Hanna said, clearly not wanting to be left out of the conversation.

"And Sydney's on her way with your food right now," Marco said, gently nudging his wife away from the table.

"See you at the park tomorrow," Jordyn called back over her shoulder, though Josh wasn't sure if she was talking to him or—more likely—her sister.

Charlotte polished off her chicken fingers and ate most of the fries on her plate; Emily ate two slices of the individual cheese pizza she'd wanted; and Hanna ate one slice of her pepperoni pizza—but only after picking off all the pepperoni—and half of Tristyn's garlic bread. Josh offered her some of the spaghetti that came with his chicken parmesan, which was what she'd originally wanted, but she wrinkled her nose and shook her head.

He was waiting for the check when Tristyn noticed that Hanna had fallen asleep at the table.

"Because she didn't have her nap at two o'clock," Charlotte said matter-of-factly. "And now she's going to be awake until midnight."

"How was I supposed to know that she should have a nap at two o'clock?" he wondered.

"It's in the book," his eldest niece informed him.

"And when did I have time to read the book?" he asked.

Charlotte just shrugged.

"The book?" Tristyn said.

"Is actually a binder," he told her. "Filled with about four hundred pages of instructions from my sister on what her daughters like and don't like, dosages for medications, if required, and apparently nap times."

"Only Hanna has a nap," Charlotte said. "Emily and me are too big for naps."

He looked at his youngest niece, her head flopped back against the chair. "What do you think the odds are of me getting her home and into bed without waking her up?" he asked Tristyn.

"Not anything that I'd wager on," she told him.

But when they got back to his condo, she guided Charlotte and Emily into the elevator while he carried Hanna. He laid her carefully on the narrow cot his sister had brought along with all their other paraphernalia, then helped Tristyn supervise while Emily and Charlotte had their baths and got ready for bed. By the time their teeth were brushed, it was almost eight o'clock—and he was ready for bed, too.

And then, as soon as the other girls were tucked in, Hanna woke up, and he got to go through the whole routine again with her. But being ready for bed didn't mean that she was ready to sleep. In fact, she seemed completely revived after her "nap" and ready to play.

"I'm thinking Charlotte was right," Tristyn told him. "She's going to be awake now until midnight."

"Lucky me." He sighed. "And the other two will probably be awake at the crack of dawn, like they were this morning."

"You should take them to the parade tomorrow," she said.

"Why?"

"Because I think they'll enjoy it, and you know the whole Garrett clan will be at the park to help you keep an eye on them afterward."

"I almost forgot tomorrow was the Fourth of July," he admitted.

"It follows the third every year," she pointed out.

He laughed softly. "That's assuming I knew today was the third. I'm not even sure what day of the week it is."

"Monday," she said, heading toward the door.

"Thanks for all of your help," he said.

"You're welcome."

"I hope canceling your date tonight wasn't a problem."

She shook her head. "I'll see him tomorrow."

That revelation surprised him. "You guys must be pretty serious if you're introducing Rafe to your family," he commented.

"He's already met my family," she said, then she frowned. "Wait a minute—I never told you his name."

"Your sister mentioned it."

"What else did she mention?"

He shrugged. "She didn't tell me how long you've been dating him…or if you're sleeping with him."

Tristyn rolled her eyes. "You really don't understand the concept of boundaries, do you?"

"I'm guessing that's a 'no,'" Josh continued. "If your relationship was at that stage, you wouldn't have bailed on him tonight."

She frowned. "What kind of logic is that?"

"The undisputable kind. Because if you were sleeping with him—and he was able to satisfy you in the bedroom—you wouldn't have let anything interfere with your plans to be with him," he said.

"Of course, the other possibility is that you *are* sleeping with him but he's lousy in bed." Then he shook his head. "But no, I can't imagine you would still be with a man who wasn't able to meet your needs."

"You do realize this whole conversation could be categorized as sexual harassment," she noted.

"Are you feeling harassed?"

No, she was feeling…aroused, she realized uneasily.

Which, she was certain, had absolutely nothing to do with Josh but was simply a result of the topic of their conversation—and the fact that she hadn't had sex in almost two years. A sexual hiatus that she'd considered ending tonight.

She wondered what it said about her relationship with Rafe that she hadn't hesitated to break their plans—that she had, perhaps, even been a little relieved to have an ex-

cuse not to take that next step right now. She liked Rafe—she really did. He was handsome and sweet and kind, and she always had a good time with him. But for some inexplicable reason, she wasn't eager to get naked with him.

Or maybe the reason wasn't inexplicable at all.

Maybe the reason was standing right in front of her.

She pushed that unwarranted and unwelcome thought to the back of her mind. "I'm going home now," she told Josh.

"And if you were sleeping with him," he continued, as if she hadn't spoken, "you'd probably be stopping by his place on your way home to—"

"Good night, Josh." And with those final words, she opened the door and made her escape.

Unfortunately, it wasn't as easy to escape her own thoughts and feelings. Because the truth was, simply being in the same room with Josh stirred her up far more than being in Rafe's arms ever did.

Chapter Four

The Independence Parade was always the opening event of Charisma's Fourth of July celebration. Although Josh enjoyed the festivities at Arbor Park, where the processional ended, he didn't usually seek out a spot on the parade route to watch the various groups and floats go by. Of course, he didn't usually have three little girls with him, but as soon as Jordyn had mentioned the parade and fireworks at the restaurant the night before, his nieces had been clamoring to attend. On the plus side, because they were in a hurry to get out of the house, they didn't grumble too much about having sandwiches for lunch.

Shortly before one o'clock, Josh was piling the girls into his truck again because he knew that all the best viewing spots would be gone at least an hour before the parade started. It was a beautiful, clear day, which meant that the sun was in full force. Thankfully, Charlotte had reminded him about the bottle of sunscreen that her mom had packed, and he'd rubbed them all down before they left his condo and brought the bottle along to reapply as necessary. They were all wearing hats, too, but he still worried that they were likely to bake in the North Carolina sunshine.

There were some trees along the parade route, but those

coveted spots were all occupied by the time he'd parked and herded the girls toward the end of the route, where they would be closer to the park for the other festivities when the processional ended. He hadn't gone too far before he found Tristyn's other sister, Lauryn, with her husband, Ryder, and their kids, Kylie and Zachary. Lauryn and Ryder rearranged their grouping to make room for Josh and his nieces to join them. Charlotte and Emily sat on the curb with Kylie, while Zach and Hanna perched on top of the chest cooler behind them.

He saw the speculation in Lauryn's gaze as she looked at the three girls, so before she could ask, he turned to Ryder and questioned him about the restoration he'd recently completed in Watkinsville, Georgia. That topic kept the conversation going for a while, then Ryder said, "But we've got an even bigger project under construction right now."

"What's that?" he asked, at the same time Lauryn rolled her eyes at her husband.

"We were going to wait awhile before we told the whole world," she reminded him.

"Josh isn't the whole world—he's practically a Garrett," Ryder argued. "And since we've told the rest of the family—" he turned back to Josh "—he should know that we're going to have another baby."

"Congratulations," Josh said, offering his hand to the handyman.

Though technically the baby that Lauryn was expecting would be her first with Ryder, her new husband had formally adopted the children from her previous marriage on the same day he'd married her, so that they officially became a family.

Josh couldn't resist teasing Lauryn, asking, "One baby or two?"

"One," she said quickly, firmly. "I have them one at a

time. Jordyn's the overachiever—and the twin gene came from Marco's family."

"One at a time works for me," Ryder said. "Because making them is half the fun."

"Yeah, we'll see how much fun you think it is when you don't get to sleep through the night for the first three months," his wife quipped.

He snaked an arm around her waist and drew her close to his side. "You won't be doing it on your own this time," he told her.

She looked up at him, her expression filled with love and gratitude. "I know," she admitted. "But I still think your plan to fill our house with six kids is a little over the top."

"Six?" Josh echoed, stunned. Because six was twice as many as he was responsible for now, and after three days, he was beginning to doubt whether he would make it through the summer with his sanity intact.

"I think he just wants an excuse to build a really big house," Lauryn confided.

"Actually, I've been thinking about an extension—" Ryder stopped abruptly when his wife held up a hand.

"I think I hear something," she said.

"Is it starting?" Kylie asked.

"I think it might be," her mom said.

Josh could hear it now, too—the drums and pipes that indicated the approach of a band from somewhere in the distance.

"I can't see," Hanna said.

"There's nothing to see right now," he told her.

But as the parade drew nearer, so did the crowd, edging ever closer to the curb. As a result, the little ones had trouble seeing past the bigger bodies, so Ryder lifted Zachary onto his shoulders and Josh did the same—a little uneasily—with Hanna.

The firm grip his youngest niece had on his hair suggested that she was as uneasy as he was—at least in the beginning. But she giggled when the fire department squirted the hot crowd with a hose and clapped when the majorettes paused in front of them to twirl and spin.

After the parade, he thanked Lauryn and Ryder for sharing their curb space, then directed the girls toward the park—where they spent almost an hour in line to have their faces painted before they went to get ice cream. As they made their way toward a cluster of picnic tables, his gaze avidly searched the crowd for a familiar face. He saw plenty of people he knew, but not the one person he most wanted to see.

They succeeded in snagging a picnic table in the shade—a minor miracle—and Charlotte and Emily mostly managed to finish their snacks before they melted. Hanna wasn't nearly as successful, and by the time she'd given up on the soggy remnants of her cone, she was covered nose to chin with chocolate ice cream.

"Apparently you've got a lot to learn," Tristyn teased as she set her cousin Andrew's youngest daughter, Lilly, onto the bench with her ice-cream cone and offered Josh a container of wet wipes.

He hadn't seen her approach, but his initial jolt of surprise was quickly supplanted by pleasure. And the pleasure grew as his gaze skimmed over her, from the ponytail on top of her head to the skimpy tank top that molded to her curves and short shorts that highlighted her mile-long legs.

"The first rule of child care," she continued, "is never go anywhere without wet wipes."

"I'll keep that in mind," he promised, gratefully removing a disposable cloth from the container and clumsily attempting to remove the sticky residue from his niece's face and hands. He glanced up at Tristyn. "Where's your boyfriend?"

He was hoping she would object to the label, but she only said, "He's helping set up the tables."

Then, in a not-so-subtle attempt to change the topic of conversation, she turned her attention to his nieces to ask, "Did you guys see the parade?"

They responded enthusiastically and in great detail, their words spilling over one another so that he wondered how Tristyn could understand anything they were saying. As he continued to clean up Hanna, out of the corner of his eye, he saw that Emily had stood up on the bench and was wiggling around.

"What are you doing?" he asked, horror dawning along with comprehension.

"I got ice cream on my shorts," she told him, attempting to push the offending garment over her hips.

"Well, you can't just take them off," he admonished.

"But they're sticky."

The glint of amusement in Tristyn's deep green eyes had him fighting to contain his own smile.

"Let's see if I can help you get rid of the sticky," Tristyn offered, taking a wipe from the container and scrubbing at the drip on Emily's shorts.

Josh appreciated her help. He'd quickly discovered that taking care of three little girls was a lot more work than he'd anticipated—and gave him a whole new respect for his sister. He'd also realized that sharing the responsibility with someone else—with Tristyn—made it not just easier but more enjoyable. He continued to wipe ice cream from Hanna's hands and face while Tristyn cleaned Emily's shorts and Lilly sat quietly eating her ice cream.

"There you go," Tristyn told Emily.

The little girl frowned at the wet spot.

"They'll dry in just a few minutes," Josh promised, anticipating her complaint. "Probably less in this heat."

"Look, Unca Josh," Hanna implored. "Bawoons!"

He turned to follow the direction her finger was pointing and saw a couple of clowns making balloon animals for the kids who had gathered around.

With a sigh of resignation, he returned the container of wipes to Tristyn. "When are the fireworks?" he asked wearily.

She laughed softly. "Not for hours and hours yet."

"Do you want to come with us to get balloon animals?"

"Sorry," she said, not sounding sorry at all. "But I promised Rachel I would bring Lilly right back after she had her ice cream."

"I guess I'll see you later then," he said, letting Hanna tug him away from the bench.

"No doubt," she agreed.

After the girls each had a balloon animal in hand, Josh steered them toward the Garretts' usual picnic spot.

His best friend's family had expanded over the past several years, as Daniel and his brothers and cousins all got married and started families of their own. Now there were kids ranging in age from nine months to twelve years, and his nieces were immediately accepted into the fold.

Although Charlotte was a few years younger than Maura and Dylan, they were letting her hang out with them; Emily was playing on a nearby climbing structure with Kylie and Oliver; and Hanna had apparently become new best friends with Jacob and Zachary. The family wasn't finished expanding yet, either. Ryan's wife, Harper, was about six weeks away from her due date and, as he'd learned a few hours earlier, Tristyn's sister Lauryn was scheduled to add to her family around Christmas.

In fact, looking around at the various couples and groups, he realized that Tristyn was the only one of Daniel's cousins who wasn't yet married—and he wondered if the guy she was with planned to change that.

Marco had introduced Josh to Rafe when he arrived,

which was how he'd learned that Tristyn's date was also Marco's cousin and the head chef at Valentino's II.

"So you're the reason that Tristyn canceled our plans last night," Rafe commented, as he shook Josh's hand.

"Yeah, sorry about that," he said, as Marco moved away to help his wife set up a portable play yard for their boys.

"No need to be," the other man assured him. "She explained the situation, and I know she'd never walk away from a friend in need of help."

Though Josh couldn't deny the accuracy of the description, it still grated on his nerves that Rafe was so dismissive of the time Tristyn had spent with him. It was as if the guy was so secure in his relationship with her, he had no worries about his girlfriend hanging out with another man. Admittedly, she'd been hanging out with another man and three kids, but still.

"There you are," Tristyn said, a smile lighting her face as she made her way toward them. And for just a second, Josh thought she was talking to him. Then she linked her arm through Rafe's, effectively dispelling that notion. "Your nonna's looking for you."

"And I'm hiding from her," Rafe admitted. "It's my day off and I don't want to talk about tweaking any of my recipes or any other restaurant business today."

"Then let's take a walk before dinner," she suggested, leading him away. "I saw your aunt brought cannoli, which means that I need to get a head start on burning off the extra calories."

Not wanting to watch them wander off together, Josh purposely turned in the other direction.

Josh spent some time hanging out with Daniel and Kenna and their kids; chatted with Harper about her return to WNCC—the local television station for which she now produced the morning show—and her plans for jug-

gling her promotion with a new baby; and congratulated Braden and Cassie on their recent engagement. All the while, he kept a close eye on his three nieces, who were more than happy with their new friends. When the food was finally set out—the selection covering most of two picnic tables—everyone dropped what they were doing to get in line. Since Josh hadn't brought anything to contribute to the potluck, he bought a couple platters of burgers and sausages from the Fireman's Picnic—another Fourth of July tradition, which brought together the local ladder companies to cook up various offerings, with the proceeds going to support the children's wing of Mercy Hospital.

"I haven't seen you eat anything," Jane Garrett said, handing him a plate piled high with a double-decker cheeseburger, potato wedges, pasta salad and baked beans.

"I wasn't going to go hungry," he assured her. "I just wanted to make sure the girls were taken care of first."

"Tristyn helped the little one with her plate, but the other two managed to take care of themselves."

"The little one's Hanna," he said. "Emily is playing with Kylie, and Charlotte is with Maura and Dylan."

Jane smiled. "They're beautiful girls."

"Those Slater genes always come out on top," he teased.

"And still, you don't have any of your own running around here."

"And still, I somehow ended up responsible for three kids," he noted wryly.

"Your sister obviously trusted you to take care of her daughters."

"My sister obviously had no other options," he countered.

His friend's mother shook her head. "Don't go selling yourself short."

He chuckled. "No one's ever accused me of doing that before."

"I've known you a lot of years," she reminded him. "And I've admittedly known you to coast if you thought you could get away with it. High school English class, for example, when you decided to watch a movie rather than read the book it was based on in order to write a report."

Josh took a bite of the burger, so that he'd be too busy chewing to be able to respond to her allegation.

"I've also known you to show an incredible amount of focus and determination when something matters to you," she continued. "The success of GSR in such a short period of time is proof of that."

He swallowed. "Thank you," he said cautiously.

"Now I'm wondering when you're going to show that same level of commitment in a personal relationship."

"You don't need to worry about me," he assured her. "I'm perfectly happy with my life just the way it is."

"I do need to worry about you," she countered. "My other boys are all married now and have wives to take care of them. You're the only holdout."

He smiled. "You do realize I'm not actually your fourth son?"

"Of course I do. And lucky for you that you're not, or the thoughts you have when you look at my youngest niece would be highly inappropriate."

He nearly choked on a potato wedge. He coughed, cleared his throat. "You think you can read my mind now?"

"I don't need to be a mind reader to recognize lust in a man's eye," she told him.

"Jesu— Jeez," he hastily amended. "I don't— I mean—" He blew out a breath. "Okay, this is incredibly awkward."

Jane just chuckled. "I've watched you watch her for years," she admitted. "And I've been wondering when you're going to stop watching and actually do something to get the girl."

"I'm not," he told her. Reminded himself.

"Why not?" she demanded.

"Because Tristyn's a keeper," he answered honestly. "And I'm not the kind of guy who's looking to keep a woman."

She smiled knowingly. "It's been my experience that most guys think they're not that kind of guy—until the right woman comes along."

Tristyn was pleased to see that Josh had brought his nieces to the Fourth of July celebration. She wasn't pleased to realize how often her attention wandered in their direction throughout the afternoon. She told herself that she was just making sure the girls were having a good time, because she could imagine how difficult it was for them to be away from everything and everyone that was familiar for the summer. But after some initial hesitation, they appeared to have found their niche with the other kids. And the truth was, she spent a lot of time watching Josh watch the girls.

"Has your friend figured out what he's going to do with his nieces for the summer?" Rafe asked, proving that he was aware of the focus of her attention.

"I don't think so," she said. "But they were only dropped on his doorstep a few days ago."

"You mentioned that when you called last night."

She tipped her head back to look at him. "I'm really sorry I bailed on you at the last minute."

"It's okay," he said. "If I had three kids dumped on me, I'd be grateful for an extra set of hands."

"If you had three kids dumped on you, your mother and nonna would both be there in a heartbeat. Josh's family is…scattered. His other sister is in London, his parents are in France—or maybe Germany. His grandparents are local, but I don't know that they'd be able to keep up with three kids."

"Then he's lucky he has you," Rafe said.

Though his tone was casual, his word choice seemed deliberately odd to her. "He doesn't *have* me," Tristyn replied.

"Are you sure about that?" he probed.

She felt her cheeks flush. "Of course I'm sure."

"Because while you're doing a pretty good job of pretending that you're not looking at him, he's not even trying to hide the fact that he's watching you," Rafe said.

"Josh is Daniel's best friend and business partner, which means he's like another cousin to me—as if I didn't already have enough," she said lightly.

"One of the things I've always liked about you is that you're forthright and honest," he told her. "So I'm going to assume that you're not being deliberately deceitful now but are in denial of his feelings and your own."

She frowned, not finding either of those options particularly appealing.

He took both her hands. "When I first met you, at Marco and Jordyn's wedding, you completely took my breath away. After I spent some time with you, I was pleased to discover that a woman so incredibly beautiful could also be warm and witty and fun. And while it's been frustrating—for both of us, I think—to try to mesh our schedules to spend time together, I always suspected that wasn't the only obstacle between us."

"Rafe," she began, not sure what else she planned to say, just certain that she didn't like the direction she could see this conversation headed.

But he didn't seem to expect her to say anything else. He only dipped his head to kiss her. On the forehead.

"I have to go to the restaurant to do the prep for tomorrow," he said.

"I thought you'd decided to stay for the fireworks and save the prep for the morning," she reminded him.

"I think I'd rather get it done tonight," he decided.

Tristyn watched him walk away, feeling guilty and remorseful—and maybe just a little bit relieved.

The girls were tuckered out long before dark, but they didn't want to leave before the fireworks. So Josh, with Hanna snuggled in his lap, settled in where he could keep an eye on Charlotte and Emily, who were sprawled on the blankets spread out on the grass for the remaining children. Several of the couples with little ones had gone: Jordyn and Marco had taken Henry and Liam home after dinner; Daniel and Kenna had followed a short while later with Jacob and Logan; and Braden and Cassie had slipped away with Saige soon after that.

There was still a sizable group remaining when darkness fell—albeit not a big enough crowd that he failed to notice that, about an hour after Tristyn disappeared with Rafe, she returned to the gathering without him. Apparently he wasn't the only one with questions about their relationship, as he caught their names mentioned in a conversation from somewhere behind him.

"So…Tristyn and Rafe," he heard Rachel say. "How long has that been going on?"

Of course, he didn't know who she was talking to until he heard Lauryn respond, "I'm not sure anything's really going on. They've only been out three times in the past three months. Four times, I guess, if you count today as a date."

Then Justin's wife, Avery, joined the conversation. "It can be hard to sustain a relationship when people are on different schedules," she noted.

"Maybe they'll figure it out," Lauryn said, though she sounded dubious. "But watching them together—there just seems to be something missing."

"There's no sizzle," Rachel decided.

"I used to think sizzle was overrated," Avery admitted. "Until I met Justin."

"Still, a relationship needs more than chemistry to work," Lauryn pointed out.

"Says the woman who got knocked up by 'America's Hottest Handyman,'" Rachel teased.

It occurred to Josh that he should move away so he wasn't eavesdropping on their conversation, but the window of opportunity for doing so had passed when Hanna fell asleep in his arms.

"I'm not saying that chemistry isn't important," Lauryn said, and though he couldn't see her face, he could hear the blush in her voice. "I just think that it's not a complete foundation for a relationship."

"But without it, there's no foundation," Avery argued.

"I like Rafe," Rachel said. "But I'm not sure he's the right guy for Tristyn."

"No one thinks he's the right guy for Tristyn, because everyone's waiting for her to hook up with Josh," Avery said matter-of-factly.

Now Josh was really wishing he'd moved away when he had had the chance. It was bad enough that Daniel's mom had picked up on his never-to-be-acted-upon attraction to her niece, but to discover that the rest of the family was aware of the chemistry between him and Tristyn was more than a little unnerving.

"I'm not sure that's ever going to happen," Rachel said in response to Avery's comment. "I mean, the guy's had plenty of time and opportunities, and he's never made a move."

There was a beep and then, "Oh, that's Justin wondering where I wandered off to," Avery said.

"I should track down Andrew before the fireworks start,

too," Rachel said. "And that looks like Ryder heading this way—no doubt looking for you."

And with that, the women went their separate ways, leaving Josh in the dark—both figuratively and literally.

Chapter Five

Since Josh hadn't yet been able to make any long-term plans for his nieces, he took them with him to the office on Wednesday. He packed up some of their DVDs with the intention of settling them in front of the TV in the conference room while he caught up on the emails and phone calls that he'd missed while he was away and couldn't seem to focus on at home with the girls running around. He also saved himself more kitchen chaos by taking the girls to The Morning Glory for breakfast rather than attempting to cook for them. Confident that they were adequately fueled and content with their movie, he settled behind his desk and got to work.

About an hour later, he got up to refill his mug of coffee from the seemingly always full carafe in the reception area and spotted an RV parked in front of the offices.

"Why is there a fifth wheel outside?" Josh asked, when Daniel walked past with a handful of papers.

"Oh, I didn't realize he was here already," his partner said, dropping the papers onto Stephanie's desk.

"Who?" Josh prompted.

"Eric Voss," Daniel said, naming the team's former

crew chief, who had retired at the end of the previous season to take care of his ailing wife.

"Is he living in his RV now?" Josh wondered.

"No. I ran into him at Arbor Park yesterday and he told me that he's thinking of selling it—or possibly renting it out for the summer. And I realized it would be a convenient way to travel with a family."

Josh swallowed a mouthful of coffee. "Are you planning on taking Kenna and the kids on the road this summer?"

"For part of it, maybe," Daniel said. "But Eric's RV is probably bigger than what we'd need. On the other hand, it would be perfect for you and the girls."

Josh immediately shook his head. "I don't think so."

"Have you figured out what you're going to do with them this summer?" his friend pressed.

"No," he admitted, watching as the side of the RV slid out to expand the interior space. "I've looked at some summer camps, but Hanna is too young for most of them and those that would be appropriate for Emily and Charlotte are already at capacity."

"We could manage without you, if you needed to take some time off," Daniel assured him.

"I know," he agreed. "But I don't see how a couple of weeks of vacation is going to alter the situation when my sister expects to be gone for eight to ten."

His business partner whistled. "That long, huh?"

"She said she would try to wrap up as quickly as possible, but she warned me that it could be the beginning of September before she's back."

"Do you really plan to sit out eight to ten weeks of the season?"

Josh understood his friend's skepticism. Although it wasn't a requirement for team owners to be at the track, he'd always considered attending races as one of the perks of the position. He loved the energy and atmosphere of

race day and rarely missed an event. "I'd rather not," he admitted now.

"Then maybe you should check out the RV," his friend suggested, as their former crew chief walked into the reception area.

"Unless the RV is equipped with a full-time babysitter, I'm not sure it will solve my dilemma," Josh told him.

"I'd say it comes with everything but the kitchen sink," Eric said. "However, it *has* the kitchen sink, just no babysitter."

The retired crew chief grinned as he shook hands with each of his former employers. "Team GSR has had some good results already this season—congratulations."

"There are still a lot of races to be run," Daniel pointed out.

Eric nodded. "A lot of potential for D'Alesio to move even further up in the standings if he continues to drive the way he's been driving."

Out of the corner of his eye, Josh saw Charlotte look around as she exited the conference room, then make her way toward him. "Hanna wants to know..." Her words trailed off as she spotted the RV. "What's that?"

"It's a house on wheels," Eric responded.

Her expression was skeptical. "It doesn't look much like a house."

"Inside it does," he assured her. "Do you want to see?"

She looked from Eric to the RV and back again. "Can I?"

"Sure," he said.

"You were saying something about Hanna," Josh reminded her.

"Oh, right." She suddenly remembered. "She wants to know where the bathroom is."

"I'll be right back," Josh told the other men, then hurried to the conference room.

When Hanna was finished in the bathroom, he saw that Emily had joined the group gathered in the lobby and heard Charlotte inviting her sister to "look at the house on wheels." Although Josh had barely had a chance to get his head around his friend's suggestion of taking the girls on the road with him, he figured there was no harm in looking at the RV.

At Eric's urging, Daniel led the girls up the steps and into the living area, while Josh walked around the outside with the vehicle's owner.

"You've got a similar truck to mine," Josh commented.

The other man nodded. "You don't need anything bigger for this size RV."

"But I bet hauling an extra twelve-to-fifteen-thousand pounds would wreak havoc on my gas mileage."

Eric shook his head. "You won't get me to take that kind of sucker bet," he said. "On the other hand, the nightly rate at an RV park is a heck of a lot less than a hotel. With the added benefit of having a full kitchen to do your own cooking."

"How is doing my own cooking a benefit?" Josh wondered, as he stepped inside to check out the interior.

"Well, my wife did the cooking," Eric admitted, gesturing for Josh to check out the interior. "So it was a benefit to my wallet. And my stomach—Lainie was a helluva cook."

But Josh wasn't, and remembering the disaster of his kitchen when he'd tried to keep up with the numerous and various demands of feeding three little girls made him shudder. On the other hand, logic dictated that a disaster in a kitchen half the size of his own would also be half the size.

"Feel free to poke around," Eric said. "Open doors and drawers, sit at the dinette, bounce on the beds."

At those words, Charlotte, Emily and Hanna all glanced up.

"No," Josh said firmly, looking at each one in turn. "No bouncing on the beds."

The matching hopeful expressions on their faces instantly faded.

Eric chuckled. "Okay, I'll leave you to explore while I go into the shop to see what modifications the crew is making for the next race."

"There's more space than you would guess, once the living area and master bedroom are opened up," Daniel commented.

"But only one bathroom," Josh noted. Not that he'd expected there would be more than that, but he did wonder about the logistics of sharing limited facilities with three little girls—especially when one of them seemed to be going to the bathroom every five minutes.

"And bunk beds, Uncle Josh," Emily chimed in excitedly.

"Bunk beds, huh?"

She nodded. "Can I sleep on the top?"

"No, I want the top," Charlotte said.

"Whoa!" Josh said. "What makes you think anyone will be sleeping in here?"

"Mr. Daniel said we might get to live in this for the summer," his eldest niece told him.

Josh slanted a look at his friend.

"Might," Daniel emphasized. "I said *might*."

"Can we, Uncle Josh?" Charlotte asked.

"Please," Emily added.

"P'ease," Hanna echoed.

"Knock knock," Tristyn said, climbing into the RV, Kenna on her heels.

Daniel's face immediately lit up at the sight of his wife. "What are you doing here?" he asked, sliding his arm around her and drawing her close for a kiss.

"I thought I'd see if I could steal my husband away for a lunch break," she told him.

"You shouldn't steal," Emily said solemnly. "Stealing's bad."

"You're right," Kenna confirmed. "Stealing is very bad. But in this case, it's just an expression."

"Okay," Emily said, but she still looked uncertain.

"Where are the boys?" Daniel asked.

"Having a teddy bear picnic with their cousins at your parents' place." She glanced around. "This looks like a fun way to travel."

Emily tugged on Tristyn's hand. "It has bunk beds," she said again.

"Wow, bunk beds are pretty cool," Tristyn acknowledged. Then, to Josh, "Are you really thinking of doing this?"

"I haven't come up with any other options," he admitted. "But I'm not sure this one is viable."

"The girls seem to like it," Daniel pointed out.

"But managing the vehicle and three kids on my own is—"

"Tristyn could come with us," Charlotte interjected.

"What?" Tristyn said, obviously taken aback by the suggestion.

"Yay!" Emily said, clapping her hands together in obvious agreement with her sister's plan.

It was Josh's immediate instinct to nix the suggestion, but no sooner had the words come out of Charlotte's mouth than the idea began to take root in his mind.

"It would certainly help to have an extra set of hands—and eyes—on three kids," he agreed.

But Tristyn was already shaking her head. "Sorry," she said to the girls. "But I have to stay here to work."

"Actually, you've often said that as long as you have

Wi-Fi, you could work almost anywhere," Daniel reminded her.

"Except that someone needs to cover reception while Stephanie is in Michigan for six weeks," she pointed out.

"My friend Laurel was supposed to teach a summer school course, but it was canceled," Kenna chimed in. "She's a huge racing fan and I know she'd love to have something to do for the summer."

Tristyn frowned. "Didn't Laurel and Ren have a…" She trailed off and glanced at the girls, obviously trying to censor her words in their presence.

"Orgy?" Emily piped up, completely *un*censored.

Kenna's brows rose; Daniel coughed to hide a chuckle.

Josh closed his eyes. "Kill me now and save my sister from doing it when she comes home and hears that word coming out of the mouth of her five-year-old."

"Where did she hear that word?" Kenna wondered.

"It was my fault," Tristyn admitted, her cheeks flushing. "And it's a bad word that I should never have used," she said, addressing Emily now. "So please don't say it again or your mommy will be very mad at me."

"Okay," Emily agreed easily. "So will you come with us?"

"I'm not sure your uncle has made any final decisions yet," she hedged, looking to Josh for help.

"Don't wait too long to decide," Daniel advised his friend. "Eric's ad just went up on craigslist this morning, and he's already had a dozen inquiries."

Josh nodded.

"Why don't we take the girls back so you and Tristyn can talk about this?" Kenna suggested, already ushering his nieces toward the exit.

"You're actually thinking about it, aren't you?" Tristyn mused when they'd gone.

"Are you thinking I'm crazy to even consider it?" he asked her.

"No," she said, wandering through the RV. "In fact, I think it's a good idea."

"Really?"

She nodded. "It will give you the opportunity to spend some quality time with them, something more than the few days you usually have a couple of times a year."

"You can't honestly think that spending the better part of the summer in a tiny house on wheels with me is the best option for three little girls."

"It's hardly tiny," she chided. "In fact, this RV is bigger than my first apartment. And actually, I do think spending the summer in this with you is the best option for your nieces."

"Really? Because just last week you referred to me as—" he tapped a finger to the dimple in his chin "—just a minute, I want to get the words exactly right. I think you said I was 'an immature and unreliable jackass.'"

"I said you were *behaving* like an immature and unreliable jackass," she acknowledged. "But I believe you have the potential to be so much more."

"Thank you for that vote of confidence," he said drily.

"And spending the summer with your nieces would prove it."

"If it doesn't drive me insane in the process."

"Eric Voss used to travel in this RV with his wife and four kids," she said, pointedly ignoring his remark.

"Okay, I'll do it," he decided. "If you come with us."

Tristyn laughed. "You can't honestly think *that's* a good idea."

"It's the only way I can imagine this working."

"Really? Because when I think about spending my sum-

mer in an RV with you, I imagine having to call my sisters to bail me out of jail after the police find your body."

He lifted a brow, his expression more amused than worried. "I don't think there's as much animosity between us as you like to pretend there is."

"We can hardly be in the same room together for ten minutes without snapping at one another."

"You spent four and a half hours with me the other night with no bloodshed," he pointed out to her.

"Because your three nieces were there to act as a buffer."

"And they'll be there every mile of the road trip."

She shook her head. "There's a huge difference between a few hours and several weeks."

He deliberately stepped in front of her. "I don't think it's the possibility of conflict that worries you," he said. "I think it's the attraction."

She snorted. "Get over yourself, Slater."

His lips curved, just a little. "I think you're the one who needs to get over me."

"I did that. A long time ago."

"Did you?" he asked softly.

"Twelve years ago," she assured him.

Twelve years ago, she'd been a senior at Hillfield Academy, eagerly getting ready for the Spring Fling, when she got the call from Mitch, her steady boyfriend of almost eighteen months. Actually, it was Mitch's mom who had called because Mitch was in bed with the stomach flu and a bucket.

Tristyn had felt bad for Mitch, and selfishly disappointed for herself. Because the senior prom was *the* biggest social event at Hillfield Academy and she'd been looking forward to this day since her freshman year. To miss it would be unthinkable. To show up without a date only slightly less mortifying.

Enter Josh Slater—best friend of her cousin Daniel—who rode to her rescue like the proverbial white knight. Josh had also graduated from Hillfield, where he'd been an honor roll student and quarterback of the varsity football team in his junior and senior years. He'd been one of the popular kids—genuinely liked by all the guys and wanted by all the girls. So when Tristyn Garrett showed up to her senior prom on the arm of Josh Slater, there were whispers. She told everyone that she and Josh were just friends, but sometime during that night, she was the one who forgot that basic fact.

She'd been seventeen years old—a naive and hopeless romantic who had, over the course of several months, built the night up in her mind to be something truly special. And when Josh asked her to dance, her knees had trembled. When he'd taken her in his arms, her breasts had tingled. At twenty, his lean, youthful frame had started to fill out, setting him apart as a man in a room filled with boys. They'd danced a few more times throughout the evening, and then they'd walked hand in hand in the moonlight.

When he finally took her home at the end of the night, she'd tipped her head back to look at him, silently urging him to kiss her. His gaze had dropped to her lips, lingered. But when he made no move to breach that distance, she'd decided that she would—and nearly fell off the porch when he took a deliberate step back and walked away from her.

She pushed the humiliating memory to the back of her mind.

"Then spending a few weeks in a motor home with me and my nieces shouldn't be a problem for you." His statement drew her attention back to the present—and the present dilemma.

"You're just trying to get a free babysitter," she accused.

"Not at all," he denied. "I'm acknowledging that I'm

going to need help with the kids—and I'm willing to pay for your help."

She was annoyed that he would offer, because then she couldn't be mad at him for trying to take advantage of her. And because she would never accept money for doing a favor for a friend. Which was the trump card he played next.

"You also said," he continued, "that I should reach out to my friends for help."

"And you questioned whether we were, in fact, friends," she reminded him.

"That was before you came through for me the other night."

"I didn't really do anything," she pointed out.

"You canceled your date to help me out. Or is that the real reason for your hesitation now?" he asked. "Are you worried that Rafe will disapprove?"

She shook her head. No, far more worrying to Tristyn was the fact that she hadn't once considered how the other man might respond when he learned of her plans. Even if her relationship status with Rafe was unclear, she should have at least considered how he might feel. "I can't imagine why he would have any objections," she finally said.

"Can't you?" Josh asked. "Because I promise that if I was dating you, I wouldn't be happy to hear that you were making plans to spend the better part of the summer in the company of another man."

"Well, you're not dating me, and Rafe isn't you."

"Does that mean you'll come with us?"

She stood in the middle of the living area and looked around, then slowly nodded. "On one condition."

"Anything," he promised.

"I get the master bedroom."

Chapter Six

"Anything but that," Josh said in response to Tristyn's suggestion.

"That's my only condition," she said. "And it's non-negotiable."

"Why should you get the bedroom?" he challenged.

"Because I'm doing you a favor," she reminded him.

"You can do me another one by giving me the bed."

She shook her head. "I don't think so."

"Come on, Tris—I'm about a foot taller than you."

She lifted her gaze from his chin, which was at her eye level, to meet his. "If you think that's a foot, then your concept of six inches is probably equally exaggerated."

He narrowed his gaze. "Let's just agree that I'm a lot taller than you."

"And that sofa bed is probably seventy-six inches long when it's opened up."

"And not even the width of a double bed."

"Since you won't be entertaining any female friends while you're taking care of your nieces, I'm sure that won't be a problem."

"Okay, I have another idea," he told her.

"No."

"You haven't even heard my idea."

"I don't need to hear it," she said.

"A king-size bed is the equivalent of two double beds," he pointed out. "So two people sharing a king is almost the same as each of them having a double."

"No," she said again.

"Let's be logical about this," he urged. "Since I'm the only male, it will afford everyone more privacy if my sleeping area is separate and apart from all of the females."

"You want logical? Consider this—I get the bedroom or I stay home," she said.

He sighed. "I guess you get the bedroom."

Because in the brief time that she'd been around his nieces, he'd finally grasped how much he needed her. Not just because she was a woman, but because she had a lot more experience with kids than he did. She was "Auntie Tristyn" not only to her sisters' kids but to the offspring of her numerous cousins, and she was obviously comfortable surrounded by little ones of all ages—as she inevitably was whenever the Garrett family gathered.

He still had reservations about the trip—he'd have to be crazy not to—but he was confident Charlotte, Emily and Hanna would enjoy the experience a lot more with Tristyn around. Unfortunately, he didn't expect to enjoy the experience at all. Because he knew that being with Tristyn 24/7 would be more than a challenge—it would require him to continue to ignore his true feelings for her.

On the plus side, he had a lot of practice with that—he'd been doing it for twelve years already.

When Tristyn got home from work that afternoon, she called her sisters and invited them to come over. Because Marco was at Valentino's, Jordyn brought the twins with her, and Lauryn brought Kylie and Zachary, too, so the kids could all "play" together. Not that Henry and Liam

did much playing yet, but Kylie certainly liked playing "mommy" to the little ones.

When the children were settled with their toys and the adults with their wine—except for Lauryn, who was drinking herbal tea—Tristyn said, "I need some advice."

"About what?" her oldest sister asked.

"Something I agreed to do that now I'm thinking I shouldn't have."

"Sounds intriguing," Jordyn said. "What did you agree to do?"

"Help Josh look after his nieces for the summer."

"That doesn't sound like any cause for concern," Jordyn said.

"You're great with kids," Lauryn pointed out. "And it was apparent at the Fourth of July picnic that Josh's nieces are already taken with you."

"It's not the kids I'm worried about," Tristyn admitted.

"Ahh." Jordyn nodded. "Now we're getting somewhere."

"And the first somewhere is Kentucky."

"Now you've lost me," Lauryn admitted.

"We're going to spend the next few weeks—or eight to ten—on the road together in an RV."

Jordyn's lips curved. "Now this is getting *really* interesting. You and Josh…in close proximity to a bedroom."

"Me and Josh *and* the three girls."

"Who are—if I remember correctly—about seven, five and three?" Lauryn said.

She nodded.

"So I wouldn't count on them being very effective chaperones," her oldest sister warned. "Even Charlotte will probably be lights out by eight o'clock and asleep by nine. Which means that you and Josh will have to find something else to occupy your time together during those evening hours."

"Have you both forgotten that I've been dating Rafe?"

Jordyn snorted. "You talked about dating more than you actually did."

"Although it would be courteous to tell him that you're shacking up with another man for the next couple of months," Lauryn suggested.

"I'm not shacking up with anyone," Tristyn retorted. "And Rafe—" she blew out a breath "—he left the picnic early last night because of Josh. He said it was because he had prep to do at the restaurant, but it was right after he decided that Josh was an obstacle to our relationship."

"Obviously he's more intuitive than most guys," Lauryn noted.

"And he's right," Jordyn said. "You've been with Rafe for three months and you still haven't slept with him."

"We only managed to sync our schedules for three dates in those three months," Tristyn reminded her sisters. "And how do you know I haven't slept with him?"

"There's not a sense of intimacy between you."

She frowned. "What does that even mean?"

"She's talking about the casual, easy touches and shared glances that communicate without a word being spoken," Lauryn explained.

"Anyway, I do think this trip could be a good opportunity for you," Jordyn said.

"An opportunity for what?" Tristyn asked warily.

"To finally get over your teenage crush on Josh."

"I stopped being a teenager a lot of years ago," she reminded her sisters.

"That doesn't mean you ever resolved your feelings for him," Lauryn pointed out.

"Trust me, those feelings were resolved," Tristyn said firmly.

She didn't know if her sisters believed her claim, because as confident as she'd tried to sound, she wasn't sure she believed it herself.

* * *

Josh offered to do the grocery shopping, to stock up the RV, while Tristyn stayed with the girls. She declined the offer, because although she suspected that dragging three kids around the grocery store wasn't likely to be fun for any of them, she wanted to ensure that he purchased foods and snacks that his nieces would actually eat.

Tristyn didn't usually do major shopping. She tended to pick up a few things here and there, because as much as she liked to cook, she never knew what she wanted to eat from one day to the next. Obviously cooking for three kids—and Josh—was going to require a little more planning.

When she'd asked the girls what they liked to eat, she got the usual responses: chicken fingers, macaroni and cheese, and hot dogs. When she asked specifically about vegetables, she learned that Charlotte liked corn and carrots but not peas; Emily liked broccoli and carrots but not corn; Hanna hated anything yellow but would eat almost anything else. Fruit was more of the same. Charlotte liked red grapes and bananas; Emily liked apples, but only if they were cut into wedges, and oranges; Hanna liked grapes, bananas—because apparently the ban on yellow applied only to vegetables—and apples. But they hit the jackpot in the freezer aisle when they discovered that the girls unanimously loved ice cream and ice-cream sandwiches.

The cashier—Nikki, according to her employee ID tag—looked from Josh to the three girls and back again. "I haven't seen you in a while," she said. "But I didn't think it had been *that* long."

He looked at her blankly.

"Nikki Bishop," she told him. "You dated my sister, Katie, a few years back."

He nodded, as if he suddenly remembered. And maybe he did. On the other hand, Josh had dated so many women,

Tristyn suspected he had trouble keeping all their names straight. "And the kids aren't mine," he explained. "They're my sister's."

"They're pretty girls," the woman remarked, as she began to scan and bag the groceries.

He nodded again but said nothing to explain Tristyn's presence.

"I'm the babysitter," she piped up, continuing to transfer the contents of the cart to the conveyor belt. "So if you wanted to write your number on the receipt for him, I'm not going to be offended."

Nikki looked at Josh again, a speculative gleam in her eye.

Tristyn held back a smile as Josh slid her a look.

"Although the reason I'm buying all these groceries is that I'm heading out of town on a road trip," he explained to Nikki. "I'll be gone most of the summer."

She processed his payment, then tore the register receipt off and scrawled on the back of it. "Since I have no plans to move out of town, you can give me a call whenever you get back."

"Thanks," Josh said, taking the receipt and stuffing it into the last bag.

When they got back to his condo, the girls went into the living room to play Candyland—one of the many games their mother had sent to keep them busy while they were at Uncle Josh's—and Tristyn helped Josh unpack the groceries.

"Whoops! I almost threw this away," she said, folding the receipt and tucking it under the edge of his coffeemaker so that Nikki's name and phone number were prominently displayed.

Josh grabbed the piece of paper and crumpled it in his fist, then dropped it into the garbage can under the sink.

Tristyn tsked. "Eventually you'll make your way through the legions of women who line up at your door and might need that number," she warned.

He didn't respond to her provocative comment.

"Such are the charms of Josh Slater that not even the presence of three children dissuades the ladies," she mused, unable to resist needling him a little more.

"I thought, when you agreed to come on this trip, it was a sign that you had my back," he grumbled.

"I do," Tristyn assured him.

"Then why did you just throw me to the wolves?"

"That pretty little blonde didn't look anything like a wolf," she argued. "More like a...bunny."

"If bunnies were bloodthirsty predators," he grumbled as he began packing dry goods into the boxes they would be taking in the RV. "Why did you tell her that you're the babysitter?"

"Isn't that what I am?" she queried. "Besides, I didn't want to interfere in any way, shape or form with your romantic prospects."

"No worries," he said, shaking his head. "She's not my type."

"You have a type?"

"As a matter of fact, I do."

"Let me guess...female, naked and willing?"

"And *not* seventeen," he told her.

Her gaze narrowed in response to the direct hit.

"But you're not seventeen anymore, are you, Tris?" he asked, his tone speculative now.

"No, I'm not," she acknowledged. "And you lost your chance to take advantage of an infatuated schoolgirl a long time ago."

"Because it would have been taking advantage," he acknowledged. "But now we're both adults, standing on equal ground."

"Now we need to stop standing around and get the ice-cream sandwiches in the freezer before they melt."

"You keep insisting that you're over what happened that night, but you refuse to talk to me about it."

"There's nothing to talk about. *Nothing* happened."

"And you still haven't forgiven me for that," he noted.

She opened the refrigerator door and began putting the fruits and vegetables away.

Josh found the ice-cream sandwiches, tossed the box in the freezer, then closed the door and turned back to her. "You were seventeen," he said again. "And you had a boyfriend. Remember? That's why I ended up taking you to the prom—because your boyfriend was sick."

"I remember," she said tightly. "And I don't really think this is the appropriate time or place to take this conversation any further."

"You might be right," he admitted. "But in twelve years, you haven't been willing to talk about it..."

"It was my prom, I tried to kiss you good-night, you weren't interested," she acknowledged. "End of story."

"You had a boyfriend," he said again.

"And you've *never* kissed a girl who had a boyfriend?"

"Not if I knew about the boyfriend."

"Really?" she asked skeptically.

"Really," he confirmed. "But even if you didn't have a boyfriend—even if you'd needed a date that night because you'd broken up with him—I wouldn't have kissed you."

"Thanks for that clarification."

"Not because I didn't want to," he told her. "But because I couldn't be sure that I'd be able to stop after one kiss."

"I would have stopped you after one kiss," she assured him.

"Would you?" he asked softly. "Maybe you don't remember the way you looked at me that night, but I do. You were young and beautiful and curious. I could see it

in your eyes—the way you looked at me when we walked along the path under the magnolia trees—the wanting and the wondering. And there was no way in hell I was going to be the man who took your innocence."

Except that he had taken a part of it. Even without touching her body, he'd taken the innocence of Tristyn's heart.

It was almost midnight by the time Tristyn finished packing. Though her body was exhausted when she fell into bed, she couldn't sleep. She couldn't stop thinking about what Josh had said about the night of her prom.

He was right about her feelings. She *had* wanted him. But only because she'd allowed herself to get caught up in the romantic ambience of the evening. And Josh had been so incredibly handsome in his tux.

When she saw him standing in the foyer of her parents' home, waiting for her with a corsage box in his hand, her heart had fluttered wildly inside her chest. She'd had to hold on to the railing as she descended the stairs, because her knees were trembling so much she was afraid they would buckle.

Her stomach had been so tied up in knots, she'd barely been able to eat. And when his thigh inadvertently brushed against hers beneath the table, heat had rushed through her veins. She'd been relieved when their plates were taken away and the DJ took the stage. But dancing with Josh had been another new and incredible experience. She'd danced with other boys, of course, but Josh was no longer a boy. And being held close to his body had stirred her own in ways she'd never before imagined.

If he'd kissed her beneath those magnolia trees—and oh, how she'd wanted him to kiss her beneath those magnolia trees—she might have suggested that they go for a drive instead of him taking her directly home.

But he hadn't kissed her then—or later.

And it wasn't just the recollection of that night that kept her awake—it was the memory of the way he'd looked at her tonight. That night, his rejection had been sharp and brutal, cruelly cutting. His eyes had been cold, leaving her with absolutely no doubt that he didn't want any of what she was offering. Tonight, there had been nothing but heat.

Maybe she was tempted. Maybe there was a part of her that still wondered what it would be like to be kissed by Josh, touched by Josh, loved by Josh.

That part wasn't invited on their road trip, she decided.

Instead, she would be the babysitter that she'd told Nikki she was. She would focus on the girls to the exclusion of all else. She would not succumb to Josh's considerable charms, and she definitely wouldn't give him an opportunity to reject her again.

Chapter Seven

It turned out that Josh's plan to be on the road by 10:00 a.m. was a little optimistic. By the time the girls were all dressed and had eaten breakfast—he made a mental note to ensure they ate *before* getting dressed in the future, since Hanna required a complete change of clothes after spilling juice down her front, and Charlotte needed a new shirt because she leaned over her plate as she reached for the bottle of syrup—it was almost that time already.

Tristyn showed up at nine forty-five, fresh and well rested and so beautiful it made him ache just to look at her. She quickly surveyed the situation and took charge of the chaos, instructing Josh to finish packing the RV while she cleaned up. As a result, they were only half an hour late pulling away from his building.

They'd been driving for just over an hour when Emily suddenly put down the beginner book she'd been reading and said, "I don't feel so good, Uncle Josh."

"What's the matter, Em?"

"My tummy feels icky."

"We're going to be stopping in about thirty miles," he told her.

"It hurts now," she insisted.

"Well, there's nowhere for me to stop right now, so you'll just have to wait."

"But—"

Tristyn, quickly assessing the situation, dumped the snacks and juice boxes out of the small cooler at her feet and shoved it into the backseat—just as Emily threw up her breakfast. Mostly into the cooler.

"Eww!" Charlotte said. "She barfed on the back of your seat, Uncle Josh."

"Eww!" Hanna echoed.

Emily started to cry.

"It's okay," Tristyn soothed, reaching back to rub the girl's knee. "As soon as Uncle Josh can pull over, we'll get it cleaned up."

"Lucky I've got leather," he muttered.

"It stinks," Charlotte grumbled.

Josh didn't disagree.

Tristyn uncapped a bottle of water and passed it back to Emily. "Small sips," she instructed.

It seemed to take forever to travel those thirty miles to the next rest stop. Tristyn opened Emily's window in the hope that the flow of air would help her feel better, but his middle niece continued to cry softly, Charlotte complained that there was too much noise with the window open and Hanna kept kicking the side of his seat.

When he finally pulled over, Tristyn found a change of clothes for Emily and took her into the restroom to wash up.

"Emily always gets carsick," Charlotte said, as Josh attempted to clean the now-dried spots of vomit off the back of his seat with the wet wipes he'd stocked up on, pursuant to Tristyn's advice on the Fourth of July.

He continued to scrub the leather. "And you didn't think to tell me this earlier?"

His eldest niece shrugged. "I didn't think about it earlier, but it's probably in the book."

When he finally got the last remnants of vomit cleaned up, he pulled out the damn book his eldest niece kept referencing. Sure enough, it was noted that Emily had a tendency toward motion sickness when she was in a car for an extended period of time and recommended that she be seated in the middle of the backseat with an unobstructed view out the front windshield.

"'If planning any extended trips, be sure to give her children's Dramamine beforehand,'" he read aloud.

Charlotte nodded approvingly. "I told you it would be in the book."

There was also a parenthetical reference to the fact that Emily had no problem with roller coasters, probably because the air flow that accompanied the motion ensured that she didn't feel nauseated.

When Tristyn came back with Emily, he crossed his fingers and went into the convenience store attached to the fast-food options and restrooms. Perhaps car sickness was more common than he suspected, because he found what he was looking for on a shelf with Tylenol, cough syrup and Band-Aids.

"I got the Dramamine," he told Emily, triumphantly holding up the box for her inspection.

But she shook her head. "That's not the medicine Mommy gives me."

"It's in the book," he told her, since the girls seemed to believe all the important information had been duly noted in the book.

Emily shook her head again. "The one Mommy gives me is purple."

"And it says 'children' on the label," Charlotte offered.

"They didn't have one specifically for children," Josh explained. "They only had this one, but it says right on

the label, 'for children two-to-six, give half of a chewable tablet.'"

"I like purple," Emily said.

"When we get to a town with a real pharmacy, we'll try to find the purple one," he promised. "But right now, I need you to eat the orange one."

Emily still looked wary, but she took the half tablet from his hand and put it on her tongue. As soon as her taste buds registered the unfamiliar flavor, she spat it out on the ground. "I don't like it."

"I'm sorry that you don't like it," Tristyn said gently. "But you have to take it so that your tummy won't feel icky while we're riding in the truck."

The little girl's eyes filled with tears. "I don't wanna take it."

Desperate to figure out a solution to the dilemma and get back on the road, Josh asked, "What's your favorite treat?"

Emily blinked, seeming surprised by—and perhaps a little wary of—the abrupt change of topic. "What?"

"If your mom lets you pick a favorite treat, what would you choose?" he prompted.

"Skittles."

"Gummy bears," Hanna chimed in.

"What do you like?" he asked Charlotte.

"Kit Kat."

"Okay—let's make a deal," he suggested. "I'll go back into the store to get some Skittles, gummy bears and a Kit Kat bar if Emily chews and swallows the other half of the pill."

"Maybe you should get the Skittles first," Emily bargained, after considering his plan. "Then I can put the candy in my mouth right away to get rid of the taste of the medicine."

"Alright," he relented. "I'll go get the candy first."

When Emily had finally taken the medicine and the kids were settled back in the truck with their candy—Emily in the middle seat now, as per his sister's suggestion—he glanced over at Tristyn and saw her looking at him.

"You just bribed a five-year-old," she commented.

"And you disapprove," he guessed.

"Actually I don't," she said. "In fact, I'm impressed with your quick thinking."

He shrugged as he pulled back out onto the highway. "Isn't there some saying about sugar helping the medicine go down?"

"Look at you—quoting Mary Poppins," she teased. "Although the recommended dosage is a spoonful and I don't want to think about how many spoonfuls of sugar are in that candy."

"The candy got the job done," he pointed out. "Now, fingers crossed, we won't have any more mishaps between here and Sparta."

"Fingers crossed," she agreed.

The Dramamine didn't just help settle Emily's tummy, it made her sleepy. Before they'd driven another half hour, she was conked out. A short while later, Hanna was asleep, too. Charlotte, on the other hand, was wide-awake and growing increasingly impatient with the journey. Her steady and repeated requests of "How much longer?" had Josh clenching his jaw and his hands strangling the steering wheel. Still, he answered patiently every time. Tristyn tried to distract her with word games and stories, but Charlotte was nothing if not focused.

Then Hanna woke up and had to go to the bathroom. Again, they were nowhere near a rest stop and Josh's entreaties for her to "hold it just a little longer" were met by Hanna's increasingly frantic assertions that she had to go "now." He finally gave up on making it to a rest stop and pulled onto the shoulder of the highway so that she could

use the toilet in the RV, but by then, it was too late. So Tristyn found a change of clothes for Hanna and put her dirty clothes in the bag with Emily's.

"Looks like our plan for once-a-week laundry is going to need to be tweaked," she commented.

Josh nodded as he pulled the vehicle back onto the road. "I'm thinking a lot of this plan needs tweaking—if not outright scrapping."

"It's only day one," she said.

"Are you trying to reassure or discourage me?"

"There's always a steep learning curve with kids."

"Maybe too steep," he said.

"And you should be prepared for the possibility that they'll test you a little bit," she warned.

"Are you saying that the last few hours haven't been a test?"

She shook her head. "Not a deliberate one, anyway," she clarified. "Motion sickness and bladder limits are just facts of life."

"Facts I never considered before I agreed to make this trip," he admitted.

When he finally saw the sign for Halliday RV Park & Campground, he wanted to exhale a grateful sigh of relief—but he knew there was a lot of work still to be done. First he had to check in, then follow the map he was given to their allocated hookup spot, which was partly shaded by a stand of evergreen trees and had its own picnic table and fire pit.

"I didn't think we were ever going to make it," Josh said, when he'd finally parked the vehicle.

"We probably should have done today's trip over two days," she acknowledged. "But then we wouldn't have made it in time for the race."

"We're here now," he said.

"Finally," Charlotte said emphatically.

"I saw on the map that there are toilets and shower facilities over by the playground and pool," Tristyn told him. "Why don't I take the girls there to wash up while you take care of the hookup?"

It wasn't a quick process, but by the time Tristyn got back with the girls, he was done and ready to put his feet up and relax with a cold beer. But apparently that wasn't an option. As she explained, the girls had been cooped up in the truck for hours and needed to burn off some energy, so she gave him the choice of taking them to explore the campground or make dinner while she went exploring with them. They both knew there wasn't a choice to be made, since Josh was a pretty lousy cook.

Tristyn made spaghetti for dinner, because it was easy and all the kids liked pasta. Of course, Charlotte wanted meatballs, Emily wanted meat sauce and Hanna didn't want any sauce. She served the spaghetti with a garden salad and garlic bread. Charlotte picked the cucumbers out of her salad, Emily pushed aside the cherry tomatoes and Hanna ate only the cucumbers and tomatoes. Josh, at least, cleared his plate—and a second.

They'd made a deal that Tristyn would do the cooking and Josh would take care of the cleanup, but since he'd spent most of the day driving, she volunteered to handle his chores—just this once. He suggested that one of them could wash and the other dry, but she immediately nixed that idea. The kitchen, though beautifully designed and well-equipped, was still small—too small for two adults to navigate without bumping into one another.

By the time she'd finished, it was nearly eight o'clock. Josh reported that both Hanna and Emily were almost asleep in their respective bunks, while Charlotte was settled into hers with a reading light and a book, but even she was struggling to keep her eyes open. Tristyn folded

the dish towel over the handle of the oven and went to say good-night to the girls.

When she returned to the kitchen, she saw that Josh had opened a bottle of wine and poured two glasses. He held one out to her. Tristyn eyed the offering warily.

"I haven't poisoned it," he assured her. "If nothing else, today's adventures confirmed that there is no way I'd be able to do this without you."

"If that's a thank-you, you're welcome," she said.

"To the conclusion of day one," he said, and touched the rim of his glass to hers.

"And the power of Dramamine," Tristyn added.

Josh sipped his wine. "I just wish Charlotte had thought to mention the car sickness thing before we left Charisma this morning."

"She's seven," she reminded him. "She didn't withhold the information on purpose—she probably didn't even think about it until Emily said that her tummy hurt."

"Well, I'll definitely find a pharmacy and get some of the children's Dramamine before we have to hit the road again."

"Or at least another bag of Skittles," she said.

"Why don't we go outside so our conversation doesn't keep the girls awake?" Josh suggested.

She nodded and followed him, closing the door quietly behind her.

They sat side by side on the top of the picnic table, with their feet on the bench. It was the height of tourist season and the camp was almost filled to capacity, so there were plenty of other people around—some sitting around fires, roasting marshmallows and singing camp songs. But though it wasn't quiet, it was peaceful, and the display of stars winking against the black night was absolutely breathtaking.

Except that Josh was having trouble focusing on the

stars in the sky with Tristyn sitting so close, her enticing feminine scent clouding his brain and stirring other parts of his body.

"Can you see the Big Dipper?" she asked.

He tipped his head back to search for the constellation, then nodded.

"Do you see anything else you recognize?" she asked him.

"Orion's Belt," he suggested. Although he didn't know much more than that it was a line of three stars, there were so many stars he figured those three had to be up there somewhere.

But Tristyn shook her head. "You can only see Orion's Belt in the northern hemisphere between November and February."

"How do you know so much about the constellations?" he asked her.

"I took a few courses in astronomy and astrology in college, just for fun."

His idea of fun at college had obviously been a lot different than hers, and he suspected that mentioning that now would destroy the tentative peace they'd established. "What else do you see?" he asked instead.

"The Little Dipper, with Polaris at the tip of the handle. Then there's Cassiopeia, Cepheus and Draco—all circumpolar constellations."

"How do I know you're not just making all these names up?"

She laughed softly. "I guess you don't," she admitted. "But you don't need to know the names of the constellations or what stars they're comprised of to appreciate the view."

"You're right about that," he agreed, watching her watch the sky.

I've been wondering when you're going to stop watch-

ing and actually do something to get the girl. The echo of Jane Garrett's words both taunted and tempted him. But making a move on his best friend's cousin would be crazy. Especially as Tristyn was the type of woman a man could really fall for—and Josh had no intention of falling.

She lifted her glass to her lips and sipped her wine. "I know this view isn't all that different from my backyard at home," she admitted, "but it feels like a different world— to be surrounded by nature instead of the city."

"I'm really glad Charlotte suggested that you come with us," he confided.

"It's only day one," she reminded him.

"True," he said. Then, after another minute had passed, "I have to admit that I've been wondering about something."

"What's that?"

"Why you agreed to this trip."

"I've been wondering the same thing myself," she acknowledged.

"It could be that you couldn't resist the opportunity to spend some time with me."

"I spend more time with you than I want to at GSR," she noted.

"But we're rarely alone at the office," he pointed out.

"And we're not alone now."

"For all intents and purposes we are."

"I'm not interested in your intents or purposes," she said.

"You're interested," he said. "You're just pretending not to be."

"You're delusional," she countered.

"What did Rafe say when you told him you were coming on this trip with me? Or didn't you tell him?"

"I told you, I'm not discussing my relationship with Rafe with you."

"But a few dates isn't really a relationship, is it?"

"What do you know about relationships?" she challenged.

"Not a lot," he admitted. "In fact, probably about as much as I know about kids."

"You did okay today."

He shook his head. "I couldn't even get them out of the condo without your help this morning."

"You were managing," she said generously. "You were just a little behind schedule."

"And you managed to get us back on schedule—or very near," he noted.

"Aren't my organizational skills one of the reasons you and Daniel hired me at GSR?"

"They're why Daniel wanted to hire you," Josh admitted. "I added my vote because I like the way you look."

She shook her head, but she was smiling a little.

"Seriously, though, you handled Emily like a pro today. I was happier cleaning up puke than trying to soothe a distressed little girl."

"I've got a lot of experience soothing distressed kids," she reminded him.

"The number of little Garretts running around seems to increase at every holiday," he agreed.

She nodded. "There were fourteen at the Fourth of July celebration," she told him. "Harper and Ryan's baby will be number fifteen, and Lauryn and Ryder's will be sixteen. My cousins in Pinehurst have eight more between them, but they don't visit very often."

"Do you have any thoughts of adding to that number?" he asked.

"Someday," she said lightly. "I'd never thought of marriage and motherhood as life goals—there were so many other things I wanted to see and do. But recently, I've started to see the appeal of sharing my life with someone."

"Do you think Rafe is that someone?"

"You don't take a hint, do you?"

"I'm just curious if he's the type of guy you see your-self settling down with someday."

"I don't know," she admitted. "He's a really great guy—and a fabulous cook."

"But?" Josh prompted.

She shrugged. "Maybe there is no 'but.' Maybe he's perfect for me and we'll get married and have half a dozen kids and live happily-ever-after."

"There is a 'but,'" he insisted. "If you really believed Rafe was perfect, you wouldn't be here with me now."

"I'm not *with* you," she argued.

"And the 'but' is chemistry," he continued, as if she hadn't spoken.

"What?"

"There's no chemistry between you and Rafe."

She frowned. "How can you make a statement like that?"

"Because I saw the two of you together."

"For all of about five minutes," she pointed out.

"And it was obvious to me in the first two of those five minutes," he told her. "And confirmed when he left the picnic and you stayed to watch the fireworks with your sisters."

"The fireworks are the best part of the Fourth of July."

"If you and Rafe had chemistry, you would have been happy to make your own fireworks."

She shook her head. "Not everything has to be about sex."

"Maybe not," he allowed. "But I don't see that there's much hope for the future of a relationship if you don't want to get naked with your partner."

"Forgive me if I choose not to take relationship advice

from a man who's never had a relationship that lasted more than a few weeks."

"Maybe I haven't had a long-term relationship," he acknowledged. "But I've had a lot of great sex along the way."

She stood up, shaking her head. "You truly are a Neanderthal."

"Anytime you want me to drag you back to my cave to show you what you're missing, just let me know."

"A charming invitation, to be sure," she said drily, "but I think I'll pass."

He shrugged. "Your call."

She turned and walked back into the RV without even saying good-night.

He couldn't blame her for being annoyed with him—not when he'd deliberately antagonized her. But it had been a matter of self-preservation. Sitting under the stars and chatting about family and future plans with a woman should have sent him into a panic. Instead, because that woman was Tristyn, it had felt comfortable and easy.

And feeling comfortable and easy about those kinds of things could lead a man down a dangerous path.

Chapter Eight

"It's not right," Josh grumbled from beneath the pillow he'd pulled over his face, "that the person with a private bedroom should get to invade the public space where someone else is sleeping."

"Wake up, Grumpy Bear," Tristyn said.

"Grumpy Bear?"

"It's what Lauryn calls Zachary when he's in a mood."

"I'm not in a mood," he denied . "Unless sleeping is a mood. In which case, I'm definitely in a sleeping mood, and you're ruining that mood by banging around in the kitchen."

"I made coffee," she said.

He reluctantly moved the pillow aside and sat up to take the proffered mug. He sipped the strong, hot brew and blinked, attempting to focus. "What the hell are you wearing?"

"They're called pajamas," she said drily.

His gaze skimmed over her—from the notched collar of the long-sleeved, button-front shirt to the matching full-length pants. Aside from the fact that they were pink with a subtle white stripe, they looked more like a man's pajamas. Or an old lady's. "You sleep in granny jammies?"

She frowned. "These aren't granny jammies."

"They are so granny jammies." He lifted the mug to his lips again.

"Well, I thought—since I would be sleeping in close proximity to three impressionable young girls—that I should wear something…modest." She returned to the stove and dropped a slice of egg-soaked bread into one of two pans already on the burners.

Now that the first jolt of caffeine had hit his brain, he could hear sizzling. He sniffed the air and sighed happily. "Where are the girls?"

"They were up early, so I let them go into my room to watch the TV there so they wouldn't wake you."

"Then you came in here to bang around in the kitchen and do that yourself," he noted, shoving back the covers.

"I'm making breakfast," she pointed out. "If that's too noisy for you, I'll let you go hungry tomorrow."

"The scent of bacon is making me forget my annoyance," he admitted, moving to the pot to refill his mug of coffee. "But not my curiosity."

She flipped the bread in the pan. "I'm sure I'm going to regret asking, but what are you curious about?"

"What you usually wear to bed," he admitted.

"Not granny jammies," she told him.

He swallowed another mouthful of coffee, and though he knew it was a dangerous road for his mind to travel, he couldn't resist. He leaned closer and dropped his voice to a seductive whisper, "What do you prefer to sleep in? Whisper-thin silk? Peekaboo lace? Maybe a cute little baby doll with a ruffled hem that barely covers your—"

"No," she interjected firmly, pointing at him with the spatula in her hand.

"No baby doll?" he pressed.

"No to all of the above."

Which didn't, as far as he could see, leave any other options. "Ha! You do sleep in granny jammies."

She shook her head as she added the slice of French toast to a platter warming in the oven, then dipped another slice of bread in the egg mixture before transferring it to the pan. Finally she turned to face him. "Do you really want to know?"

"Yes, I really want to know."

"Nothing."

"Nothing," he echoed, his brain not comprehending—or maybe not wanting to comprehend—her response.

Her lips curved, just a little. "I usually sleep in the nude."

It wasn't often that Tristyn had the pleasure of seeing Josh Slater at a loss for words, but he was apparently speechless now. She read the shock in his eyes—and maybe a hint of arousal, too, and decided to play with him a little.

"I like nice clothes," she said, lifting the bacon out of the pan and setting it on paper towels to drain the grease. "But after wearing them for ten or twelve hours, it feels good to finally strip them away and slide naked between the sheets. There's nothing like the sensation of Egyptian cotton against my body."

She hummed with pleasure as she added two more slices of toast to the stack in the oven. "Except maybe the touch of a man…the slide of strong hands over my silky skin… lingering in all the right places."

"I would suggest you not casually throw around mention of your lovers," he warned.

"Why not?"

"Because I might be tempted to take you to my bed and make you forget the names of everyone else you've ever been with."

"And here I thought there wasn't anything about me that ever tempted you," she mused.

"You could tempt a saint," he told her. "And we both know that's one thing I'm not."

"Then I guess I have nothing to worry about."

He reached past her to snag a piece of bacon. "You're feeling pretty brave this morning—after running away last night," he remarked.

"I didn't run away," she denied. "I was tired."

"You were scared."

"You don't scare me, Josh."

"I know—it's your own feelings that you're afraid of."

"You might be right," she acknowledged, her tone a seductive whisper that awakened his body more effectively than the caffeine he'd consumed.

"In fact, there are times—" she looked up at him, then dropped her gaze, deliberately fluttered her lashes "—I'm not sure I can control the overwhelming urge—" she fluttered her lashes again "—to brain you with a frying pan."

He grinned and tugged on the end of her ponytail. "Please try—at least until after you've finished cooking breakfast."

"I'd be more successful if you'd give me some space," she told him.

"Okay." He snagged another piece of bacon. "I'm going to grab a quick shower while you're finishing up."

Tristyn silently cursed Josh as she tossed two pieces of burned toast into the sink and dipped new slices of bread. Making French toast was a simple task—but he'd managed to unnerve her so completely that she hadn't realized the bread was burning. Yeah, a lot of years had passed since she was a seventeen-year-old girl with a crush on her cousin's best friend. Unfortunately, her visceral response

to his nearness was unchanged, but no way was she going to let him know it.

It's your own feelings that you're afraid of.

Maybe she wasn't as adept at hiding her emotions as she wanted to believe. Or maybe he was just being Josh—teasing and flirting because that was his natural response when he was in the company of anyone female. And she teased and flirted back, because it helped preserve the illusion that she was unaffected by him. Except that the burned toast in the sink and the quivers in her belly proved otherwise.

When the bread in the pan was cooked, she added it to the platter in the oven along with the bacon and began to set the table for breakfast. She was pouring juice for the girls when Hanna came into the kitchen, holding the front of her shorts.

"I has to go potty."

"Your uncle Josh is in the shower, so you're going to have to wait a few minutes," she warned the little girl.

"I has to go now," Hanna insisted. Which, based on their experience the day before, meant that Tristyn didn't have time to walk the girl halfway across the camp to the public facilities.

"Pee pee or poop?" she asked, thinking it wouldn't be a big deal to take the little girl outside and let her squat behind a tree.

"Poop!" Hanna told her, then giggled.

Tristyn sighed. "Okay—just a sec." She went to the narrow door and knocked. "Hanna needs the toilet."

"Can she wait five minutes?" Josh replied through the door.

She looked at the little girl, who was still holding the front of her shorts and shifting impatiently from one foot to the other. "I doubt it."

He responded by shutting off the water. Thirty seconds

later, the door opened and he stepped out with only a towel wrapped around his exquisitely muscled and dripping-wet torso.

Hanna immediately pushed past him and into the bathroom.

Tristyn stood where she was, her feet rooted to the floor, her gaze riveted on the droplets of water that were sliding over Josh's taut and tanned skin. She curled her fingers into her palms to resist the urge to touch him. Because she did want to touch him. She wanted to run her hands over all his body, tracing the contours of those rippling muscles. She wanted to step closer and breathe in his clean, masculine scent, to press her lips to his skin and—

"Tristyn," Josh said.

She lifted her eyes and saw the hunger she felt reflected in his.

"I go pee pee," Hanna announced from inside the bathroom.

Tristyn shifted her attention from Josh and stepped toward the door. "You said you had to poop," she reminded the little girl.

"Poop," Hanna echoed, and giggled again.

"I think she just likes saying the word," Josh remarked.

Unbidden, Tristyn's gaze slid in his direction again, lingering on the shampoo lather that had dripped from his hair to his broad shoulders...to his wide chest...the six-pack abs...and lower.

"You're staring," he said softly, amusement mingled with the heat in his tone.

She tore her gaze away, and reached into the bathroom to grab the little girl's arm and turn her toward the door.

"I has to wash up," Hanna protested.

"You can do that in the kitchen."

Josh moved past them into the bathroom to resume his shower. She heard the door latch, then the water start again.

He would be discarding the towel now, exposing the rest of his hard, lean body—

She shoved the tantalizing image firmly to the back of her mind and focused her attention on serving up breakfast.

The girls had never been to a stock car race, so the whole experience was a little overwhelming to them. Hanna, in particular, was terrified by the crowds and the noise, and she wrapped her arms around one of Josh's legs as if she wouldn't ever let go. Even Emily and Charlotte dutifully stuck close when he bought them Ren D'Alesio T-shirts and hats at the souvenir hauler so they would be appropriately attired for the race.

Charlotte wrinkled her nose when he handed her the goodies. "Why can't I have a purple T-shirt like that one?" she asked, pointing to a girl wearing the colors of a rival team.

"Because then you'd be showing your support for Scott Peterson's car. Our car is green and gold."

"Who picked those colors?"

"They match the Archer Glass logo," he explained, naming the major sponsor of the GSR team.

Though she still didn't look thrilled, she dutifully put on the shirt when Tristyn escorted them to the bathroom to change. Of course, it probably helped that Tristyn was wearing her GSR polo shirt in the same colors. After ensuring they were settled in the owners' suite, she'd disappeared for a meeting with Ren's PA, leaving Josh with the three girls.

"Why are there so many people?" Emily asked, leaning forward in her seat and craning her neck to survey through the glass the crowd that packed the grandstands.

"They're here to meet the drivers and watch the race."

She seemed satisfied with that answer—at least for the

moment. After about ten minutes had passed, she looked at him again. "They just go round and round in a circle?"

"Well, it's a little more complicated than that," he said, though he couldn't think of an explanation that would make sense to or satisfy an inquisitive five-year-old girl.

"How do you know who's in front?" Charlotte asked, since the cars were spread out around the track.

"The blue-and-white car—number 535—is leading right now."

"How do you know?"

"Because I've been watching the race. But also because the numbers of the leaders are posted on that tower," he said, pointing it out to her.

"Oh," she said.

Hanna was paying more attention to her frayed shoe-lace than the action on the track, but at least she was sitting quietly.

"I'm hungry," Emily told him.

Hanna looked up. "I tirsty."

He glanced at Charlotte, who shrugged.

So he got them set up with food and drinks and was just replying to a text message from his business partner when the door opened and Paris Smythe, a stock car fan and racing blogger, slipped into the room. Over the past few months, she'd made it clear to Josh that she would be happy to give his team some extra coverage—if he got under the covers with her. She was a beautiful woman and he couldn't deny that he'd been tempted, but so far he'd managed to resist her overtures.

He hit Send, then tucked his phone away again.

"I missed you in Daytona," Paris said to him.

"I wasn't at the race," he admitted. "I had to go back to Charisma early to deal with a family situation."

"Well, you can make it up to me tonight," she suggested, shifting closer and tipping her head back to brush her lips

over his. "I'm at the Courtland Hotel—room 722." She slid a key card into his pocket. "I figured you'd be able to remember that number."

He took the card out of his pocket and put it back in her hand. "I'm sorry," he lied. "But I won't be able to make it tonight."

The teasing glint in her eye faded. "Why not?"

"Because I'm still dealing with the family situation I mentioned," he said.

"What family situation?" she finally asked.

He turned her to face the front of the box, where Charlotte, Emily and Hanna were seated. "You see those three little girls?"

Her eyes went wide. "They're not yours."

"No," he acknowledged. "They're my sister's—but they're my responsibility for the summer."

"Jeez, you had me worried there for a minute," she said, and laughed weakly. Then she looked at him again. "Three kids? For the whole summer?"

He nodded.

She traced one of the buttons on his shirt with a fingernail. "Well, can't you find someone to watch them for at least one night?" she implored.

"Not tonight," he told her. "They've only been with me for a couple of days and we're still getting accustomed to roles and routines. On the other hand, if you wanted—"

"No," she cut him off abruptly. "Kids aren't really my thing—not even with a man as handsome as you as the potential reward." She trailed her fingers down his shirt, hooked a finger in his belt and tugged playfully. "But if you find yourself free, you know where to find me."

He nodded. "Enjoy the race."

"I always do," she said.

Then she was gone.

"Who was that?"

He jolted at the question, then turned to find his eldest niece standing behind him. "Who?"

"The lady who just left."

"Oh, um, that was Paris Smythe. She's writes about racing."

"Paris is a place not a name," she informed him.

"Charlotte is also a place," he pointed out to her.

"No, it's not," she denied.

"Sure it is. In fact, it's the largest city in North Carolina."

She frowned at that for a minute, before she asked, "Is Paris your girlfriend?"

"What? No."

"Then why was she kissing you?" she pressed.

"I don't know what you think you saw—"

"I saw her kissing you," Charlotte said. "And your lips are pink now."

He wiped a hand over his mouth to erase the remnants of Paris's lipstick. "She was just being friendly."

"Mommy says that a girl should never kiss a boy unless she means it."

"Means what?" Josh wondered.

Charlotte shrugged. "How should I know? I'm only seven."

He fought against a smile as he attempted to redirect the conversation. "What do you think of the race so far?"

"It's okay," she said, then, "Is Tristyn your girlfriend?"

"No, she's just a friend."

"Does she kiss you like that?"

"No," he said. "What's with all the kissing questions?"

"I'm just trying to figure things out."

"Let's try to figure out if our car is going to win this race," he suggested, guiding her back to the seat beside her sisters—including one who was now topless.

He closed his eyes as he drew in a slow, steadying breath. "Emily, where's your shirt?"

She pointed to the floor.

He picked up the discarded garment and tried again. "*Why* is your shirt on the floor?"

"'Cuz it's scratchy."

He hunkered down beside her chair. "Sweetie, you can't just take off your clothes in a public place."

"I only taked off my shirt," she told him.

"Please put it back on."

"It's scratchy," she said again.

He looked around. "Where's the backpack with your other shirt?"

Then he remembered that Tristyn had it and that she'd gone to Ren's hauler for the meeting.

"You're going to have to put this one back on until we can find Tristyn," he told Emily.

"Can we find her now?"

"Not right now," he said, tugging the shirt over her head. "She's in a meeting."

"When can we go back to the trailer?" Charlotte asked.

"When the race is over," he promised.

"When's it gonna be over?" Emily asked. "They've gone round and round lotsa times."

He glanced at the tower to check the lap number. "They've gone around sixty-two times," he told her.

Which meant there were only 205 laps left to go.

And it was definitely time to find Tristyn.

Chapter Nine

Tristyn didn't say much on the return trip, but Josh suspected that might have been because the girls were chattering nonstop and it would have been difficult to get a word in edgewise. Although he was preoccupied with his own thoughts about the race—grateful that the top-ten finish would help both D'Alesio and GSR in the overall standings—he sensed that her mind was focused on something else.

It was dinnertime when they got back to the RV, but the girls had eaten so much at the track—hot dogs and popcorn and ice cream—that they weren't really hungry. Tristyn claimed that she wasn't, either, although she'd had almost continuous meetings while they were at the track, and even during the race, so he didn't know when she would have managed to grab a bite. He made himself a grilled-cheese sandwich while she took Charlotte, Emily and Hanna to the playground so that they could burn off their excess energy.

When they came back, Tristyn instructed them to get their pajamas on. Of course, that was when they decided they needed a snack, so she fixed them each a bowl of cereal. After the girls were finished eating and had brushed

their teeth and were tucked into bed, she busied herself with wiping the table and washing the dishes.

"You're going to wash the stripes right off that bowl," he said, when she'd swiped the cloth over it for the fifth time.

"What?"

He looked pointedly at the bowl in her hands.

"Oh." She rinsed the soap off and set it in the dish drainer to dry.

"Are you going to tell me what I did to piss you off?"

She was silent for a minute, as if considering how to answer the question, but she didn't deny that she was pissed off.

"Charlotte told me that she saw you kissing Paris," she finally said.

"I didn't kiss her," he said. "*She* kissed *me*."

"I don't really care who was kissing whom," Tristyn said. "I'm just asking you to remember that you have three impressionable little girls watching your every move this summer."

"I'm well aware of that," he told her.

"Which means you're not going to be able to...socialize to the extent you're accustomed to."

"Socialize?" he echoed.

She rolled her eyes. "Are you really going to make me spell it out?"

"I think that would be good."

"Okay," she relented. "You're going to have to leave the fence bunnies at the fence."

Josh knew there was as much action to be found away from the track as on it. And while he couldn't deny that he got a kick out of the attention that came from owning a race team, he'd never—not once—said yes to any of the frequent and explicit offers that had been whispered in his ear by eager groupies. Sure, he sometimes partied

with fans in celebration of a victory, but he'd never spent the night with one of them.

There were other women involved with the sport who he'd crossed paths with on a regular basis. Sometimes they hung out together, sometimes it was more than hanging out. But those women knew the circuit, they knew the rules and they didn't want anything more than he did. And he'd be damned if he would apologize to Tristyn for indiscretions that didn't exist anywhere outside of her own mind.

Instead, he only nodded. "No worries. As you know, girls who throw themselves at me aren't my style."

Twin spots of color appeared high on her cheeks. "Touché."

Dammit. He closed his eyes and silently cursed himself for lashing out. Yeah, she'd pissed him off, but he shouldn't have hit back at her. He shouldn't have hurt her. Again.

Not that she would ever admit to feeling hurt. She kept her chin up and her gaze level, but he saw the truth in those deep green eyes. And for that he would apologize. "I'm sorry, Tris."

She shook her head. "Don't ever apologize for being honest about your feelings."

Which sounded like good advice, except that he'd never been honest with her about his feelings. He was barely capable of being honest with himself.

His nieces had crashed a long time ago and Tristyn had firmly closed the door of her bedroom more than an hour earlier, but Josh still couldn't sleep. He thought about the key card Paris had slipped into his pocket earlier—the key card he hadn't hesitated to give back. The explanation he'd given was a valid one—he was responsible for his nieces and had no intention of abandoning them for the pursuit of personal pleasure. But it wasn't the complete truth, which was that he knew a few hours of fun in another woman's

bed wouldn't make him forget the one woman he wanted. The one woman he couldn't have.

The woman who was sleeping less than fifteen feet away, snuggled beneath the covers of a king-size bed in granny jammies despite her alleged preference for sleeping in the nude. Fact or fiction? He wasn't entirely convinced she'd been telling him the truth. More likely, she'd made it up for the sole purpose of keeping him awake at night. Which it was.

Because as much as he'd made fun of the shapeless boxy pj's, Tristyn had looked sexy even in those, and the buttons that ran down the front of the top started low enough to reveal a tantalizing hint of cleavage. Which he definitely should not be thinking about when he was trying to sleep, because now his body was wide-awake and ready for action.

He never should have agreed to do this road trip. And as far as bad ideas went, inviting Tristyn to come along with them ranked right up there with the worst of them. They were at the end of only their second day together, and he couldn't sleep for wanting her.

Though Josh would never admit it to anyone, she'd haunted his dreams for years. Twelve years, in fact. Since the night of her senior prom, when he'd decided to be a nice guy and save Tristyn—and Daniel—the humiliation of her being escorted to the event by a relative. That was the solution her mother had originally proposed, when Tristyn's boyfriend came down with the flu and was unable to attend, and Josh had stepped up as a favor to his friend. He'd certainly never expected to feel anything for his best friend's cousin.

Tristyn had been done up for the big event as if the Spring Fling was a royal wedding. Her dress had even been white, though that wasn't the first thing he'd noticed about it. No, what he'd noticed was that the tight, elaborately

beaded bodice of the strapless gown drew his attention—
and probably that of every other guy in the room—to her
no-longer-flat chest.

In that moment, Josh had realized his best friend's little
cousin wasn't so little anymore and that this "favor" wasn't
going to be nearly as effortless as he'd anticipated. That
was when he'd begun to sweat inside his tuxedo jacket.

Her long dark hair had been done up in some fancy
twist with sparkly pins artfully arranged in it. Stunningly
beautiful even without any cosmetic enhancement, a subtle
touch of makeup had made her eyes look bigger and darker,
her lips glossy and kissable. She'd been the embodiment
of temptation, and when he'd taken her arm and led her to
his car, he hadn't been certain that he'd be able to resist.

It had taken an extreme force of will—and consideration of how Daniel might react if Josh made a move on
his best friend's cousin—but he'd delivered her home at
the end of the night as untouched as she'd been at the beginning. After eight torturous hours with Tristyn being
close enough to touch—and not being allowed to touch her.

He'd barely survived those eight hours—and now he'd
signed up for eight weeks in close proximity to her.

What had he been thinking?

When Charlotte had impulsively invited Tristyn to join
them, he should have said no, firmly and unequivocally.
That he'd implored her to say yes was proof he hadn't
been thinking—at least not with his brain. Now he was
trapped in less than three hundred square feet of living
space with a beautiful woman who turned him inside out
just by breathing.

He was pretty sure the attraction he felt wasn't entirely
one-sided. He'd caught her staring at him when he stepped
out of the shower, and the look in her eyes had not been that
of a disinterested woman. And since they were both unat-
tached adults—because he didn't believe that her claims

of a relationship with Rafe were anything more than a smoke screen—why shouldn't they explore the attraction between them?

The primary reason, of course, was that she was still his best friend's cousin. And if Daniel had any idea that Josh was even thinking about getting Tristyn naked—well, he didn't want to imagine what his friend might say or do, how it would affect not just their friendship but their business partnership.

Still, he suspected that one night with Tristyn might be worth the fallout. His fear was that one night would not be enough.

The following morning, Josh didn't wake up to the sounds of Tristyn banging around in the kitchen. He woke up to whispers.

It took him a minute for the words to register, and another few seconds for him to be able to identify the individual speakers.

"We're not s'posed to wake him up," Charlotte admonished.

"But how long is he gonna sleep?" Emily asked.

"Maybe he's jus' 'tendin' to s'eep," Hanna suggested.

"Adults don't pretend to sleep," Charlotte informed her.

"How d'you know?" her youngest sister pressed.

"Because no one would get mad at them for not being asleep when they're supposed to be."

"Do you think he'll be mad if we wake him?" Emily asked.

"Tristyn told us not to," Charlotte reminded her.

"We could poke him. Pokin's not wakin'."

"No—don't poke him!"

"Mommy usually wakes up when we stand by her bed."

"Because she's got 'tuition," Emily said. "Uncle Josh doesn't got kids so he doesn't got that."

"He does have ears, though," Josh said softly. "So maybe if you keep talking, he'll hear you."

"He's awake," Emily announced, clearly pleased by the discovery.

"But his eyes is c'osed," Hanna protested.

He finally, reluctantly, lifted one eyelid, then the other.

Hanna rewarded him with a beaming smile. "*Now* he's awake."

He scrubbed a hand over his face. "What time is it?"

"Seven thirty-seven," Charlotte told him.

Which wasn't insanely early—it only felt insanely early because he'd slept so poorly the night before.

He glanced toward the closed door of the master bedroom. "I guess Tristyn's still sleeping."

The three girls all shook their heads. "She went for a walk," Emily said.

"To get buttermilk," Charlotte added.

"Fo' pancakes!" Hanna chimed in.

He wondered where she could have walked to for buttermilk at such an early hour. Connected to the campground office was a small store with basic groceries and other essentials, but he doubted she would find buttermilk there.

"So you didn't wake me up to make your breakfast," he guessed.

"We wanna go swimmin'," Hanna announced.

Only then did he notice that they were all wearing their swimsuits and holding beach towels.

"At seven thirty-seven in the morning?"

They nodded enthusiastically.

"It's seven forty now," Charlotte pointed out.

"And the splash pad and pool don't open until ten," he told them.

"Oh."

But he got out of bed now and stumbled toward the coffeemaker, which—thanks to Tristyn—had already brewed

a fresh pot of coffee. He poured the hot liquid into a mug and sipped carefully.

"Why do you drink coffee?" Emily asked.

"Because I like it," he told her.

"Caffeine's not good for you," Charlotte informed him. "It will stunt your growth."

"Since I'm pretty sure I'm finished growing, that's not really a concern," he said.

Tristyn returned just as he was starting on his second cup of coffee. She wished him a good morning and immediately set about making breakfast.

Charlotte looked at the container she'd brought back from the store.

"That's not milk, it's yogurt," Charlotte said.

"I like yogurt," Emily said. "Especially the kind with blueberries."

"This is plain yogurt," Tristyn explained. "They didn't have buttermilk, so I'm going to improvise."

"What's improvise?" Emily asked.

"It means to make something from what's available."

"Are we still gonna have pancakes?" she wondered.

"Yes, we're still going to have pancakes."

"And then we can go swimming?"

"Then we can go swimming," Tristyn confirmed, then she looked pointedly at Josh. "And that 'we' includes you."

He could think of few things less appealing than a public pool crowded with screaming kids and weary parents. But then he added something to the picture in his mind: Tristyn in a bathing suit. A teeny, tiny bikini. And that prospect silenced any remaining protest. Lucy called just as the girls were finishing up their breakfast. Because of her work schedule and the time difference, she hadn't been able to talk to the girls every day, although Josh did send her regular updates and occasional pictures of them. When each of the girls had talked to her for a few min-

utes and Lucy finally said goodbye, Hanna started to cry. "I miss Mommy."

"Don't be a baby," Charlotte snapped at her.

Emily's eyes filled with tears, too, but she valiantly held them in check.

Hanna's fell freely down her cheeks as she climbed into her uncle's lap. "When's she comin' home, Unca Josh?"

"She's hoping to be back by the twenty-ninth of August, but she's doing a very important job in Spain and it might take longer than that," he cautioned.

Emily was already looking at the calendar Tristyn had hung up on the fridge, counting the days. "The twenty-ninth isn't so long," she said.

"That's the twenty-ninth of July, dummy," Charlotte told her.

"Oh." Emily's face fell.

"Don't call your sister names," Josh admonished.

"Your mom will be home as soon as she can, because she misses you guys as much as you miss her," Tristyn assured them.

"How do you know?" Charlotte challenged.

"Because she's your mom—and there's nothing harder for a mom than to be away from her children."

"How do you know?" Charlotte asked again. "You don't have any kids."

"No, I don't," Tristyn acknowledged. "But I have two sisters and they both have kids, and I know they don't like to be away from them for more than a few hours."

"Why don't you have kids?" Emily asked curiously.

"Um…" She glanced at Josh, who was fighting a smile, clearly amused by her interrogation at the hands of two little girls. "Because I'm not married," she finally responded.

"You don't have to be married to have kids," Charlotte pointed out matter-of-factly. "Our mom wasn't married when she had Emily and Hanna."

"That's true," she acknowledged cautiously. "But I guess I always hoped to get married before I had kids."

"When are you gonna get married?" Emily asked her.

"I have no idea," Tristyn admitted.

"You could may-wee Unca Josh," Hanna piped up.

The amusement on Josh's face vanished and a slightly panicked expression took its place.

Tristyn shook her head. "I don't see that happening."

"Why not?" Charlotte asked. "You wouldn't have agreed to come on this trip if you didn't like Uncle Josh."

"Of course, I like your uncle Josh," she agreed. "But the real reason I decided to come on this trip is that I didn't know if he could cook, and I wanted to be sure you guys wouldn't starve."

Emily giggled at that.

Charlotte rolled her eyes. "He wouldn't let us starve."

"Living on fast food is almost as bad," Tristyn said.

"I fed them fast food twice," he pointed out.

"Twice in two days."

"And you're trying to distract us from talking about your wedding plans," he chided.

"Why don't we talk about *your* wedding plans?" she countered. "Oh, right—because you don't plan to *ever* get married."

"Why not?" Emily asked, shifting her attention to her uncle.

Josh's narrowed gaze promised retribution for Tristyn.

"Because he wants to…date…a different girl every night," she said.

"Maybe I'd change my mind if I met a woman who could convince me that the advantages of spending my life with her outweighed the disadvantages of marriage."

Tristyn was surprised by his response, until she realized he was simply attempting to appease his nieces.

"Can we go to the pool now?" Charlotte asked, clearly bored with the topic of conversation.

"As soon as your uncle gets his bathing suit on," she agreed, grateful for the reprieve.

He went to put on his bathing suit.

Tristyn was spraying sunscreen on the girls when he came out of the bathroom. Unfortunately, he couldn't tell if she was wearing a teeny, tiny bikini because she was wearing one of those cover-up things on top of her bathing suit. Even when they got to the pool, she stayed in the shallow end with Hanna—and kept the cover-up on.

Though both Charlotte and Emily claimed that they'd had swimming lessons, Josh bought them inflatable armbands to provide some extra peace of mind—probably for him more than the girls.

After almost two hours in the pool, they went back to the RV for lunch.

"When I was at the store this morning, I talked to Mrs. Halliday about extending our reservation," Tristyn said, as she buttered slices of bread to make sandwiches.

"We can't extend our reservation," he argued. "Not if we're going to make it to New Hampshire by next weekend."

"I don't think the girls are eager to head to another racetrack, especially not one that's more than nine hundred miles away."

"Wasn't that the whole point of getting the RV?" he asked. "So that we could travel with the girls?"

"It was," she confirmed. "And we will. I just think that it will be easier on all of us if we stay here and you fly to New Hampshire for the weekend."

"The girls are my responsibility," he reminded her. "And I'm not sure how I'd feel about being so far away from them when their mother is in another country."

"I'll be with them every minute of every day that you're gone," she told him.

"That's a lot of minutes," he warned.

"We'll be fine. The girls have wanted to play mini-putt and I'm sure we'll spend some more time at the pool and the playground. And if it rains, we've got a bin full of games, puzzles and books. Plus there's an activity room in the community center with more games and dress-up clothes and craft supplies." She assembled the sandwiches, cut them in halves—and Hanna's in quarters—then set them on plates. "Besides," she said, "Paris will most likely be in New Hampshire."

"How is she a factor in any of this?"

Tristyn shrugged. "I understand the value of maintaining good relationships with the media."

"You're not suggesting I seduce a writer to get GSR mentioned on some racing blog?"

"Of course not," she said quickly, her cheeks flushing. "Although that blog has twenty-two thousand subscribers."

"Including you?" he guessed.

"She's a good writer and does a nice job showing fans the human side of the sport." She was also blonde, beautiful and built, but Tristyn tried not to hold that against her.

"Even so, I have no interest in extracurricular activities with Paris Smythe," he told her.

"It's none of my business," she said. "I realize I might have come down a little hard because of what Charlotte saw at the track, but that was more about your lack of discretion than Paris."

His brows lifted. "So now you're sending me off to New Hampshire on my own so I can be…discreet? Or are you trying to get rid of me in the hope that some distance might lessen the…tension…between us?"

Chapter Ten

Though she didn't look at him, Josh saw Tristyn's cheeks flush with guilty color, confirming his suspicions. Living in close proximity was making it increasingly difficult—for both of them—to deny the attraction that simmered beneath the surface. And it was only a matter of time before the heat between them turned that simmer to a full boil.

"I'm just trying to come up with a plan that works for everyone," she told him now.

"We had a plan," he reminded her. "And it was for the girls to come with me on the road."

"I'm only suggesting a minor amendment to that plan—to spare them another nine hundred miles on the road, which we'd then have to do all over again to make the trip from New Hampshire to Indiana the following weekend. But if we stay here, we're only a two-hour drive from Indianapolis."

"Okay," he relented. "If they want to stay here, I won't object."

He wasn't really surprised when Charlotte, Emily and Hanna unanimously voted to skip the journey to Loudon. Day one of their road trip hadn't been a lot of fun for any of them—especially Emily. And Hanna. But while

he could understand that they weren't eager to get on the road again—and maybe sitting out the longest leg of the journey was a good idea—they would have to get back on the road eventually. But at least they were equipped with Dramamine now.

Not having to drive nine hundred miles gave Josh more free time with the girls before he left. He was surprised to discover that he really enjoyed hanging out with them— swimming in the pool, playing Candyland, patiently, and repeatedly, explaining the basics of stock car racing in an effort to foster some appreciation of the sport.

It was the time he spent alone with Tristyn, after the girls had gone to bed at night, that was much more of a challenge for him. The RV was spacious, as far as RVs were concerned. But after only a week of sharing that space with a gorgeous, sexy woman, the temptation was proving stronger than his will to resist.

The night before his flight, Tristyn was in the kitchen, making muffins. He'd noticed that she didn't seem to spend much time sitting still, and he didn't know if she had a constant need to be busy or if she didn't want to sit down because there was nowhere to sit that wouldn't be close to him. Whatever the reason, she was in the kitchen while he was watching a ball game on TV.

During the seventh-inning stretch, he got up to grab a beer from the fridge and, as he turned with the bottle in hand, Tristyn leaned over to put the batter in the oven. Their movements coincided in a way that caused the sexy curve of her behind to brush the front of his shorts. The inadvertent contact nearly made him groan.

Tristyn did gasp as she straightened up again and turned. "You're in my space."

"Yeah," he agreed, making no effort to move away.

A tiny furrow appeared between her brows. "Could you please get *out* of my space?"

"I could," he agreed, taking a moment to give her idea some thought. "In fact, I'd say we've done a pretty good job of maintaining our separate spaces over the past week."

"Until now," she said pointedly.

"Uh huh."

She looked at him, her gorgeous green eyes filled with wariness—and maybe a little bit of desire.

She was so damn beautiful. But her beauty was only part of the appeal for Josh. She was also warm and sweet and funny and smart. And that whole package was pretty close to irresistible.

"Twelve years," he murmured.

"Josh," she said.

A warning or request?

"It's a long time to wonder, don't you think?" he asked softly.

"I guess that depends on what you're wondering." Her tone was deliberately neutral, but the slight breathlessness gave her away.

"The same thing you are," he told her.

The way he was looking at her was making everything inside of her tremble. Not with fear, Tristyn realized, but desire. But going down that path with Josh—especially now—would be dangerous.

"Whether Ren will get the pole in Loudon?" she suggested, desperately trying to shift the conversation to safer ground.

Amusement flickered in his eyes for just a moment before the heat took over, sizzling between them.

"I'm not thinking about the race," he said. "And neither are you."

Before she could argue the point, because she had no intention of admitting that he was right, his mouth was on

hers. And with the first brush of contact, any thought of resistance—any thought at all—fizzled away.

In that moment, there was nothing but Josh.

Nothing but Josh and the exquisite, intoxicating sensation of his kiss.

The pressure of his mouth on hers was every bit as glorious as she'd imagined—and yes, she'd spent a lot of time imagining his kiss since she'd seen him making out with Missy Harlowe when she was thirteen. More time than she was willing to admit.

Except for the finger and thumb that held her chin immobile, he touched her only with his lips. That was all he needed to hold her under his spell, simultaneously captivating and mesmerizing her. He kissed like a man who knew how to kiss a woman, who could take her to the edge with just the masterful seduction of his mouth on hers.

He didn't just taste, he savored. And she savored his flavor in return. Twelve years ago, she would have given almost anything to experience his kiss. Twelve years ago, she'd been totally unprepared for something like this. Even now, she wasn't sure what to do with the desire that spread through her veins, the desperate need that clawed at her belly.

She curled her fingers into her palms, digging her nails into the soft flesh to prevent herself from reaching for him. Because she was afraid that if she touched him now, she wouldn't be able to stop. She wouldn't want to stop.

It was Josh who finally, eventually, ended the kiss, easing his lips from hers with obvious reluctance.

She exhaled, a slow, unsteady breath, and finally dared to look at him. He rubbed a thumb over her bottom lip, swollen from his kiss. The sensual caress made her shiver.

"And that," he said, his gaze lingering on her mouth, "is why I didn't kiss you twelve years ago."

She swallowed, but she didn't respond to his comment.

There was nothing really to say, no way to avoid the truth that had been revealed by the meeting of their lips.

That kiss was only the beginning.

Josh's flight was delayed because of a storm, and he'd just arrived at the track when his cell phone rang. A quick glance at the display had him cringing—and considering letting the call go to voice mail. Unfortunately, that would only delay the inevitable argument that probably could have been avoided if he'd thought to call his sister and advise her of the change of plans in advance of changing them.

"Hey, Luce—how is Madrid?"

"Right now, it's raining," she told him.

"Here, too," he said, as thunder rumbled overhead. "How are my girls?"

"Great," he said. "They're having a lot of fun in the pool at the campground."

"They do love the water," she confirmed. "What are they doing now?"

"Oh, um, I'm not actually sure," he admitted. "They're with Tristyn."

"And where are you?" she asked.

"New Hampshire."

There was silence on the other end of the line.

"Luce?" he prompted.

"I'm here," she admitted. "I'm just trying to figure out what to say in response to discovering that my brother—who I entrusted with my three daughters for the summer—has abandoned them with a babysitter in another state."

"First of all, you didn't 'entrust' me with your daughters—you dumped them on me," he pointed out.

"Because there was no one else that I trusted to take care of them."

"Second, you know that Tristyn isn't a babysitter."

"Excuse me—your girlfriend-of-the-week," his sister amended.

"She's a friend who's helping me out because I was overwhelmed by the prospect of taking care of three girls on my own all summer."

"Those three girls are your nieces," she reminded him.

"Who barely know me because, for the past six years, you've refused to come to Charisma for a visit."

"You're supposed to be getting to know them now. Instead, you're in New Hampshire."

"I'll be back in Kentucky tomorrow night," he promised her.

"I have to go," she said. "I've got another call coming through."

"I'll text you Tristyn's number," he said.

But she'd already hung up.

Tristyn and the girls kept busy while Josh was in New Hampshire. They played mini-putt, spent some time at the splash pad and swimming pool, made friends with the neighbors and even went to a movie. She also watched the race on TV, pleased to see that Ren and his team put in a solid performance, consistently in the top twenty, sometimes even breaking the top ten. GSR's driver seemed poised for another strong finish until the third turn of lap 296, and her heart nearly stopped as she witnessed the 722 car get clipped by the 416 and then, seemingly in slow motion, spin into the wall.

Accidents weren't an uncommon occurrence on the track, but even the commentators noted that it didn't look much like an accident and speculated that Curtis Bond, the driver of the 416, was still mad at D'Alesio for sneaking past him on the outside and taking the checkered flag in Kansas City a few weeks earlier. The race officials would review the tapes and decide what—if any—disciplinary

measures to take against the driver, but Tristyn knew that was little consolation for Ren and his team, who worked hard to prepare for every race.

As the damaged cars were moved off the track, Hanna climbed into Tristyn's lap, dropped her head back and slid her thumb into her mouth—a telltale sign that she was sleepy. Tristyn lifted a hand and brushed her soft, wispy bangs away from her face. Cuddling with the little girl, she felt a tug of longing deep inside. She'd always assumed that motherhood was in her future somewhere, but she hadn't been in any rush to head in that direction. Recently, she'd started to feel differently.

She blamed Lauryn and Jordyn for that. She'd been perfectly happy with her life—she had a great house and a fabulous job and a wonderful family. But the recent marriages of both of her sisters had made her realize that she wanted more. That she wanted to meet someone to share her life and raise a family with, too.

Tristyn had been only twenty-four when Kylie was born—thrilled to be an aunt but definitely not ready to even think about being a mother. Two years later, she'd had a much more hands-on role for Zachary's birth and was actually in the delivery room with her sister, coaching Lauryn in place of her deadbeat husband, who had already left town with the yoga instructor.

Tristyn had felt the first twinges of longing then, not just because she was the first to hold the baby—after his mom, of course—but because it had been such an awesome and amazing experience to play even a small part in the process of bringing a new life into the world. In addition to having a front-row seat for the birth, she'd had a front-row seat to the chaos that was her sister's life at the time. Sure, Lauryn had a beautiful toddler daughter and an adorable newborn son, but she also had a mountain of debt and a broken heart. Tristyn had no desire to experi-

ence that kind of upheaval and turmoil. Now Lauryn had a new husband and another baby on the way, and Tristyn was thrilled for her.

A few months after Lauryn and Ryder's wedding, Jordyn had given birth to her twin sons. Marco had been right there, holding his wife's hand and breathing with her through every contraction, so Tristyn didn't have the same front-row seat for that event—thank God for small favors—but the pure and sweet love that filled her heart when she held those tiny babies for the first time was the same. Yet it was more than just the babies that had changed her focus. It was seeing Jordyn and Marco cuddling the precious lives they'd created and brought into the world together. That was the moment when it had hit her, when she'd realized that she wanted what they had—the partnership, the commitment, the love.

Someday, she promised herself, as she tucked Hanna into her bunk.

As a result of Ren's DNF—Did Not Finish—Josh was in a lousy mood when he got on the plane in New Hampshire, and his disposition hadn't changed at all by the time he landed in Kentucky. He arrived at the campground just as Tristyn and the girls were returning from the splash pad. His nieces seemed happy to see him and chattered away about everything he'd missed while he was away. Tristyn, sensing his mood, gave him a wider berth.

She'd just finished helping Hanna dress as a knock sounded.

Josh's scowl deepened when he saw a man standing on the other side of the door, holding a square glass pan.

"Hey, is Tristyn around?" he asked.

"I'm right here, Sean," she immediately responded from behind him.

The other guy's—*Sean's*—eyes lit up when he saw her.

Josh stepped away from the door but not out of earshot.

"I just wanted to return your pan," Sean said. "And to thank you again for the brownies."

"They're gone already?"

"They were gone the first night," he admitted. "It just took us two days to get around to doing the dishes."

Tristyn laughed, a warm, seductive sound that stirred Josh's blood—and likely had the same effect on the guy who was staring at her with adoring eyes.

"The girls and I are going to make chocolate chip cookies later," she told him. "I'll bring some over when we're done."

"You don't have to do that," Sean said. "But we'll certainly enjoy them if you do."

"I'll see you later," she promised.

"I'll look forward to it."

Josh watched through the kitchen window as the other man walked away—a whole twenty-five feet to the RV parked directly beside theirs.

"Who was that?" he asked, as Tristyn moved past him to put the pan in the cupboard.

"Sean."

"Yeah, I caught the name," he admitted. "I was looking for a little more detail than that."

"He's an electrician from West Virginia. He and Blake and Owen grew up together and they still take a few days to get away together every summer. It used to be a week, but since Owen got married a couple of years ago, they cut it back to a few days."

"Do Sean and Blake have wives?"

She shook her head. "Blake's engaged, though, and getting married in the fall."

"And how did you meet these guys?" he wondered.

"They rescued our dinner Friday night," she told him. "I'd just put the burgers on the grill when the flames sput-

tered and died. Blake saw me attempting to unhook the tank and offered to throw our burgers on their grill. After we ate, he switched out the tanks for me, so I made them some brownies to say thanks."

Which was, Josh knew, exactly the kind of thing she would do and absolutely no reason for the petty jealousy gnawing at the pit of his belly.

"And when I took the brownies over, they asked me to be their fourth for euchre, so I spent a few hours playing cards with them."

"While the girls were…where?" he prompted.

"At the pool," she said, picking up the wet towels they'd dumped on the table when they came back from swimming.

He frowned at that.

Tristyn shook her head, clearly exasperated with him. "Honestly, Josh—where do you *think* they were?"

"With you," he guessed.

"Of course, they were with me." She pushed open the door and headed outside to hang up the towels.

He followed. "Playing euchre?"

"PlayStation," she corrected. "Because apparently 'roughing it' does not mean living without video games for some people."

"I hope you had Hanna in bed at her usual bedtime."

"She fell asleep on their sofa."

"How late were you there?"

"Since I was unaware that I had a curfew, I didn't actually make note of the time when we left," she told him.

"Lucy said it's important for the girls to have a consistent schedule."

"A couple of late nights isn't a big deal."

"A couple of nights?" he echoed.

"Yes, Josh. We were over there last night, too. While you were banging Paris Smythe into next week, I was cor-

rupting your three young nieces with euchre and video games."

"I wasn't banging Paris Smythe—or anyone else, for that matter," he retorted.

"Well, that might explain your lousy mood," she acknowledged.

"Did you really think I'd kiss you on Thursday and sleep with another woman on Friday?"

"Truthfully, I didn't think about that kiss at all."

The words might have stung his pride except that the flush in her cheeks and the rapid beating of the pulse point below her ear told a different story. He took a step closer, forcing her to tip her head back to meet his gaze. "Liar," he said softly.

She put her hands on his chest and shoved. Though her effort was ineffectual, he took a deliberate step back. He wasn't in the habit of intimidating women, but he'd never known a woman like Tristyn. She had an uncanny ability to make him crazy without even trying, to make him want her just by breathing.

"I waited twelve years to kiss you," he reminded her. "I won't wait that long to kiss you again—or take you to my bed."

She lifted her chin. "Nobody takes me anywhere I don't want to go."

"Lucky for me, you want me as much as I want you."

"Lucky for you, you've got that enormous ego to fill your bed, so you won't be lonely without me in it."

And with that parting remark, she walked away.

Chapter Eleven

Tristyn knew that she could walk all the way back to Charisma and not walk off her frustration with Josh. So she went only as far as the end of the lane before she pulled her phone out of her pocket. She knew that she could count on either of her sisters to commiserate with her, and dialed Jordyn's number because she was first in her alphabetical list of contacts.

"The man is driving me insane," she said without preamble when her sister had connected the call.

"Hold on a sec," Jordyn said. "Lauryn's here, so I'm going to put you on speakerphone so we both know what's happening."

She heard a click, then her oldest sister's voice. "Hi, Tris. What's happening?"

"He's driving me crazy."

"Josh?"

She huffed out a breath. "Of course, Josh."

"What's he done now?"

"Nothing new, really," she admitted. "He's just being his usual arrogant, annoying self."

"Something must have happened to prompt this call," Lauryn remarked.

"Yeah—he got back from Loudon and started criticizing how I spent my time with his nieces while he was away."

"He was probably upset that Ren crashed with only five laps left," Jordyn said, revealing that she'd watched the race, too—or at least the highlights.

"There's no excuse for being a jerk," Tristyn said.

"I'm guessing his behavior is a sign that you haven't gotten naked with him yet," Lauryn mused.

"What? Of course not."

"It's not completely outside the realm of possibility," Jordyn noted.

"I'm *not* going to get naked with Josh," she said firmly. But, because she had no secrets from her sisters, she confided, "He did kiss me, though."

"Finally," Lauryn said.

"And then?" Jordyn prompted.

Tristyn frowned. "Isn't that enough?"

"Not if it was a good kiss," Jordyn said.

"And Josh Slater looks like a man who would know how to kiss," Lauryn chimed in.

"He does know how to kiss," she acknowledged.

"And then?" Jordyn said again.

"And then I remembered what happened the last time I let myself fall under the spell of Josh Slater."

"That was twelve years ago," Lauryn reminded her. "Neither of you are the same people now."

"I know I'm not the same naive girl I was then, but I'm not sure Josh has changed at all." She sighed. "I never should have agreed to this road trip. There's no way I can spend another six weeks in that RV with him without killing him."

"You could try jumping his bones instead," Jordyn suggested.

Tristyn choked on a laugh. "I guess that is another pos-

sibility—except that I'm not giving him another chance to push me away."

"He's not going to push you away," Lauryn assured her.

"How do you know?"

"Because we've seen the way he looks at you when he thinks no one else is looking," Jordyn said.

"Well, it's not likely I'd have an opportunity to jump his bones with three kids around, anyway."

"I have two babies at home, but I can assure you, I jump Marco's bones every chance I get."

"Please," Lauryn interrupted. "Even between sisters, there's such a thing as too much information."

"As if you're not riding Ryder every night."

"La-la-la," Tristyn sang, attempting to drown them out as she'd done when they were kids and she didn't want to hear what they were saying.

"My point," Jordyn said, speaking loudly enough to be heard over the singing, "is that the bedroom door has a lock."

"Can we talk about something else?" Tristyn suggested, because the more she talked about the possibility of getting naked with Josh, the more tempted she was—despite the fact that he was acting like an idiot.

"Uh uh," Jordyn said. "You called to talk about Josh, so that's what we're doing."

"I called so that you could agree he's being an idiot."

"He's being an idiot," Lauryn said loyally.

"Probably because the memory of that kiss is keeping him up at night—and I don't just mean awake," Jordyn added.

"Not helpful," Tristyn said.

"Okay, let's forget about what Josh wants for a minute," Lauryn said.

"Thank you."

But her sister's next words made her realize that her expression of gratitude was premature.

"What do *you* want?" Lauryn asked gently. "Honestly. Because if you're really unhappy or uncomfortable with the situation, you can leave. You don't owe Josh any favors."

She thought about her sister's question for a moment before responding, "I want to not have the feelings I'm feeling."

"Will those feelings go away if you come home?" Lauryn asked.

She sighed. "Probably not."

"Then try to forgive him for being an idiot, enjoy being with him and see what happens."

Talking to her sisters helped a little; walking around the campground helped some more. When she got back to the RV, Josh was on the phone with Daniel, giving what sounded like a play-by-play of every adjustment made to Ren's car for the previous day's race. The girls were anxious to do something, so she got out the ingredients for chocolate chip cookies, then enlisted their help with the measuring and mixing.

She'd planned to make a pot of chili for dinner, but she'd forgotten to pick up chili powder at the grocery store and decided on meat loaf instead. When she served it up, Emily eyed the slice on her plate skeptically.

"What is it?"

"Meat loaf," Josh answered.

His niece poked it with her fork. "What kind of meat?"

"Ground beef."

"That's cow," Charlotte informed her sister. "Moooo!"

"Charlotte," her uncle said, a warning in his tone.

"I don't like ground beef," Emily announced.

"It's the same kind of meat we had the other night in the form of a hamburger," Tristyn told her.

"So this is like a hamburger?" Emily asked skeptically.

"Sort of," she agreed.

"Can I have it on a bun?"

"It's like a hamburger but it's not a hamburger," Josh tried to explain. "It's meat loaf, and you eat it with a fork."

"I wanna eat it on a bun," Emily insisted.

Josh looked at Tristyn.

She shrugged. "I guess it doesn't matter how she eats it as long as she eats it."

He found the leftover bag of buns and opened one up, then put the slice of meat from Emily's plate on it.

"I wanna bun, too," Hanna decided. "An' ketchup."

He looked at Charlotte, who was nibbling tentatively on a tiny piece of meat. She nodded.

So the girls ate their meat loaf as if it was a hamburger. Emily even put her mashed potatoes and corn on top of the meat, as if the vegetables were condiments.

"Well, I think we can take meat loaf off the menu for next week," Tristyn decided, as the girls cleared their plates from the table.

"I thought it was delicious," he told her.

"Your nieces weren't exactly thrilled with it."

"You've read the book," he reminded her. "According to Lucy, they eat what's put in front of them or they don't eat."

"Still, if I'm going to cook, I'd rather cook something that's going to be eaten—and enjoyed—by everyone."

"Well, the chocolate chip cookies were a hit."

"Who doesn't love chocolate chip cookies?"

"I like brownies, too," he said, nudging her away from the sink. "But I guess there were none of those left."

"You guessed right," she said. "What are you doing?"

"Dishes. That's my job," he reminded her.

"Can we go to the playground?" Charlotte asked.

Tristyn glanced at the clock. "I guess we can go for an hour, and then it will be time for your showers and pajamas."

Although it was undoubtedly convenient to have a bathroom in the RV, the narrowness of the shower stall and the limited capacity of the hot water tank made it awkward to get the girls cleaned up and ready for bed. After scoping out the public facilities, Tristyn had decided that they should shower and get ready for bed there. The first night, Charlotte had been embarrassed to walk across the campground in her pajamas—until she saw several other kids, some even older than her, doing the same thing. Now they were all accustomed to the bedtime routine, which was much more efficient than taking turns in the trailer.

By the time they returned, Josh had the dishes washed, dried and put away, and was watching a baseball game on TV.

"It's sto-wee time, Unca Josh," Hanna announced, as soon as she stepped into the RV.

Josh didn't know how or why he'd become the resident storyteller, but he found he enjoyed the time with Hanna before she went to bed at night. And although Charlotte and Emily could both read age-appropriate books, they sometimes listened in to story time with their little sister, too.

He muted the sound on the television. "Okay, go pick out a book to read."

When he came back to the living area after story time, Tristyn was sitting on one end of the sofa with her iPad in hand. "Are the girls tucked in?"

He nodded and lowered himself onto the sofa, facing her instead of the television.

"I owe you an apology," he said.

"Yes, you do," she agreed.

"I was in a lousy mood earlier and I took it out on you."

"That's an explanation, not an apology."

"I'm sorry," he said.

She nodded, her attention still on the iPad screen. "I accept your apology."

"That's it? You're not going to make me grovel?"

She sent him a sideways glance. "Would you?"

"Probably," he admitted.

"Well, I appreciate the thought," she said, her gaze back on the article she was reading, "but it's really not necessary."

He took the iPad from her, closed the cover and set it aside. "We need to talk about this."

She frowned. "I thought we just did."

"Not about what happened earlier," he said.

"About what?" she asked warily.

"The fact that you make me crazy."

"*I* make *you* crazy?" she said incredulously.

He nodded. "You were right—Paris was at Loudon, and she invited me to spend the night with her. And I wasn't the least bit tempted, because even when I was more than nine hundred miles away from you, I couldn't stop thinking about you. I couldn't stop wanting you."

He kissed her then—a kiss full of frustration and need. And she kissed him back, because she was just as frustrated and needy as he. And because this was Josh, and she'd wanted him for too long to deny herself now. His tongue swept along the seam of her lips, parting them so that he could deepen the kiss. She hooked her hands over his shoulders, holding on to him as the world spun around her.

It was just a kiss, and not even their first. But that kiss had been a tentative exploration. Now, she was more than ready to surrender to the passion that pulsed in her veins.

Except that he pulled back and raked a hand through his hair, already disheveled from her fingers. "See what you—"

She silenced him with her lips.

If Josh was surprised by her initiative, he didn't show it. He certainly didn't protest. And while his mouth was busy with hers, he slid his hands beneath the hem of her T-shirt. His fingertips glided over her stomach and his thumbs traced the underside of her breasts through the lace of her bra.

It was barely a graze, but her body immediately responded. Her nipples grew taut as heat pulsed in her veins. His hands shifted a little higher, and his thumbs brushed the peaks of her nipples this time. She gasped softly.

"Yes?" He whispered the question against her mouth.

She could say no.

She *should* say no.

This was her chance to put on the brakes, to take a step back. But she didn't want to put on the brakes. She didn't want to step back. She wanted Josh.

After an almost imperceptible hesitation, she replied, "Yes."

He unhooked the front fastening of her bra and pushed the cups aside. Then his hands were on her breasts, cradling their weight in his palms as his thumbs continued to trace and tease her nipples. It had been a long time since she'd had a man's hands on her, and the exquisite sensation of Josh's hands on her now nearly made her whimper.

Desperate to touch him, too, she tugged his T-shirt out of his shorts and slid her hands beneath the hem to explore the rippling muscles of his abdomen and chest. He pushed her shirt up and lowered his head to capture one turgid nipple in his mouth, suckling deeply. She gasped again as arrows of sensation shot toward her center.

He eased her back on the sofa and settled himself between her thighs. Even through her shorts and his, she could feel the rigid length of his erection. She instinctively lifted her pelvis to rub provocatively against him.

He grasped her hips in his hands. "You're killing me, Tris."

"I warned you that might happen if I came on this trip with you."

He chuckled softly. "Do you have any—"

She put a hand to his lips. "Shh."

He immediately stilled.

"I thought I heard something," she whispered to him.

"What?"

"A click. Like the latch of a door."

The words were barely out of her mouth when the toilet flushed—a definite and timely reminder that they weren't alone.

She pushed him away and scrambled up off the sofa. She fumbled in her efforts to refasten her bra with unsteady hands, but finally got it done. She tugged her shirt back into place while the bathroom taps turned on, then off again. Her breathing was unsteady; her knees were trembling. Thankfully, it was almost dark now, so he probably couldn't see the hot color that filled her cheeks.

The bathroom door opened, then Charlotte turned back to her bedroom, giving no indication that she'd seen or heard anything.

Tristyn exhaled a shaky sigh.

"Tristyn—"

She shook her head. "Don't."

"Don't what?"

"Don't say anything."

"All I was going to say is that I'm sorry we're not alone," he told her.

She was sorry, too.

And grateful.

And unbearably aroused and incredibly confused.

She wanted him—she could no longer deny that simple fact.

But she didn't want to want him.

She especially didn't want to end up nursing a broken heart, and she knew that getting involved with Josh could only end in heartache.

She'd been so certain that she was in control of her emotions. That she could spend the better part of the summer with Josh and not be affected by his proximity. She'd managed to hold out for all of ten days.

She lifted her hands to her face, appalled by her own wanton behavior. If she hadn't heard Charlotte go into the bathroom—if they hadn't been reminded that they weren't alone—how far would they have gone?

She was ashamed to admit that she didn't know. That she couldn't be sure she would have put on the brakes. She'd been so incredibly aroused by his kiss and his touch, almost desperate for more.

"On the other hand, your bedroom door has a lock," he noted.

She shook her head. "You just want to sleep in my bed," she said lightly, attempting to shift the conversation back to safer ground.

He was silent for a moment, then he nodded, taking her cue. "Can't blame a guy for trying."

Josh went to bed alone.

After Tristyn retreated into her room, he pulled open the sofa bed and stretched out on top of the mattress. He tried to focus his thoughts on anything but Tristyn, but his efforts were futile. He didn't need to wonder about what might have happened if Charlotte hadn't woken up to go to the bathroom. There was no mistaking the fact that Tristyn had been as hot for him as he was for her. And if they hadn't been disturbed, they would have stripped their clothes away and finally given in to the passion that had burned between them for so long.

He didn't know whether to be grateful or annoyed that they'd been interrupted before that could happen. He did know that he was still aroused—rock hard and aching for her. Only her.

It took him a long time to fall asleep, and it seemed like only moments later that he felt something jab into his shoulder. And then again.

He opened one eye to find Hanna standing beside his bed, her favorite teddy bear clutched in one hand. "I had a bad dweam, Unca Josh."

He sat up and scrubbed his hands over his face, resigned to the fact that he wasn't going to get much sleep at all tonight. "What was your bad dream about?"

"I don't 'member," she told him.

"Then how do you know it was a bad dream?"

"'Cuz I woke up wif my tummy hurtin'."

"Do you need a drink?"

She shook her head.

"Do you want me to tuck you back into your bed?"

She shook her head again.

"What do you want?" he asked, unable to think of any other options.

"I wanna s'eep wif you."

"With me?"

She nodded. "P'ease."

He shifted over so Hanna had room to climb up. She was asleep again within two minutes—on his pillow.

Women, he mused, settling back on the edge of the mattress with his hands clasped behind his head and trying not to think about the woman who was sleeping on the other side of a very thin wall.

The only woman he wanted.

Chapter Twelve

Tristyn was awake first, as she usually was. Following her morning routine, she tiptoed into the kitchen to start the coffee brewing, then moved past the sofa bed where Josh was sprawled out, still sleeping, to the back bedroom, where the girls slept in their bunks.

As usual, Charlotte was on her tummy, her covers bunched up at her feet, her pillow on the floor. Emily was spread out like a starfish, using every inch of her mattress. Seeing the way she slept, Tristyn could understand why Charlotte had been unhappy about having to share a bed with her at Uncle Josh's condo. Hanna was...not in her bed.

Tristyn's breath caught in her throat and her heart started to race. She bent down to pull back the covers, in case the little girl was so tangled up inside she couldn't see her. She found four plush animals but not Hanna—and her favorite teddy bear was missing, too.

She rushed back to the living area—no longer worried about tiptoeing, not thinking about anything except that Josh's youngest niece was gone.

"Josh." She choked out his name as she shoved at his shoulder to wake him. "Josh—wake up. Hanna's gone."

"What?" He immediately bolted upright. "Where?"

"I don't know," she admitted, trying to quell the panic rising inside of her. "I went to check on the girls, like I do every morning, and—oh." Relief flooded her system and tears filled her eyes as she spotted his youngest niece curled up under the covers on the other side of the mattress. Tristyn smacked him again then, even harder this time.

"Ow." He rubbed his shoulder. "What was that for?"

"For letting me think that I'd lost your niece."

"I didn't let you think anything," he protested. "I didn't know what you were thinking until you came in here and started yelling—"

"I wasn't yelling," she retorted.

"You weren't whispering."

Of course, his voice was raised now, too, and Hanna shifted restlessly in the bed, her little brow furrowed.

Tristyn turned on her heel and retreated to the kitchen area. Though her heart hadn't yet settled back into its usual place inside her chest, the rhythm wasn't quite as fast and frantic as it had been a few minutes earlier.

She didn't realize Josh had followed until she turned around and nearly ran right into his chest. His broad, tanned and naked chest. She immediately stepped back—and bumped into the stove. He caught her shoulders to help steady her, except that she could feel the imprint of each and every finger through the thin fabric of her pajama top, and the effect was anything but steadying.

"I'm sorry you were worried," he murmured. "She had a bad dream and wanted to sleep with me."

"It wasn't your fault," she acknowledged, blinking back the tears that had filled her eyes. And maybe, if she hadn't been so deliberately averting her gaze from the tempting image of those broad shoulders, she might have noticed the little girl was tucked in beside him. "A bad dream, huh?"

He nodded and lifted a hand to brush away a tear that trembled on her lashes.

The unexpected gentleness of his touch sent a shiver down her spine. "And she went to Unca Josh to slay her dragons," she said, managing a weak smile.

"I'm no one's hero," he said, the words an unmistakable warning.

"Last night you were Hanna's," she pointed out.

"All I did was share my pillow."

"Sometimes a little kindness is all it takes."

He took two mugs from the cupboard and filled them with coffee from the pot, sliding one across the counter to her. "Do you ever have bad dreams?" he asked.

"Not bad enough to entice me to climb into your bed for comfort," she assured him.

"When you climb into my bed, it won't be for comfort," he said.

She wanted to take issue with his arrogant tone as much as his words, but she suspected that challenging his assertion would lead them down a dangerous path. A path that her mind warned could lead to heartache even as her body urged her to follow wherever he wanted to go.

"I need to get dressed," she said, and headed for the sanctuary of her bedroom instead.

Daniel and Kenna decided to bring their boys to the race at Indianapolis. They arrived on the Thursday night, so that Daniel could be at the track for qualifying on Friday, and came to the campground to visit with Josh and Tristyn and the girls. After spending some time at the playground—a much bigger park than at Sparta but which the girls agreed did not make up for the lack of a swimming pool—they went back to the RV, where Josh was going to barbecue chicken and ribs for dinner.

Over the past few days, Tristyn and Josh had gone back to tiptoeing around one another while the attraction between them continued to simmer just below the surface.

Thankfully, Josh's nieces were unaware of the tension between the adults, but Tristyn worried that her cousin and his wife wouldn't be. A worry that proved founded when Daniel caught Tristyn alone in the RV as she was putting together some snacks.

"So—how have things been going?" he asked.

"Good," she said, but kept her attention focused on the vegetable platter she was making.

"Do you think you could expand on that response a little?"

"What else do you want to know?"

He slid the platter away from her, forcing her to look up at him. "Do I need to beat up my business partner?"

She shook her head. "Absolutely not."

He held her gaze for another few seconds, then shook his head. "I should have discouraged you from doing this."

"Putting out snacks?" she asked, deliberately misunderstanding him.

"Spending your summer in close quarters with Josh."

"It was your idea," she reminded him.

"For Josh and his nieces," he agreed. "I didn't know he was going to ask you to go with them."

"It was actually Charlotte who asked. And while I wouldn't say it seemed like a good idea at the time, I wanted to help Josh—to help Charlotte, Emily and Hanna."

"And now?" he prompted.

She shrugged. "You know me and Josh are like oil and water much of the time, but we're managing."

Daniel pinned her with his gaze. "Do you still have feelings for him?"

She turned her focus back to her task. "I was infatuated with him for a short while when I was seventeen," she said. "I'm a lot older and a lot wiser now."

"And living with him," her cousin pointed out.

"A temporary arrangement."

Daniel nodded, but he still looked worried. "What if I said I needed you back at the office?"

Tristyn spooned dip into the bowl she'd set in the center of the platter. "Is Laurel struggling with things?"

"No, she's doing a great job," he admitted. "The only problem is that I don't like the way Josh has been looking at you."

"How has he been looking at me?"

"Like he wants to see you naked."

She felt her cheeks flame as she remembered how close they'd come to that actually happening, but for the grace of a seven-year-old's bladder. "I'm sure you're mistaken."

"I'm sure I'm not," he told her.

"Can we maybe switch to a less awkward topic of conversation?"

"I've known Josh a long time," Daniel continued, ignoring her request. "He's not just my business partner, he's my best friend."

"I know all of that," she reminded him.

"He's kind and generous and sincere—the type of guy who wouldn't hesitate to give the shirt off his back to help someone else."

"Is there a point to this?"

"The point is that he's generally a really great guy, but he doesn't have a clue when it comes to romantic relationships."

"No worries," she assured him. "Because we don't have a relationship—romantic or otherwise."

"And you're not just my cousin, but a valued member of our team. I don't want to lose you at GSR because Josh steps out of line."

"Stop worrying," she said again. "I can handle Josh."

"I hope so," Daniel said. "Because Kenna had the bright idea of inviting the girls for a slumber party in our hotel suite tomorrow night."

That gave her pause, but she was careful not to let Daniel know it. "You have two kids of your own already—why would you want to add three more?" she asked.

"Well, she suggested it to give you and Josh a break, and I agreed because she's been making noises about having another baby and this seemed like a good opportunity to see what a house full of kids would be like."

"You're counting on Josh's nieces to make your case in favor of birth control?" she guessed.

He shrugged. "I realize the plan may very well backfire. Kenna's always wanted a big family, and I think she'd really like to try for a girl."

"And if your plan does backfire?" Tristyn prompted.

"Then I guess we'll be talking to Ryder about an addition for our house."

Tristyn smiled, because the resignation in his tone was tempered by the overwhelming love that she knew her cousin had found with his wife. Four years earlier, Daniel had married Kenna for the sole purpose of gaining access to his trust fund and with the intention of divorcing her at the end of twelve months. Long before that deadline, they'd fallen in love.

Daniel's willingness to agree to anything his wife asked was proof of his love for her, and warmed Tristyn's heart. The prospect of spending a night in the RV alone with Josh heated the rest of her body.

And that was exactly what made her apprehensive about an evening without their pint-size chaperones.

While Daniel was catching up with Tristyn, Kenna was sharing her proposed plan with Josh.

"A slumber party?" he said dubiously.

"Kids love sleepovers," Kenna assured him.

"I'm not sure it's a good idea."

"You don't trust me with your nieces?" she asked, sounding hurt.

"You know that's not it," he told her.

"Then what is it?" she demanded.

"I just think you'll be pulling your hair out with five kids underfoot—and it's really pretty hair."

She smiled. "Always the charmer, aren't you?"

His gaze automatically shifted to the RV, with Tristyn inside. "Not everyone would agree with that assessment."

"A woman who's had her heart bruised is understandably going to be wary," Kenna told him. "Especially around the man who did the bruising."

Josh said nothing.

"I know why you did it," she said gently. "You deliberately hurt her a little because you were afraid of hurting her a lot."

"I didn't want to hurt her at all," he said.

"Have you explained that to Tristyn?"

"I've tried," he admitted. "But she won't listen. And maybe it's better that way—because nothing has really changed."

"Really?" Kenna looked at him skeptically. "Nothing has changed? Your feelings for her are exactly the same now as they were twelve years ago?"

"Well, I'm no longer denying that I want to get into her pants," he said.

Kenna merely lifted a brow. "I grew up on the south side," she reminded him. "I'm not shocked by a few crude words—and I'm not convinced, either."

"You don't believe I want to get into her pants?"

"I don't believe that's all you want," she said. "And if you do believe it, you're kidding yourself."

* * *

The next day, Josh dropped the girls off at the hotel with Kenna—as per her suggestion—so they didn't have to hang out at the track all day. While Josh and Daniel met with Ren and his crew chief, Tristyn was dealing with various administrative tasks. After the first round of qualifying was finished, Ren had the fastest time and was awarded the pole for Saturday's race.

"I guess the slumber party is a go," Josh said, when Tristyn came out of a meeting with Ren's personal assistant.

Tristyn shook her head. "Kenna is a brave woman."

"What about Daniel—doesn't he get any credit for agreeing to the plan?"

"No, because he had ulterior motives," she said, and went on to explain her cousin's rationale.

"So I guess they'll be having another kid," Josh said.

Tristyn laughed. "I guess they will."

"While Daniel and I were growing up, it was always our dream to be surrounded by fast cars and faster—" He glanced at her and abruptly closed his mouth.

"Women?" she guessed, and laughed again.

He shrugged. "My point is, I never would have pictured my best friend as a devoted husband and doting father, but there's no doubt those roles look good on him."

"They lucked out," Tristyn agreed. "They might have got married for the wrong reasons, but they decided to stay married for all the right ones."

"Yeah," Josh admitted. "But I didn't come in here to talk about Daniel and Kenna—aside from the fact that their offer to keep the girls overnight made me wonder if you'd want to go out for dinner tonight."

She raised an eyebrow. "Really? You're asking me to go out for dinner…with you?"

He shrugged. "I thought it might be a nice change for both of us."

"We've eaten dinner together almost every night for the past three weeks. How would this be a change?"

"For starters, you won't have to cook it," he told her.

"That would be a plus," she agreed.

"And since we won't have to worry about the dangers of children around an open flame, we could even dine by candlelight."

"That sounds…romantic," she said, her tone tinged with suspicion.

"Do you have something against romance?"

"No," she admitted. "But don't make the mistake of thinking that I'm going to let you share my bed just because you buy me a romantic dinner."

He didn't deny that he wanted to share her bed but only said, "What's your answer, Tristyn? Yes or no?"

She knew that he was asking about more than dinner. And if she said yes, she would be saying yes to more than dinner. She wanted to say yes, because the prospect of a night out, with wine and candlelight and adult conversation, was incredibly appealing.

The prospect of a night out with Josh—and taking their relationship to the next level—was undeniably unnerving. It had taken only one kiss for her to accept that there was some potent chemistry between them. The second kiss, which had very nearly led to a lot more, proved that any attempt to deny her attraction would be futile. But was she ready to give in to that attraction? Was she willing to be yet one more woman in a long line who had succumbed to the seductive charms of Josh Slater?

"Yes or no?" he asked again.

After a long moment during which she waged an internal battle over her decision, Josh nodded.

"It's okay," he said. "I understand."

"What do you understand?" she asked warily.

"You're afraid that, without the kids to act as a buffer, you won't be able to keep your hands off me," he said.

Tristyn rolled her eyes. "Maybe I'm afraid you won't be able to keep your hands off *me*," she countered.

"You shouldn't be," he told her. "If I find myself tempted, all I have to do is picture you in your granny jammies and the temptation will pass."

She knew she was being played—just as he knew she wouldn't be able to resist the challenge he'd issued.

"In that case, and because you do owe me a steak, my answer is yes," she said, and secretly vowed to make him eat his words before dinner was served.

Since Tristyn had mentioned wanting steak, Josh made a few inquiries, then a reservation at The Chophouse for seven o'clock. The restaurant was about a fifteen minute drive from the campground, so at six forty, he knocked on her bedroom door.

"Just a sec," Tristyn said.

Josh turned away to scoop up his keys and cell phone from the counter. He was occupied for no more than a second, and when he turned back, she was exiting the bedroom, as promised.

He expected her to be punctual. He didn't expect his tongue to nearly fall out of his mouth when he saw her.

It was his own fault. He realized that now. He'd issued the challenge and she'd responded—with devastating effectiveness.

Though he'd been joking about her granny jammies—mostly—at the moment, he couldn't even remember what they looked like. Because the dress she was wearing right now wrapped around her curves like a second skin. The skirt fell just a few inches above her knees, and the neckline dipped low between her breasts, revealing a shadowy

hint of cleavage. Her long, shapely legs were bare, her feet tucked into sexy sandals with four-inch heels. Her usually smooth and sleek hair was teased and tousled as if she'd just crawled out of bed—an image that made him want to march her back through the door and topple onto the king-size mattress with her.

On any given day, she was beautiful. Sexy. Tempting. Tonight, she was stunning. Scorching. Irresistible.

He vaguely registered the movement of her lips—painted the same scarlet color as her dress—but he couldn't hear what she said over the roar of blood through his veins. "What?"

Those lips curved into a smile that was a lot sexy—and just a little bit smug. "I said I was ready to go."

He was ready to go, too, directly to her bedroom—

"Dinner," she prompted.

"Dinner. Right."

He looked around for his keys, then remembered he had them in his hand.

He put his other hand—without the keys—on the small of her back to guide her toward his truck. She sucked in a breath, a response that assured him she wasn't as unaffected by his touch as she pretended to be.

He opened the passenger-side door for her and she eyed the distance between the ground and the seat doubtfully. "Clearly I wasn't thinking about our mode of transportation when I bought this dress."

"What were you thinking about?" he asked, as he lifted her onto the seat.

"Making you drool," she admitted.

His gaze raked over her again. "Mission accomplished."

Chapter Thirteen

The hostess seated them at a table for two and handed them menus in embossed leather folders. The ivory linen tablecloth was pristine, the silverware gleamed, the crystal sparkled. The overhead lighting was subdued, supplemented by the flame of a votive candle that flickered behind a hurricane shade.

Tristyn had just started to peruse the menu when a waitress came by to deliver warm bread and offer drinks. After they'd ordered, they shared a few minutes of easy, casual conversation before Josh looked at her across the table and said, "You're going to make me admit it, aren't you?"

She folded her arms on the table and leaned forward, well aware that the posture pushed her breasts up to the neckline of her dress. "What is it that you don't want to admit?"

To his credit, he kept his eyes locked on hers. Mostly.

"That the way you look in that dress is enough to make me forget about your granny jammies."

"That almost sounds like a compliment," she mused.

"You've probably been told that you're beautiful more times than you can count."

The Last Single Garrett

Brenda Harlen

D0040413

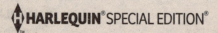

HARLEQUIN® SPECIAL EDITION®

"Maybe," she acknowledged. "But I've never heard *you* say those words."

"Do you need me to say them?"

"Only if you believe them."

His gaze held steady on hers. "You, Tristyn Garrett, are the most beautiful woman I've ever known."

"Hmm...that sounded like the well-rehearsed line of a man who's hoping to end the evening in a woman's bed."

"I'm not going to deny that I'm hoping, but that doesn't make the words any less true," he told her. "And if they sounded rehearsed, it's only because I've thought them a thousand times in my mind."

And when he looked at her the way he was looking at her now, she almost believed him. Then she reminded herself that this was Josh—and Josh had probably charmed more females out of their panties than she wanted to count. Thankfully, the arrival of the servers with their plates saved her from having to respond, because she was afraid that anything she said would reveal the effect his words had on her.

She'd opted for a thick, juicy rib eye, and it was prepared just the way she liked it, served with a fully loaded baked potato and broccoli florets. Josh had the prime rib with mashed potatoes and baby carrots. While they ate their food and sipped a delicious Cabernet Sauvignon, they chatted about various current events and shared news from home.

Thinking about her sisters and her cousins, she was reminded of her promise to herself that she would never settle for anything less than the forever-after kind of love each of them had found with their respective partners. So why had she agreed to this date with Josh tonight when she knew that he wasn't the man to give her what she wanted?

Okay, he could give her some of what she wanted— because she also really wanted to get naked with him and discover if he lived up to his reputation. But getting involved with him, even temporarily, could screw up a lot of things. Not just because they had to work together when they went back to Charisma, but because he was practically a member of her family.

"What are you thinking about?" Tristyn asked, when she realized that Josh had also been silent for several minutes. Then she shook her head. "That's a silly question to ask the night before a race—of course you're thinking about Ren's chances tomorrow."

"Actually, I wasn't thinking about the race," he admitted. "In fact, I haven't thought about the race or the team or anything related to GSR since you walked out of your bedroom in that killer dress."

"Then I guess it was worth every penny that I paid for it," she mused.

"Except it's not only the dress."

"You're one of those guys who likes a woman in high heels, aren't you?"

"Well, yes," he agreed, lifting the wine bottle to top up her glass. "But that wasn't what I meant, either."

"What did you mean?"

"It's the woman inside the dress—and the shoes—who continues to intrigue me," he told her. "I've known you for almost twenty years. I spend more holidays with your family than my own. And for the past three years, I've seen you almost every day at work."

She picked up her glass, sipped.

"After all that time, you'd think I'd know everything about you," he continued. "That we'd run out of things to talk about. But you continue to fascinate me, and I'm never bored in your company."

"So why do you look as if you're worried about something?" she asked.

"Because you worry me," he confided. "I look at you and I know you could be the perfect woman for me.

"But I'm not looking for the perfect woman," he hastened to add. "What you said to the girls about me was true—I'm not looking to settle down. I don't want to give up my lifestyle for a ring on my finger, rug rats at home and a woman in my bed—not even a woman as beautiful and tempting as you."

"Well, you can stop worrying," she told him. "Because I'm not looking to be your perfect woman. I do want what each of my sisters has found with her husband—someday. But I'm not looking to settle down right now, either." Okay, that was a little white lie, but she decided it was a forgivable one under the circumstances. "And I promise you, even if I was, I know better than to look in your direction."

"So what are you looking for now?" he asked her.

She thought about his question for a minute before answering, "To satisfy my curiosity."

He reached across the table and stroked the back of her hand. "I can satisfy more than your curiosity."

The way her body responded to his casual touch, she had no doubt that he could. But admitting as much would be a boost that his ego didn't need.

"Give me a chance to prove it," he urged.

"I'm thinking about it," she admitted.

His eyes lit with wicked promise, but before he could say anything, the waitress came by with dessert menus.

"I'm not sure I could eat another bite," Tristyn said, even as she skimmed the offerings. "Oh, but they have a tiramisu cake."

"You do have a sweet tooth, don't you?"

"I do," she agreed. "But the cake probably wouldn't be as good as Rafe's tiramisu."

Josh's jaw tightened perceptibly at the mention of the other man's name. "Are you still seeing him?"

"I've been on the road with you for the past three weeks. When would I have seen him?"

He nodded in acknowledgment of her point. "Okay, maybe what I should have asked is—are you planning to see him again when you get back to Charisma?"

"I don't know," she admitted. "We kind of left things open-ended."

"We're going to close that opening," he told her. "You and me—tonight."

A quick thrill of anticipation raced through her veins, but Tristyn refused to let him see it. Instead, she lifted her wineglass, sipped.

"Have you decided on dessert?" the waitress returned to their table to ask.

"Yes," Tristyn said. "I'll have the tiramisu cake."

"To go," Josh said firmly.

"Yes, sir." The server nodded and slipped away again.

Tristyn lifted a brow. "What if I want to eat my dessert here?"

The heat in his gaze practically melted her bones. "Finish your wine, Tristyn."

Though it wasn't in her nature to blindly follow orders, she picked up her glass and finished her wine.

Josh ignored the speed limit as he drove to the campground. Tristyn didn't object, because the truth was, she was just as eager as he was to get back to the RV. By the time he pulled up beside the fifth wheel, her heart was pounding so loudly she was certain he must be able to hear it.

Tonight, she thought, with almost giddy relief.

Finally, tonight, she was going to experience the bliss of making love with Josh. And the way her body responded to his kiss, his touch, she didn't doubt for a minute that it would be bliss.

He came around to open her door and helped her out of the truck. When he set her down, he took her hand, his thumb brushing the inside of her wrist, where her pulse was racing. He unlocked the RV and gestured for her to enter.

"You're having second thoughts," he guessed, when she hesitated inside the door.

"Not about tonight," she told him.

"About what?"

"Tomorrow," she admitted. "I don't want things to be awkward and weird in the morning."

"So don't act awkward and weird in the morning," he advised.

A smile tugged at her lips as she shook her head. "Is it really that simple for you?"

"I'm a guy," he reminded her. "It's not in my nature to overthink things."

"You don't have *any* concerns about how this will affect our working relationship?"

"My only worry right now is that you might change your mind. But it's your choice, Tristyn. If you tell me you don't want me, don't want this, I'll walk away."

Of course, she couldn't do it. Maybe she did have some reservations, but she knew that if she backed out now, she'd regret it for the rest of her life. Still, she couldn't resist teasing him, just a little.

She tipped her head back and kept her gaze steady on his as she said, "I don't want…"

His eyes narrowed when she paused.

"…to waste any more time talking."

His only response was to draw her into his arms and cover her lips with his own.

Her physical reaction was immediate and intense. If this was the chemistry he'd referred to, she'd never experienced it—not to the same extent—with anyone else. She willingly parted her lips as he deepened the kiss, and the erotic stroke of his tongue stirred a new hunger inside her.

She lifted her arms to link them behind his neck as she pressed herself closer to him. His hands skimmed down her back, to the hem of her dress, then dipped beneath it to slide up her thighs to her buttocks. He groaned, a sound of pure male appreciation. "You're wearing a thong."

"I don't like panty lines."

"I don't care why—I'm just grateful," he told her, his hands kneading her bare flesh. Then he pushed her skirt up and dropped to his knees in front of her.

Her stomach quivered; her thighs trembled. "Josh."

He glanced up, his eyes hot and intent. "Do you have any objections?"

She could only shake her head.

"Good," he said, and pressed his mouth to the triangle of lace at the apex of her thighs.

She reached behind to grab hold of the edge of the counter for balance as he explored her intimately with his tongue and his teeth. The barrier of lace was hardly that, but he paused long enough to yank it away and gain un-fettered access. He drove her quickly toward the verge of climax…then ruthlessly pushed her over the edge.

The orgasm ripped through her body, so fierce and strong her knees actually buckled, and she would have crumpled to the floor if Josh hadn't been holding her up. With a satisfied grin, he rose to his feet and scooped her into his arms and carried her to the bedroom. He set her on her feet beside the bed and ripped back the covers.

"The first time is going to be fast," he warned.

"Not fast enough," she said, tugging at his tie, then im-mediately going to work on the buttons of his shirt.

"And I thought I was impatient," he teased, kicking off his shoes and socks.

"I feel as if I've been waiting for you forever," she admitted, pushing his shirt over his shoulders and running her hands over the smooth, hard muscles of his chest.

"Not much longer," he promised, unfastening the buckle of his belt, then quickly discarding his pants and knit boxers.

She reached for him then, wrapping her fingers around the velvety length of him. He sucked in a breath.

"It's going to be too fast if you keep that up," he warned.

She opened the drawer of the night table and pulled out a little square packet, because there had never been any doubt in her mind about how this night would end and she'd wanted to be prepared. She carefully tore the wrapper and removed the condom, then deftly unrolled the latex over his rigid shaft.

"Now," she told him.

At any other time, Josh might have been amused by her bossy tone. Right now, he was too aroused to do anything but obey. He dumped her unceremoniously onto the bed and spread her legs, then finally positioned himself between them.

He was rock hard and aching for her, desperate to take what she was offering. He drove into her, groaning in satisfaction as he was enveloped by her wet heat. She cried out his name as another series of tremors rippled through her body—and his. The clenching of her inner muscles around him was almost more than he could stand. He fisted his hands in the bedsheet and counted his ragged breaths while he waited out her climax.

When the tremors began to abate, he slowly withdrew, then pushed in again, steady strokes that increased in speed and had her breath coming in shallow gasps.

"I don't… I can't… Oh…my…oh…yes… Josh."

When the next waves of pleasure began to roll through her, he let himself ride along with her until they were dragged under together.

* * *

It was a long time later before Josh managed to catch his breath again, before he rolled away from Tristyn and went to discard the condom. When he came back from the bathroom, she still hadn't moved. Her hair was spread out on her pillow, her skirt was bunched around her waist and one strap of her dress had fallen down to her elbow, exposing the luscious curve of one creamy breast. She looked like she'd just been ravished, and the smile that curved her lips assured him that she'd thoroughly enjoyed the experience.

"I didn't even take your dress off you."

"You can take it off me now," she suggested.

He reached for her hand and helped her up off the bed.

"I really do like the way you look in this dress," he told her, nudging the other strap from her shoulder. "But I think I'm going to like you naked even more."

He found the zipper hidden at the side, then peeled the garment slowly down her body. Undressing Tristyn was like unwrapping a coveted birthday present, and he sincerely regretted skipping this step earlier. Especially when he discovered that she was wearing a lace demi-cup bra that matched the thong he'd dispensed with much earlier. There was something about the contrast of the sexy black lingerie against the creamy silk of her skin that had an immediate and predictable effect on him.

His body's reaction did not go unnoticed. "Apparently the rumors about your stamina were not exaggerated," Tristyn said.

Over the years, he'd done nothing to dispel the rumors he knew she would hear, because he'd trusted that his reputation would be an effective barrier between them. And it had worked—maybe too well. Because now that he finally had her where he'd wanted her for so long, he didn't want any obstacles in the way. But he wasn't quite ready to bare his heart and soul and admit that, for the past twelve years, she was the only one he'd wanted, so he only said, "Let's see if you can keep up."

He hooked his fingers in the straps of her bra and tugged them down, then dipped his head to kiss the curve of her breasts. First one, then the other. Her nipples strained against the fabric, a silent request that he couldn't ignore. He took one of the turgid peaks in his mouth and suckled gently. A low sound of pleasure hummed deep in her throat as her fingers slid into his hair.

"This time isn't going to be fast," he told her. "This time, I'm going to take my time exploring every inch of your delectable body."

And he did. He traced every dip and curve with his hands and his lips, pausing only to turn her onto her stomach so he could continue his exploration on her backside.

"You have a tattoo on your butt."

She glanced at him over her shoulder. "Do you have a problem with tattoos?"

"No," he assured her. "I guess I'm just…surprised." He traced the outline of the tat with his thumb. "Is it Celtic?"

She nodded. "It's a quaternary knot. Some people believe the four sides represent the four seasons, others claim that they're representative of the four cardinal directions."

"Why did you choose to get a quaternary knot tattooed on your butt?" he asked.

"I like the symbolism of it. The unending paths illustrate continuity and eternity, and the weaving together of the different strands suggests unity."

"I like it, too," he said, then slid down her body and kissed the inked flesh.

"Now I can tell everyone that Josh Slater kissed my butt," she teased.

His lips curved as he tore open another condom. "You've told me to often enough—although I think you used a word other than *butt*."

"That's because you're often a pain in my...butt."

"Yeah, we do have a tendency to rub one another the wrong way," he acknowledged, as he covered himself to protect both of them.

"I like the way you're rubbing against me now," she told him.

"Let's see what else you like," he said, and slid into her.

Her eyes closed on a sigh. "That," she said. "I really like that."

"And this?" he asked, and began to move.

"Oh, yeah," she agreed.

Later, Josh fell asleep with Tristyn in his arms. But they came together again and again in the night, unable to get enough of one another. When he woke up in the morning, he automatically reached for her and was disappointed to discover that he was alone.

He glanced at the clock just as she walked through the door carrying two mugs.

"I know you can't function in the morning without your caffeine," she said, offering coffee to him.

He took the mug and set it on the table beside the bed, then reached for hers and put it down, too.

She frowned. "What are you doing?"

"Apparently, I need to show you that my function is just fine in the morning."

She laughed softly. "I wasn't disparaging your manhood," she assured him. "I just thought you'd want coffee."

What he wanted, what he couldn't seem to get enough of, was Tristyn. But he wasn't going to think about that now. Because if he thought about it, he'd worry about it, and he didn't want to waste any of the time they had together worrying.

As he'd told her the night before, he didn't like to over-think things. *Keep it simple*, he reminded himself.

"There are some things that are even better than coffee in the morning," he said, tugging her down onto the mattress and rolling on top of her to prove it.

Chapter Fourteen

A long time later, while Josh was in the shower, Tristyn reheated the coffee that had gone cold while they'd lingered in bed. She had no complaints. In fact, she thought she might be able to give up coffee completely if she could wake up with him in her bed every morning—but that was dangerous thinking.

Because as spectacular as it had been to make love with Josh, she knew she couldn't let it happen again. She'd wanted to satisfy her curiosity; he'd done that and more. Expecting, or even allowing, one night to become two would be a mistake.

"We need to get to the track," she said, when he was showered and dressed.

"Yeah, we do," he agreed, though he slid his arms around her and drew her close.

"And Ren has the pole today," she said, though it was unlikely he needed a reminder.

"I have a pole, too," he said, rubbing against her.

A laugh bubbled up inside her even as her body began to respond to his. "Unfortunately, we don't have time to deal with your…pole—again," she said.

"Maybe later?" he asked hopefully.

She shook her head. "I don't think so."

Josh frowned at her response, no doubt unaccustomed to a woman saying no to him—especially a woman who had already said yes. But it was important to Tristyn to put their relationship back on the friendship track. It was the only way she could be sure she wouldn't fall for him again.

"So this was a one-night stand?" he asked.

"Well, technically one night and one morning," she said lightly.

"What if one night and one morning wasn't enough?"

She couldn't let his question sway her. Even if he wanted more nights and more mornings now, he would eventually decide that there had been enough, and she'd be the one left nursing a broken heart.

"Last night was incredible," she admitted. "But pretending it was anything more than a night of really great sex would be a mistake."

He didn't dispute her characterization, but he did ask, "Why is one night of really great sex okay, but two nights—or two weeks or two months—would be a mistake?"

"Because our lives are too closely entwined," she pointed out. "You're not just my boss and my cousin's best friend, you're practically an honorary member of my family."

"So this is it? We just go back to the way things were, as if last night never happened?"

"I'm not likely to forget it—and I don't want to," she admitted. "But it can't happen again."

"I said that it was your choice, and I meant it," he said. "But I can't pretend I'm not disappointed."

"Better to be disappointed now than heartbroken later," she said lightly.

"Maybe you're right," he finally agreed.

Josh wasn't happy with Tristyn's unilateral decision to put on the brakes. He wasn't looking for a long-term relationship, but he had hoped that they could continue to enjoy being together throughout the summer. Before they'd made love, being around her and not being able to touch her had almost been impossible. Now that he knew how she responded to his touch, not being able to touch her was going to be torturous.

Pretending it was anything more than a night of really great sex would be a mistake.

Maybe she was right. Maybe he was trying to make it into something more because he felt guilty about getting naked with his best friend's cousin. But he'd had one-night stands before without obsessing about any of the women afterward. So why was he obsessing about Tristyn now?

He'd walked away from her twelve years earlier, not because he wanted to but because he knew it was necessary. Somehow, even then, he'd known that if he touched her, if he tasted her, he'd never want to let her go.

For so long, he'd wanted no one but her. But he'd ignored the truth and he'd turned his attention to other women, certain that they could satisfy the aching need inside him. He'd been wrong.

He hadn't expected making love with Tristyn to change anything—except maybe to alleviate the sexual tension they'd been living with. He didn't expect to feel any differently about her or their situation. Now that he'd experienced the thrill of making love with Tristyn, he wondered if he could ever be satisfied with anyone else, anything less than her hungry kisses, eager touches and unbridled passion.

And he wanted more than one night, dammit. He wanted more conversations under the stars, more lazy mornings, even more games of mini-putt and arguments over laundry duty. He especially wanted more opportunities to make love with her all through the night until the sun began to rise.

Wanting those things should have created a full-scale panic. He wasn't supposed to want those things. He'd never wanted them before.

But the wanting didn't scare him. What scared him was the realization that if he let her go, he might forever lose his chance to have everything he'd ever wanted. And Tristyn was that everything.

Tristyn had worried that there would be tension between her and Josh when they went back to the RV, but the presence of his nieces—and their incessant chatter—ensured otherwise, allowing them to fall back into the routines they'd already established.

After the first day, she was relieved to note that Josh didn't seem inclined to challenge her "one night" directive. But sometimes when she was in the kitchen, he'd come in to get a drink or a snack and make a point of squeezing past her in the narrow space, ensuring that his body brushed against hers. If she asked him to pass her something at the dinner table, he'd let his fingers graze hers in the transfer, and linger longer than was necessary.

It all had the appearance of innocence, but she knew better. There wasn't an innocent bone in Josh's body and he was deliberately attempting to stir up her hormones. What he didn't know, what she wouldn't admit, was that his actions were unnecessary. Because she hadn't stopped wanting him, and being in close proximity to him day after day—even without his deliberately provocative touches—was quietly but steadily driving her insane.

Every once in a while, she'd catch him looking at her with undisguised hunger in his eyes. It was admittedly thrilling—and arousing—to know that he still desired her. Though none of her reasons for not wanting to get involved with him had changed, ultimately none of them proved strong enough to counter her own desire.

After Indianapolis they headed to Pocono, breaking up the six hundred plus mile journey into two parts. When they got to their scheduled stop after the first part, it was right in the middle of a torrential downpour. By the time Josh finished the hookups—having rejected Tristyn's suggestion that he wait to see if the storm would pass—he was soaked and the girls were cranky from being cooped up in the truck for six hours.

Searching online, Tristyn found a family fun center not too far away. After Josh had dried off and changed, they headed out so the kids could climb and jump at the indoor jungle gym. Then Tristyn slipped away while Josh and his nieces were bumper bowling to do a little personal shopping. When she returned, everyone was "starving," so they went next door for pizza.

The rain had stopped by the time they got back to the RV, and soon after that the girls were snuggled into their respective bunks and fast asleep. Josh took some time then to catch up on emails and phone messages while Tristyn debated with herself the wisdom of changing the rules in the middle of a game.

Josh was on the phone with Daniel when Tristyn came out of her bedroom. And she wasn't wearing the familiar pink-striped pajamas he liked to tease her about. He felt his body stir as his gaze skimmed over her—from the top of her head to the tips of her toes, lingering on the fantasy of silk and lace that barely covered up all his favorite parts in between.

He heard a voice in his ear, but he was no longer following the conversation. As if of its own volition, his thumb tapped the screen, disconnecting the call.

Tristyn arched a brow, her green eyes dancing with amusement. "Did you just hang up on your business partner and best friend?"

"I think I did."

"And how are you going to explain that to him?" she asked.

Josh couldn't tear his eyes away from the feminine curves showcased in fantasy lingerie. "Bad cell phone coverage in this area." He cleared his throat. "Um…what happened to your granny jammies?"

"They're in the laundry."

He swallowed. "Oh."

Her lips curved then. "You're not going to comment on what I'm wearing instead?"

"No," he said, then changed his mind. "Except that maybe you should put on a robe. You look…cold."

"I'm not cold," she assured him, stepping forward to stand directly in front of him.

"Okay," he said.

"I saw this when I was shopping today, and I thought it fit your description of peekaboo lace."

The delicate lace panels did provide tantalizing glimpses of her skin. And the silky fabric seemed to caress her shapely curves. "You were thinking of me when you bought this?"

"Actually…I was thinking about how much I'd like you to take it off me."

He swallowed again. "What about your one-night rule?"

She lifted the hem of her silky slip, exposing several inches of shapely thigh, then bracketed his hips with her knees. As she settled onto his lap, all of the blood from his brain did, too.

"I've decided that it requires a minor amendment," she told him.

"An amendment?" he echoed, because he didn't seem capable of finding words of his own.

"Mmm hmm." She tugged his T-shirt out of his shorts and slid her palms beneath it.

He cleared his throat. "What kind of, uh, amendment?"

"That so long as we're together this summer, we should have as much sex as often as possible."

"That's a...major...amendment," he noted, struggling to maintain his train of thought as she raked her nails lightly down his chest.

"I was concerned that having sex again would complicate our relationship," she admitted, leaning forward to press her lips to his jaw. "But not having sex these last four nights hasn't done anything to simplify our relationship, has it?"

"That's true," he agreed, in a strangled tone.

"And if we both want the same thing—" she nipped lightly at his chin "—why are we denying ourselves?"

"I have no idea."

She looked at him now, and he saw that there was a hint of uncertainty in her desire-clouded eyes. "Do we both want the same thing?"

He wondered how she could possibly question the effect she had on him, and he silently vowed to eliminate the last of her doubts here and now. "If the same thing is me buried deep inside you, then I'd say yes."

Her lips curved. "Do you want to discuss this some more or do you want to take me to bed?"

"I want to take you—right here, right now," he told her, his gaze hot and hungry. "But considering that there are three little girls sleeping less than thirty feet away, your bed is probably a better idea."

"Probably," she agreed.

He wrapped his arms around her and lifted her with him as he stood. She hooked her legs behind his back so that their bodies were aligned from chest to hip and all the erogenous points in between. He carried her like that to the bedroom, pausing only to ensure the door was closed and locked before he tumbled on top of the mattress with her.

* * *

The first night they'd spent together had been an introduction to the exquisite joy of sex with Josh Slater. This time, Tristyn thought she knew what to expect. She was wrong.

Every time she believed that he'd taken her to the limit, he showed her that there was more. It was as if he knew her body better than she did. He certainly knew where to touch, when to linger, to enhance her sensual pleasure.

"I didn't expect it to be as good this time," she admitted.

Josh lifted a brow as he leisurely stroked a hand down her back.

"I figured part of the rush was the realization of long-term anticipation, and that once that mystery was gone, the intensity would fade."

"You were wrong."

She nodded. "You could become an addiction."

"You already are," he said, drawing her close.

He kissed her again, and Tristyn realized it had never been like this with anyone else. Probably because she'd never before had a lover of Josh's caliber and experience, and she wasn't going to delude herself into thinking that a shocking number of orgasms was indicative of anything other than that.

"Hey," he said, drawing her attention back to him. "Where'd you go?"

"Sorry, I guess my thoughts wandered."

"Wherever they wandered, they put a line between your brows," he observed, touching a finger to the crease. "Do you want to tell me about it?"

"Not really."

He waited patiently.

She sighed. "I was just thinking about how you acquired your intimate and extensive knowledge of the female body," she admitted.

"I haven't lived like a monk," he acknowledged. "But the stories you heard me tell may have been exaggerated a little—for your benefit."

"For *my* benefit? Why?"

"Because I wanted to give you a reason to stay far away from me," he confessed. "But I haven't been with as many women as you think."

"The number doesn't matter," she decided. "As long as the number of women you're involved with right now is one."

"You are the only one," he assured her. "The only one I'm with—the only one I want."

"For now but not forever," she reminded him.

"You do like your rules," he mused.

"And another of those rules is no overnight guests."

"You're trying to kick me out of your bed, aren't you?"

"It wouldn't look right if one of the girls woke up and found you were in my bed instead of your own," she told him.

"Alright," he finally relented, unable to dispute her point. "Do I at least get a good-night kiss?"

"I think you've already had more than a few good-night kisses," she said, nudging him toward the edge of the mattress.

"Uh uh," he denied. "Those were precoital, midcoital and postcoital kisses."

She was smiling as she shook her head. "It will probably be quicker for me to give you a good-night kiss than to debate your categorizations, won't it?"

"Probably," he agreed.

So she kissed him good-night, and by the time she eased her lips from his, she was tempted to break her own rule and invite him to spend the night in her bed. But she was afraid that breaking one rule would set a precedent that encouraged her to disregard others. And if she did that, she might foolishly open up her heart and fall in love with him—and that was a risk she wasn't willing to take.

Chapter Fifteen

Of the three sisters, Emily was usually the first awake. In the mornings, while Tristyn sat outside enjoying a cup of coffee, the five-year-old was often there to keep her company. The first morning in Pennsylvania, she'd barely taken a sip from her cup when the little girl said, "Look, Tristyn—my tooth is really wiggly now."

"Wow," she said, trying to sound more impressed than repulsed when Emily managed to push the tooth with her tongue so that it was practically horizontal in her mouth. "I don't think it's going to be much longer before that comes out."

"An' then the tooth fairy comes," the little girl announced.

"Does she?" Tristyn said, wondering if there were guidelines as to what the tooth fairy was supposed to give in exchange for a tooth. "And what does the tooth fairy do?"

"She gives money!"

"Like an ATM?"

Emily giggled. "Not that much money. Just a dollar."

"Still, a dollar for a tooth—that seems like a pretty good deal to me."

The child's smile slipped. "Do you think the tooth fairy will be able to find me here?"

"I'm sure she'll be able to find you, wherever you are," Tristyn assured her.

Emily's tooth came out when she was brushing her teeth before bed that night. The gentle pressure of her brush was all it took to set it free. As a result, there was hardly any blood, for which Tristyn was extremely grateful.

"Do you have a dollar for the tooth fairy?" she asked Josh, after the girls had all fallen asleep.

"Isn't she supposed to leave the money?"

Tristyn rolled her eyes as Josh opened his wallet.

"The smallest bill I have is a ten," he said.

"You can't give her ten dollars for losing a tooth," Tristyn protested. "Or Charlotte and Hanna will be trying to pull out their teeth, too."

"I'm guessing you don't have a dollar?"

She nipped the ten out of his fingers as she shook her head. "I used the last of my cash to buy ice-cream cones for the girls this afternoon."

"So what are you going to do with that?"

"I'll go to the little store beside registration and ask for change."

She came back less than ten minutes later with a package of candy in her hand.

He shook his head, as if disappointed. "You traded the cow for magic beans?"

"You read *Jack and the Beanstalk* to Hanna tonight, didn't you?" she guessed.

"Last night," he admitted.

"Gummy bears not magic beans," she said, showing him the package.

He made a face. "Gummy bears?"

"You have something against gummy bears?"

"The last time I had gummy bears, they got stuck in my braces," he told her.

"I knew that perfect smile had to have orthodontic help," she mused.

"You didn't have braces?"

She shook her head and leaned close to whisper, "Everything about me is au naturel."

"Except the tattoo," he said, pulling her down into his lap. "Did you get a dollar for the tooth fairy?"

She drew the change out of her pocket and set it on the table, then tore open her package of candy. "Do you want to share my gummy bears?"

"No, thanks. I'll have my treat later—in accordance with the amended agreement."

She nibbled on a piece of candy. "When I said as much sex as often as possible, I didn't realize you were insatiable," she teased.

"Are you growing bored with me already?"

"Not quite yet," she said. But the truth was just the opposite. The more time she spent with Josh, the more she wanted to be with him. As phenomenal as the sex was, it wasn't all about the sex. They would often snuggle together in her bed for hours afterward, talking about all manner of things and nothing in particular. She'd known Josh for a lot of years, but there were a lot of things she still didn't know about him and she was enjoying the discovery process. She definitely wasn't bored, and she suspected that she could spend a lifetime with him and not tire of his company and companionship.

For now, not forever, she reminded herself.

And focused on enjoying the now.

Emily woke up in the morning, panicked and crying. "It's gone! It's gone!"

Tristyn rushed into her room, wondering what could

have put the little girl into such a state of distress. "What's gone?"

Tears streamed down the child's face. "My tooth."

She exhaled a slow breath, confident the crisis would pass when Emily found the payment she'd received in exchange for the tooth. "Well, the tooth fairy must have come to get it," she said, attempting to soothe her. "Is there any money in its place?"

Emily nodded and held up the crumpled bill, but the tears continued to fall. "The tooth fairy isn't s'posed to take it."

Josh—standing in the doorway after being awakened by the little girl's cries along with everyone else—exchanged a look with Tristyn. "She's not?"

The distraught child shook her head. "Not the first one. Only the ones that come after."

The adults exchanged another look.

"That's a new one to me," Tristyn admitted.

"Maybe the tooth fairy didn't realize it was your first one," Josh said, as Charlotte looked at the adults suspiciously.

"Mommy kept Charlotte's first tooth in a special box," Emily said. "An' she has boxes for me an' Hanna, too. An' now my box is always gonna be empty."

Desperate for a solution to the dilemma, Tristyn impulsively said, "Maybe we can get your tooth back."

Emily sniffled. "How?"

"We can write a note to the tooth fairy."

Charlotte immediately shook her head. "That won't work—the tooth fairy only comes when someone loses a tooth, so she wouldn't be here to see the note."

Emily started to cry harder.

"There's got to be some way we can get her attention," Tristyn said, looking desperately at Josh for help.

"Smoke signals," he suggested.

Emily lifted her head and wiped her tear-streaked cheeks.

"What are smoke signals?" Charlotte asked suspiciously.

"It's an ancient way of communicating over great distances, developed long before cell phones."

His eldest niece still looked skeptical.

"That's a great idea," Tristyn declared, though she wasn't at all convinced that his plan would satisfy the girls—or that Josh knew the first thing about creating smoke signals.

"How do you make smoke signals?" Charlotte asked.

"First, you build a fire," he said.

Emily stopped sniffling long enough to ask, "Can we make s'mores at the fire?"

He glanced at Tristyn. She nodded, mentally adding the necessary ingredients to her shopping list.

"Sure," he said. "But only after we summon the tooth fairy."

"How will we know if she got the message?" Emily asked worriedly.

"We won't know for sure until tomorrow," Josh admitted. "But if it doesn't work tonight, we'll try again and again until it does."

Worried that he might set the camp on fire in his effort to generate smoke signals, Tristyn offered an alternate suggestion. "Maybe the tooth fairy's on Twitter."

"That would certainly be easier," he agreed.

"Why don't you come into the kitchen and we'll see if we can figure this out after we've had breakfast?" Tristyn suggested.

The girls immediately complied, and when everyone had eaten, Tristyn opened her tablet and linked to the social media site, then searched for "tooth fairy." The screen filled with potential matches.

Emily, sitting up on her knees now, peered at the screen, her brow furrowed. "But which one's the *real* tooth fairy?"

"The real tooth fairy will find our message," Tristyn assured her.

"What should we say?"

"Maybe something like 'recall requested hashtag tooth fairy'?" she suggested.

"But that doesn't tell her who or where," Charlotte pointed out.

Which was true, because Tristyn had hoped to keep the message deliberately vague. "What if we add 'by Emily at Pocono Mountain RV Park'?"

Emily nodded her approval; her older sister still looked dubious.

"Let's give it a shot," Tristyn urged. "If it doesn't work, we can try the smoke signals tomorrow, okay?"

"Can we still have s'mores tonight?" Emily asked.

"We can still have s'mores tonight," she confirmed. "*If* you all get washed up and dressed and come shopping with me."

"But you haven't hit Send," Charlotte pointed out.

"Oh, right." With the three girls and their uncle looking on, Tristyn tapped the button and the message went out into the world.

Lucy called while Tristyn was out shopping with the girls, which gave Josh an opportunity to fill her in on the tooth fairy fiasco. She laughed when he told her about the tweet, then she sighed wistfully.

"I didn't realize she had a loose tooth, or I would have told you about the tooth fairy."

"That would have been good," Josh agreed. "I'm just glad that I actually did keep the tooth for you rather than tossing it in the trash."

"Her first tooth," Lucy said, with a little sniffle.

"She'll lose a lot more before she's through," he pointed out.

"I know," she admitted.

"How are things going there?" he asked, in an effort to divert a complete meltdown.

"Good," she said. "We're actually a little bit ahead of schedule."

"I guess that means you haven't taken much time to see the sights."

"There's nothing here that I want to see as much as my girls," his sister said.

"It won't be too long before you're home again," he soothed. "And then I'll finally get my life back."

Except that the life he had before embarking on this road trip with Tristyn didn't hold the same appeal anymore. Because in that life, he crossed paths with Tristyn at the office and Garrett family events, but he didn't have the right to drag her into a corner to steal a kiss, or sneak into her bedroom at night, or even just sit out under the stars and talk about anything and everything.

"I know I didn't really give you a choice about any of this," Lucy admitted, drawing his attention back to their conversation. "But I appreciate everything you're doing."

"I'm enjoying spending time with them," he admitted, no longer surprised to realize it was true.

"And how are things going with Tristyn?" she prompted.

"Even from another country and across an ocean, you can't resist meddling in my life, can you?" he muttered.

"I just want you to find someone and be happy."

"Why don't you focus on your own life?" he suggested.

She sighed. "You're right—I have no business telling you how to live your life when I've screwed up mine."

"You haven't screwed up anything," he denied. "You're a wonderful mother to three fabulous kids."

"It's hard to believe that when I'm almost four thousand miles away from them," she acknowledged.

"Then get back to work so you can come home," he advised.

"I'll do that," she agreed. "Give my girls big hugs and kisses from me and tell them that I love them."

"Every day," he promised.

Tristyn could recall listening to her aunt Ellen and aunt Jane talk about how much food teenage boys could put away at a meal. Over the past few weeks, she'd begun to suspect that active little girls could probably give teenage boys a run for their money.

When they got back to the RV after shopping, Josh was there to help them carry the bags inside and put the groceries away. Though she wouldn't ever comment aloud, she couldn't help but notice that Josh had stepped up in a big way—not just with the girls, but tackling his share of the domestic chores. And though she knew it was sometimes difficult for him to juggle the responsibilities of his job with the demands of his nieces, he never balked at spending time with them. And Charlotte, Emily and Hanna had all thrived as a result of his attention.

"We're gonna make s'mores, Unca Josh."

"It looks like you're going to make a lot of s'mores," he noted, holding an enormous bag of marshmallows.

"The big bag was on sale," Charlotte told him.

"And then, of course, we needed enough chocolate and graham crackers to go with the marshmallows," Tristyn said.

"Of course," he agreed drily, as he continued to unpack. "You even bought sticks?"

She nodded. "They were conveniently located beside the other ingredients."

He shook his head. "Real s'mores are made with marshmallows toasted on the end of sticks hunted up in the woods and sharpened with a knife."

"I wanna make *real* s'mores," Emily announced.

"Me, too," Hanna chimed in.

"They will be real s'mores," Charlotte assured her sisters. "They just won't have real bugs in them that might crawl out of sticks picked up off the ground."

Hanna wrinkled her nose. "I don' 'ike bugs."

"There are no bugs in these sticks," Tristyn promised. "Plus, there are two prongs, so you can roast two marshmallows at the same time—or cook hot dogs."

"But we're havin' s'ghetti tonight," Emily reminded her.

"I meant we could use them to cook hot dogs at another time," Tristyn clarified.

"Are we having meatballs or meat sauce?" Charlotte asked, more interested in what they would be eating today than in the future.

Tristyn had taken the meat out of the freezer but hadn't decided what she was going to do with it, so she was surprised when Josh responded to his niece's question.

"Both," he said. In response to Tristyn's questioning look, he shrugged. "You were out with the girls, so I thought I'd take care of dinner tonight."

"Mom usually just throws the meat into the sauce," Charlotte said. "She says it's too much trouble to make both."

"Well, since I don't have to do it all the time, I don't mind," he said.

"Are we gonna have garlic bread, too?" Emily asked.

"Yes, we'll have garlic bread, too," he confirmed.

"With or without cheese?"

"Half with and half without," he said, because over the past few weeks he'd learned that they had very different preferences about such things.

Tristyn held back a smile.

When it was time for dinner, he dished up Charlotte's pasta, added sauce and meatballs, and a slice of plain garlic bread; Emily got pasta and meat sauce and garlic bread with cheese; Hanna had her noodles with butter and parmesan and plain garlic bread.

"What do you prefer?" Josh asked Tristyn. "Meatballs or meat sauce?"

"I'll let the chef decide," she told him.

He served up a plate of pasta with meatballs and a side of garlic bread with cheese for her, then took his own to his seat at the table.

"This is really good, Uncle Josh," Charlotte said.

"Contrary to popular belief, I don't live on frozen dinners and fast food," he said.

"What can you make besides spaghetti?" Tristyn asked.

"Penne, rigatoni, ravioli, tortellini—basically anything that cooks in boiling water."

Charlotte and Emily giggled. Hanna probably didn't understand why her sisters were laughing, but she joined in.

"You make hamburgers, too," Emily pointed out.

"Well, yes, I can grill," he acknowledged. "But most women don't consider that cooking."

"Anything that puts food on the table is cooking in my book," Tristyn assured him.

Emily finished her pasta and reached for another slice of garlic bread. She nibbled on the corner, then looked at Tristyn and tentatively asked, "Do you think the tooth fairy got your message?"

"I think she probably did," Tristyn told her.

"But how do you know?" she persisted, obviously worried that her first tooth might be lost forever.

"Because the tweet Tristyn sent out has been retweeted two hundred and eighteen times," Josh said.

Tristyn looked at him, stunned. "No kidding?"

"No kidding," he confirmed. "Of course, that's probably because Ren D'Alesio was one of the first to retweet the message, with a plea to his fans to spread it far and wide. Which they've apparently done." Josh ruffled Emily's hair.

"So I think the odds are pretty good that the tooth fairy got your message."

"But what if she doesn't still have the tooth?" Charlotte wondered.

Tristyn groaned inwardly. "Let's deal with one issue at a time," she suggested.

"I'm just saying—no one knows what the tooth fairy actually *does* with the teeth. And if she picked up a lot of teeth last night, how will she know which one to give back?"

Emily's brow furrowed as she mulled over the dilemmas her sister presented.

"Let's not borrow trouble," Josh said to her.

Charlotte frowned. "What does that even mean?"

"It means that we should wait and see what happens tonight before we worry about all kinds of other possibilities."

Emily apparently agreed with his philosophy, because her next question was, "Can we have s'mores now?"

Chapter Sixteen

Tristyn cleaned up the kitchen while Josh assembled a tower of kindling and wood and started the fire. When everything was ready, Tristyn sat with Hanna on her lap and let the little girl help her turn the stick with the marshmallow on the end. Both Charlotte and Emily insisted that they were big enough to do their own, so Josh let them, though he was seated between the two girls to keep a close eye on both of them.

Charlotte was very precise and methodical, and her marshmallows were always evenly toasted and golden brown. Emily was a little more impatient and held her stick closer to the flame to cook the marshmallow more quickly. As a result, hers were often dark on one side and uncooked on the other, but she didn't seem to mind. By the time the older girls had each eaten two s'mores, Josh had consumed at least three, while Tristyn and Hanna had shared one—which was still more sugar than she thought the three-year-old should have right before bed.

And it was apparent that Josh's youngest niece was ready for bed, so she lifted the sleepy girl into her arms and took her inside to get her washed up and changed into her pajamas. Hanna's eyes were drifting shut even before

Tristyn tucked her favorite teddy bear under her arm and pulled up the covers.

"You're next, Emily," Tristyn said, when she returned to the campfire. "It's already past your bedtime."

"Can I make one more? Please?" she asked.

"Me, too," Charlotte implored.

Tristyn looked to Josh, who could hardly say no when he'd just put another marshmallow on his stick.

"If you have another one, you have to brush your teeth twice," he told them.

Both girls nodded their agreement, already reaching into the bag for more marshmallows.

But Tristyn suspected they didn't really want any more s'mores as much as they wanted to delay bedtime a little longer. A suspicion that was confirmed when she saw Charlotte's attention had waned from her task, the marshmallow at the end of her stick hovering dangerously close to the fire.

"Charlotte, your marshmallow is smoking," Tristyn said.

Before the girl could pull her stick away, the spongy sugar confection burst into flame.

"It's on fire. It's on fire," Charlotte said. "What do I do?"

"Gently shake the stick to—"

Before Josh could finish issuing his instructions, his panicked niece jerked the stick so hard that the flaming marshmallow flew right off the end and landed on the back of Josh's hand. He swore and shook his arm in an attempt to dislodge the marshmallow, but melted sugar was sticky and a fair amount of it remained on his skin. Tristyn instinctively dumped her glass of water onto his hand.

Charlotte looked up at him with wide eyes filled with horror and tears. "I'm so sorry, Uncle Josh."

"S'okay," he said, through gritted teeth.

Emily had dropped her stick, with the marshmallow still attached, to the ground, her request for one last s'more forgotten. Her eyes were worried, too, as she looked at her uncle, who was obviously in more pain than he wanted them to know.

"Go put some ice on that while I help the girls get ready for bed," Tristyn suggested.

He nodded tersely.

"He didn't stop, drop and roll," Emily said worriedly.

She fought against the smile that wanted to curve her lips. "It was just the marshmallow that was on fire, not Uncle Josh."

"Is he going to be okay?" Charlotte asked.

"His hand might be a little swollen and red for a while— and he'll probably use it as an excuse to get out of doing dishes—but he's going to be fine," Tristyn assured her.

"I'll do his dishes," she immediately offered.

Tristyn brushed a hand over Charlotte's hair. "It was an accident. There's no need for you to do penance."

Emily giggled. "She said dishes, not pens-itch." Then she tilted her head, as if trying to figure something out. "What is pens-itch?"

This time, Tristyn let the smile come. *"Penance,"* she clarified. "It's kind of like punishment you give to yourself—a way of showing that you're sorry."

"But I am sorry," Charlotte said, her voice tearful.

"I know," Tristyn agreed. "And Uncle Josh knows, too. So why don't you go give him a hug, then get washed up and brush your teeth?"

After the girls were tucked into bed, she dug the first-aid kit out of the bathroom cabinet.

"How is it?" she asked Josh.

"It feels a lot better already," he said, lifting the bag of ice away so that she could see for herself.

She winced when she saw the skin, angrily red and already blistered. "It doesn't look like it feels too good."

He made a fist, stretching the skin. "I just hope it doesn't scar."

"Are you worried that a permanent mark will detract from your masculine beauty?"

"Of course not," he replied. "Scars add character and intrigue—except when they're caused by flaming marshmallow, which is not a story I'd ever want to share."

She smiled as she opened the first aid box. "Let's get you bandaged up so that we can reduce the likelihood of that being necessary."

She applied some antibiotic cream to a square of sterile gauze, then gently set the gauze on his wound and wrapped it with medical tape.

"Aren't you a regular Florence Nightingale," he mused. "Any chance you have a nurse's uniform tucked in your closet?"

"Is that one of your fantasies—to play disciplinary doctor and naughty nurse?"

"My only fantasies are about playing with you," he told her.

"Well, right now you should go in and say good-night to the girls," she suggested. "And reassure Charlotte that you're not going to die."

"I'm sure she doesn't think I'm going to die," he chided.

"She's worried—and feeling guilty," Tristyn told him. "And she probably won't sleep until she sees for herself that you're going to be okay."

While he was doing that, she went back outside to put out the fire and retrieve the sticks that had been discarded.

"Everything okay?" she asked, when Josh came out of the girls' bedroom.

He nodded, then sniffed. "You smell like smoke."

"I put out the fire."

"Thank you." He lifted his uninjured hand to her mouth, rubbed his thumb gently over the bottom curve of her lip. "You scarfed some more chocolate, too, didn't you?"

"Guilty," she admitted, her tongue instinctively swiping over her lip where his finger had touched.

He lowered his head and brushed his lips over hers. "Mmm, you taste sweet."

"That would be the chocolate and marshmallow."

But he shook his head. "It's you," he insisted. "It's always been you."

Her heart swelled with hope and joy, until her brain cautioned it not to read too much into a few simple words. Josh was a master at saying and doing all the right things to make a woman feel good. She refused to believe that his offhand remark meant anything more than that he was focused on her now, and for now, that would be enough.

"Is your hand really okay?" she asked instead.

"It would feel a lot better if it was on your naked skin."

She smiled. "I think that can be arranged...*after* the tooth fairy puts Emily's tooth back under her pillow."

When that task had been completed, he took her to bed and proved that—even with an injury—his hands were capable of working magic. After, while their bodies were still joined together, she found herself thinking back on everything that had happened over the past several weeks, and she couldn't help being impressed at how willingly and competently he'd handled almost anything that came up.

"You surprise me sometimes," she said to him now.

"That's what all the girls say."

She narrowed her gaze. "Do you really want to remind me of 'all the girls' when my knee is positioned where it could jeopardize your future romantic pursuits?"

"Of course, the only girl who really matters is the one in my arms right now."

"Nice save," she told him.

He grinned and pressed his mouth to hers. "I do some of my best work under pressure."

"Such as your suggestion to summon the tooth fairy with smoke signals?"

"And sometimes desperate men say stupid things," he acknowledged.

"Aside from the fact that dropping a wet blanket over a fire is potentially much more dangerous than a flying, flaming marshmallow, you would have looked ridiculous."

"Maybe," he acknowledged.

"But you would have done it, anyway, for Emily, wouldn't you?"

"Sure," he agreed without hesitation.

"I'm starting to suspect that you might make a half-decent father someday," she mused.

The hand that was stroking down her back faltered for the space of a single heartbeat. "Are you making an observation or offering to bear my children?" he asked.

"Just an observation," she said immediately, emphatically.

"Well, that was certainly an unequivocal response," he noted. "No worries about my ego inflating around you."

"I didn't mean to sound so horrified," she told him. "I just meant to reassure you that I'm not looking for any kind of happily-ever-after with two kids and a dog and a white picket fence."

"You don't want what everyone else in your family has? What each of your sisters has?" he pressed.

"Well, sure. Someday," she admitted.

"Just not with me."

"I thought you would be relieved," she said, wondering at the hint of anger—and maybe even hurt—in his tone. "We agreed that whatever happened between us when we were on the road this summer would end when we returned to Charisma."

"You're right," he said, in that same clipped tone.

"So why are you acting all pissy because I'm abiding by the terms of our agreement?"

That was a good question—and not one that Josh had a ready answer for, so he opted for denial. "I'm not."

Tristyn looked skeptical.

"Okay, maybe I was," he acknowledged. "And I shouldn't have been. Because you're right—we have an agreement. And that agreement is for as much sex as often as possible, right?"

He didn't wait for a response but crushed his mouth down on hers.

He was hurt and angry and punishing her for nothing more than being honest with him. Which he knew was irrational, and that knowledge only pissed him off more as his hands moved over her body, not coaxing a response but demanding it. He was trying to pick a fight, but Tristyn wasn't interested in fighting back. She didn't balk at the pressure of his mouth or the roughness of his hands, but responded willingly, even eagerly, with a passion that, even after more than two weeks together, never failed to take his breath away.

She was so open and warm and giving, and as her hands moved over him, stroking and soothing, his own touch gentled. Because this was Tristyn. The most beautiful, sweet and loving woman he'd ever known. She was the kind of woman a man might think about settling down with, if he was a settling kind of man. Which Josh wasn't.

He should be glad she'd reminded him of that before he did something stupid—like fall in love with her.

Order was restored in Emily's world when she awakened the following morning and discovered that the tooth fairy had, in fact, returned sometime during the night and put her tooth back under the pillow. A few hours later, they were on their way to the track. The number 722 car experienced some engine problems that held it back early in the race, and Ren finished twenty-second in the field.

When they got back to the RV, they started to pack up in anticipation of the journey back to North Carolina. A two-week break in the race schedule meant that they would be able to spend a chunk of time in Charisma before they had to focus on the next race in Tennessee.

Tristyn had plotted out all their driving routes, noting food options and rest stops available along the way, but she generally didn't pay too much attention to anything but the scenery while Josh was driving. She trusted that he could follow the directions given to him by his GPS, until she watched him drive past the turn she'd expected him to take.

"Where are you going?" she asked.

"We're making a slight detour," he told her.

"Why?"

"Because I have a surprise for the girls."

"What kind of surprise?" Charlotte asked, proving that though she usually had a book in front of her face, she was listening to every word of their conversation in the front seat.

"If I told you, it wouldn't be a surprise," he pointed out.

Which meant that he wouldn't be able to tell Tristyn, either, without potentially ruining the surprise.

"I like s'prises," Emily said—awake because the children's Dramamine didn't seem to have the same sedative effect on her as even a child dose of the adult medication.

"S'prise!" Hanna agreed.

Another half an hour passed before they arrived at their destination—thirty minutes during which all three girls, excited about the unknown surprise, entertained the adults with an unending chorus of "Are we there yet?"

There, when they did arrive, turned out to be Hershey-park.

The girls were speechless when they discovered what their uncle had planned—for all of about three seconds. Then the questions started, their words rushing over one another: "How long can we stay?"

"Where's the biggest roller coaster?"

"I has to go potty."

They stayed three days, and it turned out that Emily—who couldn't ride in the backseat of a car without feeling sick—loved the roller coasters. The bigger the better. Charlotte seemed a little more apprehensive, but she had too much competitive spirit to let herself be outdone by her younger sister. Tristyn and Josh traded off between the older girls and the thrill rides and Hanna and the family-rated attractions.

At the beginning of the summer, if anyone had dared to suggest that Josh would choose to spend three days at an amusement park with his young nieces, Tristyn would have laughed out loud. It was amazing how five weeks on the road with him and the girls had made her see him differently—*want* to see him differently.

"This was a wonderful surprise," she said, as they exited the gates after their last day at the park, the girls each carrying a bag filled with souvenirs and treats. Well, Charlotte and Emily were carrying theirs, Tristyn was carrying Hanna's, and Josh was carrying Hanna—who had protested, after three days of running on excitement supplemented by candy, that her legs couldn't possibly walk another step—on his shoulders.

"They've been pretty good sports about being dragged around from racetrack to racetrack, so I thought they deserved a break from that routine."

"You definitely delivered," she told him. "No doubt these last few days are going to be the highlight of their summer."

He nudged her shoulder as they headed toward the RV parked in the adjacent campground. "What's been the highlight of yours?"

She knew what he wanted to hear, and the truth was, every day with Josh had been a highlight surpassed only by every night he'd shared her bed. "Actually, I'm not sure mine has happened yet, but I've got a bottle of chocolate syrup in this bag that has definite potential."

He lifted his brows. "Chocolate syrup?"

She smiled at him then. "I didn't buy it as a topping for ice cream."

The closer they got to Charisma, the more excited and apprehensive Tristyn was. She had missed her family while she was away, but returning to North Carolina meant returning to the real world—and in the real world, she and Josh were colleagues and friends, not lovers. Josh seemed to have mixed feelings about their return, too, though neither of them seemed inclined to talk about what was going to happen next.

They'd made an early start that morning, and the girls—still tired out from three days of excitement at the park—had quickly fallen asleep again when they were on the road. It was only when they'd crossed the border into North Carolina that Josh remarked, "I'm finally going to be back in my own place tonight, but I'm still not going to get to sleep in a real bed."

"I don't think you have any cause for complaint. You've spent a lot of time in a real bed over the past two-and-a-half weeks."

"I have absolutely no complaints about the time I spent

in that bed," he assured her. "But very little of it was sleeping."

"It's not my fault you're insatiable."

"But you're the one who kicked me out whenever I started to fall asleep."

"Because I'd rather your nieces not go home at the end of the summer and tell their mom that Uncle Josh was sleeping in Tristyn's bed."

"Better than Emily telling her that we had an orgy," he teased.

Tristyn shook her head. "I think she's finally forgotten that word."

"You better hope so," he said. "Because I won't hesitate to lay the blame for that one at your feet."

"I would never have said it if you hadn't baited me with your comments about three females keeping you up," she reminded him.

"Lately it's only been one female keeping me up," he commented, reaching across the console to take her hand and link their fingers together. "And I'm going to miss her tonight."

It was hardly a declaration of undying love, but the sincerity in his tone tugged at her heart. "I'll be thinking of you trying not to fall off your sofa while I'm stretched out between the crisp, cool sheets of my own bed...naked," she teased, attempting to lighten the tenor of their conversation.

"You're a cruel woman," he said. Then, curiously, "You really do sleep in the nude?"

"I really do," she confirmed.

"Damn, I'm going to miss you tonight," he said. "Unless—"

"No," she said.

"You don't even know what I was going to say," he protested.

"Yes, I do. And yes, I have a three-bedroom house, but there are only beds in two of them and there would be a lot of questions from a lot of people if your truck was parked outside my house overnight."

He sighed, because that was a truth he couldn't deny.

When they got back to his condo, where Tristyn had left her car parked, he felt like he should kiss her goodbye. Except that this wasn't really goodbye, only a temporary break in their schedule. After six days in Charisma, they would pack up again and head toward Tennessee.

He didn't make any plans to see her during those six days, because he suspected that after five weeks away, her family would claim every minute of her time. Besides, it was only six days, and he decided spending that time apart would provide him with the perfect opportunity to get his head on straight again. Because some of the crazy thoughts and outrageous ideas that had nudged at his mind recently proved to Josh that his head was skewed.

Crazy thoughts of a future with Tristyn, not just for the last few weeks of summer, but always. The outrageous idea that she might actually want him, not just for now, but forever.

Yeah, a few days apart from Tristyn would definitely help him get his head on straight.

Really good sex could become addictive, and that's what he'd shared with Tristyn over the past two-and-a-half weeks. Sure, they also shared a lot of common interests. And maybe he even enjoyed talking to her about topics on which they disagreed, because she challenged his opinions and ideas and listened when he challenged hers. Plus, living in close proximity to someone for a period of time was bound to create a feeling of connection. Add in the fact that he'd known not just Tristyn but her whole family a long time, and a guy could be forgiven for thinking he might fit into that close-knit circle.

None of that was cause for panic—was it?

Chapter Seventeen

When Tristyn told her sisters that she would be home on Saturday, Lauryn and Jordyn immediately cleared their schedules, left the children in the care of their grandparents and booked an afternoon at the spa. After seaweed wraps and hot stone massages, the sisters reunited in the pedicure room.

"So...five weeks on the road with Josh and you both came back alive," Jordyn mused, as their feet were soaking in adjacent tubs of bubbling scented water.

"There were a few moments, especially in the beginning, when I wasn't sure we would," she admitted.

"What changed?" Lauryn asked.

"We learned to...coexist."

Jordyn snorted. "Is that what the kids are calling it now?"

Tristyn felt a smile tug at her lips. "And yes, having lots of scorching-hot sex probably helped ease some of the tension, too."

Lauryn grinned. "Good for you."

"It's been amazing," she admitted.

"So why are you chewing on your bottom lip like you do when you're worried about something?" Jordyn asked.

"Because it's been amazing," she said again. "So amazing I almost wish this summer would never end."

"You've fallen in love with him," Jordyn realized.

"No," she immediately denied. "Maybe." She blew out a frustrated breath. "I don't know."

"You do know," Lauryn said gently. "You're just scared."

"There are days—or at least brief moments—when I wish I'd never agreed to go on this road trip."

"Why would you say that?"

"Because being with Josh, helping to take care of his nieces and spending time with him—in and out of the bedroom—it's almost felt like we were a family."

"Why is that a bad thing?" Jordyn asked.

"Because this time that we've had together is like an alternate reality—definitely a fantasy. And I know that. But, every once in a while, I find myself wishing that the fantasy could become reality."

"Of course it can," Lauryn insisted.

But Tristyn shook her head. "If there's one thing Josh isn't, it's a family man."

"Well, he's done a pretty good imitation over the past few weeks," Jordyn pointed out.

"He is great with his nieces," she agreed. "Because they're his nieces and he knows that, as soon as his sister comes back from Spain, they'll go back to Seattle with their mom again."

"And then his life will feel empty and lonely and he'll finally realize that he wants a family of his own, but only if you agree to be the mother of his children."

Tristyn smiled at the fanciful picture her sister was painting, but she shook her head again. "Not likely. Besides, we talked about this, in the beginning, and we both agreed that whatever happened between us while we were away would end when we got back to Charisma."

"So when this road trip is over, you'll go back to working at GSR, seeing him every day, and you won't want to jump his bones?" Jordyn asked skeptically.

"I can't promise that I won't want to," she acknowledged. "Only that I won't actually do it."

Her sisters exchanged looks.

"She won't last a week," Lauryn declared.

"Five days, tops," Jordyn voted.

Tristyn rolled her eyes. "Thank you both for your overwhelming confidence and support."

"We do have confidence in you," Lauryn assured her.

"Which is why we're confident you won't give up on the only man you've ever loved," Jordyn added.

After Tristyn said goodbye to her sisters and left the spa, she impulsively stopped at the grocery store and picked up what she needed to make the chicken-and-broccoli casserole that had been a big hit with Josh and the girls. She didn't expect a woman to answer when she knocked on the door of his condo, and she was so surprised that it took her a minute to recognize the woman as his sister.

"Lucy—when did you get back?"

"Just a few hours ago," she said.

"Does this mean your project in Madrid is finished?"

Lucy nodded. "I had to burn the midnight oil every day, but I didn't want to be away from the girls any longer than absolutely necessary. And I'm jet-lagged, so I've forgotten my manners," she apologized, opening the door wider. "Please, come in."

"I don't want to intrude on your reunion," Tristyn said.

"It's not much of a reunion right now," Lucy said, tugging on Tristyn's arm to draw her inside. "Josh popped out for a minute and the girls are playing with the castanets I brought back for them."

She could hear them now, although the sound—not

quite of a caliber that could be called music—was distant and muted.

"The instruments seemed like a good idea when I was in Spain—not so much now that the girls are clicking away with them," she admitted. "Which is why Josh shut them in the bedroom."

Tristyn smiled. "They must have been so thrilled to see you."

"I think they were," Lucy agreed. "And thank you for helping Josh with the girls while I was away."

"It was a pleasure."

Lucy chuckled. "I'm sure it was at times—and other times, not so much."

"My sisters and cousins all have kids," Tristyn told her. "So I was prepared for almost anything—except the tooth fairy fiasco."

"Which, I understand, you handled very creatively."

"Well, tweeting seemed a little less dangerous than your brother's idea of sending smoke signals."

"Ohmygod—he didn't actually suggest that?"

"He did."

"I think he learned how to send smoke signals in Boy Scouts, about twenty years ago."

"He really was a Boy Scout?" Tristyn asked dubiously.

Lucy nodded. "He really was."

"Well, that former Boy Scout was really great with your daughters."

"I knew he would be. Although he did warn me that he thinks my middle child might have a future as a stripper due to her penchant of taking off her clothes wherever and whenever."

"It only happened three—or maybe four—times," Tristyn said, smiling a little at the memory of how shocked and embarrassed he was each of those times. "He's going to miss them when you go back to Washington."

"And they'll miss him, too," Josh's sister acknowledged. "Which is why we've already decided to come and visit more often."

"That's great," Tristyn said. "Are you planning to stay for a few days now?"

"I'm eager to get home and get the girls settled back into their normal routines, but we might hang out for a while first."

"Speaking of routines, I really should..." Her words trailed away when Josh walked through the door with three flat boxes in his hands.

His lips curved when he saw her standing just inside the doorway. "Tristyn—hi."

"I'm just on my way out," she told him.

"Why?"

"Because I didn't realize Lucy was back."

"And I'm going to go tell the girls that dinner is here," Lucy said, slipping out of the room.

"I should have called to tell you," he said. "But I thought you were probably busy with your family and enjoying a much-needed break from all of us."

"I had breakfast with my parents, then spent the afternoon with my sisters, but they both had other plans for dinner, so I picked up a few groceries and took a chance that you guys might be hungry, too."

"You've spent the past five weeks with us—you know we're always hungry."

"But you obviously had a different dinner plan."

"Stay and eat with us," he urged. "There's more than enough pizza to go around."

Tristyn shook her head. "Thanks, but your sister's been away for a long time and I'm sure you have a lot to catch up on."

He touched a hand to her arm. "I'll give you a call later."

"Sure," she agreed. But she knew it would be foolish to count on it.

She took her groceries home and cooked the chicken and broccoli, anyway. She even opened the bottle of wine she found in the fridge and drank two glasses while she was cooking, then a third while she picked unenthusiastically at her meal.

Since Jordyn had married Marco, Tristyn had lived alone in the house they used to share, and she was generally content with her own company. But after spending the past five weeks with Josh and his nieces in the RV, her house seemed too big and too empty.

Which was crazy, especially considering that she'd been so excited about coming home and having a little bit of breathing room. But now that Lucy was back, it was the end of the road for her and Josh—literally. She blinked away the tears that stung her eyes. She absolutely would *not* cry over the end of a relationship that was never intended to be anything more than a summer fling.

But she hadn't expected it to end so soon.

And she hadn't expected to miss Josh so much already.

Tristyn had just finished putting her dishes in the dishwasher when the doorbell rang. Wiping her hands on a towel, she went to peek through the sidelight, her heart immediately pounding harder and faster when she saw Josh standing on her porch. She drew in a long, deep breath and turned the knob.

"There's a distinct shortage of beds in my condo, especially with Lucy there now, too," he said, in lieu of a greeting.

"And you thought I'd take pity on you and let you share mine?" she guessed.

"Actually, I hoped that you wouldn't want to sleep without me—because I don't want to sleep without you."

How was a woman supposed to resist a man who told her exactly what she wanted to hear?

Tristyn didn't know that she could, but she felt compelled to at least make an effort to protect her heart. "This is a violation of the rule," she pointed out.

"Yeah, I was hoping you might consider another minor amendment," he said.

And then he kissed her, and the illusion of any resistance melted away under the seductive pressure of his mouth on hers.

She'd lost count of the number of times they'd made love over the past two-and-a-half weeks, but somehow, this felt different. Being on the road with Josh had supported the illusion that this wasn't real, that whatever feelings she had for him were a product of the situation and circumstances. Allowing Josh to be here, in her house, in her bed, made her feel more exposed and vulnerable.

Twelve years earlier, she'd been a naive and innocent girl with a huge crush on her cousin's best friend. She was neither naive nor innocent anymore. She'd had a handful of lovers and she wasn't ashamed of the fact, because she'd never fallen into bed with a man without at least feeling some affection for him. But she'd never made love with a man she loved...until now.

When Tristyn woke up in the morning, he was gone.

She couldn't deny that she was disappointed, but she understood that he needed to get back to his own place, to spend some time with his sister and the girls before Lucy headed back to Seattle with her family.

She took a quick shower, then headed to the kitchen for a much-needed cup of coffee—and found Josh standing at her stove, cooking eggs.

"You're still here."

He looked up from the pan, his brows raised. "Did you think I'd leave without saying goodbye?"

"I had no expectations," she said.

"Sometimes I think that's the problem," he said.

She poured a mug of the coffee he'd already brewed. "What's that supposed to mean?"

"Did you really expect that we would spend the better part of the summer together and then just go our separate ways?"

"That was the agreement."

"Screw the agreement," he said. "I'm not ready for this to end."

They were almost the words she wanted to hear him say, and probably the closest to a declaration of affection that she would get from him. Unfortunately, they weren't enough to change her mind.

They were good together—on so many levels. She knew their connection was about more than just sex; she also knew that they ultimately wanted different things. She wanted to get married and have a family someday—and Josh didn't. He'd been clear about that from the beginning.

So when he said he wasn't ready for their relationship to be over, she knew he wasn't thinking of a forever-after future for them together but a few more weeks—maybe even a couple months. And Tristyn couldn't do it. Because the more time she spent with Josh, the more completely she would fall in love, and she needed to get over him so she could move on with her life.

"Being with you over the last few weeks has been… amazing," she admitted. "But it was easy when we were on the road."

He divided the eggs onto two plates, added a couple slices of toast to each. "Were we on the same trip? Because there are a lot of words I might use to describe the last five of weeks, and *easy* isn't one of them."

She smiled at that. "The you and me part was easy," she amended. "Once you stopped acting like an idiot, I mean."

He smiled, clearly unoffended by her remark, as he set her plate in front of her. "It can still be easy."

But Tristyn shook her head. "Not here. Not in a town where I have not just my parents and sisters, but aunts, uncles and cousins ready to offer commentary on everything I do. And especially not with both of us working at GSR."

"You think your family would disapprove of our relationship?"

"No, Josh. I think my family would read too much into the relationship, and when we eventually parted ways, it would be awkward for everyone."

"How do you know that we'd eventually part ways?"

She pushed her eggs around on her plate. "Because you told me—in clear and unequivocal terms—that you're not looking to settle down."

He was quiet for a minute before he finally said, "Maybe that could change."

A tentative blossom of hope bloomed in her heart as she bit into a piece of toast, because she knew he was trying to make this work for her. And from a man who had eschewed personal commitment for so long, his words were a major concession. If he'd said, "My feelings have changed," she would have thrown all the rules out the window and gone for it. But "could change" was too much like a consolation prize—and it wasn't enough. Giving him her heart in the hope that he might someday reciprocate her feelings was too big a risk.

"I've still got the RV," he said, when she remained silent. "Let's take it to Bristol like we'd originally planned."

She wanted to say yes, to extend this magical summer a little bit longer. But she knew that going with him to Tennessee would only prolong the inevitable. Not to mention that Daniel would surely wonder why she was still road-tripping with his business partner when Josh's nieces—her explanation for being with him in the first place—would not be with them.

"I don't think that's a good idea," she finally said.

"You don't think *we're* a good idea," he accused, pushing away his half-eaten breakfast.

She stood up to clear away their plates. "I think, if we try to make this into something more than it is, it could mess up our working relationship, our friendship and your partnership with Daniel."

"You might be right," he finally decided.

But if she was wrong, she might have just let her best chance at happiness walk out the door.

On Monday, Lucy brought the girls to GSR before heading home to Seattle, and Tristyn teared up when she hugged each of them goodbye. On Tuesday, she reconsidered Josh's invitation to go with him to Bristol. On Wednesday, she affirmed her decision to stay home, concluding that she needed some time away from him to rebuild the shields around her heart.

She almost changed her mind again when she learned that Ren won the pole. She'd actually started to look for flights and was about to input her credit card data when she stopped herself.

Was she really eager to be there in case Ren won?

Or was it just an excuse to be with Josh?

She'd long ago promised herself that she would never be the type of woman who became so infatuated with a man that she would follow him to the ends of the earth, and she was certain now that her feelings for Josh were nothing more than infatuation. Being with him, she'd deluded herself into thinking it was love. But that was crazy.

Probably spending time with her sisters and their husbands had made her believe in fairy tales and happy endings—and she was pleased that both of them had found theirs. But she wasn't unhappy with her life. She didn't need a man to complete her. Sure, she'd love to have kids someday and she'd had a lot of fun hanging out with Josh's nieces, but she'd known going in that it was only temporary.

So why did she feel like her heart was breaking every morning that she woke up without him? Why did she think she was going to have to walk away from a job she loved at GSR because she didn't know if she could stand seeing him every day and not be with him?

Worse than not being with him would be seeing him with someone else. Or numerous someone elses. Daniel used to be the same way—a serial monogamist who dated countless beautiful women. Until he fell in love with Kenna. But just because Daniel had altered his ways didn't mean that Josh could—especially since he'd shown no indication that he wanted to. And a vague "maybe that could change" wasn't a guarantee of anything but heartache.

So she stayed home and watched the race on TV. And she was thrilled to see Ren take the checkered flag at Bristol. It was his fourth win of the season—a new record for the young driver and a definite reason to celebrate. Social media showed him out and about, with most of the guys from his pit crew and a few fans, doing just that. And in the background of one of the most widely circulated photos, Tristyn recognized Paris Smythe—with her arms around Josh.

Chapter Eighteen

Jordyn stopped by Sunday afternoon to drop off Gryffindor, because Tristyn had offered to take care of the cat when she heard that her sister and brother-in-law were planning to sneak away for a few days to Braden's house on Ocracoke. She set the cat's pillow in the corner of the living room, where it had always been when he'd lived there.

"Not a lot of treats," Jordyn cautioned, turning to her sister. "The vet said…" Her words trailed off. "Tristyn—what's wrong?"

Tristyn shook her head as she blinked back the tears. "Nothing."

"Then why does it look as if you're trying not to cry?"

"Allergies," she decided.

Jordyn narrowed her gaze. "You don't have allergies."

"Allergies can be acquired," she pointed out.

"What are you allergic to?"

"Cats," she said.

Jordyn fisted her hands on her hips. "Do I need to go and kick Josh Slater's butt?"

"No." Tristyn sighed. "It's really not his fault."

"What's not his fault?" her sister pressed.

She swiped at an errant tear that spilled onto her cheek. "That I fell in love and he didn't."

"Oh, honey," Jordyn said, and enfolded Tristyn in her embrace.

The dam cracked. Tristyn thought she'd done a pretty good job holding it together, but suddenly the tears broke through. Anguished sobs, wrenched from the bottom of her bruised and battered heart, burned her throat as she finally gave in to the storm of emotion that had been building inside her. She didn't know how long she cried, just that the tears seemed endless. Jordyn didn't offer any useless platitudes, only strong and familiar comfort.

A short while later, Lauryn showed up with a bottle of Pinot Noir and a box of dark chocolate covered cherries. Somehow, in the midst of the back rubbing and tissue passing, Jordyn had managed to text their other sister.

So Tristyn told them what had happened, because she needed to tell someone. But she felt like an idiot, blubbering to her sisters who had each endured much worse heartache than simply being dumped. In comparison to the death of a fiancé and a cheating husband, watching Josh walk away was nothing.

"Except that it doesn't sound like it was his choice to walk away," Lauryn pointed out.

"But he did," she insisted.

Jordyn shook her head. "Only after he asked you to go to Bristol with him."

"You can't get mad at him for being with someone else when you told him you didn't want to be with him," Lauryn admonished gently.

"I agree with that, with the added proviso that you have no reason to believe Josh is actually *with* Paris," Jordyn said.

Tristyn shoved her iPad toward her sister. "This clinch

that's circulating all over social media looks pretty real to me."

"I'm not saying that Paris wasn't there with him. But without knowing the details of how or why, you can't be mad at Josh."

"Yes, I can," she insisted. "This picture was taken six days after he walked out of my house. Six days after he spent the night in my bed, making love with me, he was with someone else."

"I don't believe for a minute that Josh was with her," Jordyn said.

Tristyn dabbed at her eyes with a tissue. "I wanted him to fight for me," she admitted softly. "I wanted to believe our relationship was worth fighting for—that *I* was worth fighting for."

"Where is this coming from?" Lauryn asked.

"Brett Taylor," Jordyn said.

Lauryn looked blank. "Who?"

"You were already married," Jordyn remembered. "Tristyn was in her second year at Duke, he was in his third. They were going to build houses together in Costa Rica that summer, but at the last minute, he decided to go to Europe instead."

"But that would have been…what—ten years ago?" Lauryn asked.

Tristyn nodded. "And then there was Kevin Wakefield, the second baseman for the Durham Bulls."

Lauryn smiled. "*Him* I remember."

"Do you also remember that he asked for a trade—to Pawtucket?"

"As I recall, he thought he had a better chance of being called up to Boston than Tampa Bay."

She nodded again. "But he never considered that the trade would signify the end of our relationship. I wasn't even a factor in his decision."

"Because he was an idiot," Lauryn said gently.

"And Josh went to Bristol without me," she pointed out to her sisters.

"You told him to go," Jordyn reminded her.

"Because I wanted him to say that he didn't want to go without me. And if I didn't want to go, he would stay with me. I wanted him to want me more than he wanted to be in Bristol."

"That's not really fair, Tris. You know that he feels obligated, as an owner of the team, to represent GSR."

She swiped at the tears that spilled onto her cheeks. "I know," she admitted. "But the fact that he went out to celebrate with Paris proves that I never mattered to him any more than any other woman he's ever been with."

She wasn't the type to wallow—at least not for very long. Talking to her sisters, along with the wine and the chocolate, helped her put things into perspective a little.

She'd given her heart to the wrong man and it had ended up in pieces. Now she had to put those pieces back together—and she had to do it before Monday morning, when she would be back behind her desk at GSR. Because she was determined not to let anyone—especially Josh—see that she was hurting.

Ren D'Alesio was having the season of his career, and Josh was thrilled to be a part of it. The only thing that dampened his enthusiasm when he watched his driver take the checkered flag at Bristol was that Tristyn wasn't there to witness the victory. But that had been her choice, and he wasn't going to skip the celebration just to sit around his hotel room and wish she was there.

So he went out with the team. In the past couple years, Ren had steadily moved up the ranks, showing not just skill but smarts in his racing, and the other drivers—and the media—had begun to pay attention. As a result, there were reporters shoving microphones in his face and photographers snapping pictures everywhere he went—especially on race day. Josh had never craved the spotlight and was happy to hover in the background when fans or media asked for photos. So he didn't see the picture that was circulating on social media until the next day, when his sister sent him a copy attached to an email with "WTF" in the subject line.

WTF, indeed.

He didn't know what to say to Tristyn when he saw her in the office Monday morning. He wanted to explain, but she'd made it clear that whatever they'd shared was over and done. As it turned out, she was on the phone when he walked by her desk and she never even glanced in his direction. It wasn't until he returned from lunch that she called him over.

"What's up?" he asked, attempting to match her easy tone.

"Phone messages," she said, handing him a pile of pink slips. "Apparently your voice mail is full."

"I turned off my ringer during my meeting with Daniel and Archie this morning," he said, using the nickname of Calvin Archer, the owner of Archer Glass. "I guess I forgot to turn it back on." He glanced at the message on top, and winced inwardly when he saw Paris Smythe's name and number in Tristyn's familiar handwriting.

"You should call her," she said, finally looking up at him.

"Why?"

"Because you're not the kind of guy who doesn't call."

"I didn't spend the weekend with her in Bristol," he said, wanting to be clear about that.

"It's none of my business if you did or didn't," Tristyn said.

"I didn't," he said again, holding her gaze.

She nodded. "You should call her, anyway."

"Tristyn—"

"I saw Rafe last night."

She blurted the words out before he could say anything else, and the impact of her statement made him feel as if he'd been kicked in the chest. When he'd managed to draw air into his lungs, he asked, "Is this your way of telling me that you've moved on and I should, too?"

She nodded.

He took the messages and retreated to his office.

It was just his luck that Tristyn's sister Jordyn was at the restaurant when Josh stopped by later that afternoon. "Is Rafe working tonight?"

"Yes," she admitted warily. "Why?"

"I need to talk to him."

"Why?" she asked again.

"Because I'm in love with your sister."

Her lips curved into a smile so reminiscent of Tristyn's, it actually made his heart ache. And the possibility that he might never again be the focus of Tristyn's smile was one that he refused to consider. Whatever it took, he was going to win her back.

"We were beginning to think you would never figure it out," Jordyn said to him now.

"We?" he asked, though he wasn't sure he wanted to know.

"Me and Lauryn. And Kenna," she admitted.

He shook his head. "I shouldn't have asked."

"Now I'm asking—what does any of this have to do with Rafe?"

"Tristyn told me that she was with him last night," he finally confided.

"So you came here to—what? Fight for her?"

"If that's what it takes."

"Against a man who has an impressive assortment of

knives capable of chopping, dicing and carving within arm's reach?"

He answered without hesitation. "There isn't anything I wouldn't do for her."

Jordyn touched a hand to his arm. "Then before you go storming into the kitchen and making a fool of yourself, you should know that Tristyn only saw Rafe last night because she was here for dinner."

He took a moment to absorb the implications of her words. "She wasn't out on a date with him?"

Jordyn shook her head. "She wasn't out on a date with him."

He frowned. "She deliberately misled me."

"Or maybe you misinterpreted what she said," she countered.

"No," he stated. "She deliberately misled me because she wanted me to think that she'd already moved on. And the only reason she'd want me to think that was if it wasn't true."

"While I'm not entirely sure I followed all of that, I'd like to make a suggestion," Jordyn said.

"Okay," he agreed, the realization that Tristyn still had feelings for him already making his heart lighter.

"Go have this conversation with my sister. Tell *her* how you feel."

"I will," he promised.

But there was one more stop he had to make first.

Tristyn had just settled on the sofa with a bowl of popcorn in her lap and a glass of Pinot Noir beside her, intending to spend the night binge-watching *Game of Thrones*, when a knock sounded at the door. She hadn't been expecting any company and was comfortably dressed in a pair of denim cutoffs and an old Duke T-shirt. She decided to ignore the summons. If it was either or both of her sisters, they had keys they could use. If it was anyone else, she wasn't in the mood for company.

"Come on, Tris—open up."

She immediately recognized Josh's voice. What she didn't know was why he was here.

"I know you're in there," he continued, when she failed to respond. "I can hear the *Game of Thrones* theme playing."

Inwardly cursing the single-pane windows as an ineffective sound barrier, she finally, reluctantly, pushed herself off the sofa and went to the door. She opened it with the intention of sending him away, but the words slid back down her throat when her gaze landed on him.

He was wearing a tuxedo.

And holding a corsage box in his hand.

Her heart thudded against her ribs.

Of course, any woman would probably have the same reaction. Josh always looked good, but in black tie, the man was absolutely devastating.

Without waiting for an invitation, he stepped past her and into the foyer.

She finally found her voice to ask, "Why are you here, Josh?"

Instead of answering her question, he opened the plastic box and removed the corsage. "This is for you."

"I'm a little underdressed for orchids," she protested, as he took her hand to slide the band onto her wrist.

"You're beautiful," he assured her. "Even in cutoff shorts and an old T-shirt—even in granny jammies— you're the most beautiful woman I've ever known."

She swallowed around the tightness in her throat. She didn't know what game he was playing, but she didn't want to be involved. She couldn't do this anymore. She couldn't be with him and continue to pretend that she didn't love him with her whole heart. "You shouldn't be here," she said.

But the protest sounded weak, even to her own ears.

Josh gently squeezed the hand he was still holding. "Yes, I should," he said. "Because I don't want to be anywhere else."

Then he led her into her own living room, where he immediately began to rearrange her furniture—pushing back the sofa and moving aside the coffee table to clear the center of the room.

"What are you doing?" she asked, sincerely baffled.

He didn't reply until he'd finished his task. "Rewriting history," he finally said. "*Our* history. I want to show you how I wish the night of your prom could have ended twelve years ago."

Then he tapped the screen of his iPhone a few times and the first notes of a familiar Savage Garden tune spilled out of the tiny speaker. He set it on the table and held out his hand. "Will you dance with me?"

She didn't think she'd made a move, but somehow her hand found its way to his. The way her knees were trembling, she wasn't sure she'd be able to dance, though. Then his arm, warm and strong, was at her back, drawing her closer, and she let herself relax into his embrace and move with him to the music.

"Do you remember this song?" he asked.

She nodded. "'Truly Madly Deeply.'"

"It's the song that was playing the first time we ever danced together," he reminded her.

"I didn't think you remembered," she admitted.

"I remember every second of that first dance," he assured her. "Of our first kiss, and the first time we made love."

He kissed her then—a soft and surprisingly sweet kiss, the kind of kiss that she'd yearned for the night of her prom. But she wasn't a naive seventeen-year-old girl any-more, and her yearnings weren't nearly as innocent as they'd been twelve years earlier.

"I didn't call Paris," he told her now.

"Why?"

"Because even if you're okay with me dating other women, I'm not. I don't want any woman but you."

Her heart swelled inside her chest, but her brain continued to urge caution.

"For twelve years, every other woman I've dated has been a pale substitute for the one woman I really wanted but didn't believe I'd ever have—you. And I don't want to spend the next twelve years doing the same thing in a futile effort to get over you, because I know it won't ever happen."

"It's only been two weeks," she pointed out.

He tipped her chin up so that she could see the truth of his feelings in his eyes. "Two weeks, two months, two years—it doesn't matter," he told her. "It's always been you for me. Only you."

And those words, spoken from his heart, began to heal the broken pieces of her own.

"It's always been you for me," she admitted, as she led him to her bedroom. "Only you."

He framed her face in his hands and kissed her again.

"I've missed you." He whispered the confession against her lips. "I was going crazy, wondering if I'd ever be here with you like this again. If I'd ever have the chance to hold you, touch you, love you."

"Love me now," she suggested.

"I will." He kissed her once. "I am." Then again. "I do."

They quickly dispensed with their clothing, then fell together on top of her bed, a tangle of limbs and needs. Their mouths collided, clung; hands stroked, seduced; bodies merged, mated. The rhythm of their lovemaking was familiar—and somehow different. This time, all the illusions and pretensions had been stripped away by the acknowledgment of their feelings for one another, discarded like the garments that littered the floor. Now they were just a man and a woman, loving one another—and it was all either of them wanted or needed.

"I love you, Tristyn," he said.

To hear the words now, to know they were true, filled her heart to overflowing. "I love you, too," she admitted. "I tried not to—but I couldn't seem to help myself."

"I'm not sorry about that," he said. "I think I started to fall for you twelve years ago, but I wasn't nearly ready to acknowledge the depth of my feelings for you then." His lips curved in a wry smile. "Who am I kidding? I wasn't ready to acknowledge the depth of my feelings for you even a few weeks ago. Because I knew that you were the perfect woman for the rest of my life—and I was having too much fun in the moment to think about the rest of my life.

"And then, you were no longer with me in the moment. And I realized that I didn't want anything else as much as I wanted to be with you. Not just for the moment, but for always."

"Really?"

"Really," he assured her. "Over the past few weeks, I realized something else, too."

"What's that?"

"I think I'd like to have one or two kids of my own someday—if I could have them with you."

"I really like the sound of that," she told him.

"But while I was thinking about what I wanted for our future together, it occurred to me that your family—especially your cousin, my business partner and best friend—might not approve of us making plans to start a family before I put a ring on your finger."

"Well, I didn't think we were going to try to make a baby just yet," she noted.

"Not just yet," he confirmed, reaching into the pocket of his discarded jacket for the small velvet box. "But still— I'd like to do things in their proper order."

Then he flipped open the lid to reveal the three-carat, emerald-cut diamond centered on a platinum band set with pavé diamonds.

Tristyn gasped. "Oh, Josh."

"Daniel said that you'd have to be dazzled to ever agree to marry me."

And she was dazzled—as much by his revelation as the ring. "You told Daniel you were planning to propose?"

"I needed to make sure my best friend would be my best man," he told her. "So what do you say, Tristyn Garrett— will you marry me and turn 'for now' into 'forever'?"

She threw her arms around his neck and drew his mouth down to hers. "There isn't anything I want more."

Epilogue

Over the past six years, nine of Tristyn's cousins and both her sisters had married. Now, *finally*, it was her turn.

Once Josh had put his ring on her finger, he'd been eager to move from "engaged" to "married" as quickly as possible. Tristyn was excited about starting their life together, too, but she wanted to share the happy occasion with all their family and friends. They decided on an early spring date—on a non-race weekend, of course—at Trinity Church in downtown Charisma, with a bridal party reminiscent of a royal wedding.

Both Tristyn's sisters stood up with her, and Charlotte, Emily, Kylie and Hanna were all flower girls. On the groom's side, Josh had Daniel as his best man, champion race-car driver Ren D'Alesio as an usher, and though there were only two rings to be exchanged, there were five ring bearers: Jacob, Zachary, Logan, Henry and Liam.

"Afraid she's going to be a no-show and leave you standing at the altar?" Daniel asked the question under his breath, as they watched the procession of flower girls make their way toward the front of the church.

"No," Josh denied, unfazed by his friend's teasing.

He didn't believe for a minute that Tristyn would bail

on him—on them. It might have taken them a long time to find their way to one another, but there was no doubt in either of their minds that this was it for both of them.

And when she finally appeared at the back of the church, the sight of her made his heart race like the number 722 car on the straightaway at Talladega. He didn't know that the dress she was wearing was a tulle ball gown with a sweetheart neckline, back corset, chapel train and lace appliqués on the bodice and hem. He only knew that she took his breath away.

The ceremony did not go off without a hitch. Of course, with so many little ones in the wedding party, no one expected that it would. In the middle of the vows, Emily piped up to complain that her dress was scratchy and Henry pushed Liam off the dais, but through it all, Tristyn and Josh remained focused only on one another.

When the minister pronounced they were husband and wife, it was the end of the ceremony but only the beginning of the celebration. Hundreds of pictures were taken of the bride and the groom—alone and with various members of the wedding party, then more with other family members who were in attendance, including all the Garrett cousins from Pinehurst who had traveled to Charisma with their spouses and children for the occasion.

"How long do we have to stick around and make conversation with all these people?" Josh asked Tristyn.

"Considering that 'all these people' are our wedding guests—and many of them are family—a little while longer," she told him.

"I'm eager to get my wife back to the honeymoon suite so that I can peel that gorgeous wedding dress off her gorgeous body and we can consummate our marriage—and maybe get started on a family of our own."

"You don't want to take some time to get used to being husband and wife before we become daddy and mommy?"

"I'm ready." He pulled her into his arms. "I'm ready for anything with you by my side."

"And that's where I'm going to be," she promised him. "For now and forever."

He kissed her then—not at the direction of the minister or for the benefit of their wedding guests, but simply because she was his wife now and he could kiss her anywhere and anytime that he wanted to. When he released her, he caught a flutter of movement out of the corner of his eye.

Tristyn laughed, obviously having noticed Ren waving the checkered flag, too. "I bet you've been looking for an opportunity to do that all day."

"I have," the driver agreed, then winked at her before passing the flag to the groom. "Because he's obviously the big winner today."

"He's right," Josh agreed as Ren moved away. "Today, I am the luckiest man in the world."

"I think I got pretty lucky today, too," his bride said.

"What do you think about saying goodbye to our guests and going somewhere that we can get luckier?" he asked.

She smiled. "That idea gets a definite green flag from me."

And that's what they did.

* * * * *

Catch up with the Garrett sisters!

Look for
Lauryn's story,
BUILDING THE PERFECT DADDY

And Jordyn's story,
THE BACHELOR TAKES A BRIDE

Available wherever Harlequin books
and ebooks are sold!

And watch for

MATCH MADE IN HAVEN

the new miniseries from
award-winning author Brenda Harlen
Coming soon to Harlequin Special Edition!

Available May 23, 2017

#2551 WILD WEST FORTUNE
The Fortunes of Texas: The Secret Fortunes • by Allison Leigh
Ariana Lamonte is making her name as a journalist by profiling the newly revealed Fortunes. When she finds three more hidden in middle-of-nowhere Texas, including the sexy rancher Jayden Fortune, she thinks she's hit the jackpot. Until she falls for him! Will this professional conflict of interest throw a wrench in their romance?

#2552 A CONARD COUNTY HOMECOMING
Conard County: The Next Generation • by Rachel Lee
Paraplegic war veteran Zane McLaren just wants to be left alone to deal with the demons his time in the army left behind. Fortunately, his service dog, Nell, has other ideas that include his pretty neighbor, Ashley Granger.

#2553 IN THE COWBOY'S ARMS
Thunder Mountain Brotherhood • by Vicki Lewis Thompson
Actor Matt Forrest has just landed his first big-budget role when scandal forces him to flee Hollywood for the Wyoming ranch he grew up on. His PR rep, Geena Lysander, hopes to throw a positive light on the situation, never expecting their cool, professional relationship to heat up into something more personal!

#2554 THE NEW GUY IN TOWN
The Bachelors of Blackwater Lake • by Teresa Southwick
Florist Faith Connelly has sworn off men, but sexy newcomer Sam Hart tempts her, even though both of them have painful pasts to look back on. Because he buys flowers from her, she knows he's a "two dates and you're out" kind of guy, so what's the harm in flirting a little? But when a wildfire forces Faith to take shelter with Sam, both of them confront the past in order for love to grow.

#2555 HONEYMOON MOUNTAIN BRIDE
Honeymoon Mountain • by Leanne Banks
When recently divorced Vivian Jackson and her sisters decide to take over their deceased father's hunting lodge, Vivian runs into her long-ago crush, Benjamin Hunter. He turned her down as a teen, but he's giving her more than a second look now. Their affair burns out of control, but it'll take more than heat to deal with Benjamin's secrets and Vivian's fear of failing at love again.

#2556 FALLING FOR THE RIGHT BROTHER
Saved by the Blog • by Kerri Carpenter
When Elle Owens returns to Bayside, she hopes everyone has forgotten the embarrassing incident that precipitated her flight from town ten years ago. They haven't, but Cam Dumont, her former crush's sexy older brother, doesn't care what anyone thinks—he's determined to win her over. Can Elle forget about the ubiquitous Bayside Blogger long enough to tell Cam how she truly feels about him?

**YOU CAN FIND MORE INFORMATION ON UPCOMING HARLEQUIN® TITLES,
FREE EXCERPTS AND MORE AT WWW.HARLEQUIN.COM.**

SPECIAL EXCERPT FROM

HARLEQUIN

SPECIAL EDITION

Zane McLaren just wants to be left alone to deal with the demons his time in the army left behind. Fortunately, his service dog, Nell, has other ideas—ideas that include his pretty neighbor, Ashley Granger.

Read on for a sneak preview of
CONARD COUNTY HOMECOMING,
the next book in New York Times
bestselling author Rachel Lee's
CONARD COUNTY: THE NEXT GENERATION
miniseries.

Things had certainly changed around here, he thought as he drove back to his house. Even Maude, who had once seemed as unchangeable as the mountains, had softened up a bit.

A veterans' group meeting. He didn't remember if there'd been one when he was in high school, but he supposed he wouldn't have been interested. His thoughts turned back to those years, and he realized he had some assessing to do.

"Come in?" he asked Ashley as they parked in his driveway.

She didn't hesitate, which relieved him. It meant he hadn't done something to disturb her today. Yet. "Sure," she said and climbed out.

His own exit took a little longer, and Ashley was waiting for him on the porch by the time he rolled up the ramp.

Nell took a quick dash in the yard, then followed eagerly into the house. The dog was good at fitting in her business when she had the chance.

"Stay for a while," he asked Ashley. "I can offer you a soft drink if you'd like."

She held up her latte cup. "Still plenty here."

He rolled into the kitchen and up to the table, where he placed the box holding his extra meal. He didn't go into the living room much. Getting on and off the sofa was a pain, hardly worth the effort most of the time. He supposed he could hang a bar in there like he had over his bed so he could pull himself up and over, but he hadn't felt particularly motivated yet.

But then, almost before he knew what he was doing, he tugged on Ashley's hand until she slid into his lap.

"If I'm outta line, tell me," he said gruffly. "No social skills, like I said."

He watched one corner of her mouth curve upward. "I don't usually like to be manhandled. However, this time I think I'll make an exception. What brought this on?"

"You have any idea how long it's been since I had an attractive woman in my lap?" With those words he felt almost as if he had stripped his psyche bare. Had he gone over some new kind of cliff?

Don't miss
CONARD COUNTY HOMECOMING
by Rachel Lee, available June 2017 wherever
Harlequin® Special Edition books and ebooks are sold.

www.Harlequin.com

Copyright © 2017 by Susan Civil Brown

HSEEXP0517

Celebrate 20 Years of

Love Inspired

Inspirational Romance to Warm Your Heart and Soul

Whether you love heart-pounding suspense, historically rich stories or contemporary heartfelt romances, Love Inspired® Books has it all!

Sign up for the Love Inspired newsletter at **www.Loveinspired.com** and connect with us to find your next great read from the **Love Inspired, Love Inspired Suspense** and **Love Inspired Historical** series.

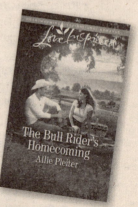

The Bull Rider's Homecoming
Allie Pleiter

www.Facebook.com/LoveInspiredBooks

www.Twitter.com/LoveInspiredBks

www.LoveInspired.com

LIBPA0517

Turn your love of reading into rewards you'll love with
Harlequin My Rewards

**Join for FREE today at
www.HarlequinMyRewards.com**

Earn **FREE BOOKS** of your choice.

Experience **EXCLUSIVE OFFERS** and contests.

Enjoy **BOOK RECOMMENDATIONS**
selected just for you.

PLUS! Sign up now
and get **500** points
right away!

Earn **FREE REWARDS**
Join Today!
HarlequinMyRewards.com

MYR16R

THE WORLD IS BETTER WITH

Romance

Harlequin has everything from contemporary, passionate and heartwarming to suspenseful and inspirational stories.

Whatever your mood, we have a romance just for you!

Connect with us to find your next great read, special offers and more.

 /HarlequinBooks

 @HarlequinBooks

www.HarlequinBlog.com

www.Harlequin.com/Newsletters

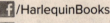

HARLEQUIN®

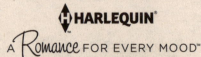

A *Romance* FOR EVERY MOOD™

www.Harlequin.com

SERIESHALOAD2015